SIN
UNDONE

LARISSA IONE

GRAND CENTRAL
PUBLISHING

NEW YORK   BOSTON

Cover design by Claire Brown
Cover photography by Herman Estevez

Grand Central Publishing
Hachette Book Group
237 Park Avenue
New York, NY 10017
Visit our website at www.HachetteBookGroup.com.

Grand Central Publishing is a division of Hachette Book Group, Inc. The Grand Central Publishing name and logo is a trademark of Hachette Book Group, Inc.

The publisher is not responsible for websites (or their content) that are not owned by the publisher.

Printed in the United States of America

First Printing: September 2010

10 9 8 7 6 5

Q-MART

"Come here." His voice was low and rough, and Sin's furious glare burned a hole right through him.

"Screw you."

"Been there, done that," he growled. "Now, come here."

She shot him the bird and started toward the door. "I don't respond well to orders."

He was up in a flash, and he had her backed up against the wall. "Then what do you respond to, little demon?"

She struck out, but before her fist could knock his teeth loose, she hissed and grabbed her head as the anti-violence enchantment kicked in.

More gently than she deserved, he peeled her bleeding hand away from her head and swiped his tongue over the needle puncture. God, she tasted decadent, with a bite like fine brandy, and he couldn't help but let his tongue linger on her skin.

The air between them crackled with sudden heat, and his hips surged as he pressed his palm to her delicate throat.

Power swamped him...She was life. She was death. She was the most dangerous female he'd ever met, and if he was smart, he'd run like hell.

***

"Ione knows how to make your heart race."

—CHEYENNE MCCRAY, *New York Times* **bestselling author of** *The Second Betrayal*

MORE PRAISE FOR LARISSA IONE
ECSTASY UNVEILED

"4½ Stars! Rich with passion, mystery, and mythology. Ione is a master worldbuilder, and one can't help but fall head-long into this imaginative and compelling story."

—RT Book Reviews

"Compulsively readable...intensely interesting...this book was awesome." **—LikesBooks.com**

"Great...fast-paced...a strong tale that has the audience believing that demons and angels walk the earth."

—Midwest Book Review

"An astonishing addition to Larissa Ione's Demonica series...fast-paced and totally captivating...The most action-packed and suspense-driven Demonica novel to date, readers will be hard pressed to put *Ecstasy Unveiled* down."

—RomanceJunkies.com

"Overwhelmingly moving at times, totally hilarious during others, and always a captivatingly magical adventure...The Demonica series is always fascinating and the fourth book superbly demonstrates why its gifted creator is an unequaled storyteller. Larissa Ione cleverly combines plots and memorable characters with her special brand of humor to craft outstanding paranormal tales." **—SingleTitles.com**

"Paranormal romance at its finest...a fast-paced thrill ride of epic proportions that will have you on the edge of your seat, cheering for the good guys...This series holds no punches and is becoming a serious must-have...it will definitely not disappoint." **—Examiner.com**

"Fast-paced and fun...The action in this book is nonstop and I never once wished I was doing anything but reading the book while the story lasted." **—DearAuthor.com**

"Ione's best yet...a fast-paced read that kept me flipping the pages as fast as I could. I couldn't wait to find out what happened next!...Each Demonica book just keeps getting better and better. The momentum of the story and pacing keeps you drawn in until way past your bedtime." **—FictionVixen.com**

"A wicked and exhilarating ride full of provocative and arousing love scenes and intense physical and emotional encounters that left me beyond a doubt captivated from cover to cover." **—BittenByBooks.com**

PASSION UNLEASHED

"4½ Stars! The third book in Ione's supercharged Demonica series ignites on the first page and never looks back... Adventure, action, and danger leap off every page. The best of the series to date!" **—RT Book Reviews**

more...

"Fast-paced from the onset and never slows down until the exhilarating climax...Readers will be enthralled by the action and the charmed lead couple."

—*Midwest Book Reviews*

"Larissa Ione pulls no punches...The love scenes are scorching hot and grab at your heart with their emotional intensity. Dark moments are written with just the right touch of hope that leaves the reader begging for a happy ending. I couldn't have loved *Passion Unleashed* more and hated for it to end. Raw, gritty, and tremendously passionate...It was awesome!"

—**RomanceJunkies.com**

"5 Stars! Larissa has outdone herself with the story of Wraith. I was pulled into this story from the first page. The action is intense and nonstop. I was engrossed and enthralled...and highly recommend adding this series to your library."

—**BittenByBooks.com**

"Awesome...Everyone loves a bad boy and Wraith is *so* the poster bad boy. Another great novel...Ione gives us a great spin on the relationship between her 'Buffys' and the demons of the world, along with a good apocalypse."

—**LiteraryEscapism.com**

"Heart-pounding...outstandingly superb...an adventure-filled romance where passion and danger continuously mount...The plot and characters are truly unforgettable."

—**SingleTitles.com**

"A delightful paranormal romance with strong world-building and a suspenseful plot. *Passion Unleashed* will captivate readers... The seducer is about to be seduced, and fans won't be disappointed." **—DarqueReviews.com**

"Plenty of steamy love scenes... nicely balanced with a high-octane plot... Larissa Ione is fast becoming a master at telling dark, edgy, and highly complex paranormal tales." **—BookLoons.com**

"Absolutely fabulous! Wraith is the ultimate bad boy who is just begging for salvation and Serena is his perfect complement. Ms. Ione will have paranormal fans begging for more." **—TheRomanceReadersConnection.com**

DESIRE UNCHAINED

"4 Stars! Rising star Ione is back in this latest Demonica novel... Ione has a true gift for imbuing her characters with dark-edged passion... thrilling action and treacherous vengeance... a top-notch read." **—*RT Book Reviews***

"Wicked... decadently sinful... prepare to be burned!" **—Gena Showalter, *New York Times* bestselling author**

"A fabulous tale... The story line is fast-paced from the opening sequence... Fans will relish a visit to the Ione realm." **—*Midwest Book Review***

more...

"Warning! Read at your own risk. Highly addictive…Rising star Larissa Ione takes her already well-crafted and unique demon world to new heights. The sex is darker, hotter, wickeder, and wonderfully erotic; the vengeful enemy is diabolical, and the story line is unparalleled. Ione is a master at creating tortured, sexy bad boys who are full of flaws and make you melt…*Desire Unchained* may only be book two in her Demonica series, but I'm completely head-over-heels in love. I have never been so enthralled with a series before. With the end of each book, I'm left desperately wanting more."   **—FreshFiction.com**

"Imaginatively riveting…Emotional intensity is the driving force behind every Larissa Ione book. Scenes may be packed with suspenseful peril or steamy passions or even quick humor and clever banter, yet it is the emotions behind the reactions of the characters that really grab the reader."
—SingleTitles.com

"Five Stars! Recommended read. I have to say that I absolutely love this book. Larissa Ione has become one of my favorite authors, and I crave more of her books. The first book in her Demonica series was fantastic, and this one is even better…[Shade] is the perfect romance hero…The whole world and all the other characters have taken a place in my heart…I wish I could go back and read *Desire Unchained* again for the first time. It was just that good."
—FallenAngelReviews.com

PLEASURE UNBOUND

"What a ride! Dark, sexy, and very intriguing, the book gripped me from start to finish—totally recommended."
—Nalini Singh, *New York Times* **bestselling author of** *Mine to Possess*

ALSO BY LARISSA IONE

THE DEMONICA SERIES

Pleasure Unbound

Desire Unchained

Passion Unleashed

Ecstasy Unveiled

Sin Undone

THE LORDS OF DELIVERANCE SERIES

Eternal Rider

Immortal Rider

Lethal Rider

Rogue Rider

For all the medical personnel out there. You've been the inspiration behind these books. I admire the work you do, and I thank you for the risks you take with your own health and safety. I've imposed on many of you for advice regarding some of my medical scenarios, and I can't thank you enough.

Also, for my sisters-in-law, Stephanie Rice, Andrea Etheridge, and Anna Walker. Your support means so much to me...and it's a bonus that you like the books!

And for Steve Gitre. I know you would have been proud. You are missed.

Acknowledgments

As always, I have about a million people to thank for their help, support, and just plain awesomeness.

First of all, thank you to everyone at Hachette who has done such a fantastic job with these books! Huge thanks to Amy Pierpont, Alex Logan, Anna Balasi, and Melissa Bullock. I'm sure I make you crazy at times, but you never let on. And I can't forget everyone in the art department, who has given me some seriously man-chesty goodness on my covers!

Special thanks to Renee, Karissa, and Arlene for Karlene, and Ashley Hopkins and Christy Gibson for their helpful medical advice.

Thank you to Lea Franczak, Melissa Bradley, Michelle Willingham, Ann Aguirre, and Stephanie Tyler for their help and reads. I owe you margaritas. With double shots.

And I owe so many people for just being cool and supportive, not just to me, but to the romance community, readers and authors alike. So a big shout-out to Valentina Paolillo, Larissa Benoliel, Jodie West, Joely Sue Burkhart, Heather Carleton, Diane Stirling, Ryan Rohloff, Tigris Eden, Mandi Schreiner, Hasna Saadani, Sarah Gabe, and Ericka Brooks.

Finally, thank you to all my wonderful readers. I'm truly blessed to have you.

Glossary

The Aegis—Society of human warriors dedicated to protecting the world from evil. *See:* Guardians, Regent, Sigil

Carceris—The jailors of the underworld. All demon species send representatives to serve terms in the Carceris. Carceris members are responsible for apprehending demons accused of violating demon law, and for acting as guards in the Carceris prisons.

Council—All demon species and breeds are governed by a Council that makes laws and metes out punishment for individual members of their species or breed.

Dresdiin—The demon equivalent of angels. *See:* Memitim

Fakires—Derogatory term used by vampires to describe humans who either believe themselves to be real vampires or who pretend to be vampires.

Guardians—Warriors for The Aegis, trained in combat techniques, weapons, and magic. Upon induction into The

Aegis, all Guardians are presented with an enchanted piece of jewelry bearing the Aegis shield, which, among other things, allows for night vision and the ability to see through demon invisibility enchantment.

Harrowgate—Vertical portals, invisible to humans, that demons use to travel between locations on Earth and Sheoul.

Infadre—A female of any demon species who has been impregnated by a Seminus demon.

Maleconcieo—Highest level of ruling demon boards, served by a representative from each species Council. The U.N. of the demon world.

Marked Sentinel—Humans charmed by angels and tasked with protecting a vital artifact. Sentinels are immortal and immune to harm. Only angels (fallen included) can injure or kill a Sentinel. Their existence is a closely guarded secret.

Memitim—Earthbound angels assigned to protect Primori. Memitim remain earthbound until they complete their duties, at which time they Ascend, earning their wings and entry into Heaven. Also known to demons as *dresdiin. See: Dresdiin*, Primori

Orgesu—A demon sex slave, often taken from breeds bred specifically for the purpose of providing sex.

Pricolici—Werewolves who are born as such. *Pricolici* can only conceive during the breeding heat, and offspring are almost always born werewolves, even if the father is varcolac. *Pricolici* are born with a mark that identifies them as *pricolici*. See: *Varcolac*

Primori—Humans and demons whose lives are fated to impact the world in some crucial way.

Regent—Head(s) of local Aegis cells.

Renfield—Fictional character in Bram Stoker's *Dracula*. Also, derogatory term for any human who serves a vampire. A vampire groupie.

S'genesis—Final maturation cycle for Seminus demons. Occurs at one hundred years of age. A post-*s'genesis* male is capable of procreation and possesses the ability to shapeshift into the male of any demon species.

Sheoul—Demon realm. Located deep in the bowels of the earth, accessible only by Harrowgates.

Sheoul-gra—A holding tank for demon souls. The place where demon souls go until they can be reborn or kept in torturous limbo.

Sheoulic—Universal demon language spoken by all, though many species speak their own language.

Sigil—Board of twelve humans known as Elders, who serve as the supreme leaders of The Aegis. Based in Berlin, they oversee all Aegis cells worldwide.

Swans—Humans who act as blood or energy donors for vampires, either actual undead or *fakires*.

Ter'taceo—Demons who can pass as human, either because their species is naturally human in appearance or because they can shapeshift into human form.

Therionidryo—Term a were-beast uses for a person he or she bit and turned into another were-beast.

Therionidrysi—Any survivor of a were-beast attack. Term used to clarify the relationship between the sire and his *therionidryo*.

Ufelskala—A scoring system for demons, based on their degree of evil. All supernatural creatures and evil humans can be categorized into the five Tiers, with the Fifth Tier composed of the worst of the wicked.

Varcolac—Werewolves who were once human, turned into wargs by the bite of another. Both born and turned werewolves can infect a human with lycanthropy. Offspring conceived outside the breeding heat are always born human. Offspring conceived during the breeding heat are occasionally infected with lycanthropy in the womb and are born as werewolves. *See: Pricolici*

Classification of demons, as listed by Baradoc, Umber demon, using the demon breed Seminus as an example:

Kingdom: Animalia
Class: Demon
Family: Sexual demon
Genus: Terrestrial
Species: Incubus
Breed: Seminus

Prologue

"The wargs must die."

Sin paced back and forth in the master chamber of her assassin den, her mind working overtime to process Bantazar's words. The Assassin Guild's messenger stood near the cold fire pit, outstretched hand holding a parchment scroll. Sin snatched it from the Neethul male, who must stand seven feet tall even without the platform Goth boots he wore. With them, he was at least two-and-a-half feet taller than she was. Still, the Guild's lackey didn't intimidate her. She'd killed much larger demons than him.

"Eight of them?" Sin asked. "Eight werewolves at once?"

He nodded, his shoulder-length, snowy hair catching on his pointed ears. The Neethul were—externally, anyway—a beautiful race, elven in appearance. "An entire pack."

Which included a two-year-old cub. She cast a covert

glance at the male standing in the corner, saturated in shadow and silence. Lycus, her only warg assassin, might as well have been a stone statue. The news that the contract would end the lives of several of his own people didn't faze him at all. Not that she'd expected it to. He was a professional. Cold, efficient, and ruthless.

Biting back a curse, Sin stopped pacing. She couldn't afford to show nerves or reluctance. The Guild was watching her closely for signs of weakness, would seize any excuse to crush her and take her assassins for themselves. She had to be more ruthless than ever right now, especially since she'd already declined to bid on nearly a dozen contracts, and she'd only been an assassin master for three weeks.

She scanned the details scrawled on the parchment in Sheoulic. "Who else has this job been presented to?"

"You know I can't tell you that." Bantazar's ruby lips peeled back in a lecherous smile. "But if you use some of your succubus talents on me, I might let some names slip in a moment of passion."

Sad as it was, she was actually tempted to screw the bastard if it would get her the information she needed. She had to offer on this job, but she needed to ensure she overbid and wouldn't win the contract. Knowing who else was bidding would give her an edge.

"I'd tell you to go to hell, Bantazar, but no doubt you own a large chunk of it." The Neethul were wealthy slave traders whose holdings included massive sections of Sheoul, and as a minor assassin master, Bantazar was definitely on the same path.

"Deth would have taken me up on the offer," he purred.

"I wouldn't brag about that." She studied the ring on

her left index finger that used to belong to her dead boss. "Deth would have screwed a spiny hellrat if he could catch one."

Bantazar laughed as he moved toward her, sinuous as a serpent. "Your assassin slaves grow restless, half-breed. Are your human morals interfering with your ability to manage them?"

She snorted. "I have no morals." Maybe she'd started out with them, back before she found out she was a demon, but all the things she'd done in her life, both forced and of her own free will, had chipped away at her heart and soul, and there wasn't a lot left.

At least, there hadn't been until she'd started a plague that was killing werewolves all over the globe. Something about that action had scraped her emotions raw, exposing a nugget of regret that sat inside her like a pebble in a shoe.

And now there'd been a mysterious increase in the number of hits put out on werewolves—wargs, as they liked to be called—and she was having a hard time bidding on contracts that would set her assassins against them.

She was already killing them by the dozens, without ever having touched them.

Absently, she rubbed her right arm, her palm registering the difference in temperature between her bare skin and the sharp lines of the tattoo that had appeared when she was twenty. The *dermoire*, a paternal history of her demon heritage, had come with a raging libido and the ability to infect anyone she touched with a disease that killed within minutes. As sucky as that was, her twin brother, Lore, had gotten off much worse. She could at least control her "gift." He couldn't touch anyone but his siblings and mate without snuffing them.

"Well?" Bantazar cracked his knuckles, an annoying sound that echoed off the chamber's smooth stone walls. "Will you bid, or will you let your slaves mutiny?"

Thanks to the bond that connected her to her assassin slaves through the assassin-master ring, they couldn't raise a hand against her—not so long as she remained in the den or at assassin Guild headquarters, or in a place protected from violence, like Underworld General. But they *could* attack her anywhere else in Sheoul or aboveground, in the human realm—which was why assassin masters rarely left their dens.

For the millionth time since she had accepted the position of assassin master, she cursed her situation. She hadn't wanted it, but she would never let her brother know that she'd taken it to prevent his angelic mate from being forced into the job Idess had won by killing Detharu. Idess would have lost her soul over this job, and since Sin figured she'd already lost hers . . .

Yeah. No big deal.

Snagging a double-ended penknife from the hip pocket of her leather pants, she scrawled an absurdly high monetary figure on the parchment. She signed, and then flipped the pen over and sliced her thumb with the sharp blade. A drop of blood splashed onto the page, and instantly, red, pulsing veins sprouted from the fluid and wove their way through the document. Within seconds, the parchment had gone from a crisp, stiff square of dried skin to a pliable, warm scrap of flesh that would become a binding contract if the individual behind it accepted her bid.

Disgusted, Sin handed the thing back to the Neethul, her stomach churning as he sauntered to the exit.

"That was hard for you," Lycus said, after the huge

door slammed shut. From behind her, his hands came down on her shoulders, his fingers kneading, but his touch made her tense up only more. "Take me up on my offer. Mate with me. We'll rule the den together."

"Are you deaf, or just really stupid?" Not once since taking this job had she committed violence against one of her underlings, but she really was tempted to turn around and introduce her knee to his balls. "How many times do I have to say no?"

His lips brushed the top of her right ear. "I can say no, as well."

She stiffened. "Blackmail, Lycus?" He was one of her few, precious bedmates now; since becoming master of the den, most of her assassins, the ones who had shared her bed for years, had become wary or afraid of her. Although it was within her rights to force them to service her, she would never do so. Lycus allowed her full use of his body, but it wasn't because he knew that she'd die without sex.

He wanted her job, wanted her as his mate so he could assume shared control over the den. But as nice as it would be to shove off the hard decisions on someone else, she couldn't give Lycus what he wanted. She could never, ever be someone's mate. Could never belong to anyone again.

Funny how she'd considered sleeping with Bantazar for information, but she had issues with bonding with a male in order to pass off distasteful but necessary duties that kept the den running and her assassins happy.

Something was going to have to give soon.

So, as she shoved Lycus away, she did something she hadn't done since she found out she was a demon.

She prayed.

One

*"There are nights when the wolves are silent
and only the moon howls."*

—George Carlin

"You *damnedpire motherfucker!*"

Con barked out a laugh at Luc's shouted insult, even as he hit the snow hard enough to shatter a human man's thigh bones. But Con was a dhampire, a rare cross between a werewolf and a vampire, and he was made of stronger stuff. As a werewolf, Luc was equally strong, but he wasn't nearly as fast, as Con had proven by hot-loading out of the helicopter before Luc had even tugged his ski goggles down over his eyes.

Con hopped his skis twice to pull himself out of the snow-pack that still glazed the peaks of the Swiss Alps, and then he was zigzagging down the mountain. The sky was clear and blue, and here above the timberline, the silence was broken only by the soft *whoop-whoop* of the helo blades and the swish of his Rossignols as they cut the fresh powder.

The lulling quiet lasted only until Luc hit the snow and hurled insults at Con again.

The helo sounds faded as the pilot, who had called them all kinds of insane but had agreed—for quadruple his usual fee for heli-skiing—to bring them up higher on the mountain, hauled ass out of there. The dude had nearly stroked out when Con told him to hover at thirty feet instead of the inches he normally held at when letting human skiers off the bird.

But no, Con didn't do anything the easy way, or even the same way twice. The last time he and Luc had heli-skied, the drop had been shorter.

And the risk of avalanche had been far, far less.

The powder was thick on top of an unstable snowpack, the slope steep, and the effort it took for Con to navigate it all would have him trembling with exhaustion by the time they reached the Harrowgate in the valley miles below.

Ahead, the mountain face became a sheer cliff, and he leaped, catching air under his skis. The ground was impossibly far beneath him and scattered with boulders, but the wind was in his face, the scent of pine was in his lungs, and adrenaline was pumping hotly through his body.

This was the best way to live—or die, depending on how he landed.

Sometimes, he didn't really care either way.

He came down hard in an explosion of snow and nearly took a header, but he caught himself just before he hit a patch of wind-loaded crust that would have sent him flying.

Behind him, he heard Luc's skis scratching out turns . . . and then came the sounds of something more ominous.

Con turned in time to see Luc leap off a snowcapped boulder, but behind him, a giant sheet of snow had begun to crack and slide, an avalanche being born.

"Luc!" Heart pounding painfully against his ribs, Con tucked and pointed his skis down the hill, angled toward Luc and a massive boulder stabbing out of the side of the mountain. Luc couldn't see the potential shelter, was too close to the leading edge of the slab of white death coming at him.

Luc, never one for delicate maneuvers anyway, left finesse behind as he shot straight down the slope, barreling through drifts like an oil tanker through thirty-foot seas, but shit, he wasn't going to make it. The avalanche behind him was gaining, and though Con could veer to the left and avoid it, he headed straight into its path.

The wind seared his face as he gained speed, getting closer to Luc...closer to the rock...closer to the fucking wall of ice and snow. They had one shot at this, and his mind shut down, taking him to a place of calm as he hit Luc at the last second, knocking them both off their feet and into the boulder as the monster wave of snow rolled over them.

Con landed on top of Luc, gripped his shoulders hard as he turned his face away from the assault of frozen chunks that broke apart against the rock. The noise was deafening, the rumble so fierce that it vibrated Con's body and seemed to shock his heart into a new, frenzied rhythm.

Sixty seconds later, he lifted his head. Excellent. They were still alive.

"Get the hell off me, you damned pervert," Luc muttered.

Con eased himself off the werewolf and brushed snow out of the gap between his jacket and his neck. "Nice way to thank a guy who saved your miserable life."

Luc sat up and patted himself down, as if checking

to see whether he was missing any parts. "Fuck," he breathed. "This means I owe you."

"Damned straight." Con lifted his leg and discovered that one boot had snapped out of its binding, but thankfully, he had a ski leash, so the ski hadn't gone anywhere. "I can't wait to cash in."

"You'd better not make me do something stupid. Like run with the bulls." Luc dug inside one of his jacket pockets and pulled out a flask. "Naked."

Con grimaced. "Trust me, I have no desire to see your pale, bare ass." He snatched the flask from Luc and took a swig, relishing the burn of the rum as it slid down his throat. "But I wouldn't mind seeing you trampled by bulls. You're an asshole."

"Ditto." Luc grabbed the liquor away and took a deep pull. "You ready to go?"

Con snapped his boot into the binding. "Yep."

"What are we gonna do after this?"

A flare of regret jerked in Con's gut. Eidolon had sent all warg hospital employees into isolation to keep them from contracting the virus that was attacking the werewolf population, and Luc was going stir-crazy. Though Con and Luc had never been friends, exactly—they'd gotten their introduction in a bar fight with each other—they were paramedic partners and they hung out together occasionally, mainly to see who could beat who at whatever they did.

But ever since Luc had gone into isolation, he'd been even more eager to do crazy shit. Con was always game, but he *did* have a job, and he was working more than ever to make up for Luc's absence.

"I gotta work. But we'll go skydiving next week."

Luc nodded, and though his expression was as stony as ever, Con didn't miss the flash of disappointment in the guy's dark hazel eyes.

"When's the last time you got laid? When you were in Egypt? That Guardian chick?" Con shoved to his feet. "You need a woman."

Luc snorted. "Women are a pain in the ass," he said, and wasn't that the truth.

In fact, the biggest pain in the ass female he'd ever met was responsible for the very epidemic that was killing wargs. And Doc E had requested—well, ordered—a meeting with Con this afternoon, and he had a sickening feeling that the pain in the ass female, aka Sin, was going to be there.

Fuck. Once more, Con grabbed the flask from Luc, put it to his lips, and finished it off. Then he punched down the mountain.

Oh, yeah. Rum and adrenaline mixed well. Much, much better than he and Sin ever would.

Sin had been summoned.

Here she was, the freaking head of an assassin den, master of more than three dozen highly skilled killers, and she'd been summoned like some lowlife imp to an audience with her brother.

The great demon doctor.

She'd already given him her blood, her DNA, her pee, her spinal fluid...whatever samples the doctor wanted for his research, she'd handed over. Sin was, after all, responsible for the disease that was wiping out the werewolf race.

What a claim to fame.

A couple of days ago, she'd even come into Underworld General to channel her power into an infected male in an attempt to kill the virus, but if anything, she'd only accelerated its spread.

And she hadn't thought it could get any worse.

Sin muttered to herself as she traversed UG's dark hallways on the way to Eidolon's office. Her boots clacked on black stone floors that were unusually in need of a good sweeping, and the echo bounced in eerie vibrations off the gray walls. She trailed a finger over the writing on said walls—protective antiviolence spells scrawled in blood. She had to give credit to her brothers for that; the hospital serviced nearly all species of demons, many of which were mortal enemies.

She rounded a corner to enter the administrative area, only to curse fiercely. Wraith, the only one of her four brothers with blond hair and blue eyes—neither of which were original parts—stood in the doorway as though he'd been waiting for her. His arms were folded over his broad chest, the *dermoire* on his right arm blending in with his T-shirt's Celtic print—Celtic print that was cleverly designed to form the words "Fuck off."

"Well, if it isn't Typhoid Mary."

"Read your shirt." She pushed past him to enter the office, missing a step when she saw not only Eidolon, MD, but also Conall, SOB.

Great. When she'd last seen the vampire-werewolf a few weeks ago, they'd parted on shitty terms. He'd assumed the worst of her, threatened her, had been an utterly unlikable ass. Oh, sure, she'd led him to believe she'd intentionally started the epidemic that was killing his warg relatives, but if he hadn't been such a jerk, she might have told him the truth.

Not that the truth was much better.

"Sin." Eidolon remained at his desk, his espresso eyes bloodshot and framed by dark circles. His short, nearly black hair was mussed, probably from repeated rakes of his fingers. He pretty much looked like hell itself had beaten the crap out of him. "Sit."

The command ruffled her feathers, but she hooked a chair with her foot, yanked it as far from Conall as possible, and planted her ass. "What now? I don't have any blood left, and if you think you're getting a stool sample, you can—"

"I don't need a stool sample," Eidolon interrupted. "I need your help."

She felt Con's silver eyes boring into her like drill bits, and to her annoyance, her body flushed with warmth as though remembering another drilling he'd given her. That was *so* not happening again. "Look, you should know that the Assassin Guild has been flooded with requests for hits on wargs. I don't know if the sudden surge is related, but I figured I'd tell you."

Wraith's sharp gaze cut to Eidolon. "I've heard the same thing. Word on the street is that some of the other were-species are worried that the wolves will transmit the disease to them, so they're being a little . . . proactive."

Both Eidolon and Con uttered the same raw curse.

Sin settled back in her chair and forced herself to stay calm, when all she wanted to do was scream at this disaster she'd created. "You said you needed my help. What kind?"

Eidolon reached for the water bottle on his desk and

took a swig before speaking. "Thanks to Harrowgates
and the ability to travel instantaneously, the virus has
now made its way to every continent except Antarctica.
The death toll is climbing. The disease has a one hundred
percent mortality rate, a practically nonexistent incubation period, and no victim has lived longer than seventy-
two hours after infection. Basically, by the time a patient
arrives, we don't have a lot of time for treatment."

Jesus. It was worse than she'd thought. "Haven't you
made any progress at all?"

"A little." Leather squeaked as Eidolon leaned back
in his chair. "We've discovered a half-dozen wargs who
were exposed but didn't contract the infection. The R-XR
is trying to determine what makes them immune."

The U.S. Army's paranormal unit was involved now?
And Eidolon was working with them? She'd known that
their brother Shade's mate, Runa, used to be a member,
and that Runa's brother Arik still was, but *holy crap*—it
just didn't feel right for the government to be involved in
any way with Underworld General.

Especially not a military unit that killed, captured, and
experimented on demons.

Then again, UG had several strong ties to The Aegis,
a civilian demon-slaying organization—hell, Eidolon was
even mated to an Aegis Guardian—and so far, the asso-
ciation had benefitted both UG and The Aegis.

"So I'm here, why? Are you in need of assassination
services, or what?" She threw that out just to get a reaction from her uptight, always-in-control brother, but to her
surprise, it was Con who made the noise.

"You're here because wargs are dying, and it's your
fault," he growled, a hint of an odd British-ish accent

tweaking his words. It happened when he got all pissy, and it was strangely . . . hot.

But she still didn't like him, and she wrenched her head around to peg him with a glare. Which might have been a good plan if he hadn't looked so damned good in his black paramedic uniform, which set off his deeply tanned skin and sun-streaked blond hair so beautifully. Toss in those shimmering silver eyes, and there was no glaring at him. Only admiring.

"Why are you even here?" she snapped, more irritated by her reaction to him than anything. "I didn't think the disease affected dhampires."

"I'm on the Warg Council. I'm keeping them informed."

"Well, good for you."

Eidolon cleared his throat imperiously. "Actually, you're both here for a reason. Sin, it's time that we put some serious effort into working with your gift. We've got to determine a way to use it to treat the disease."

"We tried that before. My 'gift' kills. It doesn't cure." Her "gift" was something she'd really like to give right back to her Seminus father. Too bad he was dead.

"Yeah, well, technically, you shouldn't exist, so I'm not ready to write off the impossible."

Oh, she loved the reminders about how she was a freak of nature, the only female Seminus demon to ever have been born. A Smurfette, as Wraith liked to call her.

"So what's your plan?"

"Can you use your gift to determine what kind of disease resides inside a body? If you touch someone who is ill, can you tell what they are sick with?"

"Sort of. I can feel the arrangement of the virus or

bacteria or whatever. And once I learn it, I can replicate that specific disease." She shot Conall a smirk. "Khileshi cockfire is a favorite."

Wraith laughed. Conall paled. Eidolon looked at her like she was responsible for every case of the excruciating, dick-shriveling venereal disease he'd ever treated. The guy was so freaking uptight he probably starched his freaking underwear.

"As disturbing as that is," Eidolon said flatly, "it's exactly what I wanted to hear."

There was a tap at the door, and Lore strode past Wraith, who was still playing doorjamb sentinel. Lore held a folder in his leather-gloved hand, and Sin didn't think she'd ever get used to seeing her twin brother in scrubs. "I read the R-XR's initial report on the immune wargs, and something jumped out at me. The wargs who didn't catch SF after being exposed were born wargs. So I examined the bodies in our morgue and ran some tests. I know not every warg that's been infected has come through the hospital, but the ones who have? *Turned* wargs."

Sin frowned. "SF?"

"Sin Fever," Wraith chimed in a little too enthusiastically.

Sin Fever? They'd named the fucking disease after her? Bastards.

E flipped excitedly through the folder Lore gave him. "Just when I thought we'd never find a link between the victims. I'll call the R-XR and let them know. Excellent work, Lore."

Despite the grim subject matter, Sin couldn't help but be thrilled that her brother, who had, as an assassin, known nothing but killing and loneliness until just weeks ago, was now mated, happy, and working in the hospital—the morgue, where his death-touch couldn't accidentally kill anyone.

"Wait," Sin said. "How can you tell the difference between turned and born werewolves?"

"Born wargs usually have a birthmark somewhere on their bodies, but we can't always go by that." Before Sin could ask why, Eidolon finished. "Outcasts are required to have them removed, and some turned wargs have them artificially applied, so we have to perform genetic testing to determine if they're born or turned."

Huh. Who would have thunk it? "So, what was it you wanted with me?"

Eidolon looked up from the paperwork, and the circles under his eyes seemed to have lightened a little. "About that . . . see, that's why I called Con to this meeting."

Bracing his muscular forearms on his knees, Con leaned forward in his chair. When he spoke, his fangs flashed as fiercely as his eyes. "What are you saying?"

"Your weekly blood tests for SF have been coming back negative," Eidolon said. "Until yesterday."

"*What?* I have the disease?" Con exploded out of his chair, but Eidolon held up his hands in a stay-calm motion.

"Not exactly. It's in your blood. Your body isn't attacking it, nor is it attacking you, and you aren't producing antibodies. But when we introduced Sin's blood to the mix in the lab, your white blood cells and hers joined forces to attack the virus."

Sin's skin prickled with foreboding. Eidolon was dancing around something. "Skip the buildup and backstory. Bottom line, what do you want from us?"

"I need Con to feed from you," he said with uncharacteristic awkwardness. "And I need it to happen now."

I need Con to feed from you.

Con cursed softly. "As much as I'd like to help you out, Doc, I can't do what you're asking." Yeah, he'd tasted Sin's blood before—and it had been damned good—but that was exactly why he couldn't do it again. He'd been addicted to a female's blood before, and he would never allow it to happen again.

"I get that she's not your favorite person—"

"He said he can't do it," Lore interrupted. "Let it go."

Eidolon tapped a pencil on his desk, the dull thud of the eraser on wood punctuating his words. "Unfortunately, there's no 'let it go' option. This might be our only shot at an immediate solution."

"I don't understand," Sin said. "What do you mean, a solution?"

Eidolon spun one of the papers around to show Sin and Con where he'd scrawled a lengthy column of numbers. "I can't inject the amount of Sin's blood required to destroy the virus into Conall without killing him. He needs to ingest it. As a dhampire, he has a double-chambered stomach, the second chamber working the way a vampire's works—to deliver a victim's blood almost directly into the vampire's bloodstream. So if my calculations are correct, a normal feeding will allow him to take in enough blood to start attacking the virus. Once that's done—"

"I can monitor his blood to learn how the virus is killed and then use my power to try to destroy it myself," Sin finished.

"Exactly." Eidolon grinned. "You really should be working here instead of as an assassin."

At some point, Sin had produced a throwing knife and was now flipping it between her fingers, and Con had a feeling the speed directly related to her level of agitation. The sucker was whirling like a helicopter blade. "Bite me."

Eidolon gestured to Conall. "That'll be his job."

"No," Con said grimly. "It won't. There has to be another way."

"I agree." Sin rose to her feet, her blue-black hair swishing angrily around her waist. "I don't let anyone fang me."

You let me, you little liar. Hot, little liar. Man, Con wanted to call her out on exactly how she'd let him, but at least two of her brothers in the room were a little on the overprotective side, and the other didn't need an excuse to kill things. Come to think of it, none of them needed an excuse.

Neither did Con.

"If there was any other way," Eidolon said, "I'd find it. But there's not." He wadded up a sheet of paper and tossed it at the overflowing garbage can in the corner. "You have the virus—it's just not attacking you, and I don't know why yet. It's a slightly different strain from what's attacking the wargs...it's adapted to your species, but it might be trying to mutate into something that *can* attack you, which is why we need to eliminate it as soon as possible. As for the wargs...that's what was so weird about the blood samples the R-XR took. It was as if the uninfected wargs were a different species and unable to catch the virus."

"You mean like how horses don't catch measles from humans," Sin said, and Eidolon nodded.

"Exactly. I still don't know what would make born wargs so different from turneds." The frustration in Eidolon's voice was echoed in his expression as he turned to Con. "And you, even with your vampire status, you're somehow more closely related to turned wargs than born ones."

A tremor of unease went through Con. That was just one of the dhampire race's dirty little secrets, but it was one he was going to have to share with the doctor. Anything to help get this damned epidemic stopped. Well, not *anything*. He'd leave out the minor details. Though he supposed he didn't owe his people the courtesy of keeping their secrets, since they'd all but exiled him. Oh, they kept track of him because, ultimately, he was too valuable to completely throw away, but he'd shamed them, and they were happy to punish him for it.

"Dhampires aren't exactly born this way."

Eidolon scowled. "What do you mean?"

Con leaned forward and braced his forearms on his thighs. "I mean that when we hit our late teens, our fangs come in, we start craving blood... and then we get sick. On the first night of the full moon after our fangs have fully developed, we have to be bitten by a warg or we'll die."

"Interesting," Eidolon murmured. "So dhampires are basically turned werewolves who drink blood. Guess that explains why you ended up with a form of the virus, but there's something else to consider."

Con didn't like his tone. Not at all. "What else?"

Eidolon paused as though searching his brain for the right words, and Con's gut hollowed out. "The virus inside you isn't likely to want to *only* attack you. It wants out."

"So what you're saying," Con ground out, "is that I'm a carrier. I could have infected people."

"Unfortunately, yes. The disease seems to be transmitted via both direct and indirect contact, as well as by air, but as an asymptomatic carrier, you might transmit it differently. I tested your saliva, and it's definitely present. We need to run tests to be sure, but since Luc hasn't come down with the virus, you probably aren't breathing it out or passing it on by casual touch. But you need to avoid intimate contact with werewolves and other dhampires."

Oh, bloody hell. How many females had Con fed from and slept with in the last month? His mind raced as he counted and eliminated those who weren't werewolves. Only one had been a warg...a *turned* warg. And ironically, a female who he'd avoided sleeping with for years because he cared about her, and she deserved better than a one-off with him.

Shit. "Hold on, Doc." Con dug his cell from his pocket, dialed, and Yasashiku, a member of the Warg Council, answered on the second ring.

"Con. You're missing the meeting. Valko's about to have a freaking puppy. Where are you?"

"I'm at work. I'll be there as soon as I can." Moving toward a corner, he lowered his voice. "Have you heard from Nashiki lately?"

Yasashiku's silence made Con suddenly, achingly, aware of the pounding sound of his heartbeat in his ears. "You didn't hear?"

"Hear what?" *Don't say it. Don't. Fucking. Say it.*

"She caught the virus," Yas said, his faint Japanese accent thickening with emotion. "She died last night."

Con didn't even reply. Numbly, he closed the phone.

He'd done his share of killing in his thousand years of life, some of it justified, some not. But there was something truly obscene about killing someone with pleasure. Especially because, years ago, he'd saved Nashiki's life after she'd been attacked by a pride of lion-shifters, and though he didn't normally keep in contact with his patients, she'd been special, bubbly and bright, one of the few people he'd met in his life who never let anything get them down.

So he'd saved her . . . only to kill her.

Sure, there was no proof that *he* had given the virus to the gorgeous, honey-skinned warg, who hadn't deserved how he'd screwed her while fantasizing about Sin, let alone how he'd given her a disease that had turned her organs to mush. No proof at all, but the timing was right, given the time frame from onset to death.

Crimson washed over his vision as both nausea that he'd killed an innocent female and anger that the person ultimately responsible was right there in the room with him collided. This had to end, and at this point, the risks of repeated feedings from Sin were the least of his concerns.

Especially since all of the risk would be Sin's.

"Con?" Wraith's deep voice was a mere buzz among the other noise in Con's head. "Dude. You okay? You look like you're about to take a header."

"Then I'd better feed." Conall's voice was cold as he swung around to Sin. "And it looks like you're lunch."

Two

This was such bullshit.

Sin got that this might be the answer to the epidemic, but Con didn't have to look at her like she was a juicy steak. He could at least try to be as repulsed as she was.

"Sit." Con's voice had deepened to a compelling, husky rasp that nearly had her complying with his demand like a well-trained dog.

"We're going to do it here?"

He cocked a sandy eyebrow. "You'd rather do it in a patient room? Or maybe a supply closet would be more to your liking?"

Oh, the bastard. They were *not* going to a patient room, where a bed would make it way too easy to do more than the blood thing, and the supply closet remark was a jab at the first—and *last*—place they'd been together.

She sank down into a chair. "Fine. Get it over with."

"How sweet," Wraith said. "You sound like an old married couple."

She flipped him off as Con turned to her brothers. "Could we get some privacy?"

"No." Sin jabbed a finger at Eidolon. "You. Stay." Mainly, she was being a bitch, but also, the little flutter in her belly at the thought of being alone again with Con was a dangerous sign that she *shouldn't* be alone with him.

Lore stepped forward. "I'll stay."

"It's okay, bro," she said. The last thing she needed was Lore's hovering. He'd been doing it for thirty years, and he seemed to be having a hard time breaking the habit. "This will be strictly a clinical procedure. Eidolon can oversee it." *Clinical?* That was a joke and a half, because she knew having Con's fangs slide into her flesh would be pleasurable no matter how much she wanted to deny it.

For a long moment, Sin was sure Lore would argue. Fists clenched, he stood there glowering, his *dermoire* writhing angrily. Like hers, it was a faded imitation of their purebred brothers' markings, but it still behaved the same way, appearing to move during periods of high emotion. He finally nodded and, after shooting Con a look of scathing brotherly warning, took off.

She made a shooing motion at Wraith. "You, too. Scram."

"Smurfy." Wraith took off, whistling the theme to *The Smurfs* as he went.

"We don't need Eidolon," Con said. "I've been doing this for a thousand years. I know when to stop."

Sin wasn't worried about being drained, but she wasn't about to admit that her real fear was that without a chaperone, she'd end up doing a lot more than playing Happy

Meal. Fortunately, she didn't have to say anything, because Eidolon got that stern expression on his face, closed the door, and propped a shoulder against it, long legs crossed casually at the ankles. He wasn't about to budge, and Con must have come to the same conclusion because he muttered something under his breath and sank to his knees beside her.

With him kneeling, they were at eye level, and she gulped dryly when he locked gazes with her.

"Give me your wrist," he said, and when she hesitated, his cold smile was at odds with the heat roaring off his body. "You'd prefer the throat? Or groin? Sure, it'd go faster that way, but I didn't think you'd want that much intimacy." His eyes sparked with amusement, mocking her.

She thrust her left arm at him. "Damn skippy, I don't."

He took her wrist gingerly, as if the mere thought of touching her disgusted him. And maybe it did on some level. But she'd never met a vampire who didn't admit to getting at least a little revved while feeding.

A whisper of pain came with the penetration of his fangs, followed by sparks of pleasure so intense she had to bite back a moan.

"Sin," Eidolon said softly, "you'll need to monitor the virus levels in his blood now and then. You should get a baseline now."

Yes, a baseline. Anything to wrench her attention away from how good it felt to have Con's lips on her, his teeth in her. Concentrating, she fired up her gift until the *dermoire* on her arm began to glow, and then she gripped Con's shoulder. Beneath her fingers, his muscles bunched as though in protest, but her succubus senses picked up signs of increased arousal: the sound of his heart rate jacking up, the rapid rise and fall of his chest, the rise in the temperature of his skin.

Her own body answered with a rush of liquid heat, but she clenched her teeth and concentrated on reading his blood. Her power entered him in a focused beam and threaded through his veins and arteries. When she used her gift to create a disease, her victims didn't feel a thing, but she'd never probed around like this before.

"You okay?" she asked, and when Con's shimmering eyes flashed up at her, she regretted asking. Who cared if he was okay? She was the one getting sucked on. The one who was starting to see spots.

He gave a slow nod and went back to taking long pulls on her wrist. Closing her eyes, partly because the room had begun to spin, she focused on feeling around inside Con's veins. Shadowy black-and-white pictures formed in her head. She could see individual blood cells rushing through the narrow vessels, and with them, the virus. New cells joined the rush; hers, she was sure. Almost as though the presence of the fresh cells prodded Con's, his cells attacked the virus like a pack of wolves taking down an injured deer.

"It's working," she whispered, hoping the boys didn't notice the way her speech was a little slurred.

Con's draws began to ease off.

"Keep going. You need more of my blood to join the fight."

He grunted, a sound of refusal, and his fangs began to slide from her flesh. She grabbed his head and forced him to stay, though it took a lot more effort than it should have. "Almost, Con. We can kill it off—"

"Sin!" Eidolon's strong fingers pried hers from Con's scalp. And maybe she shouldn't have noticed how silky his blond hair was, but for some reason, she did. "He has to stop."

"Just a little longer..."

Rearing back, Con tore away from her. His eyes were swirling pools of molten metal, the carnal hunger there giving away both his fear that he'd gone too far and his desire to go further. Eidolon clapped a palm over her bleeding wrist even as she lunged forward, desperate to get Con to take more blood. She needed more time to study how the virus survived, how it died...

"We can't stop now!"

Con swore, grabbed her hand, and for a moment she thought he was going to continue, but instead, he peeled her brother's hand away even as Eidolon fired up his own gift to heal her and swiped his tongue over the punctures. Before her eyes, they sealed up, and an irrational fury grabbed her.

"You idiots!" More spots gathered in her vision and her head spun as she lurched to her feet. "The virus is going to rally in him. It's going to..."

"Shit!" Con's voice and arms closed around her as the floor fell out from beneath her.

"So, you've been feeding for a thousand years, huh?" Eidolon's sarcastic drawl grated on every one of Conall's nerves as he carried Sin to the nearest exam room and laid her gently on the bed.

Thing was, Con had no excuse. Sure, Sin kept encouraging him, telling him they were almost there, but worse than that—terrifyingly worse—was that hunger for her had overridden common sense, and he'd fed for longer than he should have.

He was just glad he hadn't wrestled her to the floor and tried to take a lot more than blood.

"Heal her," he snapped, his anger at himself putting a caustic note in his voice that Eidolon didn't deserve. Still, the doctor merely shrugged as he gathered IV supplies from the cabinet next to the bed.

"My power knits tissue and bone together. It doesn't make blood." He lined up the supplies on a tray and wheeled it toward Sin. "We'd need Shade for this. He can use his gift to force the marrow to produce blood faster."

Con brushed her glossy hair away from her face, which was far too pale.

"Then get Shade," he pressed. Sin wasn't in danger, but he didn't like how her vibrance had been literally sucked out of her. But this *was* the first time she'd ever been quiet. He should be grateful.

"He's off for a few days." E gestured to the cabinets behind Con. "Toss me a Ringer's."

Con fetched a bag of IV saline solution and lobbed it to the doctor. "So call him in."

"Runa's sick, and he can't leave the triplets."

Con's breath lodged in his throat. Shade's mate was a turned werewolf. "It isn't SF, right?"

Eidolon inserted a needle into a vein in Sin's left hand. "Thank gods, no. It's a mild stomach virus."

"Good." Con would hate to see anything happen to the female who had made Shade a lot more agreeable to work for. And speaking of work... "You going to call Bastien back in, now that you know the virus isn't affecting the *pricolici*?" Bastien, a born warg who had been run off by his pack decades ago because he'd been born with a club foot, had devoted his life to UG, and Con knew the forced "vacation" had to be killing him as much as it was Luc.

"Hell, yeah." Eidolon gestured to gauze wrappers on the floor. "The janitorial department is falling apart without him."

As Eidolon hooked the bag of saline onto a stand, Sin moaned, and her eyes opened. "What...what are you doing?"

"Hold still," Eidolon said. "Our boy here got a little carried away with his meal."

She smiled weakly. "That's 'cuz I'm so sweet and irresistible."

Con snorted. "Not the words I would use for you." Well, irresistible, maybe, but there were a lot of less complimentary words that fit her, too.

"Ass," she muttered. She lifted her hand and frowned at the line connected to it. "Hey, knock it off. I don't need this—"

Con gripped her wrist and pushed it back down to the mattress. "Yeah, you do. I took too much blood."

Eidolon shot her a stern look. "If you had banked more of your blood like I asked you to do, I could be putting it instead of saline back into your veins."

"Yeah, yeah. Whatever. I heal fast."

"One benefit of being a Seminus demon," Eidolon said as he jacked up the head of the bed so she could sit.

"There are more?" Sarcasm dripped from Sin's voice, but Eidolon ignored her to check his beeper.

"I have an incoming trauma. Con, stay with her until the bag is empty. When you're done, hit the lab. I'd like a blood sample from you. I want to see if you have any antibodies in your system now. And you"—he pointed his finger at Sin—"be good."

Sin rolled her eyes, but at least she didn't snark back at him. Instead, she waited until the doctor left, and then she turned on Con, a little bundle of ebony-eyed fury. "You idiot!"

She was sexy when she got worked up. "I said I was sorry for taking too much blood." Actually, he hadn't, but he felt a little bad about it, so he figured that counted.

"You should have taken more. You could still be contagious."

"It's not worth killing you over." Not that killing her wasn't tempting.

"Well, duh. But chugging another pint of blood wouldn't have killed me."

"Yeah, it would have." He dug through one of the drawers for a phlebotomy kit. "Why haven't you banked your blood like E wanted?"

"Who are you? My dad? It's none of your business." She shifted on the bed, the seductive rasp of her tight leather pants against the sheets making his cock twitch. Con might not like her, but his dick wasn't so judgmental.

"If you'd done it, I could be drinking it now instead of waiting for you to produce more blood." He pulled up a chair with a frustrated yank, sat, and rolled up his shirt sleeve.

"I'll see if I can speed things up just for you," she said wryly. "And in the meantime, be careful that you don't run around spreading disease."

"Ironic thing to say, coming from you, don't you think?" He snorted. "I think I can manage to not bite or fuck a warg for a few days. And do you really care?"

Crimson splotched her cheeks, and he caught the scent of irritation coming from her. "Yeah. You're right. I'm thrilled that the virus is killing people. Yay, me."

"Why did you start it, then?"

"I was bored. There hasn't been a good pandemic since the Spanish flu in, what, 1918?"

"Son of a—" He wrapped a rubber tourniquet around his biceps. "Just once, can you give me a straight answer?" Working with angry, jerky movements, he clamped one end of the tube in his teeth and tugged it tight.

Sin squeezed her eyes shut, and for a heartbeat, a startling shadow of vulnerability darkened her expression. But so quickly Con doubted what he saw, she opened her eyes and locked on him with that death ray of hers. "Killing is what I do. Do you really think I need a reason to start an epidemic?"

Jesus effing Christ. He had never met a female—or male, for that matter—with such a thick wall around them. Swearing to himself, he inserted a needle into the median cubital vein in the crook of his elbow. "I actually do think you need a reason. You might be an assassin, but I haven't met an assassin yet who didn't plan every kill very carefully."

Surprise flickered in her cool black eyes at his assessment. "Most people think we run around killing all willy-nilly."

"Most people are morons." He reached for a vacutainer, a tube for gathering blood. "Most hunters, whether animal, human, or demon, are selective and careful about their prey. You get caught or injured, and you're dead. Hunting is a matter of life or death if you need to eat."

"Like you."

"Like me." He eyed her, wished she'd stop squirming and making obscene rubbing sounds on the sheets. "Even in warg form, I'm careful about what I catch."

"I thought werewolves *do* kill all willy-nilly." The way one corner of her mouth turned up in an impish smile told him she wasn't completely serious.

"*Pricolici* wargs and dhampires maintain control. It's the turned werewolves you have to watch out for, but usually only the newer ones. The older that wargs are, the more they can control themselves during the moon phase. Younger wargs do tend to kill without a lot of skill or forethought."

Young wargs were the ones who tended to get nailed by The Aegis, and the ones who had given all werewolves a reputation for being monsters. On the other paw, the older any warg was, the less "human" he became. There was definitely a trade-off. Control while in beast form came with a loss of connection with humans while in the human body.

He pushed the vacutainer into the holder, and blood began to fill the tube. Sin frowned. "Uh...do you need help with that?"

"Nah. I'm good with one hand."

"No doubt you are."

He smirked, amused by her presumption. "I have no need to be. Females fall at my feet." Sin hadn't exactly fallen at his feet—no, she'd tried to kick his ass when they first met. But she'd eventually caved. Of course, as a succubus, she could very well cave to every male who crossed her path. And why that thought made him suddenly grumpy he had no idea.

"The day I fall at your feet," she drawled, "is the day I give up pizza."

"Pizza?"

"Mmm, love it. All kinds. Thin crust, pan crust, the works, just cheese...yum." She rubbed her flat belly, and Con had to clench his fist to keep from reaching over and joining the action. "Stomach's rumbling. Need pizza."

"Tell you what. You explain to me why you started the epidemic, and I'll bring you a pizza when I come back from the Council meeting." He also made a mental note to call Luc with an update about SF. Con had promised the warg that he'd keep him up on the latest news.

She hesitated, then shrugged. "It was a hit gone wrong. I was supposed to waste this werewolf, so I channeled my gift into him. It usually kills quickly, but I was interrupted by Idess."

"Lore's mate? Why would she interrupt?" Con remembered the first time he'd seen the gorgeous angel who gave off a glow of pure goodness, even though rumor had it that she was human now. Idess had been brought in to the hospital by Lore after a battle in which they'd tried to kill each other.

Now they were mated, happy, and practically inseparable.

Sin waved her hand. "Long story. But basically, she was all angel-fied at the time, and she was protecting the guy." She cast a sideways glance at him. "It was that first victim you brought into the hospital. Remember when I was waiting around the ER?"

Hell, yeah, he remembered. He'd brought Chase in, and Sin had been hovering. He'd left the dying werewolf in a trauma room and paused outside the door to write up the paperwork. Sin had been there.

She cleared her throat. "Hey, how is the warg?"

Con looked up, startled to see the incredibly hot female standing in front of him. "Dying. Why?"

"No reason." She rubbed her arms, which were covered by her denim jacket sleeves. "What's wrong with him? Was he in an accident? Is he sick with something?"

"You're kind of nosy."

She shrugged. "Just a concerned citizen."

He watched her for a moment, letting his enhanced vampire and warg senses reach out to detect her species. Her high temperature and low heart rate indicated demon blood, but she smelled slightly human. So demon and human, but what kind of demon? Whatever she was, she bled like everyone else. The scent came to him on a raft of air, making his mouth water and his fangs drop. As a paramedic, he'd trained himself to ignore the tantalizing scent and sight—Doc E frowned on his medics attacking patients for food—but for some reason, he was reacting to this sexy creature. "You should get your leg looked at."

Frowning, she looked down at the spot of blood that had seeped through her jeans. "It's no big—"

He didn't wait for her to finish. Hunger had hijacked his body, and if he didn't get the hell away from the little temptress, he'd soon be feeling the effects of the Haven spell when he jumped on her. Quickly, he handed the clipboard to a nurse and headed toward the parking lot.

"So," he said, "you tried to kill that warg with your gift, and he survived long enough to infect others."

Sin tucked her knees up against her and wrapped her *dermoire*-marked arm around them, giving him a tantalizing view of her tight, round ass. Not that he was looking. "Yep."

"Why not slit their throats or shoot them? Why go the disease route?"

"Why not?"

Back to the nonanswers. *Impossible female.* "Do you want the pizza, or not?"

"What, pizzas are rationed now and only you can get one? I'm outta here." She yanked the catheter out of her hand and leaped off the bed with sinuous grace and the lightest thump of boots on the floor. "I have stuff to do, people to kill, and I can get my own pizza." Blood seeped from her hand, and though Con was sated, his mouth still watered.

"Come here." His voice was low and rough, and Sin swung around, her furious glare burning a hole right through him.

"Screw you."

"Been there, done that," he growled. "Now, come here."

She shot him the bird and started toward the door. "I don't respond well to orders."

He was up in a flash, the tube of blood dangling from his arm, and he had her backed against the wall. "Then what do you respond to, little demon? Because right now, I've got a mind to turn you over my knee and spank the spoiled hell out of you and see how you respond to *that*." Her gasp of outrage was a bright spot in his otherwise shitty day. "Oh, yeah," he purred, as he wedged his thigh between hers. "You do respond to me. You responded very well to what I spilled inside you."

When she'd told him she couldn't climax until her partner came first, he'd been surprised. And then he'd made her come. Hard. He could still hear the sound of her panting breaths, could still feel her tight inner muscles clamped around him—

She struck out, but before her fist could knock loose a few of his teeth, she hissed and grabbed her head with both hands as the pain from the antiviolence enchantment that protected the hospital kicked in. She and her siblings were immune, but only if they fought with each other.

"Forgot about the Haven spell, huh?"

"I hate you," she rasped, and why that made him smile, he had no idea.

More gently than she deserved, he peeled her bleeding hand away from her head and swiped his tongue over the needle puncture. God, she tasted decadent, with a bite like fine brandy, and he couldn't help but let his tongue linger on her skin. She went taut, slowly releasing her head with her other hand.

Beneath his fingers, the pulse in her wrist pounded, matching his beat for crazy beat. The air between them crackled with sudden heat, and his hips surged as he pressed his palm to her delicate throat, wanting to absorb the sensation of her lifeblood flowing under both his hands.

Ah...*damn.* Power swamped him as though he'd completed a circuit. She was life. She was death. She was the most dangerous female he'd ever met, and if he was smart, he'd run like hell.

Licking her lips, Sin took a deep, shuddering breath that ended with "Release me."

Right now, that was the last thing he wanted to do, but he'd made his point. She might hate him, but she wanted him. Head a little fuzzy and still feeling the buzz of her blood inside his veins, he stepped back, but she surprised him when she caught his wrist.

Her *dermoire* lit up, and heat spread through his arm. "Just checking your virus levels," she said, her voice thick with the same lust that coursed through him like syrup. "You really should have drank more."

He fixed his gaze on her throat and was only half serious when he murmured, "Still can."

Her eyes glinted with mischief as she eased closer and pressed the length of her body against him. All her soft parts fit perfectly with his hard ones, but then he'd known that. "Go for it," she said, exposing her throat and calling his bluff.

She knew damned good and well that he couldn't risk taking more blood from her, especially given how he'd lost control earlier. And he wasn't about to take from her throat. Too intimate, too much contact, and way too much Sin for him.

Funny. Too much sin. *That* had never been a concern before. He'd spent the majority of his life committing all of the sins and inventing new ones.

But this little succubus was killing his people, had made him a carrier of the disease, and her brothers were hyperprotective sons of demons who would have his balls on a spit if he fanged and banged her right here, right now.

You did her in a fucking closet.

Yeah, and talk about a mistake. One he wouldn't mind repeating. Sure, he despised her, but that would keep things interesting in the sack, wouldn't it?

Images of her clawing his back, biting his neck, fighting him even as she spread her legs for him flooded his brain. A sixth sense told him she'd give as good as she got, would have no trouble keeping up with him even during the worst of the moon fever, when violent matings could kill.

Back off … back off … He took in a ragged breath, desperate to keep control, because although the full moon was two weeks away, Sin's blood had forced a high tide in his veins, and every primal urge was starting to rage.

Besides, there wasn't a breed of succubi out there that didn't steal something. Whether it was your seed, your soul, your life force, or your heart, they sucked something out of you and rarely gave back.

Sin definitely did not strike him as the giving kind.

The door flew open with a bang. Still hopped up with feral instincts, Con pivoted, fangs bared, to face the threat.

Wraith strode inside, his loose gait deceptively relaxed. Deceptive, because his bright gaze was predatory; he was fully aware of what he'd walked in on, and Con knew the cagey bastard well enough to know he'd file away the information and use it when it was to his advantage.

"Smurfette," Wraith drawled, his eyes focused on Con. "E needs you in the ER. Warg came in, circling the drain."

Sin scowled. "Circling the drain?"

"Dying," Con gritted out. "He's dying."

Wraith nodded. "Time to see if you can save lives instead of just taking them."

Three

Karlene Lucio wasn't sure what would come first: freezing to death or bleeding to death. There was another possibility as well, but she refused to consider the idea that she was going to be decapitated by Aegis hunters.

Some of the very same Aegis hunters she'd been working with for years.

Pain streaked through her right shoulder where the bullet had entered, and snow stung her face as she stumbled through the dense forest, leaving a trail of blood a blind man could follow. Damned Canadian wilderness. Who lived here?

The person you need to find, that's who.

Shivering despite the layers of clothing she wore, she stumbled over a fallen branch and did a face-plant in the crusted ice. A crack rang out, and wood exploded in shards an inch from her cheek. A muffled scream escaped from her as she rolled and came up behind a thick log. Her

hand shook as she dug in her parka pocket for her pistol—
not that she could hit the broad side of a Gargantua demon
with her left hand.

Empty. Her gun was gone.

Frantically, she looked around her, dug through the
snow, tearing her nails and fingertips, leaving bloody
smears in the pristine snow. She didn't even hear the second shot that put a slug through her upper arm and lodged
in her side. She felt it, though, like a hot poker striking
her with the force of a semi truck, and she flew backward,
slamming into a tree trunk hard enough to knock the air
from her lungs. As she lay on the ground, dazed, fire gathered in her veins, spreading through her body, and she
almost welcomed it. Anything to not feel cold anymore.

The snow and the trees began to blur together. Something crunched next to her: footsteps. Weakly, she looked
up at Wade, the male Guardian standing before her, the
barrel of his pistol aimed at her forehead.

"I'm sorry it had to come to this," he said gruffly. His
eyes were sad but resolved. She'd expect nothing else from
a Guardian who was forced to destroy someone who had
deceived and betrayed The Aegis for years. Didn't matter
that they'd fought side by side, had worked toward a common goal—to rid the earth of evil.

She was now considered one of the evil . . . and a traitor,
to boot. The Aegis's new, more lenient stance on underworld creatures was even more of a joke than a don't-ask-
don't-tell policy.

She could beg for her life, but it wouldn't do any good.
And in truth, she'd never begged for anything, and she
wasn't about to start now. Besides, maybe this was for the
best.

"Close your eyes," he said.

"Go to hell." Her death might be for the best, but that didn't mean she was going to make it easy on her killer. Wade was going to have to look into her eyes as he ended her life.

This time, she heard the shot. But she didn't feel it. Blood sprayed everywhere, splattering the trees, the snow, her face. Wade crumpled to the ground, the top of his skull missing. And standing where Wade's body had been was the very werewolf she'd come all the way into the middle of nowhere to see.

And though her vision was fading, she could tell that he didn't look happy to see her.

Son of a bitch.

Luc looked down at the female Guardian whose pale blue eyes had gone glassy, and he knew she was about to lose consciousness. Sure enough, as he plugged the butt of his rifle into the snow, she twitched like a dying beetle, face pale from blood loss and cold, and she was bleeding a hot river into the snow.

Karlene.

Jesus. The last time he'd seen her had been in Egypt, where they'd met. And screwed. And then parted without a word, and Luc had never expected to see her again.

So what the hell was she doing here? And why were her fellow Aegi trying to kill her? Did they know her secret?

Right now, it didn't matter. She was bleeding to death, the freak late-spring blizzard was getting worse, and there was, no doubt, another Aegi out here somewhere. The demon hunters rarely worked alone.

Cursing, he slung the rifle over his shoulder, gathered

Karlene in his arms, and forged his way back to his cabin.
She was bleeding badly, but he couldn't risk being followed by a Guardian and he had to take the long way
back—a path that took him along a stream bed that would
hide his tracks if the blizzard didn't.

Finally, wet, frozen, and exhausted, he reached his
cabin. Inside, the fire blazed and the scent of rabbit stew
permeated the air. In his arms, the female groaned. The
sound was reedy, weak, and he had to hurry.

Carefully, he laid her down near the hearth, and then
he peeled back the bearskin rug near the south corner of
the living room. Knots and natural wood grain concealed
the hatch he'd had installed and concealed by a sorceress,
but with one well-placed strike with the side of his fist
over one particular knot the door popped open. Instantly,
a blast of icy air blew his chin-length black hair away
from his face and dried out his eyes. He'd have to get a fire
going down there or Kar would freeze to death before she
had a chance to bleed out.

Gently, he picked her up and carried her down the steep
steps. The room beneath was dark, stealing light only
from the slats in the floor above. He lay her on the straw
pallet, lit a fire in the hearth that had been cleverly vented
through the fireplace above, and ran back up the stairs.

After grabbing his jump bag and a couple of blankets, he
kneeled beside her and gloved up. Her lightly freckled face
was pale, her short cap of strawberry blond hair matted
to her skull, and she no longer looked like the tough-bitch
Guardian who had gone toe-to-toe with him during battle-
lust-induced werewolf sex. She looked vulnerable and fragile, and right now, he was her only hope of survival.

Working rapidly and with precision, he went through

the standard ABCs—airway, breathing, circulation—ritual and was not thrilled with the results. Her pulse was rapid and thready, her breathing labored, and, damn, he wished he was a doctor instead of a paramedic.

He grabbed a pair of shears to cut away her parka, the sweater beneath it, and the thermal and silk shirts under that. The girl had definitely been prepared for the cold. Too bad she hadn't been prepared for the two bullets that had torn apart her shoulder and arm.

The flesh was mangled, and bone thrust through the hamburger-like mess. Black streaks spread like evil vines from the wounds, through her shoulder and chest, lengthening and branching off as he watched.

Silver bullets. So the Aegis definitely knew what she was—a born warg. He'd seen her crescent moon birthmark on the sole of her foot when they'd been naked. If not for that, Luc would have left her to die in the snow. He wasn't taking any chances, so lucky for her he'd just gotten a call on his sat-phone from Con, who'd given him the latest SF update. Only turned wargs were affected. Wasn't *that* just fortuitous as all hell for the bastard borns.

The wounds were bad. Kar needed to go to UG, but the nearest Harrowgate was two miles away, and in the blizzard it would take him hours to get there—*if* he could get there. He had a snowmobile, but it wouldn't do much good in this weather, and the noise would attract any nearby Aegi.

And they were still two weeks from the full moon, which meant there was no hope for Kar to shift and heal her wounds.

If he didn't get her real medical attention, these wounds would kill her.

He could buy her time, though. The silver bullets had

to come out. The poison was spreading through her body, had already reached her abdomen, and at this rate, she'd be dead within the hour.

"Kar?" He spoke in a low, soothing tone as he rummaged through the medical kit for his forceps. "This is going to hurt." She didn't reply, and he hoped she was too out of it to feel what he was about to do.

Drawing a bracing breath, he dug around in the deepest hole—the bullet had gone through her arm and entered between her fourth and fifth ribs. He eased the slug from her body and tossed it into the trash. Those Aegis bastards.

He'd despised them for more than ninety years, since the day one had nearly killed him as he shifted out of his werewolf form. But his hatred had hit a new level three years ago.

Ula.

Dammit. He didn't have time to dwell on the female he'd wanted to take as a mate. She was dead, and her death at the hands of the Aegis slayers took up too much time in his nightmares anyway.

The second bullet was harder to remove. He was forced to make an incision to widen the wound, and though Kar didn't wake, she moaned. The silver slug was lodged in her humerus, and all around it, the bone had blackened with poison.

Cursing, he worked the bullet out with the forceps, and as it pulled free, Kar screamed in agony. Her body jackknifed, and he had to use his weight to hold her down.

"Almost done," he grunted, as he pinned her and waited for her to settle. It took a minute, but she quieted and stilled, mercifully losing consciousness again.

Luc worked quickly to finish, but it took forever to get

the wounds stitched and dressed. It wasn't enough. Not nearly enough. She'd lost a lot of blood, was probably bleeding internally, and if he didn't get her to UG fast, she was going to die.

Kynan Morgan couldn't believe he was doing this. No human in his right mind would knowingly walk into the building that housed the Warg Council. Especially not if you were a member of The Aegis.

But then Kynan wasn't completely human, probably wasn't in his right mind, and he definitely wasn't without defenses. Nope, the amulet around his neck, Heofon, might have put the weight of the world on his shoulders, but it had also come with a cool invincibility charm that meant nothing but a fallen angel could harm him.

Pretty awesome.

Okay, Lore could kill Ky, but they'd worked out their differences a while back. Mostly. The demon still liked to needle him, but that went both ways.

Kynan stood at the threshold of the ancient ruin of a building that had likely, at one time, housed Russian nobility. Now it was in shambles, and when a dark-haired woman with wary eyes gestured for him to follow her inside, he noticed that the interior was in worse shape than the exterior.

Crumbling walls and chipped stone floors greeted him, though throw rugs in vibrant shades of crimson and gold had been laid out. Potted plants and trees that grew right out of the floor gave the rooms an earthy, outdoorsy feel, which made sense, given that wargs, especially the born ones, were basically wild animals.

The female stopped outside a room that might once have been a grand library. It still housed books, but most of them were yellowed with age and dust. Two males stood in the center of the room, and as Kynan stepped inside, he sensed movement behind him.

He didn't have to turn around to know that he'd just been surrounded and trapped. The wargs definitely wouldn't be taking any chances.

The larger of the two, the one with the broad nose and shaggy, reddish hair, narrowed his eyes at Kynan. "You should know that no Guardian has ever set foot in Warg Council headquarters. How did you find us?"

"The Aegis has ways." Actually, they'd been searching for this place for decades, and they still didn't know where it was. Kynan and Wraith had tracked it down just yesterday—the demon could find anything, especially now that he was as charmed as Kynan. "Who are you?"

Red sneered. "Valko." He nodded to the towhead. "This is Raynor. And your name so we can notify next of kin?"

Funny guy. "I'm Kynan."

"And why are you here, Kynan?" Raynor asked. "Do you have information about the plague that's killing our people?"

"If he did, do you think he'd tell us?" Valko scoffed. "The Aegis wants nothing more than to see us extinct."

"That's not true." Kynan removed his sunglasses and tucked them into his pocket. "The Aegis has been killing fewer werewolves than ever before, and you know it." Thanks to Tayla and Kynan, The Aegis had gone through several changes, which included a capture-instead-of-kill policy for most werewolves. As long as they didn't harm humans, werewolves were pretty much left alone. At least, they were supposed to be. Not everyone in The Aegis agreed with the new policies that made attempts to avoid killing nonharmful underworld species, and it was hard to police individual Aegis cells.

"So why are you here?"

"Because I need information about a new breed of werewolf."

Valko frowned. "New breed?"

"One that shifts during the new moon instead of the full moon."

Both wargs' eyes went utterly flat. Valko's expression turned to stone. "There is no such thing."

"There is." Kynan cracked his knuckles, prepared to crack heads, too, if that's what it took to get some answers. "One of them is on the run with Guardians after her, and I'm trying to save her life."

And then some heads were going to roll for this. The Guardian's father, an Aegi himself, had contacted the Sigil in a panic, worried that his daughter was in danger. Sure enough, after a little investigating, Kynan had learned that instead of bringing the matter to the Sigil, the Guardian's cell had decided to ignore the new policies and mete out justice according to the old laws.

"We've already lost contact with a Guardian who was hunting her," Kynan continued. "So I want to know what the hell is up with her and why she'd head to the Northwest Territories."

"Whatever she is, you need to kill her," Valko said, surprising the shit out of Ky. "Abominations are always dangerous."

Raynor stiffened, and an undercurrent of tension spun

up in the room. "You think anyone who was not *born* a warg is an abomination."

"That isn't what I said," Valko said in a mockingly pleasant voice. "You *varcolac* are too sensitive. Not everything is about you." He turned back to Kynan. "We know nothing about wargs who can shift during the Feast moon. I suggest you kill the female and let it go."

Valko was lying, but clearly, he wasn't going to give up anything. And since no one he'd spoken to, not even Eidolon or the R-XR, had heard of any kind of warg that turned on the new moon, Kynan was at a dead end.

Four

"Our species faces extinction."

The Warg Council's Prime Enforcer made his grim pronouncement while leaning over the table around which nine other members sat, his fists planted firmly on the scarred oak top. Like many born wargs, Ludolf had black hair, brown eyes, and a penchant for drama.

"That's an exaggeration," Con said calmly, though inside he was anything but. Still in his paramedic uniform, he'd come straight to the Moscow hideaway after leaving Sin, and while he'd anticipated the usual flaring tempers between the born and turned wargs, he hadn't expected them to pounce on him the way they had. Anxious for information from Underworld General from the only Councilmember with an inside track, they'd practically dragged him into the room, which was a large chamber in the basement of a building the Council had owned since moving from its Romanian stronghold more than a century ago.

The grilling, from all sides, had started the moment he'd taken his seat as the sole representative for the dhampire race.

"An exaggeration?" Valko, the Council leader, slammed his fist on the table. "Is that what your boss told you? I think he'd say anything to protect his precious sister."

No doubt about that. But Eidolon was also working his ass off to find a cure. Conall stood to address the others. "Eidolon is making progress—"

"What kind of progress?" That from Raynor, one of the four turned-warg Council members. "And Sin should have been killed a long time ago for her part in this."

For some reason, a growl took root in Con's chest, but he managed to squash it. "Sin might be the answer to the cure," he shot back. "Eidolon is experimenting with her abilities as we speak."

"Eidolon," Valko spat. "I don't trust him. He's a traitor to all underworld beings. Anyone who would mate with an Aegi is worthy of only contempt." His brows slammed down to frame a murderous glare. "Speaking of Aegi, you work with one named Kynan at the hospital?"

"I used to," Con said. "He quit a while ago." Quit so he could become an Elder, one of the twelve members of the Sigil who ran The Aegis, but Con didn't think Valko needed to know that. "Why?"

"Because he left just minutes before you arrived. Did you tell him how to find us?"

Con blinked. "Kynan was *here*?"

"Yes. Apparently The Aegis is hunting a Feast warg, and he wanted information."

That caused a stir among the crowd. Originally created

thousands of years ago by a freak mating between a demon and a warg, the resulting abominations had been enslaved and bred by demons to kill other wargs. Though they were no longer enslaved, Feasts still possessed an inbred instinct to kill werewolves. They were so despised and feared that they didn't even have a representative on the Council. Probably because they were killed on sight.

No exceptions.

Ludolf's lips peeled back from his teeth. "You didn't tell him anything?"

"Of course not," Valko snapped, because it was truly a dumb question. No one wanted The Aegis to know about Feast wargs. The fear that the slayers would use Feasts to hunt *varcolac* and *pricolici* was too great. "I hinted that any such warg is one-of-a-kind, and told him to kill her. But I've dispatched a team to hunt her."

"I did, too," Raynor said, and yeah, now there'd be a competition between turneds and borns to see who could get the female's head first. Too bad for her, but right now the Council had more serious problems.

Con locked gazes with each of the other Council members one by one, seven males and three females, starting with the lowest-ranking turned warg, to Valko. "We've learned that the virus only affects *varcolac*."

Silence fell like an ax. For a moment, no one so much as breathed. Then, just as suddenly, the room exploded in curses from the turned wargs, and not-so-subtle utters of "Thank the gods" from the born wargs.

Raynor shot to his feet with such violence that his chair flew backward and cracked against the wall. "'Thank the gods'? You racist bastards!"

Valko stood. "Calm down. No one is happy about this

turn of events, but it does mean that wargs are not doomed to extinction."

"No," Raynor snarled. "Only we second-class citizens are, but who cares about that, right?"

"Enough!" Con barked. "Arguing isn't going to solve anything. What's important is that we now know who is at risk."

"And that helps us how, *damnedpire*?"

Con hated that insult, only tolerated it from Luc because they had an antagonistic relationship anyway. His temper flared, and he bared his fangs at the turned female who'd flung the barb at him. Sonya returned the display of aggression, her teeth glaringly white against rich, dark skin he'd felt under his hands one night not so long ago.

"It means born wargs no longer need to isolate themselves," Ludolf said loudly, drawing everyone's attention back to him. "We can round up the *varcolacs*—"

"And give you 'purebreds' an excuse to treat us even worse? You going to put us in some kind of camp?" Raynor scoffed. "I wouldn't put it past the *pricolici* to have started this plague in the first place as a way to get rid of us."

Valko stepped around the table, the bitter stench of menace preceding him. "That's ridiculous."

"Is it?" Raynor moved to meet the larger male, a plan that could end with his throat ripped out.

"This was no plot to exterminate turned wargs." Conall put himself between the two males. If they wanted to shed blood, he couldn't care less, but a battle right now would require his participation, and if *he* bled, he might put the turneds in the room at risk from the virus he carried. "But one thing is certain; we can't let this get out. If members of the Council, people who *should* have level heads, believe there's a conspiracy, think about the general public. We could have a civil war on our hands."

"So you're suggesting that we continue to let *pricolici* citizens live in fear unnecessarily?" Ludolf's disgusted tone made clear what he thought of the idea.

"Oh, yes, we wouldn't want the precious purebloods to suffer along with the mutts, would we?" Yasashiku said.

Shit. This meeting was going to end up in a full-on dogfight in a minute. Every person in the room was an alpha, and though there was a pecking order within each of the *pricolici*, *varcolac*, and dhampire societies, rank meant nothing outside an individual's society. And with the way aggression was winging through the tension-thick air, this wasn't going to be a minor scuffle. Fur was going to fly.

"What do you think, Conall?" Valko asked. "Since your breed isn't affected by any of this, what's your take?"

"I've already told you what I think. We need to keep it quiet for now. We can't afford to let hysteria tear us apart more than we already are." He would also keep quiet about the fact that his breed apparently *was* affected.

"We?" Raynor sneered. "No one persecutes you dhampires. You are born that way. Not made against your will."

"For the love of Sirius, stop your whining!" Ludolf shouted.

Sonya rounded on Ludolf. "Do you blame us?"

It was true. The turned wargs were looked down on as inferior beings. *Varcolac* were underrepresented on the Council, their words and opinions weighed less than those of born wargs, and their issues were treated as trivial. They'd been given voting rights only two years ago, which still grated on most of the *pricolici* council members. Only Feast wargs were looked down on with more disdain.

"We'll put this to a vote." Con clenched his fists to keep from knocking some heads together if anyone disagreed. A diplomat, he was not. "Those in favor of keeping this under wraps for now?"

All but two members, both *pricolici*, raised their hands, sealing the decision.

"It's settled, then." Con yanked his leather jacket off the back of his chair. "We can meet again in a week, or earlier if Eidolon has a breakthrough."

"Hold up, dhampire," Valko said. "There's still the matter of what to do with Sin."

Con bristled. "What do you mean, 'what to do with Sin'?"

"She must be held responsible. You will bring her to us."

Con schooled his expression to hide his surprise. That Valko would demand justice for something that was a turned-warg issue was extremely unusual. "Sin didn't start this epidemic intentionally."

"A drunk driver doesn't set out to cause an accident, but in a human court, he's held responsible."

"Since when do you care about human issues?" Con asked. "Human laws don't apply to her, and because Sin is a Seminus demon, she's not subject to warg law, either."

Valko steepled his fingers, his expression unusually neutral. "We will present her to the Seminus Council for punishment."

Whoa. Okay, it was strange enough that Valko wanted justice, but to have it come through official channels, rather than having Sin killed, was almost unbelievable.

Something was up. "And if they decide she's done nothing wrong?"

"Then we'll involve the Justice Dealers and the Maleconcieo."

Ah, okay. Lightbulb moment. Eidolon had been raised by the Judicia, demons whose entire purpose was to mete out demon justice, and for years he'd served as they had, as a Justice Dealer. If Dealers and the Maleconcieo, the highest demonic authority that presided over all demon Councils, were involved, Eidolon would be brought into the mix, and he might very well be forced to carry out Sin's punishment—probably in the form of death.

Valko had despised Eidolon for years, since the day the doctor had failed to save Valko's son after he'd been shot by an Aegi's silver bullet. That Eidolon had later mated with an Aegi had only fueled Valko's hatred. Valko would love to see Eidolon forced to kill his own sister.

Con scanned the room. Anticipation glittered in every warg's eyes, as though they already smelled blood in the air. "Eidolon needs her to find a cure or to develop a vaccine."

"Then perhaps we should involve the Justice Dealers now," Raynor said. "If she's held in prison, she will have no choice but to submit to Eidolon's tests and treatments."

"You're suggesting she'll run?" Con asked. "She won't. She's committed to ending this epidemic."

Skepticism laced Valko's voice. "You have one week."

"One week is not enough—"

Valko shoved to his feet. "You will stick to her like glue for the week, and after that, you will bring her in. If Eidolon is still seeking a cure, we'll let the Seminus Council decide what to do with her. But she *will* face justice for this."

Cursing, Con headed for the door, refusing to stay in that room for one more minute. Those two societies were ticking time bombs. And with a disease spreading faster than the Black Death had, the last thing the world needed was a werewolf civil war.

Valko and Ludolf remained behind in the conference room after everyone else had left. Valko trusted all the *pricolici* members of the Council, but he'd been raised with Ludolf in the Botev pack, and there was no one he trusted more than the ruthless bastard who had killed their clan leader and then handed control as pack alpha over to Valko.

Ludolf sat back in his leather chair, his heavy-lidded gaze sweeping between the closed door and Valko. "You think they fell for it?"

"Fell for what, Dolf?" Valko asked innocently.

Ludolf snorted. "Don't play that way with me. I know you too well, and you're too cunning. Once you heard that only the *varcolac* were affected by the plague, your wheels started spinning." He kicked his feet up on the tabletop. "So? Did they fall for it?"

There was a long silence while Valko considered the intelligence level of each member. Most turneds were half-wits with pathetic instincts, but one couldn't underestimate them, especially not Raynor. And Con, as a dhampire, definitely wasn't stupid. "The *varcolac* don't want to believe that we possibly care about their plight, but yes, I think they believe my proposal was genuine. They're aware that I *do* want Eidolon put down, after all." Oh, yes, Valko's hatred for Eidolon was well known, so no one would suspect that his suggestion to involve the Justice

Dealers and Sem Council was about far more than punishing Eidolon and his sister.

"And Sin?"

Valko had nothing against Sin. Not now, anyway. In fact, he'd like to thank her for starting the epidemic that was killing the *varcolac*. But he had a plan for her.

"Are you still in contact with your brother?"

A slow smile stretched Dolf's thin lips. His half brother had been in hiding for three decades for crimes against other wargs, but they wouldn't have lost complete contact. "I can be."

"Good. Tell him that if he sends Sin's head to Eidolon without anyone discovering who was responsible for her death, the Warg Council will forgive his past transgressions and give him a place on the council. If Con is caught in the cross fire, even better."

"You are devious. The turneds will be blamed for taking revenge."

"And we will sit back and watch them be destroyed, if not by the virus, then by us, with the full cooperation of the Seminus Council." Valko couldn't contain the hum of anticipation in his voice.

"You truly believe the Sems would go to war over the death of one female half-breed?"

"Of course not. But they'll be angry enough to side with us when the war starts."

"And why will a war start?"

"Because," Valko said, "we're going to leak the fact that the disease affects only *varcolac*, and once the lowlife turneds start up with their conspiracy theories and assume that we are responsible for the disease—"

"They'll attack us."

Dolf grinned. "And we will finally have the excuse we've needed for centuries to destroy those abominations."

"And," Valko added, "depending on which side the dhampires fall on, we might be able to take them out, as well. The canine were-world will finally be cleansed."

As he exited the rear of the Warg Council building, Con sensed the presence of another dhampire. The parklike grounds spread over half an acre, the copse of trees near the far wall of the property concealing the only Harrowgate in a two-mile radius. The scent of warg was strong around the gate; any species with a halfway decent sense of smell would hightail it back into the Harrowgate or away from the Council building immediately.

Unless they were there for a reason, and as Bran emerged from the forest shadows, Con knew this wasn't going to be pleasant.

Bran was, as many dhampires liked to say, a scary motherfucker.

Standing seven feet tall and built like a bull, the guy didn't have to do anything to get people to move out of his way. But it was his missing right eye and the scar that ran from his right temple to the left side of his chin that sealed the deal. Well, that and the full tank of crazy that gleamed in his good eye.

He kept his long, silver mane pulled back in a ponytail so none of it obscured the mess that was his face.

"Conall." Bran's rough voice vibrated deep into Con's chest. "We need to talk."

Con crossed his arms over his chest. "I didn't think you came all the way to Moscow because the vodka is so good." Probably not the smartest way to talk to a senior Dhampire Councilmember, but Con hadn't bowed and scraped to anyone in a long time.

"Aisling has gone to the night."

A chill shivered over Con's skin. What happened to dhampires when they died was a strongly held secret among his people—the biggest secret, in fact. Speaking about it was forbidden, even within their own species. Outside their own kind, they were compelled to silence.

Compelled, in the mystical sense of the word. Every dhampire possessed an inborn inability to speak in specifics about "going to the night." The words simply would not come, and no amount of torture could force a dhampire to discuss it.

"Aisling was so young," Con murmured. He'd been fond of his three-century-old second cousin, a strong voice in the shrinking dhampire community who had borne two babes and was carrying a third. "The baby—"

"Dead."

"How did it happen?"

"Human road rage." The vicious curl of Bran's upper lip said that the driver had gotten a taste of dhampire justice. "We were fortunate to have retrieved her body—her car went over a cliff and into the ocean."

"I'm sorry about Aisling, but why deliver the news in person?"

"Because I wanted to be the one to tell you that you're taking her seat on the Council, and that you will participate in the upcoming breeding season."

Con's curse dragged out on a long breath, and damn, he wished he still smoked. But smoking had gotten boring, no matter what he'd put in the pipe or rolled in the papers.

How long had he wanted this very thing? To take on the duties of his father, to lead the clan to prosperity and good hunts? But not this way. Not because they had a seat to fill and he was the last adult in his father's royal line. They were supposed to ask him to come back because they wanted his input, his experience. Not because they needed his genes.

His stomach did a few somersaults as he leveled his gaze at Bran. "No."

Bran's fist snapped out, catching Con in the jaw. It was a light blow, a punishing nip by wolf standards, but it stung. "Whelp! You do not tell your alpha *no*."

Very slowly, so as not to provoke Bran, Con dropped his arms to his sides and widened his stance. "I have a seat on the Warg Council, a job at Underworld General—"

"You'll give them up," Bran barked. "Yordan will take your seat on the Warg Council, and I doubt the demon hospital will miss you." The big male crowded close, so close that if Con breathed deeply, their chests would touch. "You *will* come home and take your place in dhampire society. We have been patient with you, letting slide your absences during the breeding seasons, letting you run loose outside our range, but it's time for you to settle down and fulfill your duties as dhampire royalty."

Letting him run loose? Settle down? "I think, old man, you mistake me for a youngling pup. *You* expelled me from the clan. It was only Aisling's pleading that convinced the Council to allow me back during the full moon tides. Now you suddenly want me to return and never leave again, except to conduct business and feed?"

And since male dhampires were prone to blood addiction if they fed off the same individual too many times, they definitely had to leave the dhampire sanctuary to find their meals. Not that a male couldn't get addicted outside the sanctuary, as well.

Con had more than enough experience with that to know.

Bran snarled, and Con braced himself. A verbal battle was something he could win. But if Bran lashed out—

Con found himself on the ground, laid flat by a meaty fist. Pain spiderwebbed across this face, bells rang, and honest-to-God stars swirled in his vision. Bran stomped Con in the ribs, and son of a bitch, that hurt.

Rolling to avoid another strike, he kicked out, catching Bran in the back of the knees and knocking him to the ground. As the other dhampire hit the grass, Con threw a punch that sent Bran skidding on his ass for several feet. Con dove, landing another punch, the crack ringing out in the crisp evening air.

Ultimately, Con would lose this fight. Oh, he could take the three-thousand-year-old dhampire, but winning would be interpreted as an overthrow of an alpha, and Con would find himself not only back in the clan but in charge of it.

Fury lit his fuse at the lose-lose of the situation, and after he got in a few more well-placed punches, he rolled onto his back and allowed Bran, whose mouth filled with his own blood, to pin him. Bran clamped his hand around Con's throat and squeezed, cutting off his breath.

"You insolent cur," he hissed. "You are a spoiled wretch who should have been brought to heel centuries ago. We took pity on you after your mother's death, but you didn't learn from that, did you?"

Fuck you, Con mouthed, even as his lungs began to burn from lack of oxygen.

"Does it bother you at all?" Bran's voice was a gravelly purr, as though he both enjoyed and hated taunting Con. "Do you regret sinking into blood addiction? Do you ever think about the female who died because of your lack of control? Do you ever think on *how* Eleanor died?"

Go. To. Hell.

Slowly, Bran peeled his fingers away, and Con took a grateful gulp of air. "You *will* return, and you *will* take your place on the Council. You are coming with me *now.*"

"Can't." Con started to thrash, straining against Bran's heavy body and the hand that clamped down on his neck again.

"I will take you by force, Conall." His knee came up to nail Con in the groin, effectively putting an end to the struggle. And maybe to future kids, as well. "What will it be?"

"The disease that is killing wargs is a threat to us all," Con bit out. "You can have me when the crisis is over."

"Show me your throat."

Damn him. It wasn't enough that Con had willingly lost the fight; Bran was going to make him endure complete surrender. Grinding his molars so hard they hurt, Con cranked his head to the side, leaving his jugular exposed. For a long moment, Bran did nothing. Con's pulse ticked off the seconds, and the longer Bran kept Con in the submissive, humiliating position, the more Con began to sweat.

"You've made your point," Con growled.

"No," Bran said, with a sadistic laugh. "I don't think I have." He dropped his mouth to Con's throat, and Con's heart leaped up there to join the party.

"Don't. The virus is in my blood."

Bran's hot breath whispered across Con's skin. "How convenient."

Very. Being fed on in a show of dominance was never pleasant.

The scrape of teeth along Con's jugular made him tense because, like Con, Bran had never been cautious with his own life, and Con wouldn't put it past the crazy bastard to bite despite the viral infection swimming in Con's veins.

Finally, Bran leaped fluidly to his feet. "You have until the epidemic is contained or the breeding season starts. Whichever comes first." He stepped into the Harrowgate, and the shimmering curtain solidified, leaving Con alone in the courtyard.

Alone with the knowledge that his days of freedom were numbered, and with the words "Be careful what you wish for" running through his head.

Five

"Let the bodies hit the floor."

"Bodies," by Drowning Pool, blared from Sin's iPod Shuffle, and she sang at the top of her lungs as she walked with Wraith to the ER. After Con had taken off—without so much as a "Thanks for the meal"—Wraith had made her stop by the cafeteria for a quick snack to replenish her blood sugar or some crap. Apparently, Eidolon the Great had insisted. Something about passing out again.

Now, Wraith was stone silent, though a cocky smirk turned up one corner of his mouth. "So," he said, tugging her earbuds from her ears, "you banging the paramedic?"

So much for the stone silence. She'd love to make *his* body hit the floor. "Not that it's any of your business, but no." Not recently, anyway.

"But you want to." When she opened her mouth to deny it, he cut her off. "You can't lie to an incubus about sex. You should know that."

"Whatever," she muttered, and stuck the earbuds back in place.

Wraith's boots sounded like mini-bombs striking the obsidian floor even through the blaring sound of the music, and with each step, her nerves twitched. No doubt the effect was calculated, because she knew he could move like a damned phantom when he wanted to. Once again, he yanked on the headset's cord. "He wants you, too."

"Well, gee, aren't you just smarter than you look." Knowing the battle was lost, she turned off the tiny MP3 player. "Hello, he's a guy. And a vampire. He was responding to the feeding." And to her succubus pheromones, which had a tendency to attract the attention of all non-incubi males, even if only subliminally. "What's your point, anyway?"

He shrugged. "Just making conversation."

Bullshit. He was trying to get as much information about her as he could. Her new brothers all responded differently to her existence—Eidolon accepted it like she'd been around for years, Shade made extra efforts to build a relationship, and Wraith . . . he kept her at arm's length, and she had a feeling he would until he learned to trust her. She got that; she was the same way. Just because someone was biologically related didn't make them family. Definitely didn't make them likable.

Worse, family had the potential to hurt a person much more than a stranger ever could.

"You don't like me, do you?" she asked.

"I don't know you."

She stopped in the middle of the hall. "Cut the shit."

He grinned. "You're a straight shooter. I *do* like that."

"But?"

Wraith's blue eyes glazed over as he stared down the hall, going someplace she couldn't follow. "But we have a history of some real fuckwads in the family, starting with our father and ending with Roag. Lore has proven himself, but you...you're a wild card." His gaze shifted to her, and it was as cold as the arctic tundra. "I won't let you screw with my brothers."

"Screw with them? Maybe you could keep in mind that I saved the lives of two of Shade's kids. And I never wanted to meet you guys at all. The only reason I'm spending as much time with you as I am is because Eidolon and Shade won't leave me alone."

Eidolon called her to come in for stuff related to the epidemic, and Shade was always inviting her to dinner with his family to thank her for what she'd done for his sons. And sure, the triplets, Rade, Stryke, and Blade, were cute and all, but dealing with drooly little rugrats was *way* out of her comfort zone.

"But you're here now, and you're in our lives. So what happens when the plague is over and you don't need to come to the hospital anymore?" Wraith stepped closer, using his size in an attempt to intimidate her. "Will you disappear?"

She wrenched her neck to look up at him, but no way was she backing down. "That's the plan."

A low growl rumbled in his chest. "I couldn't give a hellrat's ass, but my brothers? Different story. Lore worries about you. E has accepted you into the family, and he's not going to let you go. Shade...he lost a sister he loved, and now he needs you to help him heal. He probably doesn't see that, but even as dense as I am sometimes,

I see it. So guess what, little sister? Get used to having me around because I'm going to be your shadow until I'm sure you won't hurt our family."

Sin practically shook with rage. "You don't get to tell me what to do," she spat. "And I'm not your 'little' sister. I'm older than you are, dickhead."

"Duh, the years you spent as a clueless human don't count. Everyone knows that." He narrowed his eyes at her. "Just remember what I said. Don't try to run away, because there is no place on Earth or in Sheoul where I can't find you." His voice was a rumbling, deadly murmur. "And trust me, you don't want me on your heels." He did a crisp about-face on the ball of his foot and took off down the hall, leaving her spitting mad and tempted to go after him, though she had no idea what she'd do if she caught up to him.

"Sin!" Eidolon gestured to her from the double swinging doors to the ER. "I need you. Now."

Sin mentally flipped off Wraith and hurried after Eidolon, who didn't even wait to see if she was following. He crossed to a room near the parking lot doors and flung back the heavy curtain.

There, lying in a bed, was a tawny-haired male, a teenager, maybe, his skin ashen in the few places where it wasn't mottled by black bruises, blood leaking from his nose, eyes, and ears. Machines breathed for him, pumped fluids into his veins, monitored his vital signs. A young, humanoid nurse—a shifter of some sort, according to the star-shaped mark behind her ear—checked his status, her face pinched with concern.

Sin wanted to throw up. "Was he in an accident?"

"That's what this disease does." Eidolon lifted the

patient's chart from a hook at the end of the bed. "It's a VHF, a viral hemorrhagic fever. It causes multisystem failure, including the vascular system. Organs break down, and veins basically dissolve. The patient bleeds from all orifices—"

"*Stop.*" Horrified, Sin stumbled back a step, bumping into a cabinet behind her. God, what had she done?

Eidolon gestured to the nurse. "Vladlena, can we get a minute?"

"Of course, Doctor."

Once she was gone, Eidolon gripped Sin's shoulders. "Sin," Eidolon said, his tone much kinder than she deserved. "I need your help. I need you to channel your gift into him and see if you can force the virus into compliance."

"I've already tried with that other warg a few days ago. It didn't work, and he wasn't nearly as bad off as this guy."

"I know. And this might not work either. But you've had a chance to see how the virus in Con's blood was killed. If you can cause a similar reaction inside this warg, he might have a chance."

"Dammit," she breathed. "Okay. Yeah." She curled her hands into fists in an effort to keep from trembling. It had been decades since anything had affected her so strongly, and she wasn't sure how to deal with it other than by burying her emotions down deep, the way she'd always done.

Bucking up, she gently gripped the warg's blackened, swollen hand. "Why so bruised?"

"He's bleeding subdermally as his capillaries rupture."

Dear God. She closed her eyes, digging for every ounce of stone-cold detachment she had. She'd been a killer for years, had been to hell and back—literally—and she'd seen much, much worse than this.

She just hadn't caused it.

"Why can't he drink my blood like Con did?" She opened her eyes and shifted her gaze to Eidolon, the walls, the floor, because anything was better than staring at the dying kid. "I mean, I know wargs normally don't drink blood, but wouldn't that provide some sort of defense?"

"It worked on Con because he's part vampire, and the blood he took from you went nearly immediately into his bloodstream. For anyone else, the blood goes into their stomach and is digested or regurgitated."

Ick. "Can you inject my blood into them?"

"Even if your human blood type were the same as the victim's, you're part demon. Injecting your blood directly into a werewolf would kill him."

Numbly, she nodded. Forced herself to look down at the boy, because he deserved that, at least. Slowly, so slowly, her mental walls finally slammed into place, blocking off the horror, the sorrow, the guilt. Oh, it would all come out again, painfully so, but right now, she needed to put up the shields that would allow her to handle this.

Concentrating, she opened herself up to her ability, and heat ripped down her arm from her shoulder to her fingertips, following the curves and lines of her *dermoire*. It glowed as her gift channeled into the werewolf.

The disease rolled over her, a dirty sludge of information that made her arm and mind heavy. In her head, the visuals swirled—she could see the twisted, squiggly virus strings wrapped around blood cells, squeezing the life out of them. The shape of the virus strands were different than the ones in Con, but she visualized the way Con's virus had been destroyed, and then she blasted the warg with power. Stinging gooseflesh prickled from her shoulder to her fingertips, as she imagined reversing the disease, taking it back to its beginning stages.

Nothing happened.

She concentrated harder. Sweat beaded on her brow.

Still nothing.

Breathing deeply, she unleashed the full force of her power, until it felt as though her arm were wrapped in electric fencing. Inside her skull, a hive of angry bees buzzed. Distantly, she heard Eidolon calling her name. Her eyes stung as sweat dripped into them.

Feedback streamed up her *dermoire* and into her head... Something was happening. The werewolf's blood cells vibrated, and all around them, the virus strands broke apart. First, it was just a few, but suddenly, they were exploding like popcorn. Tiny bits of the virus rushed through the vessels.

Encouraged, Sin probed the male's network of veins and arteries, and everywhere, the enemy was being destroyed. *Yes!* This had been so easy, such a great fix, and as her mind's eye played the scene in high-def, she smiled.

The virus shreds ran thick through his bloodstream... so thick that they began to pile up, clinging the walls of the arteries...clogging at the narrows.

Oh, shit. Sin dialed back her power and shifted the visuals to the area around his heart. Suddenly, beeping alarms and a flurry of activity surrounded her. She caught a glimpse of the warg's heart squeezing, then stopping, the veins and arteries around it flattening as they became clogged.

Someone tore her away, and she stood there, dazed and in disbelief, as Eidolon and half a dozen staff members worked to save the warg. Idess, Lore's mate and an ex-angel who had been given the task of escorting human souls out of the hospital, entered the room, which was a very, very bad sign. Turned werewolves had human souls, so if Idess was there...

Sickened and shaking, Sin didn't know how long she watched, but when Eidolon cursed violently and called the time of death, she walked out of the room like a zombie, unsure where she was going or what she was doing. All she knew was that her right arm itched, a warning sign that she was about to bleed.

"Sin! Stop!" Eidolon stepped in front of her, and when he raised his hand, she braced herself for a punishing blow. But instead of striking her, he gripped her shoulders, forcing her to stop. "It wasn't your fault. He was going to die anyway."

She didn't point out that it was still her fault.

"Can you tell me what went wrong?"

"Yeah," she said as she twisted out of his grip. "My psychotic mother fucked a demon, and here I am." She laughed bitterly. "She always said she was a screwup. I guess I inherited that, huh? I mean, she couldn't even abort us after eating a demon herb grown solely for killing off mistakes. Leave it to me to not get dying right."

"Hey." Eidolon reached for her again, but when she stepped back, he dropped his hand. Still, there was compassion in his eyes, compassion she didn't want or need. "What happened to you as a child, what's happening now...I'm sorry. I've been hard on you—"

"Whatever." She cut him off, way too uncomfortable

with the mushy-mushy, and impatient to find privacy so that when her guilt erupted no one would witness her pain or try to make it stop. "Let's just figure out a way to end this."

Her brother was intuitive enough to know she needed to change the subject, and he rolled with it as if he'd never tried to get all apologetic. "Tell me what happened in there with the warg."

"There was too much of the virus in his system," she said. "When it died, it clogged up his veins."

Eidolon appeared to consider that. "Do you think that if you got to someone before so much of the virus was in the blood you could kill it without the same thing happening?"

"Maybe. But how will that help you? There's no way I can cure every infected warg that way."

"No, but we might be able to use the dead virus to create a vaccine or a cure by studying how the young virus was actually killed with your power."

She frowned. "Can't you use the virus from the werewolf who just..." *Died.*

Fortunately, Eidolon spared her from having to say it. "I'll get samples, absolutely. The problem is that as the disease progresses in a patient, the virus degrades. By the time the patient dies, there isn't a lot of structure left to study or use. None of the patients have developed antibodies, either. The R-XR has gotten some samples from newly infected wargs, but the problem is that the R-XR can't kill the virus even in the lab. Nothing kills it. It has to age and die on its own. This is not a human virus, Sin. It's a demon virus, which means human research and procedures are failing us. Hugely. It doesn't behave like any human or animal virus I've ever seen. We might as well be working with a disease from outer space."

The intercom squawked, and she nearly jumped out of her skin as Eidolon was called to the triage desk.

He gestured for Sin to follow him around the corner. "I'll take care of this. Wait in the..." He trailed off, and she followed his gaze to where a nurse, a patchy-furred slogthu, was eyeing two males wearing the black jumpsuit uniform of the Carceris—underworld jailers who weren't known for their gentle methods. One, a vampire with waist-length chestnut hair, moved to meet her brother. The other, humanoid and species unknown, looked around with curiosity.

And, as if the emergency department wasn't crowded enough, Con stepped out of the Harrowgate.

"Eidolon." The vamp held out his hand, and Eidolon clasped it with a firm shake.

"Seth. How can I help you?"

Seth's ice-blue eyes shifted to Sin, sending a prickle of foreboding up her spine. "Is that your sister? Sin?"

Eidolon stiffened. "Why?"

The other demon stepped forward, overly large lips peeled back to reveal sharp teeth and a forked tongue. "Because," he said, "we're here for her. She's under arrest."

We're here for her.

Someone on the Council had changed their mind. Son of a bitch. First, Con had been ambushed by Bran, and now this. He couldn't catch a freaking break. Sin wouldn't, either.

Con had been inside a Carceris prison, and it wasn't

Disneyland. The enchanted cells neutralized all species' special powers and their unique requirements, so that vampires didn't need blood, incubi didn't need sex, Cruenti didn't need to kill. But they also left the demons powerless, unable to defend themselves from whatever punishments the jailers dished out.

If Sin were taken, she could be kept like that for years. The demon justice system operated on the premise that all were guilty until proven innocent, so dragging heels meant years, even decades, of torture behind bars.

Con knew from experience.

He eased casually toward Sin, who stared at the Carceris officers, one a vamp, the other a *wither drake*, in disbelief. Eidolon put himself between the vampire and his sister, his expression glacial.

"What is she accused of?" Eidolon asked.

"Initiating an epidemic that is destroying wargs." Seth's voice carried through the emergency department as if he'd used a loudspeaker, and everyone within earshot stopped in their tracks to gawk. Even Bastien, who had obviously wasted no time in returning to work, froze solid, his push broom hovering over a pile of trash.

Sin squared her shoulders, taking on the Carceris guys without a trace of fear when any normal person would be shitting bricks. "And who is my accuser?"

"We weren't given that information." Seth whipped a set of Bracken cuffs out of his pocket. Developed by the Judicia to negate species' abilities, these particular cuffs had tiny serrated spikes on the inside to prevent the wearer from struggling. "You will come."

Con caught Sin's arm. "Not yet," he whispered in her ear. "But don't fight. They aren't affected by the Haven spell. They'll beat the hell out of you, and there's nothing you can do."

"I'm not letting them take me," she ground out.

"Neither am I," Con said, and from the menace Eidolon was throwing off, neither was he. The *wither drake* moved to block the Harrowgate, leaving Con and Sin only one way out. The ambulance bay. "I'm going to the parking lot. Give me ten seconds, and then run to the first ambulance on the left. Try to avoid the *wither drake*'s gaze. He can reduce you to a wrinkled bag of skin in about ten seconds. Reconstitution isn't fun."

To Sin's credit, she didn't argue. She simply nodded and moved up behind E, putting her closer to the sliding-glass parking lot doors.

"Who will I have to answer to?" she asked Seth, who gave her a long, assessing look.

"The Warg Council."

"This is a Seminus Council matter," Eidolon said, but the vampire shook his head.

"You know the laws, demon. If the two Councils cannot decide on a punishment—"

"I haven't been taken before either Council," Sin interrupted.

"The wargs are not required to take their issue to your species Council," Seth said. "It's recommended, to avoid wasting Justice Dealer time with frivolous suits, but it's their choice."

"You're lucky the wargs haven't slaughtered you outright." The *wither drake*'s voice was monotone, bored, and Con suspected he was hoping that Sin would resist arrest. The dude was going to get his wish. And then he was going to wish he hadn't.

Frost formed on Eidolon's words. "The Seminus Council would have taken issue with Sin's death."

"Only if they could prove that the Warg Council was involved."

True. If some lone warg killed Sin, nothing would be done unless Sin's family took revenge on a personal level or contacted Justice Dealers, who would probably rule in a single warg's favor despite Eidolon's history as a Dealer. Con didn't think the Sem brothers were really the type to go the legal route anyway. They were much more the "hunt them down and kill them painfully" type.

Con got that.

"Well, Sin," Con said loudly, "best of luck. E, I'm heading out on a run." He caught Eidolon's dark gaze for just a second, long enough to deliver his unspoken message. *I'll get Sin out.*

He headed for the sliding-glass doors, where Wraith was waiting, big body propped casually against the frame, hands tucked in his jeans pockets as he watched. Anticipation glittered in his blue eyes. Con had no idea when the demon had arrived, but he was glad for the extra muscle. Wraith loved a good fight.

Con brushed past Wraith with a nod, climbed into the newest of three black ambulances, and started it up. As if turning the key was a signal, Sin burst out of the hospital. Wraith stepped out as well, his leather duster kicking up around his ankles, and then the Carceris officers were there, Eidolon on their heels. He wouldn't have been able to do much to stop them inside the hospital, but the parking lot wasn't protected by the Haven spell.

Sin dashed toward the ambulance while Wraith effortlessly laid the Carceris vamp out with a fist to the throat.

Eidolon grabbed the *wither drake* by the arm, but not in time to prevent him from launching a lock-dart—a weapon that, once it pierced its target, paralyzed the victim until he arrived at a Carceris prison.

Lightning quick, Wraith knocked the dart askew with his hand, but it struck a glancing blow to Sin's thigh as it corkscrewed downward. Blood sprayed, and though she yelped, she didn't slow. As Eidolon decked the demon, Wraith pinned the vamp before he could rise, and Sin leaped into the rig's passenger seat.

"Go!" she shouted, as she slammed the door shut.

Con hit a button on the dash, and the rear wall of the parking lot shimmered, revealing a human parking garage on the other side.

The rig's tires squealed as they spun out of the stall. Once they were through the portal, it closed again, turning into a solid, concrete wall. No humans, if they were ever to trespass, would see the door for what it really was.

He turned to Sin, who was looking back to make sure the Carceris guys weren't somehow breaking through the barrier. "You okay?"

"Yeah. Why?"

"You're bleeding."

She clapped a hand over the wound. "I've had worse."

Heart still pounding, he peeled out into the early-morning Manhattan traffic, his aggressive move causing more than a few honking horns. "Keep pressure on it. We'll pull over in a minute and patch it up."

"I said I'm okay."

"Don't be a stubborn idiot." He slammed on the brakes to avoid crushing a taxi that pulled out in front of him, though Con intentionally let the ambulance trade paint with the other vehicle, just to make the driver piss his pants. "You can't afford an infection right now." Besides, the scent was going to trip his crazy switch if they didn't get her wound covered.

She rolled her eyes. "How much trouble are E and Wraith in?"

"Interfering with Carceris officers and their duty?" He wondered if he should lie, then decided she could handle it. "A lot." He didn't bother telling her he was in for a good time with whips, canes, and waterwheels at the hands of torturers, too, because he doubted she cared.

"Damn," she breathed.

"They'll be okay. E's got experience with the system, and Wraith is . . . Wraith."

"I don't want to owe them. They're into my shit enough as it is."

"Ah."

"Ah, what?" She turned away from looking out the passenger window to glare at him. "What's that supposed to mean?"

She must have let up on the pressure on her cut, because a particularly strong whiff of blood made his fangs pulse. He breathed through it the way he always did when he'd failed to feed and was treating a bleeding patient. But he'd fed—from Sin—only hours ago, and he shouldn't be having this reaction.

A chill ripped into his marrow as an ugly thought came to him. What if addiction was already starting to set in? It shouldn't start until around the sixth feeding, but he was rapidly learning that, with Sin, very little was predictable.

"Earth to Con." Sin waved her hand in front of his face, breaking him out of both autopilot and the thoughts he didn't want to be thinking. "What does 'ah' mean?"

"Just wondering what makes you tick." He eased to a stop at a light and watched the first rays of the morning sun peek between two office buildings. "You didn't ask out of concern if they would be in trouble. You asked because you don't want to *owe* your brothers. Why is that?"

Surprisingly, she didn't fire off a shot at him. Instead, she went still and silent, and the tantalizing aroma of her blood—and *her*—thickened in the cab. He glanced at her leg, where a crimson flow seeped between her fingers, and his grip on the steering wheel became white-knuckled as the medical side of him that wanted to fix her battled with the dhampire side that wanted to taste her. Maybe there was a bag of O-pos in the back.

She shifted, throwing her head back against the seat, which had the unfortunate effect of making her small breasts jut forward, testing the elasticity of the black tank top she wore beneath her leather jacket.

The steering wheel groaned under the force of his grip, as the male in him leaped into the fray with the medical and dhampire sides. Damned succubi. He yanked the wheel, and with a squeal of tires, the ambulance whipped into a parking lot.

"What are you doing?" she snapped. "Oh, my God, do you even know how to drive?"

He popped a ticket from the machine, found a parking spot, and shut down the engine, unconcerned that humans would notice them. The ensorcelled ambulance wasn't invisible to human eyes, but it registered only in their subconscious. Humans would avoid the rig, react to it on the road, but they wouldn't think of it or its passengers as anything odd or interesting.

No, his concern right now was demons.

And his own desire, which was another kind of demon entirely.

"Climb in the back," he said tightly. "I'm going to treat your wound."

"I told you—"

"I don't care." His voice was cold, his body hot, and the mix was wreaking havoc with his patience. "You're on *my* turf, in *my* rig, so you follow *my* rules."

She glared. "What if the Carceris finds us?"

"They won't." He reached between the two seats and shoved open the small door to the box section of the rig. "They'll be looking for you in the obvious places first. Not city parking lots."

"And after you're done patching me up?"

Good question, and he hadn't thought that far ahead. Probably because his brain was swamped with her scent. "I'm taking you home," he said finally. "You're coming home with me."

Six

"I'm not going home with you."

"We'll talk about it while I'm patching you up." Con jerked his thumb toward the back. "Go."

Grudgingly, Sin climbed between the front seats and ducked through the hatchlike door separating the cab from the box section of the ambulance. A dull red light illuminated the space, and the same Haven spell symbols from UG were scrawled on the walls, but other than that, it could have been a human ambulance.

Her leg throbbed as she worked her way down the narrow aisle between the bench seat and the stretcher, but that wound wasn't nearly as bad as the pain spreading through her arm. She didn't have to look to know a large gash had split her *dermoire* across her biceps. The pain had struck suddenly, but she'd borne it in silence, the way she always did. As an assassin, she never gave her victims the luxury of a scream, so she figured she didn't deserve one any more than they did.

She didn't deserve for the gash to be treated, either. She'd allow Con to mend her leg, but her arm was off limits.

Con jerked down black rubber shades from rollers over each window. Every sliver of outside light was snuffed, obviously a necessity when transporting vamps and other light-sensitive demons during the day. "Take off your pants."

"Wow. Not one for foreplay, are you?"

He turned to her with lethal grace despite the limitations of the cramped compartment. "I spend hours on foreplay," he said, his voice a slow, sexy drawl. "What about you?"

Heat flooded her face. Somehow, he knew the answer, knew she'd never engaged in foreplay in her life. For her, sex was fast food, not gourmet cuisine. Oh, she enjoyed it with the right partners, but the desire to linger in bed, taking pleasure in a male's body, had been crushed out of her a long time ago. Now, sex was about staying alive. In the last thirty years especially, it had become routine, quick trysts with a couple of assassins from her den, with only the occasional roll in the hay with males like Con to shake things up.

And now that she was an assassin master, she rarely left the den except to go to Guild headquarters or the hospital, so her choices had been even more severely limited, mostly to Lycus. It would probably be that way for the rest of her life.

"Foreplay is overrated." The gash in her arm screamed with pain as she shed her pants and hopped up on the stretcher. She left her thigh and ankle holsters in place, though, because her weapons weren't going anywhere.

"Then you're not doing it right." Con snapped on some surgical gloves, somehow making the sound and the action erotic. "You've had shitty lovers."

"You were one of my lovers," she pointed out, but he didn't take the bait.

"Once. And there is something to be said for a hard, fast fuck." His voice became a mesmerizing purr. "But there's nothing like taking the time to slowly peel off every article of clothing, to kiss every inch of your lover's skin as you do it. To lick all the sensitive places until they quiver. To explore all the textures of your partner's body with your fingers, your mouth." His fangs flashed as he added, "Your teeth."

Hunger gripped her so fiercely she had to struggle to breathe. Yet somehow, she managed to speak calmly, as if Con's graphic words hadn't affected her. "The end result is the same. An orgasm. So why waste all that time? In the hour it takes you to lick someone from head to toe"— God, seriously? *Want.*—"I could have had half a dozen orgasms." Assuming she was with some fictional male who could come that many times, too—or a Seminus demon, whose ejaculate left females climaxing over and over, even if he left the room.

"Trust me," he murmured, "the wait is worth it. You'll get all those, but they'll be better. Hotter. A-fucking-mazing."

Sin went utterly wet and achy. Even if her succubus needs weren't creeping up on her, Con would have jump-started things.

"Put pressure on your laceration." The abrupt change

of tone and subject made her blink, but he turned away to paw through the glass-faced cabinets and toss supplies next to her on the gurney.

Still dizzy with the images he'd put in her head, she grabbed a paper towel from the dispenser behind her and held it to the bleeding wound. A trickle of warmth ran down her arm and into her palm, and she covertly tucked another paper towel inside her coat sleeve. Then she entertained herself by watching Con's fine ass hugged by black BDU pants. When he swiveled around back to her, she got a kick out of the way his gaze went to her bare thighs and black silk thong that was now damp with her arousal.

The longer he stared, the faster her heart beat, the more her belly fluttered.

The hotter it got inside the damned ambulance.

When his silver eyes finally snapped up, they'd darkened to a rich, smooth pewter, the hunger in them stark and undeniable, which was no surprise given what they'd just been talking about. For just a moment, she wondered if he'd act on his need, and she was both disappointed and relieved when he sank down on the padded bench across from her.

"This is pointless," she said, even though the towel under her fingers had soaked through. "I heal quickly."

"The dart the Carceris struck you with was coated with an anticoagulant. Keeps you bleeding so they can track you in the event that the dart doesn't stick."

Clever. "How do you know so much about them?"

"I've had my fair share of experience with them." He gripped her calves with both hands, spread her legs, and tugged her forward so he was between her thighs, her knees resting against either side of his ribs.

Sin tried to ignore the intimate position, but her body couldn't, and she tensed, feeling caged even though it was he who was pinned between her legs. "You've been arrested? What did you do?"

"Like I said, I have experience with them."

"Ooh," she teased, dragging her foot up his back. "A bad boy. Come on, spill."

"Maybe I killed annoying succubi for fun." His words were gruff, but his fingers were gentle as he lifted the towel to inspect her leg wound.

"I hope you gave them a bunch of those foreplay orgasms first." He snorted, but didn't offer up any details about his time with the Carceris. Clearly, he wasn't going to talk, so she studied the inside of the ambulance, with its cabinets, benches, and a station near the front that looked like a miniature chem lab for mixing potions. "So, how do vampires do this job, anyway? Doesn't the sight and smell of blood make you hungry?"

"If you've just gorged on Thanksgiving dinner, do you want to have a sandwich?"

That was a joke. She hadn't had a Thanksgiving dinner since her grandparents had been alive. But suddenly, she craved turkey, mince pie, and homemade rolls. Nostalgia, something she'd banned long ago, filled her with the same warmth she'd felt when her family gathered around the rickety old holiday dinner table. As a child, she'd envisioned futures that involved a husband, children, Uncle Loren and his family, all gathered for holidays with their grandparents. Now she knew better than to let those childish dreams in, and ruthlessly, she flexed her arm and allowed the pain to bring her back to the present, where she'd never celebrate sappy, sentimental holidays again.

"I don't want food after a large meal, no, but... Oh, so you feed before your shift?"

"And during. We keep snacks in the cooler. All medics do, depending on their species. Worked with one partner who gnawed on bones the entire shift."

Gross. "What if it's not just diet that's an issue for you guys? What if it's something else?"

"What? Like needing to kill or absorb pain?"

She shrugged. "Or screw."

One tawny eyebrow shot up. "Species who kill uncontrollably can't be medics, but we used to have one guy who fed on others' pain. This was the perfect job for him, until he decided he'd rather not make patients feel better. The sex thing... I don't know. Guess it depends on the breed of incubi or succubi. Shade manages fine for short shifts. Why? You thinking about signing up? Because I'll bet you wouldn't have any trouble getting a partner who could, ah, help you out between runs."

Oh, and wouldn't *that* conversation with Shade, who ran the paramedic program, be fun? "Thanks, but I already have a job."

He shook his head, unscrewed a bottle of something, wetted a gauze pad, and swiped it over her cut. "This is a coagulant Eidolon developed from vampire saliva. It's more effective on supernaturally inflicted wounds than anything humans have invented."

"Eew."

"Would you rather I licked you?" The dark, sultry note in his voice wrapped around her like a silk ribbon.

How to answer that? Because either yes or no would be both truth and lie. In the end, she managed a breathy "No," which she could only hope sounded more convincing to him than it did to her. She cleared her throat and changed the subject. "Look, can you step on it? I need to get to my assassin den."

He leveled her an amused, *no-deal* look, as if she had absolutely no say in her future. "I told you, you're coming to my place." He finished mopping up the laceration, which, thanks to the vamp spit concoction, was now oozing instead of gushing. "The Carceris is looking for you. They'll hit all of the obvious places first."

"Well, Captain Bossy, the den has security goons." When Con took a break from twisting the top off a small bottle of antiseptic to give her an are-you-fucking-serious look, she sighed. "I know they can't stop the Carceris, but they'll at least warn me."

"Are you sure about that? Little sting..." He squirted the liquid into the cut on her thigh and she gritted her teeth against the pain. "Aiding and abetting is a serious offense. Do your guards love you that much?"

No, they didn't. A slow roll of guilt rose up in her as she thought about how Eidolon and Wraith had come to her aid even knowing what they were risking.

And Con, too. She studied him as he worked on her wound, his gloved hands gentle, practiced. She hadn't expected that. From the moment she'd met the gorgeous male, he'd been nothing but intense. Hard. He'd thrown her against the side of the very ambulance they were in. He'd bet his paramedic partner, Luc, that he could get into her pants.

And he had.

Now he was carefully tending to her wound and trying to get her to safety. "Why are you helping me?" she blurted.

"You still owe me ten bucks."

She flashed him a fake smile. "Funny. But you're not helping me because I busted you for making a bet with Luc and taking more than half the winnings."

"Fine. How's this? You're responsible for the warg epidemic, and if you're locked up in a cell, Eidolon won't have the access to you he needs to help develop a cure," he said. "Besides, I owe your brothers."

Of course. He wasn't helping because he liked her or anything. Which was fine, because she didn't like him either. And *that* couldn't sound more childish, could it? "Why do you owe them?"

One big shoulder rolled in a half-shrug. "I was on a bad path. Self-destructive. Got into a bar fight with Luc and we both ended up at UG."

"So, Eidolon saved your life?"

"Nah. Another little sting." He swabbed the laceration with something that, yeah, stung. "Have you met Vladlena? She's a nurse. Hyena-shifter. Few years ago, her father, a doc named Yuri, had a bug up his ass about some crap that went down between me and his son years earlier, and he sicced the Carceris on me. Eidolon figured that if I was stuck in prison, I couldn't make good on my hospital bill, so he got me out. Payment was me working for him for two years."

"Guess you stuck around?"

"Guess so. Turned out to be a cool job. No two calls are the same. Keeps me on my toes."

Sin got that. She wasn't much for routine either. "So, you done yet?"

"Why so anxious?"

"Because I'm vulnerable anywhere outside the den, assassin headquarters, or the hospital. Which is why I need to go to the den instead of your place, even though the Carceris will look there." She also needed to find one of her sex partners. Fast. Before she broke down and pounced on Conall.

"Vulnerable to what?"

"My assassins."

He blinked. "Your own assassins are a danger to you?"

"Some of them covet my position. Whoever kills me gets to take over the den."

"How do you stay safe when you're with them?"

"Assassins and their masters are bonded, so they can't harm the master inside any assassin den or headquarters, or any place protected by a Haven spell. But outside those areas...all bets are off. A few of the older assassins can actually sense their masters' locations."

Con breathed a curse. "You are a pain in the ass, aren't you?"

"Your bedside manner sucks."

"Oh, I have one hell of a bedside manner," he drawled huskily, reminding her that her body ached, and not from pain. He smoothed a large bandage over the wound, his fingers roaming slowly over the fabric and her skin, turning a medical procedure into one of the most sensual experiences of her life.

Talk about pathetic.

He left his hands where they were, wrapped around her thighs, and he looked up, his sterling gaze meeting hers. The air in the ambulance seemed to thicken and heat, and would it kill Shade to install air-conditioning in these things?

"Take off your jacket," he murmured.

Sin's heart stuttered. "I'm not having sex with you."

"You want to." An easy, seductive smile turned up his sinful mouth. "But that's not why I want you to strip."

"Liar. You'd love to get into my pants."

He looked at her like she was a complete idiot. "You're bleeding still."

Oh. Humiliating. She sniffed. "No, I'm not."

"I can smell it."

Damned vampires. "Give me my pants."

"Take off your jacket. I won't tell you again."

"And I won't let you treat the wound." She jerked her legs out of his grip, but he was on his feet in a flash, yanking her jacket down to reveal the wide gash in her biceps.

She tried to wrench away, but he held her easily, his amusement gone. "How did this happen? Who did this? The Carceris?"

"I did it," she snapped, and his head jerked back.

"You're a cutter?" He reached for a gauze pad, but she gripped his wrist.

No, she wasn't. But she wasn't going to explain anything to Con. "Do not mess with this one," she said levelly. "I will fight you, and on this, I will not back down."

Con's handsome, angular features hardened with anger, and she heard the grind of his teeth and the pop of jawbone. "You can't let it bleed like that."

"I can, and I will."

"I'm on the edge right now, Sin." His voice was guttural, with a slight tremor that extended to the hand she was holding.

Shit. Her blood was tempting him. She closed her eyes, cursing silently. She'd allowed Eidolon to stitch her arm once, instead of using his healing powers. Maybe this time—

Hot breath fanned over her arm, and her eyes shot open.

Con's mouth was close, so close... Yes, just this once...
"Do it," she whispered, and for all of that, he hesitated.

His trembling worsened, and he reached for the vamp
spit. Without thinking, Sin cupped the back of his head
and brought his lips to her arm. The wound was a deeply
personal pain, and she wasn't about to let some strange
medical concoction near it. Then again, was letting Con
be a part of that pain any better?

Her emotions wobbled, and she exhaled slowly, unsure
she could handle such intimacy. No, she was sure. She
couldn't.

Just as she was about to push him away, he moaned,
let out a shuddering breath, and sank his body against
her, and in a heartbeat, her concern seemed distant. His
arousal was a massive presence against her core, and
his hands, still encased in surgical gloves, slipped under
her tank top to grip her waist. How the hell the slide of
latex on her skin could feel so erotic was beyond her, but
she wished he'd either move his hands up to her breasts
or lower to her sex so she could see just how much more
erotic it could get. Unfortunately, he kept them tamely
motionless, his grip tight, as if he were afraid that if he
loosened it, he'd do exactly what she was hoping for.

Slowly, tentatively, he swept his tongue from the base
of the cut to the crest. The soothing caress eased the pain,
and with each slow lap, it eased more, until there was
nothing left but a mildly pleasant sting.

And a throbbing lust that penetrated all the way to her
core.

Beneath Con's skin, his muscles were bunched, his
body tense, and she sensed something dark inside, something he was trying to contain.

"Con?" She slid her hand over his back, and beneath her palm, his muscles rippled and jumped.

He uttered something in a language she didn't know, but she was pretty sure it was a nasty curse. Abruptly, he leaped back, and at the same moment, someone pounded on the rear door.

A rumbling voice came from the other side. "Send the succubus out, or everyone inside dies."

Con didn't take time to think. Instinct roared to the surface, and he lunged, taking Sin down to the rig's deck, covering her body with his. Ten seconds ago, when he was battling bloodlust, he'd have gotten off on the feeling of her hard form against his harder one, of her thighs cradling him between them, but right now, his only concern was keeping her safe.

If she died, so might the only hope for getting rid of the virus in his blood.

Plus, her brothers would kill him. A lot.

"Who is it?" he whispered.

"I don't know," she whispered back. "I don't recognize the voice. Must be the Carceris."

"They couldn't have found us that quickly. Not without a hellhound or a blood tracker. It's gotta be an assassin."

She cursed. "Let me up."

There wasn't enough room in the aisle between the bench seat and the stretcher to let her up even if he wanted to. "I'm going to start the engine and get us out of here. Stay down."

She didn't argue, miracle of miracles, and he eased himself off of her, backing slowly on his hands and knees toward the opening between the box section of the rig and the cab. He paused at the tiny doorway and listened, allowing his superior hearing to search out anything out of the ordinary. All he picked up were the normal sounds of a city. Tires on asphalt, honking horns, humans chatting as they funneled in and out of subway stations. There was nothing that might indicate the number of assailants outside the ambulance.

He peered into the cab and saw a male demon just outside the driver's window. Shit. He eased back. "Nightlash at the front."

"Sparkly pink ring in his nose?"

Con did a double take. "Yeah. Real manly."

"It's Zeph." She eased to her hands and knees. "The one out back will be a Ramreel named Trag. They're partners. Never work alone."

"Your assassins?"

She snared her pants and jammed her legs into them. "Bastards."

"So that's a yes." Con blew out a breath. "I thought you didn't recognize the voice."

"Trag is an expert at disguising it. But the good news is that I know how they work." She'd produced a throwing knife, and she held it loosely in her fingers, ready to throw. "They probably don't know about the Haven spell, but they don't plan to come inside to kill me anyway. If you don't shove me outside, they'll bust open the doors and use ranged weapons to kill me."

"Guns?"

"Doubtful. More likely they'll use poison darts or fireballs."

"You have fifteen seconds," the male near the rear doors called out, and Sin leaped nimbly to her feet.

"I'll go out through the side door. I can slip around the front and take Zeph by surprise if you can throw open the back door—"

"I have a better idea." Con stood. "Which one is the most dangerous? The strongest?"

"Trag," she replied, and disappointment sliced through him. Con had fought Ramreels before, but a Nightlash assassin would be something new. "Why?"

"I'll take him." He glanced up at the roof hatch that Shade had installed precisely for situations like this. The demon thought of everything. Though Con was going to suggest an installation of external ambulance weapons when this was over. "You get the other one."

"Wait—"

Too late. He slid the hatch open and quietly lifted himself through it. Slowly, he eased onto his stomach and inched toward the rear of the rig. Behind him, silent as a whisper, Sin came up, all grace and flexible muscle. Below, Trag banged on the door.

"Time's up."

Con went over the edge, landing on the Ramreel and taking him down hard. The demon's horns made a satisfying crack on the pavement. Nice. Distantly, he heard Zeph's pained grunt, but then Con took a fist to the face, and pain brought his attention fully back to his opponent.

"You can't defeat me, paramedic," Trag spat. "I'm a trained assassin."

"Wrong." Con jammed his knee into Trag's gut. "As a paramedic, I know *exactly* how to kill you." A lifetime of fighting had taught him a lot, but learning how the body worked had made him that much more lethal.

On that energizing thought, Con thrust his fist into the

Ramreel's thick neck, crushing his larynx. Trag made an agonized bleating sound, which Con cut off with a double-tap to his broad snout. The demon rocked backward, but he recovered in a flash, doubling over and using his massive, curled horns to ram Con into the rig's back door.

Fuck, that hurt.

Con ducked, barely avoiding being impaled by Trag's dagger. With a deft spin, he wrenched the demon's arm behind his back and flipped him. Trag went down, and Con delivered another devastating blow to his throat, one that blew right through the male's carotid artery, killing him instantly. The body would disintegrate, as did most demons when they died outside of Sheoul or a demon-built structure in the human realm, and Con didn't wait around to watch.

He sprinted to the front of the rig, where Sin was mashed against the driver's-side door by the Nightlash. He held a knife to her throat, but she had her hand on the demon's shoulder, her *dermoire* glowing fiercely, and before Con could dispatch the bastard, he fell to the ground, his skin ashen and rashed, eyes sunken in.

Whatever disease Sin had pumped into the demon had brought him down hard. And grotesquely.

The reminder of what she was and what she had done slapped him in the face, bringing his brain back to the place it needed to be while dealing with her: professional distance.

"You okay?" he asked.

"Yeah." She kicked the dead demon in the ribs and winced, clutching her thigh.

Con swore. "Let me check your leg—"

"It's fine." She wheeled away and stalked to the rear

of the rig, where the Ramreel's body was already nothing but a greasy stain on the asphalt. "Son of a bitch," she breathed, and Con swore he heard a trace of regret. "He was a damned good assassin."

"Not so good with the hand-to-hand."

"It was his main weakness." The morning breeze blew her hair into her face, and Con barely resisted the urge to brush it back. "He relied on his aim and didn't focus enough on physical combat."

"And what's your weakness?"

She shoved her dagger into her boot. "I don't have one."

"If you believe that, then delusion *is* your weakness."

"Aren't you a smarty-pants," she said crisply. "Fine. My weakness is that I'm a succubus. But it is very rarely an issue when I'm working."

He doubted that, and now he wanted to kick himself for not considering that he might want her blood so badly because she was a succubus. It might not be her blood at all—it could be her pheromones that were driving his hunger, not an impending addiction.

Unless...

"What is your succubi requirement?" he snapped.

Her raven eyebrows popped up. "Uh...sex?"

"No, I mean, what is it you steal or cause?"

She jammed her hands on her hips. "Well, I don't steal souls, if that's what you're asking. I don't do anything."

Oh, she did *something*, whether or not she knew it.

A hiss, like the sound from a flattening tire, rose up behind him as the Nightlash's body dissolved. He waited until the noise died away before asking, "How long before you'll need sex?"

"Not long. And all my regular partners are at the den."

A stirring of...something...made him twitch. It couldn't be jealousy. He'd never experienced that before. Not over a female. But something definitely torqued his temper, and he herded her into the passenger seat with his jaw set so tight he practically had to pry it open to talk after he settled behind the wheel.

"We'll figure something out, but we won't have much time at my house." He cranked the engine. "The Carceris will be looking for you in all your haunts, but you can bet your ass that they're investigating me. It won't be long before they find out where I live." He had two residences—hopefully they'd check out his apartment first. "We should have time to clean up and map out our next move." Like maybe handing her off to one of her brothers. Sin didn't seem to have heard him. She was staring off into space and absently rubbing her breastbone. "Hey, you okay?"

She blinked. "Of course I am."

Right. No weaknesses. But he wasn't buying it. Her own assassins were trying to kill her, take her job, and unless she had ice water in her veins instead of blood, it had to bother her.

And he knew damned good and well her blood ran hot, not cold.

"Does your chest hurt?"

"A little. It's a dull ache from losing two assassins I was bonded to."

He grimaced, unable to imagine being able to sense someone's death like that. He got the rig moving as Sin fished a cell phone from her pocket and dialed. "Who are you calling?"

"One of my guys." She paused, said into the phone, "Lycus. What's going on?"

Con's dhampire hearing sharpened, enhanced, and homed in on the conversation.

"You're out in the open. You're a target, Sin." The male's voice was as clear to Con as if he were sitting in the passenger seat with Sin.

Fuck that. The guy would have to sit in the box section of the rig. Strapped to the gurney.

"No shit." Her voice lowered, and she turned away, as if she didn't want Con to hear. "Where are you?"

"The den. Waiting for you."

Okay, strapped to the gurney and dead. Con gnashed his teeth, annoyed at his own reaction. There was no reason to be jealous, no matter how sleazy this Lycus idiot sounded.

"Who all is after me?"

There was a pause, and then a low purr rumbled over the airwaves. *"Come back to the den, Sin. Swear to mate me, and I'll make sure they're called off."*

Son of a— Con bit back a curse as his entire body jerked, and the ambulance with it. Horns honked as he whipped the rig back into the right lane, ignoring Sin's glare. He didn't give a shit what Sin did, who she "mated" with, or what she did with her assassin business. But this Lycus fucker was blackmailing her, and that just pissed him off. The sudden image of her naked, beneath a well-muscled body didn't bother him at all. *At. All.*

Sin flushed with anger, and Con waited for her to tell the bastard off with her usual sharp tongue. So he nearly fell over when she said tiredly, "I said no."

Con could practically hear the smile in the male's

voice. *"You're weakening, succubus. Don't take too long to roll over."*

Very slowly, Sin mashed the End button, still looking at the BlackBerry's screen. "Asshole," she muttered.

Con realized he was gripping the steering wheel hard enough to put a bend in it, and forced himself to ease up. "How many more of your assassins might be after you?"

Her fingers formed fists in her lap, and she turned to fix him with a penetrating stare. "All of them," she said. "They have all turned on me."

Luc had been alternately peering through his two tiny windows, keeping an eye out for potential trouble, when he heard Kar's fragile voice rise up from the basement.

He took the steps to the room below and found her lying on the pallet where he'd left her, though she'd rolled to her uninjured side and was staring at the chains secured to his log and stone wall.

"Where...where am I?" she rasped, her Texan accent barely discernible through her pain.

He crouched next to her. "You're in my moon room." Not that he used the thing anymore. He no longer cared what he did on nights of the full moon. He refused to chain himself up, preferring to run free. Eventually The Aegis would kill him, or maybe a hunter, or, most likely, Wraith. The demon had sworn to take Luc out when the last of his humanity left him, and really, that had happened when Ula died. "What do you remember?"

Kar shifted, wincing when she tried to move her arm. "Being chased by The Aegis."

"They obviously learned the truth about you."

Firelight flickered on her face, the light and shadow making her expression hard to read, but there was a note of amusement in her voice. "Guess you can't blackmail me anymore."

He nearly smiled at that. They'd been holed up in an Aegis stronghold in Alexandria, Egypt, while they waited for the apocalyptic battle between good and evil to start, and in this particular conflict, Luc, the Sem brothers, and a lot of other demons had been there to fight for Team Good and Annoyingly Righteous. They'd actually been working with The Aegis in a fragile truce that had been laden with tension and distrust.

Kar had been there as a Guardian, all holier-than-thou, and then she'd sensed the werewolf in him.

And he'd sensed it in her.

Already revved up for the pending war, his sex drive had roared to life. And he wasn't the nicest guy in the world, so he'd made her a deal. Ten minutes naked, and he'd keep her secret.

She'd bitched and growled, but after Team Good had claimed victory in Jerusalem, she'd given him half an hour. His body hardened even now, just thinking about how he'd taken her three times in that thirty minutes. Up against the side of the building. On the ground, missionary style. On their knees, him giving it to her from behind. All couplings had been rough and raw, the way wargs did it, especially after a hardcore battle. He'd come away sore and scratched, and more sated than he'd been in a long time.

"I'm sure I can find something to blackmail you about," he said, as he settled his palm over her forehead to gauge her temperature. "You have a fever." He slid his fingers down to her throat. "And your pulse is too fast. I'm going to get some ice and meds."

Her good hand shot out to capture his wrist in a surprisingly strong grip. "No drugs."

"We've got to get your fever down."

She licked her lips, closed her eyes, but she didn't release him. "Okay, but nothing that will hurt the baby."

He stared at her. "You're pregnant?"

"Yes."

She must have gone into a breeding heat just days after he'd been with her. Thank God he hadn't sensed it coming on. He'd have been compelled to stay and fight any other males who showed up to claim her. The winner would have mated with her over the three days and nights of the full moon, both in human and beast form, and if she became pregnant during that time, their bond would be permanent.

"Where's your mate?"

"Dead." Her eyes were still closed, and he wished she'd open them so he could get a read on her.

"Did The Aegis kill him?"

"Yeah."

"Was he born or turned?"

"Turned," she said softly.

A chill bit all the way to his marrow. "The cub could be born human."

She finally opened her eyes. "I'm aware of that."

"Will you kill it?" Born warg laws were harsh in regard to human infants; they were to be destroyed at birth. Though Luc had heard of a few mothers who had left the babies at human hospitals or fire stations so the children could be adopted.

She hesitated, and for a moment, he thought she'd say yes. But then her eyes flashed, the steely glint in them hinting at what kind of mother she'd be. Fierce. Loving. "I will protect my baby with my life. That's why I'm here. The virus..."

"What about it?"

"I'm scared. You know what's going on—you have an inside track—"

He snorted. "In case you hadn't noticed, I'm holed up in the middle of nowhere. But I do know that it affects only turned wargs, so you're safe." For some reason, she didn't appear to be relieved, but then, she was as ill with her injuries and silver poisoning as she would be with SF. He palmed her forehead again, knowing damned good and well that the fever wouldn't have eased. "So that's why you're here? The only reason?"

She shifted her gaze to the fireplace, stared into it blankly. "I didn't have any place else to go once The Aegis found out about my secret."

"You shouldn't have come here." It was an asshole thing to say, but then, he was an asshole. Since the day he was attacked by a werewolf, he'd been all about taking care of himself and not giving a crap about anyone else.

"Clearly, it was a mistake." Her voice was so soft it was nearly drowned out by the crackle of the fire.

"Yeah, it was." He stood, tossed another log on the fire with a little more force than was needed, and sparks flew up, snapping angrily. "The last thing I need is to take care of a breeding female who has slayers on her tail. How'd they find out what you are anyway?" When she didn't answer, he turned around. Her eyes were closed, her breathing even. She was out again.

And he was in one hell of a mess.

Seven

They rode in silence for a good thirty minutes. Sin was grateful for the quiet at first, until her thoughts started swirling around and she realized how much trouble she was truly in. Lycus, that slimy, double-crossing dickwad. She'd known she couldn't trust him, but she'd hoped he'd use some of his considerable influence to keep most of her assassins off her back—without her swearing to become his mate.

And he was wrong; she wasn't weakening. As nice as it would be to share the burdens of being an assassin master, she couldn't bond herself to anyone, especially not a piss-head like Lycus.

Dammit. Between her own assassins wanting her head on a platter and the Carceris wanting her strung up in a cell, she was starting to feel like a deer during hunting season. So when her cell phone began to ring incessantly—calls and texts from Lore, Eidolon, Shade, and even one from Wraith—her last nerve frayed like the end of a snapped rope and she turned the phone off.

"They're worried about you." Con slid a glance at the BlackBerry. "You should answer."

"I don't need their concern."

His reply was sharp. "Selfish much?"

Okay, yeah, she was selfish. Since the day she and Lore had gone through the transition that had given them tattoos, uncontrollable sexual needs, and killing abilities, she'd been forced to leave the human world behind. Which meant leaving softness, compassion, and love in a place where it wouldn't hurt her. The world she'd been whisked into by a demon slave trader just days after Lore abandoned her had toughened her up, real fast.

She'd spent a century with demons who breathed cruelty like air, and the buildup of scar tissue, both physical and emotional, had been the only reason she'd survived. Then, thirty years ago, she'd found Lore, and his devotion had chipped away, just a little, at her shield. And now, her reason for not responding to her brothers wasn't because she didn't need their concern—though she didn't. It was because no matter how much she hated it, she found herself worrying about Wraith and Eidolon's punishment for helping her.

But she wasn't going to tell Con that. Voicing it made it real and invited pity and useless phrases like "I'm sorry." And "It'll be okay."

Goose bumps prickled her skin. Her grandma, who had raised Sin and Lore from the day they were born, used to say that a lot. *"It'll be okay, Sinead. Your mama loves you. She's troubled, that's all."* And *"It'll be okay. People can be cruel, but you'll always have me."*

Grandma had lied. Mama hadn't loved her, Sin hadn't always had Grandma, and it had definitely not been okay.

The ambulance's radio squawked, and Eidolon's strained voice pierced the silence. "Con. Pick up."

Con punched a button on the dash. "E. We're safe."

"Thank gods." Eidolon's relief transmitted over the airwaves. "Don't tell me where you're going. This frequency might be monitored. Sin, stay away from every place you've ever been."

"Yeah. Will do." An unfamiliar flare of guilt sparked in her belly, and she cleared her throat. "Hey, uh...are you and Wraith...I mean...did you—"

"Don't worry about us," Eidolon said. "Just get where you're going and we'll talk later." He disconnected, leaving Sin and Con in tense silence again.

For another long-ass hour. She spent the time gazing out the window at the passing cars, wishing she could be in one of them, behind the wheel and driving to a destiny of her choosing instead of being chauffeured to one she didn't want by an arrogant dhampire.

An arrogant dhampire whose long, muscular legs flexed as he worked the gas and brake pedals. Whose thick biceps rolled and bunched as he steered. Broad shoulders filled the driver's space, and images of her hands clinging to them as he pumped between her thighs filled her head. She was so acutely aware of him, so hypersensitive to his heat, his scent, even the sound of his breathing, that no matter how many times she averted her gaze back to the outside world, she found her eyes drifting back to him. Felt her body leaning toward him.

He was such a pain in the ass.

Finally, as the suburbs turned into pastures and

farmland, Con pulled the ambulance off the main road
and onto a gravel one lined by rows of trees.

"I'm guessing you don't drive to work very often," she
mused.

"There's a Harrowgate less than a quarter mile away
in the woods, so no, I don't drive often. A two-hour com-
mute would be a killer."

The ambulance crunched over gravel for maybe half
a mile before Con pulled into the driveway of an old but
well-kept ranch-style house set against a hill and cut deeply
into a forest that appeared to have been cultivated for privacy. She got out and did a sweep of the perimeter while
he moved his black GTO out of the garage to make room
for the ambulance. He also had a motorcycle, a snowmobile, and an ATV. The guy liked his toys with engines.

Con eased the ambulance inside—the big rig barely
fit, and she thought she heard the scrape of metal at some
point. Shade was going to pop his cork at the scratches the
vehicle had gotten today.

"Nice ride," she said, as she trailed a finger along the
GTO's sleek fender. The thing still had dealer plates on it.

Con shrugged. "It'll do until next year."

"Next year?"

"I get a new one every spring."

She peeked through the tinted glass at the leather interior. "Like the new-car smell, huh?"

"Nah," he said, as he punched the garage door button.
"I get tired of driving the same thing over and over."

"Maybe you should get a plane," she muttered, and he
nodded as if she'd been serious.

"I'm working on it. I already have my pilot's license."

Of course he did.

Once the garage door had rolled down, he disarmed the security system and led her into the house, which was a true bachelor pad. The furniture was old but well-kept. There were clothes draped over the chairs and couch, and she wondered if the windows had ever been cleaned. It looked like Lore's place, only newer. And bigger. Definitely more personal.

His shelves and walls were loaded with stuff that appeared to be ancient—pottery, framed sketches of stone cathedrals, weapons. She drifted toward one magnificent piece, a longbow hanging between a halberd and a Japanese katana.

"Impressive." She trailed a finger over the smooth yew surface. "I wouldn't have taken you for a house kind of person, though."

"Where did you think I'd live?" he asked, amusement in his voice. "A tent?"

Shrugging, she turned back to him. "Most single guys are apartment dwellers. And most single wargs live a little more rustically."

It was his turn to shrug. "Born wargs prefer the outdoors and wilderness, but a lot of turned wargs are human enough to like living with other humans."

"Until they realize that humans are food and that chaining yourself up in an apartment gets noisy."

"True." He tossed the ambulance keys onto the dining room table.

"What about dhampires? You're sort of born that way ... and then turned."

His hands went to his shirt buttons as he pinned her with a cool, remote gaze. Man, she wished she could read him better. "What's your point?"

There was a strange avoidance vibe in his answer, but she couldn't determine what, exactly, he was skirting. "Where do you fall on the warg scale? What do you do? About the full moon, I mean."

He peeled out of his paramedic shirt, and her tongue nearly rolled out of her mouth at the sight of his sharply defined muscles and honed, hard flesh. She was used to males who kept themselves in top form—no assassin let himself go flabby—but Con had a lean, powerful runner's body, the kind that was used well and often. He was made for marathons.

I spend hours on foreplay.

Oh, yeah. Marathons.

"I sure as hell don't chain myself." He tossed the shirt over the back of a chair. "I go home. To where I was born."

She had to force her eyes away from his chest to meet his. "Where's that?"

"Scotland. It's where dhampires originated. The Dearghuls—the only clan that's left—have a sanctuary there. Acres of property where we can hunt during the moon fever."

Eyes level…eyes level… "How many of you are there?"

"Our numbers are pathetically few. So few that during the mating season, all unmated males and females must participate."

Sin bit her cheek to keep from moaning at the "mating" word. "So you don't mate like other wargs? I mean, getting a female pregnant during her heat doesn't bind you to her forever?"

"No," he said huskily, and she wondered if the subject

had affected him the way it had her. "In fact, the males very rarely take permanent mates."

His skin was *so* tan. "Why not?"

"Because we tend to kill the females."

Ah, well, okay. That wasn't cool.

She wandered around the living room and down the hall to check out the bedrooms. Yep, she was a Nosy Nellie, but Con didn't seem to mind. "What do you do with all this space? You have parties and stuff?"

He looked up from checking the answering machine. "Nope. A lot of my friends are human. They'd ask too many questions."

"Human? You're tight with *humans*?"

"Not recently." He moved to the window and yanked the curtains closed. "Just had to let go of my last group of buds. When they start mentioning how you never get older, it's time to take a "permanent job" in some remote place with no communications. Right now, I'm studying nematodes in Antarctica."

"Well, aren't you a dork." But seriously...how odd that he hung with humans. He seemed like an underworld-purist kind of guy.

His cell phone rang, and he dug it out of the lower side leg pocket of his BDU pants. "E. Yeah. You're where?"

Con hung up, strode to the front door, and standing there, still in his scrubs, was Eidolon. Shade was next to him, clad from boot to neck in black leather, from his biker boots to his jacket, sunglasses hiding his dark eyes. He looked like the freaking Terminator.

"How'd you know where we were?" Sin asked.

"I'm a good guesser," Eidolon said as he and Shade stepped inside. He tossed a duffel bag at Sin. "Clothes.

Figured you might need them after getting nailed by the dart."

Con closed the door, but not before scanning the area outside. "Is Runa doing better?"

"Not good enough." Shade tucked his sunglasses into his pocket. "She made me leave. Said I was driving her crazy. Besides, I needed to do some grocery shopping."

Sin nearly laughed at the image of the big, bad leather-clad demon pushing a grocery cart through the vegetable and diaper aisles at a supermarket. "I have a hard time believing you left her alone, not feeling well, with three babies."

"I didn't. Gem and Tay are with her." Tayla, Eidolon's mate, and her twin sister, Gem, were both half-Soul-shredder demon—the worst of the worst—but they were gooey marshmallows when it came to caring for their nephews. Gem was pregnant, and Sin figured it wouldn't be long before Tayla hopped that crazy train, too.

Shade moved to Sin. "You okay? E said you were hit with a lock-dart."

"I'll live." She dropped the bag and marched back to the kitchen, talking as she went. "Con patched me up before the assassins attacked."

Both Shade and E focused on her, dark lasers of pissed-off-ness, and she knew she'd made a huge mistake by saying anything. "Assassins?" they both growled.

"Yeah." Con took a six-pack of beer out of the fridge and tossed a bottle at each of them. Sin fumbled hers. She'd been too busy admiring *his* six-pack. "Your sister can't take a freaking step without causing some sort of disaster."

Shade popped the cap off his bottle and flung the top into the sink. "Who were they?"

"They were mine. I'm walking around with a bull's-eye on my ass." She held up her left hand and wiggled her fingers, where Detharu's silver ring glinted in the light. "Any assassin who kills me and takes my ring inherits my job. I'm pretty much the underworld's most wanted right now."

"Hell's bells," Shade muttered. "What kind of defense do you have against them?"

She waggled her brows. "Besides my uber-incredible fighting and self-defense skills?"

"Yeah," Shade said flatly, and sheesh, the guy had no sense of humor. "Besides those."

I could bind myself to Lycus for the rest of my life. She shrugged. "All I can do is stay ahead of them. Most won't be able to find me, but a few can sense me. It's even possible that they've put out the word to every hired blade in the underworld. I need to keep moving."

"You'll have to do that to keep ahead of the Carceris, too," Eidolon added.

"You'll stay at the cave with Runa," Shade announced, as if he'd made the decision and Sin would have to accept it. "The entrance is hidden, and even if they track you to it, they'll never get in."

"You don't know my assassins. Trust me, they'll find a way. I'm not putting your mate and children at risk."

Eidolon raked his hand through his hair. "Then we'll take turns with you."

"Turns?"

"There are four of us," Eidolon pointed out, as if she couldn't count. "One of us will always be with you."

"No way." She twisted the cap off her beer bottle. "I can take care of myself. I don't need you guys being all big brother. Besides," she said jauntily, as she linked arms with Con, "I have this studly dhampire to keep me safe."

Con went taut, his arm and chest muscles turning to iron against her. For a second she thought he'd argue, but he shocked her by saying, "I don't have a choice. I need her blood to eliminate the virus inside me."

"Well, gee, don't sound so excited."

"Trust me," he said in a hard tone. "I'm not. I do have other obligations."

Shade knocked back half his beer. "Con can stay. That'll give you two bodyguards."

Sin jerked away from Con, partly to round on Shade, but mostly because Con's lack of a shirt was a distraction she didn't need. "Do you not understand the word no? I don't want to be responsible for you."

"Responsible?" Shade choked on his beer. "Responsible for *us*?"

"Yeah. What if my assassins use you to get to me? Or what if they kill you?"

"I think," Shade said quietly, "that you underestimate us."

No, actually, she knew her brothers were more than capable of defending themselves. But no one was invincible. "There's also the trouble with the Carceris," she reminded them.

"We're not worried about that," Eidolon said, but Sin shook her head.

"I am. I said no."

Shade was in her face so fast she didn't have time to blink. Next to her, Con tensed again, and she wondered if, possibly, he was gearing up to defend her. "This isn't up for debate," he growled. "We have each others' backs in this family, and we won't let yours be exposed."

She went up on her tiptoes, but she still only reached his shoulders. "I. Said. No. If I were a brother instead of a sister, you wouldn't be this crazy about protecting me, and you know it. I will *not* be treated differently just because I don't have a dick."

"Sin—"

She cut off Eidolon by slamming her beer down on the counter, spraying foam everywhere. "I will not put you at risk." She'd done that by accepting Lore's help with her ex-master, Detharu, and it had cost her brother years of suffering. She wouldn't do that to a sibling again, and neither would she allow herself to grow close to them. If she was stuck with them twenty-four-seven . . .

She shuddered. They were overbearing and protective enough as it was. If they got to know her, she'd be screwed.

"You don't have to do this alone." Shade's fingers circled her wrist, his hold gentle but as unyielding as shackles. "You are ours—"

You are mine. The voice of her first master, the one who had taken her off the streets where she'd been starving, craving things she didn't understand, pounded in her head. He'd run an underworld crime ring that mostly operated in the human world—gambling, prostitution, murder for hire, drug and slave trafficking. He'd been the first to own her, but he hadn't been the last.

You are mine. You belong to me. You are ours. The words of past masters kept clanging around in her skull until her throat tightened and her heart kicked madly against her ribs.

"Yours?" Sin broke Shade's hold and stumbled back so fast she bumped into Con. "I belong to no one." God, she was trembling all over, and her breath had backed up in her lungs as anxiety swamped her.

"Whoa." Shade's hands came up. "Hey, it's okay."

Con rested his palms on her shoulders, his grip strangely comforting when it should have made her feel even more trapped. "I think you boys should back off."

Eidolon and Shade glared at Con, glints of gold breaking the surfaces of their dark eyes as anger sparked. "I appreciate what you've done for her," Eidolon said, his voice scraping gravel, "but she *is* our sister, and we can handle this."

Tension pinged off Sin's skin like buckshot. She opened her mouth to tell them all off, but Con spoke first.

"She needs you," he said, in that soothing paramedic voice he'd used on her in the ambulance. "You know that. *She* knows that." He squeezed her shoulder, a silent message to roll with what he was saying. "But it might be best if you let me stay by her side while you handle things from UG."

Everyone stared, motionless, until Eidolon finally took a long swig of his beer and nodded. "You'll check in every couple of hours."

Sin clenched her fists at the command, but she resisted the urge to mouth off. Antagonizing E and Shade now would be stupid, and she wouldn't put it past Eidolon to change his mind.

"I might only have a couple of days, maybe hours, before I have to take care of some clan business, but we'll do what we can until then," Con promised.

"Good." Eidolon propped his hip against the kitchen's

island countertop and cursed with annoyance when the beer that had spilled out of her bottle soaked his pants. "Since you'll be moving around a lot, can you take her to warg areas that might be infected? I can give you the locations of the packs where my patients came from."

Con frowned. "Why?"

"Because before the Carceris interrupted us, we were working on reversing the disease in an infected warg. Sin failed, in part because too much of the virus was in the warg's blood, and what was there had degraded too badly to be useful in the lab. If she can try the same thing with someone who has been infected for only a few hours, she might have a shot at success. I need a sample of freshly killed, intact virus."

"Interesting." Con slid her a glance, one that was almost approving, and for some reason, she felt like a happy puppy that had been praised for piddling outside instead of on the carpet. Annoying. "Yeah, we can do that."

"Lore plugged all the cases into a computer program the R-XR developed to track outbreaks and cross-check them with known populations of canine-based underworld beings—"

"I thought only turned wargs were affected," Sin interrupted. "Why track anyone else?"

"Just a precaution, in case the disease mutates. Like it did with Con." Eidolon handed Con a slip of paper, Lore's handwriting scrawled on it. "That's the log-in and password."

Sin's heart lurched in her chest. "How is Lore?"

Shade cocked a dark eyebrow. "Flipping out."

She scrubbed a hand over her face. God, what she wouldn't give for all of this to be over already. "I figured.

Look, why don't you guys go do whatever it is you do. Con and I will be fine."

Both brothers shot her looks edged with doubt, and then nailed Con with eyes that said, *If anything happens to her, you're dead.*

Con acknowledged their unspoken threat with a lazy nod that also conveyed that he wasn't worried. But whether that was because he was confident in his abilities to keep her safe or if it was because he wasn't afraid of her brothers, she didn't know.

"Give me your hand." Shade held out his to Sin. "Since Con is going to need to feed from you, I'm going to tweak your system to increase your blood production. After that, you'll need to stay hydrated. Drink lots of water."

Sin put her hand in his. Instantly, a warm, tingling sensation flowed from her fingertips to her bones. She sagged, and both Eidolon and Con moved to catch her. Con was faster, and as he pulled her into his big body, tension sparked in the room again.

God, these guys were impossible. Lore had never been this bad, but then, he'd walked on eggshells around her because he felt so guilty about what had happened that one night so long ago.

He also realized she had succubus needs, something the Long Lost Trio seemed to not understand. Well, it was time to *make* them understand.

She backed away from Shade, and in a deliberate, sensual motion, she reached up and gripped the back of Con's neck. "Look, boys. You seem to think I'm some sheltered, sweet little virginal doll." She scraped her nails across Con's skin, and he hissed. Those fangs were so damned sexy. "But I'm not. I'm a Seminus demon. Think about what that means."

Shade turned an interesting gray color. Eidolon winced.

"Yeah. I need sex or I die. So stop with the obnoxious chaperone shit, because I really don't want you anywhere nearby while I'm doing it, and I don't think you want that either." She gave them her sweetest smile. "And know that the second you're gone, I'm going to ride Con until he begs for mercy."

Eidolon sighed. Shade swore. And Con muttered something that sounded strangely like "Mercy."

One type of tension left the house with Shade and Eidolon. But another remained, a less violent tang in the air, but one that was no less dangerous. Sin was a fucking menace, and no one was safe around her. Especially not Con.

I'm going to ride Con until he begs for mercy. Jesus. He was lucky Shade and E hadn't gutted him right then and there. Hell, her words alone had done that. Now his blood was pumping steam through his veins, his skin hot and itchy, and his cock was hard as a steel pipe.

She stood in the kitchen, fist wrapped tightly around her beer bottle. "That was fun," she chirped.

"What is your problem?" His bark should have made her jump, but no, Miss I'll Take on the World squared for battle.

"Excuse me?"

He stalked toward her, and the closer he got, the more her chin came up in that defiant way of hers. "You heard me." He tore the bottle from her hand and slammed it down on the counter. She made a sound of outrage as he caged her against said counter, his fists planted on either side of her. "What is your deal with your brothers? Why are you so hostile?"

She shoved against his bare chest, but he didn't budge. "Get away from me."

"Answer." He put more weight on her, which put more skin on skin. It also put his hips in contact with her stomach, and it wasn't going to be long before it would be obvious that he wasn't completely hating being this close to her.

"I'm not hostile." She squirmed, but as soon as she realized that all she was doing was wedging them together tighter and doing some interesting grinding, she stopped and said with a huff, "I just don't know them."

"Why not?"

She craned her neck to look up at him. "You don't know?"

"Know what?"

"I wasn't even aware that Shade, Eidolon, and Wraith existed until a few weeks ago. They didn't know about me until last month." She shoved again, for all the good it did her. Now that they were plastered against each other, she had no leverage. "Get. Off."

Now why in the hell did his imagination have to take those two little words and make an X-rated flick out of them? "Is that an offer? You going to follow up on that charming little announcement you made to your brothers? Because you're the one who will be begging for mercy."

Sure, he was mostly trying to antagonize her, but he knew what being inside her felt like. He knew what she tasted like. And, as with all sins, this one was addictive.

Literally.

The reality put a much needed damper on his lust, cooling him down a few degrees.

"It was *not* an offer," she ground out. "I was messing with those two meatheads because they needed a damned wake-up call."

"Agreed, but next time, put someone else's balls in a vise."

"But squeezing yours is so much more fun," she said, with a cheery bat of her eyelashes. Then she frowned. Her *dermoire* lit up, and a tingle ran through his chest. "You need to feed."

"I don't."

"Maybe not for hunger. But the virus is building again."

"It can wait. You still haven't recovered from the last feeding, not to mention the blood loss from your wounds." Shade had power-punched her blood production into high gear, but Con didn't want to push it. And the less time spent with his mouth on her, the better.

She shrugged, making her long, silky curtain of black hair swish against his chest. "Whatever. We're only going to be traveling to warg packs. But no skin off my back. Just don't blame me for any infections you cause."

Sudden anger replaced the residual lust zipping through his veins, and with a snarl, he pushed away, putting several feet of distance between them. "I blame you for all of them."

Her eyes narrowed into furious ebony slits. "Yes, I'm to blame. Are you ever going to stop reminding me?"

"Maybe when my friends stop dying." Clenching his fists so hard his knuckles ached, he pivoted around so he wouldn't have to look at her, wouldn't have to be reminded how much he both wanted her and hated her. His temple throbbed as he fought the urge to grab her, shake her until her teeth rattled, and then strip her naked and claim her right there on the kitchen floor.

Suddenly, her fists were pummeling his back. "You stupid son of a bitch! I fucked up and infected a shitload of people, but you don't have to."

She shoved him hard enough to knock him into the fridge, severing the last thread of control on his temper, blurring the line between lust and anger. Hot, potent adrenaline surged in his veins as he wheeled around, seized her upper arms, and lifted her. He knew his eyes had gone fully mirrored, so she'd see her own terror in them. His fangs punched down and his cock got hard, and shit, he was on the edge.

But instead of terror, he saw only defiance as she ground out, "Do it, asshole. Bite me. What are you fucking waiting for?"

Con slammed her against the wall and bit into her neck. She gasped, but the sound was followed by a low moan. As her honeyed blood poured down his throat, his libido went berserk, the way it had in Eidolon's office, except multiplied by a hundred. Maybe it was because they were alone. Maybe it was because they had full body contact and his anger had shot all his common sense through the roof.

Maybe it was because with each feeding, the addiction was building.

"Con..." His name came out on a whisper of breath against his ear, and it was his turn to moan. Especially when her legs came up and hooked around his waist, putting his aching shaft in contact with her core.

Her nails dug into his shoulders. "Fuck me," she murmured.

For most dhampires—and vampires—feeding went hand in hand with sex, which was why he preferred to take his blood from females. Few of his kind were picky about the sex of their bed and blood mates, but Con had long ago determined that a soft, sweet female was the best fit for him.

Except there was nothing soft or sweet about Sin, and for some reason, that fact had a far more powerful effect on him. The fight, the intensity . . . it rocked him like nothing—and no one—else.

Yes. No. Ah, damn, his body was screaming for her, but his mind swirled with doubts. Deeper involvement with her would be a bad thing on so many levels. He'd keep her safe because he owed her brothers and because she could be key in finding an answer to the epidemic, but that was as far as the relationship between Sin and Con could go.

"Con." Her satiny lips brushed his cheek, and the raw desire in her voice pummeled his resolve. "I need it."

Right. Duh. Succubi. He had to keep her safe *and* healthy. Justifying sex had never been so easy.

He couldn't tear open his fly fast enough.

Sin wrapped one arm around his neck and dropped her other between them so she could rip open her own pants. Not gently, he shoved her up on the counter, disengaged his fangs, and jerked off her pants and thong. They caught on her boots, and he growled with impatience, tearing her pants as he yanked them off.

"Hurry," she breathed.

Now was definitely not the time for finesse, and he

didn't spare her as he gripped her thighs, spread them, and plunged deep into her satin core. Her cry of passion joined his. He felt her everywhere—on his skin, in his blood. It was like drowning in ecstasy, and he could no longer remember why he'd resisted her.

"Harder," she moaned, and holy hell, she was a fucking dream come true.

He planted his palms on the wall above her head, and she leaned back, bracing herself on her arms behind her, her legs wrapped tightly around his waist in that way all males loved. A trickle of blood ran down her throat from the punctures in her neck, and he dipped his head to swipe his tongue over it. The flavor nearly had him coming.

"I love how you taste," he growled against her throat. "I want to taste you everywhere." He wanted to get her naked and then spend hours kissing her all over. Licking and nibbling and sucking every inch of skin, with a heavy emphasis on that succulent place between her legs.

"Yes." The word came out on a harsh whisper. "Come, Con. Now."

Since semen was the trigger for her, the idea of torturing her by withholding for a little while was appealing as hell, but he was too far gone to scrounge up that kind of control, not when her sex was like a glove, squeezing and massaging until he was on the verge.

He pumped into her, hard and fast, so much more wild than they'd been in the supply closet, when they'd been virtual strangers sneaking a quickie before her brothers caught them and castrated his ass.

His hip rubbed on her thigh holster, a strangely erotic sensation, and when she flexed her muscles, the sheath dug into his flesh, catapulting him to climax. It hit him like a searing wave of lava, spreading up his spine and into every limb. He spilled into Sin, and her core clenched around him as she joined him in a blatantly silent release. She was holding back, just as she had the first time.

When it was over, he collapsed onto his elbows against the wall and braced his forehead on hers in a desperate attempt to catch his breath. She was breathing hard, too, her sex still contracting and taking every last drop.

She shifted, sitting up, and he slid out of her. She gripped his biceps, and for a second he thought she was preventing him from leaving, but her *dermoire* lit up, and he realized she was checking for the virus. When she swore, he knew the news was not good.

"You didn't take enough blood. It's almost gone. Just another sip, maybe..."

"No." He stepped back and tucked himself into his pants. "We'll give you a day to recover."

"A day could get the virus back up to unmanageable levels."

"We'll see." He glanced down at her creamy, spread thighs, at the glistening juncture between them, and unbelievably, his cock swelled again. Quickly, he jerked his gaze away. "I'm going to shower and change. You can use the guest bathroom if you want. If not, why don't you log in to the hospital's records and get a map of the viral outbreaks. Computer's in my office. We'll head out after that." He walked away without waiting for an answer.

After showering, he dressed in jeans and a plain white T-shirt. He found her in his office, hair wet and dressed in the leather pants and short-sleeved black button-down Eidolon had brought.

"I've printed out the locations of all known infected

wargs," she said, not bothering to turn away from the computer screen. The printer spit out a couple of pages.

"Excellent." He jammed his feet into his boots, grabbed the papers, and considered whipping up a quick meal. He made a killer southwestern omelet.

Sin came up behind him while he was shuffling through the fridge. "Do you feel that?"

"Feel what…" The hairs on the back of his neck prickled.

"Get down!" Sin dove at him, took him to the floor in a tangle of limbs as the entire world exploded. A massive boom shattered his ears, and a whoosh of searing flame blasted his skin. Rolling, he covered her body with his, clenching his teeth against the torrent of wood and plaster that rained down on his back. Another explosion sent a shock wave of heat and pressure into them both, and almost as if they'd been picked up by a giant, invisible hand, they were lifted and hurled against the stove. Pain wrenched through his shoulder, but he ignored it as he grasped Sin's hand and dragged her, on his hands and knees, toward the garage.

"I have an escape tunnel," he shouted, and then hacked up a freaking lung as black smoke filled his chest.

Somewhere in the house, glass shattered, and the rapid pop of automatic gunfire pierced the roar of flames. Someone was very serious about making sure they were dead.

The garage was already burning, but Con shielded his face from the flames as he made his way to the rig. Coughing, he climbed inside and grabbed a jump bag. He leaped out and caught a glimpse of the blackened vehicle through the billowing smoke. Shade was going to be fucking pissed about the brand-new ambulance. It hadn't even gone on a dozen runs yet.

Sin was crouching where he'd left her, at the fridge-sized gun safe near the back wall. Quickly, he punched in the security code and spun the wheel to open the door. There were no weapons inside, but the bottom was a concealed hatch, which he tugged open.

"Cool," Sin said between coughs.

"Hurry." He nudged her to the opening. "There's a ladder down."

He cast one last, longing look at his house burning down around him. He'd liked this place, but he supposed there was no sense in mourning, since he would have had to give it all up to join the clan in Scotland anyway. He just hoped he had time to help with the warg disease situation first.

Flames in the shape of a giant hand shot out of the wall, and Con reared back as a piercing, chilling shriek froze the marrow in his bones. "What the fuck is that?"

"Not good, whatever it is!" Sin yelled. "Come on!"

He started down the tunnel, but as he did, something outside the shattered window caught his eye. He blinked, and it was gone.

"Con? What are you doing?"

He shook his head. "I could have sworn I saw a big dude on a horse. And he was wearing a fucking suit of armor."

Eight

Sin scaled the ladder, her skin feeling singed and sunburned. At the bottom, darkness closed in on her, becoming complete blackness when Con closed the door to the gun safe and the hatch over the hole. She heard his big feet hit the rungs, and then he bumped into her at the base, smelling of a weird combination of smoke, piney soap, and his own natural, dark scent. It was messed up that she noticed, and even more messed up that it stirred her even though they'd just taken the edge off her need.

But then, she'd always been turned on by danger, and they were in it up to their chins.

She heard some scritching noises, and a flashlight lit the darkness.

"Aren't you the prepared little dhampire. Handy escape route you have here."

He gestured down the tunnel with the Maglite. "You never know when you'll need a quick getaway."

"You make a lot of quick getaways?" She started moving, her feet barely making a whisper on the soft dirt floor.

"Probably no more than you do," he said dryly.

"Probably." She was always finagling her way out of tight scrapes. She took an S-curve well ahead of the circle of light behind her, and her handy-dandy demon night vision finally kicked in to help. "Where does it go?"

"Ends near the Harrowgate." His voice, magnified by the narrow passage, sounded like it was next to her ear, even though he was a few feet behind.

"The gate will be guarded to prevent our escape."

"No doubt."

He said nothing more as they scurried like rats to the end of the tunnel, which was cleverly disguised by a large boulder in a tangle of bushes and trees. The sound of rushing water helped mask the noise of their exit as they belly-crawled to the edge of the thicket. They lay in silence for a few moments, feeling out their surroundings, listening for enemies. Sin sensed the Harrowgate to the south, very close.

Once Con was satisfied that they weren't being watched, he crept out of the foliage and gestured to the stream that snaked through the forest. "The Harrowgate is just around the bend."

Sin drew a throwing knife from her boot. "Want one?" she whispered.

"Nah. I'm good with my hands," he said, and her body heated in enthusiastic agreement. "You can do the long-range shit."

Using the trees and thorny brush as cover, they moved downriver. Near the narrows, where the rapids crashed with increasing violence, the Harrowgate entrance shimmered between two massive oaks. Nearby, partially concealed by shadows and a leafy hedge, was a blond lion-shifter—one of Sin's own damned assassins.

"Mother. Fuck." She started toward him, but Con grabbed her arm.

"Let me."

"Go to hell. He's mine."

Con's lips peeled back in a silent snarl. "Is he the one who wants you to be his mate?"

He'd heard that? "Nah, Marasco already has six females in his pride. He definitely doesn't need another. Watch my back." She shrugged out of Con's grip and sent the throwing knife into the air. Her aim was deadly and perfect... but her assassins were well trained, and Marasco leaped out of the way as the blade zinged past his ear.

Smiling, the squat male wheeled around, drawing his signature weapon, a paralyzing dart, in his right hand and a pistol in his left. He carried the firearm because he hung out with human gangbangers, but few supernatural creatures actually used them. They couldn't be fired in Sheoul, but more than that, guns were considered human weapons, and most demons despised them.

Also, most demons were no more affected by a bullet than most humans were by bee stings.

Sin was not one of those demons.

"Marasco," she cooed, with a bat of lashes. "After all we've been through, you still want to kill me?"

His broad nose flared, probably seeking the scent of anyone accompanying her. Hopefully Con had gotten downwind. "Nothing personal, love. Though it's always a pity when succubi die. They're too rare as it is."

Laughing, she eased to the right as he eased to the left so they were circling in the thinned-out area between the stream and the Harrowgate. "I'm the rarest of all. One of a kind. Would be a shame to kill me."

He glanced at the ring on her finger. "I'm sure the trade-off will be worth it."

"Not for me. I like breathing." She maintained eye contact, but kept her peripheral vision on his hands. Wisely, he kept them wide apart and always moving, making it difficult to keep track of both at all times. "Who are you working with? I know you aren't alone, and you haven't been an assassin long enough to sense my presence."

"Does it really matter? The entire den wants you dead."

He lunged, and the silver tip of a dart glinted in the dappled sunlight. She hit the ground and rolled, slid her Gargantua-bone dagger from its sheath at her waist, and popped to her feet. The crack of gunfire deafened her as the whisper of a bullet brushed her shoulder. She slashed out with the dagger, knocking the pistol to the ground. Marasco snarled, and suddenly, a four-hundred-pound lion was coming at her. She blocked with one arm and buried the dagger in his side with the other, but she went down beneath the beast. Her spine cracked hard on a rock and his giant-ass paws pinned her shoulders.

Then, suddenly, he went airborne. Conall stood next to her, fists clenched, fangs elongated. He had a faint, satisfied smile on his face, and if she hadn't been in so much pain, she'd have thought it was hot.

Marasco hit a tree with enough force to splinter the trunk, but he landed on all fours and charged again. Sin launched the dagger, which had tasted his blood and would now seek him out, and never miss. It struck his chest dead center. Shock flashed in Marasco's eyes as he stumbled. He stayed on his feet, still pushing forward, but he'd lost his momentum and, staggering, he lost his hold on his lion form.

Now human, he collapsed, rolling to his side, blood gushing from his chest and his mouth. Dropping his medic bag, Con kneeled next to him. Sin cursed. Con was seriously going to pull some paramedic shit—

He twisted the knife. Marasco moaned through clenched teeth, too well trained and conditioned to react much to any kind of torture.

"Tell me who you're working with," Con said coldly, but Sin knew the lion wasn't giving anything up, for the same reason he wasn't screaming in agony.

"Go...to...hell." Marasco's golden eyes glazed over, and his chest stopped moving, and instantly, something popped painfully in her chest as the assassin bond with him broke.

Con yanked the blade out of the lion-shifter's body. "We gotta go."

"We need to double back to the house." She took the dagger from him and wiped it on the dead shifter's jeans. "I want to see who he was working with—"

She leaped to her feet as the sound of...hoofbeats?... thundered in her ears.

Con cursed. *"Now."*

He dragged her by the arm to the Harrowgate. She barely had time to steady herself before he threw her inside the capsule-like room and dove in after her. As the hazy curtain formed to seal them in, an arrow punched through the hardening veil, whispered across Sin's cheek, and pierced the wall between Australia and New Zealand on the Earth map.

"Who the hell was that?" she yelled, as Con slapped his palm on the glowing map. It burst into a dozen neon-colored lines that were etched into all four of the obsidian walls.

"It's not one of your guys?" He tapped Europe, and the continent grew larger as the others vanished. He kept tapping it out until he pinpointed somewhere in Romania. The door shimmered open, and she turned to grab the arrow—often weapons gave away clues as to their owners' identities—but it was gone. Son of a bitch. Who the hell used dissolving arrows? She'd never even heard of them.

"None of my assassins shoot disappearing arrows from horseback." Which could mean that good old King Arthur was from another assassin den. Dammit! She'd known there was a possibility that her guys would get others involved, but the reality...well, she hated to admit it, but their fierce desire to see her dead stung. And now she was truly fucked.

She stepped out of the Harrowgate and into a dismal, cold, gray day. She thought it might be afternoon, but it was hard to tell, since the sun was hidden behind the thick clouds and fog. "Where are we going?"

"A warg stronghold." Con swung around. "Test my virus levels."

She bristled. "A please would be nice." At his glare, she huffed. "Fine." She gripped his wrist, charged up her gift, and probed his blood. "You just fed, so levels are really low."

"I'm still going to be careful." His tone turned wry. "So no unnecessary biting, screwing, or bleeding on anyone."

"Do you regularly bleed on people?"

He dropped his medic bag next to the Harrowgate. "You're a ball of laughs, you know that?" He took off along a grassy, worn trail, leaving her to follow.

"Hey," she called to him. "I'm known throughout the assassin community as a funny person." Con missed a step. "See? That was funny." Better if he'd fallen on his face, but she'd take what she could get.

He ignored her, kept walking, though they didn't go far. They were, apparently, near the base of a mountain range and down in a fog-shrouded valley. Sin could make out a walled town where the mists thinned. From what she could see, only one poorly maintained road ran to and from the village. Clearly, no one came here who wasn't either lost or actively seeking the town.

"What is this place?"

"We're near Moldavia. The ancestral birthplace of born wargs." Con's long strides ate up the ground, one step for her two. "This village is the home of the largest *pricolici* pack in the world."

"Bespelled?"

"Of course."

Like many supernatural beings who lived in the human realm, the wargs had enchanted their city with the same type of magic that encased UG's ambulances. Most humans would either pass by the town without noticing it, or they'd be repelled by a feeling of deep sadness. The few who made it inside probably wouldn't be there for long.

"So, do only *pricolici* live here?"

"Mostly. *Varcolac* can come and go, but they can't live in a *pricolici* town unless they're mated to a pack member."

Sin and Con approached the main gate, an arched entrance in the wall, and Sin was not surprised to see a tall, broad-shouldered male standing just outside it, his stance casual, almost lethargic, but his shrewd eyes missed nothing. This would be a scout, a pack member assigned to alert others to an intruder. Though he wouldn't stop Sin and Con, she knew he'd broadcast their arrival the moment they were out of sight—if he hadn't already.

Before they reached the gate, Con halted. "Have you ever been inside a *pricolici* village?"

"No. Why?"

He glanced down what appeared to be the main street, which was mostly deserted. But Sin sensed activity all around, and she didn't believe for a moment that the streets weren't being watched. "Do you have any of the same limitations as male Sems? If you sense arousal in someone, are you compelled to relieve it?"

"No, thank God." That had been an interesting revelation about her purebred brothers. Before they'd taken mates, they'd been slaves to sexual desire on a scale that made her issues seem minuscule. Like her, they needed sex to survive, but they'd also been forced to satisfy a female's lust whenever they felt it, which meant that in public places like pubs, they could be trapped for days.

"Good. Then stay close and don't make eye contact with anyone unless I've introduced you to them. No one, got it?"

"I can take care of myself."

"No doubt about that. But I don't think even you can fight off a pack of horny males, or females who would see you as a threat. And since they'll be able to sense the demon in you, you'll be fair game."

"I said—"

"Yeah, you said. But I've seen wargs rip others apart with their bare hands. You upset the pack, we're both dead."

So, Con turned out to be right.

The scent of sex entered Sin's lungs like an aphrodisiac, warming her from the inside, while the feel of it in the air shimmered over her skin. She felt drugged, loose, completely dreamy. The tendrils of mist swirling around their feet as they walked up the center of the medieval-like town only added to the surreal texture of the world they'd entered.

"Con?" She brushed up against him, intentionally, and groaned at the feel of his hard body against hers. "Maybe I should wait outside the wall." She'd been inside brothels, harems, and orgies and never had she encountered anything so raw, so intense. It was as if the village itself seethed with primal instincts and hungers that were never sated.

Con must have felt it, too—the evidence made an impressive bulge in the front of his jeans. "You'll be vulnerable out there," he muttered. "We'll hurry."

He took her hand and led her along the main thoroughfares, where a few people kept to the sidewalks and glass shop fronts revealed people inside the pubs, stores, and eateries. Oddly, Sin realized they'd been passed by only a couple of vehicles. Even odder, every now and then she caught sight of couples screwing in alleys and side streets. Some were clothed, some naked, some in various states of undress. And...

"Is this a gay village?"

"No."

"Then why is most of the action male on male?"

"*Pricolici* are horny," he said roughly, as he dragged her past a couple who seemed to be doing their best to prove Con's point. "Especially during their teen-human-equivalent years, which extend into around their fiftieth year. You know how male dogs will hump anything?"

Right now *she'd* hump anything...She gulped. "Yeah."

"It's pretty much the same with young, unmated male wargs. The females are less insane with lust at that age, so the males burn off their excess testosterone with fights and sex. Usually both at the same time."

"Which explains why a lot of them are bloody."

"Winner does the loser."

Speaking of which, she watched in morbid fascination as two young males beat the crap out of each other, until one knocked the other to the ground and mounted him. The loser immediately stopped fighting, and the sudden expression of pleasure on his face, as well as his stiff cock, said this wasn't a rape situation at all.

"Are there any rules here?"

He tugged her to get her moving again. "Can't fuck, fight, or walk naked on main roads or in places like restaurants, where humans might accidentally go if they find their way into the town."

The human in her appreciated the need for rules, but the sex demon in her wanted to get down and dirty, right in the middle of the town square, just to cause a little trouble and shake things up. She shuddered at the thought, felt a wet rush between her legs, and started toward the fountain. As if Con knew what she was up to, he let out a low, erotic growl, squeezed her hand, and dragged her from the square.

They ducked down a side street—and ran into three fighting males. Fascinated and wondering how *that* was going to end, Sin stopped, digging in her heels when Con tried to force her away. She didn't get a chance to see how the males were going to settle the battle and sex, because Con grabbed her by the waist and hauled her out of there. She'd have fought him, but ... yeah, it just felt too good to have his arms around her.

She shivered with nearly uncontrollable desire as he put her down half a block away from the fighting trio, though for just a second he hesitated, his fingers digging into her hips, his panting breaths matching hers.

"Why are you affected so strongly by all of this?" She gripped his wrists, holding him there, wishing he'd come closer. "You're ... old."

He laughed, a deep, clear note that rang through her in a pleasant wave. "I'm young by dhampire standards." He sobered as he gazed at her, then took a deep breath and pulled away. "I'm not normally affected like this. It's you. You're putting off some hellacious fuck-me vibes."

"Not enough, apparently," she muttered.

He either ignored her or didn't hear her, but he took her hand again and led her down a couple more cobblestone streets until they reached the outskirts of town and the narrowest road yet, which ran alongside the town wall.

Once again, she slowed as a distant, odd sound caught her attention. "What's that? Sounds like a dogfight. Big one."

Con nodded, but kept walking. "When aggression

sparks in a large group of wargs, they shift, no matter what time of day or month, so they can battle in beast form."

She whistled, low and long. "You wolfy people have turned fighting into an art form. Living with you must be loads of fun."

For some reason, he tensed. "We 'wolfy people' can be very gentle with our families."

True enough. From what Sin had seen, Runa was a perfect example.

At the end of the street was a cul-de-sac with four small, thatch-roofed houses, each separated by several yards of land and thick copses of trees. As they approached, a muscular male wearing nothing but jeans exited one of the houses, his gaze fixed on Con. Beside her, the scent of aggression wafted off Con.

"What's going on?" she asked under her breath.

Con didn't answer right away, and as they got closer, the dark-haired male bowed his head, though with obvious reluctance.

"He's an alpha," Con finally replied. "But I'm older, stronger, and more alpha. We determined that a few years ago."

So . . . Con had beaten the crap out of the guy. That must have been interesting. "Did you make wild, passionate love to him after you proved victorious?" She was only partly teasing, was imagining the fight, the sex, and again, a primal response rose up, and God, her bones were going to melt if she didn't get Con between her legs. Soon.

One corner of Con's lush, gorgeous mouth turned up. "I passed on that." The male didn't lift his head until Con stopped in front of him. "Dante. Good to see you."

Dante gave a curt nod. "Sable is inside." He shifted his

gaze to Sin, his expression dark. Dangerous. "Who is the female? She is not warg."

"She's a colleague."

Dante's lip lifted in a silent snarl. Clearly, he didn't want her anywhere near his family, but Con didn't give him a chance to protest. Still holding her hand, he entered the house, where the scent of roast venison made Sin's mouth water, and once the door closed, her lust eased so abruptly she sagged against Con. He caught her, held her steady until she could stand on her own again.

"You okay?"

She nodded, grateful for the temporary reprieve.

Children's laughter came from somewhere in the house, and a tall, red-haired female wearing green sweats and a sweatshirt came around the corner, grinning when she saw Con.

"Father!" She hurried to him, but dropped to her knees at his feet. He lifted her into a huge hug.

"Father?" Sin asked, and he shrugged.

"Technically, I'm Sable's great-great-great-great-grandfather, but we'll pretend there aren't so many greats in there."

"What brings you here?" Sable gave Sin a warm smile before hugging Con again, giving his neck a little nuzzle and kiss, much the way pups greeted older canines. For some reason, the display of affection put an odd lump in Sin's throat. "Would you like to stay for supper?"

"I'm here for only a minute," he said. "No time to even sit."

Frowning, Sable stepped back. "What is it?"

"You've heard of SF."

"Of course." She waved her hand dismissively. "We

have guards at the gate to prevent foreign wargs who might be infected from entering."

"You need to take your family somewhere else. Somewhere isolated."

"But why, if—"

Con gripped Sable's shoulders and forced her to look into his deadly serious eyes. "Because soon it's going to become known that only turned wargs are susceptible, and security at your gate will no longer be needed."

For a moment, confusion swirled in Sable's eyes, surely matching Sin's own, and then the blood in Sable's already pale face drained, making her freckles stand out like a dalmation's spots. "Oh, gods."

"It'll only be a matter of time before a warg civil war breaks out," he said grimly. "Get your family to safety."

She gave him a shaky nod. "Just a minute." She darted out the door, leaving Sin and Con alone in the entryway.

"I don't understand what just happened," Sin said, still staring after the shaken female. "Why would the news about turned wargs be bad? Isn't your... daughter... a dhampire?"

"Not even close." A child squealed somewhere in the house, and Con smiled fondly. "Back when our numbers were far greater, female dhampires often mated with wargs. Eight hundred years ago, my only daughter did so. Her offspring followed suit, mostly breeding out the dhampire blood. Sable is *pricolici*, and her mate is as well."

"Now I'm even more confused—"

"One of her cubs is *varcolac*."

Oh, shit. "How did that happen?" She waited for a response. And waited. "Con?"

"It's not important," he said flatly, the dismissal just blatant enough to piss Sin off.

"If it's not important, then it shouldn't be a problem for you to tell me, right?" She crossed her arms over her chest. "And it's not like we have anything better to do."

"It's a very dangerous secret, Sin. Something that could destroy my family."

Her anger veered sharply to hurt, which made her ping right back to anger, because dammit, he shouldn't be able to affect her like that. "Ah. So you think I would use the information to harm them. Nice. Must have been hell to stick your dick into someone so repugnant."

Angry, guttural words fell from his lips. Good. He deserved to be as irked as she was. As the curses died down, he trained his laserlike gaze on her, his expression tight, shadowed with unmistakable warning. "When a born warg gives birth to a human baby, they are usually put down before they can utter a cry. But Sable couldn't do that. She bit the infant and had the mark of a born warg tattooed onto him."

"So I'm guessing she could get into a lot of trouble if the child is discovered?"

"Under warg law both she and the child could be executed."

Sin grimaced, though she wasn't surprised. After a hundred years in the demon world, very little surprised her anymore. But now she understood his reluctance to spill the secret. "If both parents are born wargs, how did the kid pop out human?"

Con hesitated, his eyes hooded and unreadable. Finally, he blew out a breath and answered gruffly. "Sable came into season while she was on a private sabbatical.

She mated with a turned warg, but they were interrupted by The Aegis. He was killed. Just hours after that, Dante found her, took her during what remained of the heat, and when it was over, they were bonded. She came to me when it was time for the birth and confessed that she thought the cubs might be the dead male's. She gave birth to fraternal twins—one warg and one human. She nipped the human, had him tattooed, and returned to the pack. Not even Dante knows the truth."

Jesus. That was one hell of a secret. "So they need to get the kid to a place where he can't catch the disease once the town opens up and turned wargs are free to come and go."

"Exactly."

Sin pondered what he said, and then blurted, "Where is your daughter? You know, your *daughter* daughter."

A sad smile touched his sensual lips. "She died in childbirth. I didn't know her well—I'd left the clan by the time she was born—but I felt her die."

She didn't have time to utter an awkward condolence because the door burst open and Dante stalked through, his big hand wrapped around the back of Sable's neck. Her green eyes were red-rimmed, her face streaked with tears. "Is what my mate said true? Was Roman born a... *human*?" He said "human" like he might say "filthy maggot."

Con glanced at Sable, who nodded. "Yes," he said, his eyes as cold as his voice. "And if you hurt the child or Sable, I'll hang you by your entrails and make you suffer for a month before you die."

Trembling with emotion so powerful that Sin could smell it like bitter smoke, the male warg released Sable and closed his eyes. When he opened them, crystal tears glistened on his lashes. "I would have killed the infant if I'd known back then," he said, and Sable's pained cry brought a cringe from him and a hiss from Con. "But I'm not that male anymore. The cub *is* mine, and I will defend him with my life."

With a sob, Sable flew into Dante's arms, and he held her tight, his tears joining hers.

Guarded respect softened the hard line of Con's jaw. "You'll take Roman somewhere safe?"

"We'll leave within the hour."

Sin stood aside while arrangements were made and good-byes were said, and even though they had to leave the peace of the home, Sin was more than happy to get out. She could deal with lust much more easily than she could deal with strong emotion.

"Come on." Con closed the door behind them. "I want to get out of here before—"

"Too late," she breathed. High-octane lust, even more intense than before, flooded her body, making her mind fuzzy and her sex ache.

"Shit." He took her hand and forced her to jog through the streets, using the main thoroughfares as much as possible.

Crazily, the faster they moved, the hotter she got. It was as if each step ramped her up even more, and by the time they reached the town square, she'd unbuttoned her top and was so ready for Con's hands to be on her. Unable to wait another second, she jerked him to a stop. The potent scents of desire and danger rolled off him, swirled inside her, and she swayed, reaching out to brace herself against him.

"Sin... no. Don't touch me." His eyes were wild, glinting with shards of lust. "I'm going to... lose control. I'll take you right here."

Panting, her body tingling with awareness, she ran her palms up his stomach, skimming his pecs until she reached his broad shoulders. "I wouldn't mind—"

A rough sound erupted from his throat, and lightning fast, he snared her wrists and held them away from him and against her own chest. "I will not cheapen you."

She laughed, but the sound was hoarse. "Cheapen? Seriously? With the things I've done, I can't get any cheaper." Surprise flickered in his eyes, and she realized she'd revealed a hell of a lot more about herself than she had intended. More than she ever had, to anyone. She ran her foot up his calf, as much as a distraction as because she was on the verge of jumping him. "And for Hell's sake, you did me in a freaking *supply closet* on a bet. How is this different?"

A shadow crossed his face, almost as though the reminder brought him shame, and no doubt it did; at the time, he'd implied that he'd lowered his standards to service her needs. He shifted away from her foot. "You're bitter, little demon. Your past must have a hell of a choke hold on you."

"Fuck you," she said, but even to her own ears it sounded more like an offer than a kiss-off. "You don't know anything."

Clenching his teeth, he set her away from him. "I know that I'll never take you in public, even in a place where public sex is normal and accepted."

She raised her chin. "Maybe it's normal for me."

"I don't doubt that it is." The tone of his voice was

naked, utterly lacking in the kind of judgment that should have accompanied what he'd said. "But I do doubt that you want it to be."

Damn him. Damn him for somehow looking into her soul and reading her like a damned book. Her eyes stung as she spun around and headed for the town gate.

"Sin." She ignored him. "*Sin!*"

This time, his sharp tone penetrated, along with a raising of her hackles, and she stopped. All around her, young males were watching, their eyes gleaming with hunger. Where had they come from? And why were they looking at her like that when they could be fucking each other?

"Con?" she asked quietly. "What's going on?"

"They've sensed your arousal," he murmured. "And your anger. They intend to have you."

Nine

This was not good. Sin might as well be a female warg in heat, and few males would back down from that.

Baring his fangs in warning, Con wrapped his palm around the back of Sin's neck. Unlike Dante's hold on Sable, this wasn't a domination thing; it was a sign to the advancing males that she was his, and they'd have to go through him to get her.

His. No, she definitely wasn't his and would never be. Even if he weren't destined for an isolated life with his clan, he couldn't see himself tied to her—at least, not in a nonerotic way. And yet, he was vibrating with a startling, possessive fury, and he was still drowning in hunger so intense he could hardly see straight.

A couple of the younger males hesitated, but the more aggressive, dominant males continued to stalk them, the gleam of lust—and bloodlust—glowing in their eyes. The air was thick, drenched with violent anticipation, and

Con's skin tightened, preparing for an unwelcome shift into his beast form.

"Back slowly toward the gate," Con said, his voice slurred by both need and the fact that his fangs had filled his mouth. "Don't draw a weapon. And for all that's unholy, button your shirt."

Damn, he'd been afraid of this. Sin was a magnet for trouble. How had she managed to survive this long?

One of the youngsters lunged. Con knocked him back with a powerful blow to the jaw. Yelping, the kid wheeled back into the crowd. The display instilled a little respect into the others, and the distance between Con and Sin and the mob increased.

They had almost arrived at the wall when Sin's harsh whisper cut through the fog. "The gate is closed."

Son of a— Con risked a glance over his shoulder at the sentry, whose hungry gaze was fixed on Sin. "I freaking hate pack mentality," he muttered.

"I have an idea." Sin broke away from him before he could stop her. A couple of males started to give chase, their instinctive prey drives activating at the sight of their target darting away. Con leaped in front of them with a bloodcurdling snarl that brought them up short. He'd kill them, and they knew it.

He angled his body so he could keep an eye on the horny males while checking out what Sin was doing, and he damned near swallowed his tongue.

The way the sentry was swallowing Sin's.

The guy had her pinned against the wall, his hips grinding into her as his hands clawed at her top. A wild, primitive rage spewed like molten lava through Con's veins. Seeing any female being savaged angered him, but he could still feel Sin's blood rushing through him, could still feel her as part of him, and the word "mine" was a faint buzz in his head.

But did he want *her*, or did he want her blood? Both were dangerous desires, and he needed to get over himself real damned fast.

Suddenly, the sentry jerked away. Sin kept a grip on his wrist, her expression calm, cool...but her eyes flashed black fire. She said something, and he doubled over, losing his breakfast on the cobblestones. Though his movements were jerky, he withdrew an iron key from his pocket, jammed it into a panel on the wall, and the thick wood-and-iron gate clattered open, its hinges creaking in protest.

The pack of males rushed the gate, blocking the exit, but out of nowhere, a furious roar cut through the fog.

"Let them go!"

Con let out a curse, looked up to see Valko standing on the wall walk. The Warg Council leader pointed at the group of males, and they tucked tail and slunk away like scolded curs. Con might be grateful to Valko for the save, but he didn't need the guy asking questions about why he was there. Fortunately, Valko merely gave Con a slow, meaningful nod, one that made it clear that Con owed him, and then he took off, heading toward the north wall tower.

Quickly, Con grabbed Sin's hand and got them the hell out of town, and they kept going until they reached the Harrowgate.

"Who was the dude on the wall?" she asked when they'd stopped.

"Head of the Warg Council. That was his town. His

pack." Con still didn't like the timing of Valko's appearance on the wall, even though it wasn't anything out of the ordinary. Valko would have been alerted to the arrival of visitors. "So what did you do to the guard?"

"I gave him Khileshi cockfire." An impish grin lit her expression. Gods, she was gorgeous when she smiled like that. "Told him his dick would shrivel up and burn off if he didn't open the gate."

"I thought you can't cure a disease once you give it."

"I can't." Her eyes glinted with mischief that matched her smile as she made a show of studying her fingernails. "He'll be making an emergency trip to UG."

It was his turn to grin. "Nice."

He drank in the sight of her standing proudly on the hill, her gaze feral, fierce, her raven hair catching the wind and swirling around her face and shoulders. As a sex demon, she hadn't been bred to fight, but there was something inside her that was a warrior. Maybe her human ancestry gave her that edge, or maybe it was her hard life, but something called to his own warrior blood and consumed him from the inside out.

He wanted to take her to the ground, drive into her in a mating that would be as wild as the mountains in the background. He'd mark her with his scent, his come, his teeth...

Holy hell, he needed to stop thinking about his fangs in her throat. He searched his memory, trying to remember if this was the way it had been with Eleanor, the only female he'd ever drunk to addiction. He recalled obsession with her blood, hunger that hurt, but for the life of him, he couldn't remember the insane need for sex.

Slowly, Sin's smile faded, and she spat in the dirt. "I don't think that guard has brushed his teeth in a year."

He had the strangest impulse to put his mouth on hers, to kiss her until she burned and tasted only Con.

Clearly, they were too close to the warg village, and he was still feeling the effects of the inhabitants' animal natures.

"Why are they like that anyway?" she asked. "I thought wargs were a little more...civilized."

He glanced back at the village, where the gate had opened again, and the sentry was standing just outside, watching them through the thinning mist. "Born wargs really are wolves in human clothing. It's why they live apart from humans. You'll never find a *pricolici* living in a city with them. They also are fully aware of what they do while in animal form, and they generally won't kill humans because they're smart enough not to want to expose themselves to the human race. It's one of the reasons they want to exterminate turned wargs. The *varcolac* are a risk."

"Well, they didn't seem to have any trouble with killing me."

"You aren't human."

"Thanks for the reminder," she muttered.

He couldn't help it—he reached out and tucked a tendril of her unruly hair behind her ear. "You don't accept what you are, do you?"

"I don't know what I am," she said, stepping out of his reach.

He let his hand fall back to his side. "How can you be as old as you are and not know?" Con knew very well what he was, and he'd long ago accepted it, even if he wasn't always thrilled about it.

She shrugged. "I thought I did know. Before, we were

just half-breed mongrels with no idea what kind of demon we really were. We had no expectations. Then Lore and I found our brothers. Now we know our demon, but not what it means. We know what Seminus demons are, but it doesn't do any good because the rules don't apply to us."

He hadn't thought of it that way. But then, he'd grown up keenly aware of what he was: a dhampire from a shrinking line of royalty, who had arrogantly expected to take over the clan one day—until the wake-up call that said, no, the world didn't revolve around him. He might not like the role he was born to play, but at least he'd known about it his entire life.

"You can make your own rules."

"Oh," she said silkily, "I do make my own rules. And I never break them."

"Like what? What is one of your rules?" He was starting to think one had something to do with driving dhampires crazy.

"No one will *ever* own me again." She raised her chin in that stubborn set he was beginning to admire. Especially because it bared the slender column of her throat and forced her to arch her back the way it did when he was driving between her legs. "I will never belong to anyone—I will die before I allow that to happen."

He remembered how she'd freaked out when Shade said that she belonged to them, and he wondered how encompassing her self-imposed rule was. "What are we talking about, Sin? You don't want anyone to own you... or your heart?"

She laughed bitterly, and entered the Harrowgate. "I don't have a heart for anyone to take."

Con slung his jump bag over his shoulder and followed Sin into the cavelike enclosure of the Harrowgate.

I don't have a heart for anyone to take.

Bullshit. Granted, she didn't seem to give a crap about anyone but herself, and maybe Lore, but Con had once witnessed the way she'd wrapped her body around Shade and Runa's child to protect the boy from an evil fallen angel. She'd used herself as a shield, and concern for the baby had darkened her expression when she'd seen the blood on his skin—blood that turned out to be hers.

Sin the Hardass definitely had a heart. And something inside him was itching to goad her into seeing how wrong she was. But why was proving he was right so damned important?

Because she tests you. Because she's untamed, unpredictable, and you'll accept any challenge if it seems impossible.

Yeah, okay, that was why. He was easily bored, always on the lookout for ways to keep from going out of his ever-loving mind.

It didn't always pan out. His quest for excitement had nearly gotten him killed a few times, had taken him down some dark paths, and in a roundabout way, it had gotten him in the situation he was currently in.

He'd become a paramedic in part because Eidolon had forced his hand, but there was also an allure to doing something he'd never done. He'd been partnered with Luc, who was as eager to risk his neck as Con was, and who had instigated the bet that had gotten Con into Sin's pants. Gods, life took some strange, bumpy turns.

Con palmed the map of North America, and Sin crowded close. He could smell the damned male warg on her, and his muscles twitched with the need to hightail it back to town to kill him.

"Where to now?" she asked, as he tapped out the map.

"Montana. The northern Rockies," he said, more sharply than he'd intended. "It was one of the places Lore indicated on his outbreak chart."

"Well." She gave him a fierce poke in the shoulder. "Aren't you a grumpalufagus?"

The door shimmered open, and cool air that smelled of pine trees flooded the small space. He practically leaped out into the twilight-drenched forest, needing to get away from her. "You nearly got us killed," he said, knowing it wasn't fair to blame her, but the image of her kissing that bastard wouldn't go away.

"I also got the gate opened," she pointed out, and he clenched his fists. "We could have gotten out of the town even without your Council leader buddy."

"It was reckless and stupid, and you won't do it again."

"Won't?" She jammed her fists on her hips. "*Won't?* You have no say in anything I do."

His jaw tightened. "When it comes to wargs, you *will* listen to me. I know them. I know how they react, I know how they fight, and I know how they lust—"

"Oh, for the love of God, put a butt plug in the male tough-guy crap. I know what I'm doing. I'm damned good at killing and fucking, and I'll use either of those weapons—"

Blinded by fury, he gripped her by the arms, hauled her up against him, and took her mouth. There was nothing gentle about the kiss at all. It was about wiping the other male out of the picture. It was about dominance and all that male tough-guy crap. It was about making sure that all his intimacies with her were about anger or pure lust, because he couldn't afford to soften.

Not that she'd allow that to happen. She squealed in outrage and stomped on his foot. Pounded against his chest.

Then she bit his lip hard enough to draw blood. When the blood hit her tongue, she jerked, but the sharp pleasure-pain drove him harder, and he thrust his tongue against hers, stroking, licking, forcing her to taste him.

And then she wasn't fighting anymore. She didn't need to. The razor edge of a blade was biting into his groin, and he froze as solidly as an ice sculpture.

"Kiss me again without my permission," she whispered against his lips, "and I'll geld you and sell your balls to a Ruthanian specialty meats shop. Understood?"

"You won't do that," he whispered back. "You'd miss them too much."

Sin snorted and made the blade disappear into her pocket as she stepped back. "Men are always overestimating the worth of their genitals."

That fast, his anger was gone, and he threw back his head and laughed. "Come on," he said. "We have work to do."

Ten

They hadn't gone more than a dozen yards along a worn game trail when a shot rang out, silencing the crickets and sending the squirrels that had come out for their last foray before nightfall skittering into their holes in the trees. Sin and Con ran toward the sound, and in just a few yards they were following more violent battle noises and the stench of blood.

A lot of blood.

The scent grew stronger as they rounded an outcrop of rock and found two dead people, probably werewolves, beneath a bush.

"Wargs," Con whispered, confirming her suspicions.

"Born or turned?" She didn't see any telltale marks to indicate that they were *pricolici*, but the marks could be covered by their clothing. Or blood.

"Don't know."

A scream tore through the air, and they crashed

through the brush, not bothering with stealth, not even as they broke onto a trail and into the middle of a slaughter.

"Oh, God." Sin skidded to a halt. There were two small cabins tucked away in the forest, but they must have housed several families. They were battling, some in warg form, and some still in human, using axes and knives. One male was firing a shotgun at a leaping werewolf.

The ground was soaked with blood, and a child lay dead on a porch. A *child*.

A big male swung his arm, severing a female's head with his claws as she pleaded for mercy. "Diseased *varcolac* scum." The words were warped by his animal muzzle, but the hatred was as clear as the sky above.

Rabid fury exploded in Sin, and she launched at the born wargs, whose battle gear set them apart from the others. Her throwing knives took out one, and her Gargantua dagger ended another. She lost track of time, of control, and though she knew Con was tearing through the *pricolici* like a tornado through a trailer park, her concentration was fully centered on causing pain.

Finally, nothing moved. Sin stood in the middle of the small camp, numb. Con was still hopped up from the battle, his fangs as large as a mountain lion's, his muscles twitching. Sin sensed the darkness in him, the battle and bloodlusts that should have triggered her own, but for once, she was just numb.

The born wargs had managed to take out everyone before they'd fallen victim to Sin's blades and Con's hands.

"Son of a bitch," Con said roughly. His chest still heaved with exertion from the fight. "They did it. Someone leaked the fact that only the *varcolac* are affected."

"You think it was a Councilmember? There are probably

staff members at UG who know." She didn't mention that his granddaughter and her mate knew as well.

He swept the area with his silver gaze, his entire body tense, his expression grim. "It's possible it was someone from UG, but I'd bet my left nut it was someone on the Council. The *varcolac* were furious at the meeting. I'm not sure their leader, Raynor, was convinced that SF isn't a conspiracy to kill them. And Valko...he'll take any excuse to let the *pricolici* kill off the *varcolac*."

"This whole thing just keeps getting worse." A sudden, shooting pain streaked down her right arm. She clapped a hand over her shoulder where one of her glyphs, a round sundial-shaped mark, had split in two. Odd. The gashes that usually appeared in her *dermoire* were straight lines, but this was a zigzag, a perfect Z that didn't extend beyond the faded black lines of the circle.

Con's brow furrowed. "Are you hurt?"

"No," she lied, because the truth was, she didn't care. Her little sting was nothing compared to the suffering she'd caused.

Con's hand lifted to cup her cheek, and the tender caress of his fingers on her skin might as well have been a wrecking ball, the way it cracked her shield of numbness. Her chest tightened and her throat closed up as all the deaths piled high on her conscience. All of it was her fault, and she suddenly felt like she was drowning in blood.

"I've got to fix this," she whispered. "I've got to end it, Con. My life can't have been about death."

"This *will* end, Sin—" He paused, his tawny brows drawing together. "Did you hear that?"

She started to shake her head, but then a small cry breached the silence. She didn't wait for Con. She sprinted toward the sound, and her heart nearly stopped when she saw a woman lying in the open doorway of a shed behind the cabins. She knew immediately what it was: a sick hut.

For dying wargs.

The female shrank back at Sin's approach, her watery gaze full of terror.

"Hey," Sin said softly, as she sank to her knees. "It's okay. I'm not going to hurt you."

Con sank down on his heels beside Sin, dropping his medic bag to the ground. "Are you injured?"

"Sick." She coughed, and blood sprayed onto the ground. "My family . . . are they . . ."

"I'm sorry." Con pulled two pairs of surgical gloves out of the bag and offered one to Sin, but she shook her head. "They didn't make it." At her ragged sob, Con gripped the woman's wrist gently with one gloved hand, probably to check her pulse. "When did the first symptoms appear?"

"This morning."

Con met Sin's gaze, and she nodded. "Might be early enough for me to try." Sin smoothed the female's limp brown hair away from her face as tenderly as she could. Her skin was hot, probably sensitive, and she didn't want to cause any more pain. "What's your name?"

"Pamela."

"Pamela, I'm going to try to heal you. Be still, okay?"

A shudder went through her slender body, but she nodded. Leaving her hand on Pamela's cheek, Sin powered up her gift. The familiar tingle wound its way down her arm and to her fingertips, and the moment it entered the werewolf, Pamela gasped.

Con's soothing, deep voice assured Pamela that everything was okay, and though Sin wasn't so sure about that,

she appreciated the way he was so calm, so sure, so...
sympathetic. He might have taken the job because Eidolon forced his hand, but Con belonged in the medical field,
and she wondered if he realized that.

Sin punched her power through Pamela's body, seeking out the virus. Compared to the other wargs Sin had
tried to cure, this one had very low levels, and taking out
the individual virus strands wasn't nearly as difficult as
she'd thought it would be.

Eventually, the virus was dead. Gone. A thrill of
excitement rode her as hard as exhaustion did, and she
smiled as she released Pamela and collapsed against
the side of the shack. "It's gone," she rasped. "I think
you're okay."

Con looked up from digging through his medic gear.
"What about you?"

"I could use a month of sleep, but I'm fine." Sin reached
over and helped the other female sit up. "How are you
feeling?"

Pamela swayed, but remained upright. "I'm hungry."

"That's a good sign." Con smiled, and though this
wasn't the time or place for Sin to appreciate the raw masculinity he threw off when he did that, well, she definitely
appreciated it. "I'm going to take some blood, but I want
you to head to Underworld General."

"The demon hospital?"

"Yes." He took some rubber tubing from his bag.
"You'll find the medical symbol inside the Harrowgate."

As Sin watched Con draw blood, she hoped this was
the beginning of the end for this disease. The nightmare
had gone on too long, and way too many people had died.

When Con finished, Sin helped Pamela to her feet,

angling herself to shield the warg from the sight of her slaughtered friends and family. Gripping Pamela's shoulder, she guided her toward the path to the Harrowgate, but froze when her scalp began to tingle with awareness. They were being watched.

"Sin!"

At Con's shout, she spun, felt the whisper of a blade as it sailed past her ear, heard a thud and a cry, and Pamela dropped, a throwing ax meant for Sin embedded between Pamela's eyes. Oh...*shit*!

All around, the forest came alive as assassins launched both themselves and their weapons. Sin dove behind the shed, Con on her heels. A female Croucher demon leaped from the branches of a tree, her three eyes focused on Sin with deadly intent. Con moved in a blur of motion, slipping behind the demon to wrap his arm around her throat as Sin shoved a dagger into the assassin's third eye. The Croucher's shriek was cut off by a twist of Con's hands and the snapping of her neck. He released her, and she crumpled to the ground.

It was too easy—this female was an amateur, but the others wouldn't be.

Con must have come to the same conclusion because he gripped Sin's hand and yanked her into the forest. "We have to run!"

The sounds of pursuit were hot behind them, and then, out of nowhere, a horse screamed. Sin and Con wheeled around, and Christ on a cracker, this couldn't get any worse...

"That's the dude I saw at my place," Con breathed. "Only...different. His armor is tarnished."

"Tarnished" wasn't the word Sin would use. It was

dirty, scuffed, and black sludge oozed from the cracks. His horse, a massive white beast with crimson eyes, was smashing assassins under its hooves. The rider's deadly aim sent arrows punching into throats, heads, and hearts.

"Now we need to run faster," Con barked, and, yes, she agreed. Wholeheartedly.

"There's a cabin a few miles up the mountain," he said, as they sprinted through the woods. "Belongs to an ancient spellcaster friend of mine. It's not protected by a Haven spell, but it *is* warded against demons."

Sin ducked under a branch, but caught another in the chin. "In case you haven't noticed, *I'm* a demon."

"I can get you through her mystical minefield."

She hoped so, but based on the way the day was going, she wasn't going to count on it.

Eidolon's father, Resniak, was not an easy male to talk to. And though Eidolon allowed very few people to rattle him, Resniak, a hulking Judicia demon whose expression was stuck on stern, made Eidolon's intestines twist into knots, and always had. Didn't matter that Resniak wasn't his biological father—the male had raised Eidolon as his own, and the Judicia were strict parents.

"Favors are not something Justice Dealers grant," he was saying as he stood in Eidolon's office, filling it with more than his big green body and giant rack of antlers. His forceful presence sucked up all the air and left Eidolon's chest tight, as though oxygen were at a premium.

"I'm aware of that, Father. And I admit that my request is based on the fact that Sin is my sister. But the request is reasonable. She's entitled to an investigation."

Resniak idly stroked the ends of his black beard. "An investigation can be performed while she's imprisoned."

"Agreed," Eidolon ground out. No more arguing. Either his father would find his request to be logical, or he wouldn't.

Logic. It was something Eidolon had grown up with, but as a purebred Seminus demon, instinct and emotion had trumped logic at the worst possible times. And at the best times. Logically, he should have killed Tayla the first time he'd seen her, when she'd come into his hospital, injured after killing demons. Instead, he'd been fascinated, and his desire for her had obliterated logic and common sense.

Thank the gods.

Time stretched, and the oxygen level in the office kept plummeting. Finally, his father nodded curtly. "I can guarantee nothing. But I'll see what I can do. As for the punishment that you, Wraith, and Conall face for interfering with Sin's arrest, I can make a plea for suspension until after the epidemic is over." He exited without so much as a good-bye, but that he was going to try to pull some strings to get Sin out of trouble was the same as someone else throwing a big I-love-you party, and Eidolon collapsed into his chair with relief.

He heard footsteps in the hall, prayed it wasn't his father coming back, and switched on his computer.

"E. I waited until the Vulcan ambassador was gone. We have a problem."

"I don't want to know. And stop calling the Judicia Vulcans." Eidolon didn't look up from his computer. Maybe if he pretended Wraith wasn't there—

"Then I have two problems for you."

Eidolon finally looked up to see Wraith and Kynan standing in his office doorway, both looking like Armageddon was at hand. And since Armageddon *had* been at hand not long ago, this was serious.

"What is it?"

Kynan entered, his mouth set in a grim line, his denim-blue eyes flashing. "Word's out that only turned wargs are affected by the plague." Though Ky's voice was always gravelly from damage sustained during his Army days, it was even rougher than normal now. "They're blaming born wargs for the outbreak, and born wargs are using this opportunity to destroy turned wargs."

"Shit," Eidolon breathed. "We need to prepare the emergency department for an influx of patients and get the word out to our turned staff." Though the turned staff members were still in isolation to avoid infection, isolation wouldn't necessarily protect them from extermination.

Kynan sank down in a chair and kicked his booted feet up on Eidolon's desk. Funny how comfy the human had gotten since he'd been charmed by angels and was now impervious to harm. Then again, the guy had always been fairly comfortable in his own skin. "I've already given Shade a heads-up. Runa should be safe in the cave, but he's still going into total lockdown mode."

No doubt he was. Eidolon wouldn't hesitate to do the same with Tayla.

"There's more," Wraith said, because yeah, of course there was. "Con wasn't answering his cell, so I went to his place to check up on Sin."

Eidolon frowned. Odd. Wraith didn't check up on anyone out of the goodness of his heart. "And?"

The way Wraith shifted his weight and didn't meet

Eidolon's gaze sent a tremor of dread through Eidolon. "The house has been bunker-bustered. Nothing but ashes and smoke."

Eidolon froze. *"What?"*

Wraith jammed his hand in his leather duster's pocket, doing the weapon-molesting thing he did. "It was really fucked up, E. Looked like the house had been firebombed. The ground had been all torn up by the fire department, but I did a sweep of the area. Found traces of footprints— could be the assassins after Sin. Also found horse tracks leading to and from the Harrowgate."

"Hell stallion?" Kynan asked.

Wraith shook his blond head. He'd tied back his hair with a leather thong, and the ends slapped violently against his coat. "Their hooves char the ground. These were regular tracks. Big, like Clydesdale hooves."

"Wraith." Eidolon cleared his throat, but that didn't rid it of the raw rasp in his voice. "Do you think Sin and Con are dead?"

Wraith let out a long, drawn-out breath, and Eidolon's heart plummeted to his feet. When Wraith finally spoke, his voice was strong and sure. "I found evidence of a skirmish near the Harrowgate. Con hasn't survived for centuries by being stupid, and Sin's got instinct. My gut says they got out."

Since Wraith's gut was usually right, and it was all they had to go on, Eidolon let himself relax. "Does Lore know?"

"Nope. I called him a few minutes ago to see if he'd heard from Sin. He hadn't, but I didn't tell him about the house. Didn't see any reason to freak him out until we know something."

"Agreed." Eidolon checked his watch. Still several hours until morning, when Wraith would return home and not leave his son and vampire mate until nightfall again. Not unless there was an emergency. "Can you do what you can to track Sin and find out who is behind the attack on Con's house?"

Wraith nodded. "There's something else. Whoever blasted the house used infernal fire. I could smell it in the ashes."

Eidolon's stomach wrenched. "Someone was serious about killing Sin and Con."

"What's infernal fire?" Kynan asked.

"It's like underworld napalm," Wraith said. "The shit is massively powerful, but what's special about it is that it calls fire spirits in the flames."

"Which hunt down anyone within the range of the heat," Eidolon finished. "Its use is forbidden in the human realm. So whoever is responsible was willing to risk getting caught and burned alive by Justice Dealers." Eidolon cursed. "We have to find Sin."

"I'm on it." Wraith started out the door, but Eidolon stopped him.

"On your way out, tell Bastien I need to see him."

"You got it." Wraith took off, leaving E with Kynan.

Kynan's eyes were calm, assessing. As Tayla liked to put it, when you looked at him, you knew he was reading the situation about ten seconds into the future. "You calling the R-XR?" While functioning as a local Regent in The Aegis, Kynan had worked with the Army's paranormal unit, the Ranger-X Regiment, for years after being attacked by a demon while serving in a regular Army unit as a medic.

"They're going to be in damage-control mode."

"Yeah," Kynan sighed. "This is bound to spill over into the human world. The Aegis will need to engage in damage control as well. I'll head to HQ for a conference."

"What do you think they'll do?"

"I don't know." Kynan ran his hands through his spiky, dark hair, ruffling it even more. "We've kept a lot of turned wargs under surveillance to make sure they chain up during the full moon, but we may end up guarding instead of monitoring." He laughed. "How weird is that? Not long ago we were killing them, and now we might be saving them."

"You think Guardians will protect werewolves? It's one thing to not kill them, but another to actively protect them."

Kynan looked troubled. "Yeah. There's been an incident that is going to make my argument a little harder." He shifted his feet off the desk, spread his legs, and braced his forearms on his thighs as he leaned forward, his gaze even sharper now, his military conditioning coming to bear. "A Guardian was recently outed as a werewolf. Remember when I asked you if you knew of any wargs that shifted during the new moon? Well, whatever she is, her cell put out the word and chased her into Canada. They lost her, but one Guardian is dead. On top of everything else that's been going on in The Aegis..."

Eidolon swore. Kynan didn't need to finish the sentence. A lot of what was going on was Tayla's fault. Undercurrents of dissent had been filtering through The Aegis's ranks over the fact that Tayla, a half-demon, was not only a Guardian, but also a Regent in charge of a large cell. Kynan's marriage to Gem, Tay's sister, had stirred the pot even more. And then, a couple of months ago, Tay had put a vampire on the payroll—a Guardian named Kaden, who had been turned into a vampire after being captured during an Aegis raid on a nest.

Now Guardians were quitting, while others were calling for change. This werewolf news could cause the already simmering pot to boil over.

"Tayla sure has a way of stirring things up," Kynan said, as if reading Eidolon's mind.

"Tayla wouldn't be Tayla if she wasn't always in the middle of a shitstorm." And Eidolon wouldn't have it any other way.

"You saved her life, E." Kynan's gravelly voice was quiet. "She was headed down a bad road, and you took her off it."

A sobering, pleasant warmth filled Eidolon's chest cavity. "She saved me, too."

"You're a big sap," Kynan said, as he shoved to his feet, and Eidolon nearly laughed. Tayla had accused him more than once of the same thing. "If you need any help with Sin, let me know."

"I might take you up on that. Good luck with the Sigil and your rogue werewolf." Kynan left, brushing by Bastien on his way out.

Eidolon's doorway was getting a hell of a workout today. "Bastien. Thanks for stopping by."

The warg nodded, making his mop of curly brown hair bounce into his eyes. "What do you need, sir?"

"I just learned that civil war is breaking out between the *pricolici* and *varcolac*. Do you know anything about it?"

Bastien's fingers tightened on the handle of the toolbox he seemed to always have in his hand, but other than that, he showed no reaction. "No, sir. I have no contact with my pack anymore."

"I just want to make sure you're safe. And that this won't affect your job."

"You mean, will I try to harm the turned wargs who come to the hospital?"

"Yes."

For a long moment, the werewolf looked down at the floor, and when he finally raised his gaze, his normally soft brown eyes had turned fierce. "My loyalty is to this hospital, Doctor. I won't let you down."

Man, Eidolon loved this place. Managing a hospital staffed by dozens of different species, many of whom were natural enemies, could get hairy, but ultimately, they were here because they wanted to help others, and Eidolon took a lot of pride in that. And people like Bastien, who some liked to say was "only" a janitor, were the heart of the facility, and every bit as important as the most talented surgeon.

"Thanks, Bastien. Glad you're back."

After the warg limped away, his club foot knocking harder on the floor than his other, Eidolon dialed the phone. Arik, Runa's brother and a top member of the R-XR, answered on the second ring.

"What do you want, demon?"

Arik wasn't the friendliest guy ever. "I want to know if you're aware that born wargs are out to commit genocide on the turneds."

Arik swore. "I was just going to call you about that. We've had scattered reports of wargs attacking wargs, but no confirmation yet on whether or not it's born-on-turned violence."

"Wraith confirmed it, and he doesn't get shit like this wrong."

"We'll look into it," Arik said. "Got anything new on SF?"

"Maybe, but I don't want to share anything until I hear from my sister."

There was a brittle silence. These guys didn't like being kept in the dark, especially if the one keeping them there was a demon. And even though Arik's sister, Runa, was mated to Shade, the guy still hadn't come around all that much.

Finally, Arik blew out a breath. "I think I should bring Runa to D.C."

"You want to take her to R-XR headquarters?" Eidolon laughed. "Good luck with that. You'll need an entire armored division to get her away from Shade."

"I'll get one if I have to."

Eidolon dumped the cup of paper clips onto his desk and started tossing them back in, one by one. "You know they can't be separated."

"Shade and the kids can come, too. I can't leave her unprotected."

"Trust me. The only place safer than the cave is the hospital, and if it weren't for the fact that I'm getting diseased wargs in by the dozen, they'd be here. You've got the same problem there. You might be able to protect her from born wargs, but you're working with the virus. Can you guarantee that it won't somehow find its way to her?" Silence was E's answer. "Exactly."

"Eidolon...I'm not sure I really have a choice in this."

A chill went up Eidolon's spine. "You've been ordered to bring her in."

"It wasn't an order. More of a strongly worded suggestion."

"Why?"

"For her own protection," Arik said, and just as Eidolon was about to call him on that bullshit, Arik added, "and because her ability to shift at will might provide her some resistance to SF or help us find a cure."

She could shift at will because of the R-XR. They'd used her as a test subject for an experimental cure for lycanthropy, which hadn't worked but had given her the ability to change into a werewolf any time she wanted to. Eidolon had already considered her altered DNA into the SF equation, had performed tests using her blood and the virus, but hadn't seen any encouraging results.

"I'll have Shade send you blood samples. Maybe you'll have better luck than I have. But don't you dare try to take her in," he warned.

Arik cursed. "I'll stall as long as I can. Update me on the rest as soon as possible."

"You do the same." Eidolon paused, remembering Ky's question about the new breed of warg. Could be a lead on a new direction of testing. "Arik...do you know anything about werewolves that shift during the new moon instead of the full?"

"Nope."

"That's what I thought. Keep me in the loop about the other shit."

Arik hung up just as Eidolon's beeper went off. Three more diseased wargs were incoming. Five more were being brought in...dead. But not because of the disease. Trauma.

Looked like the civil war was in full swing.

Eleven

Everything hurt. Kar groaned. Heat surrounded her, though an icy draft cut through the warmth every once in a while. She opened her eyes. Blinked. Blinked again, hoping that she was seeing things.

Nope. She appeared to be in some sort of...basement? Dungeon? The fire set into one wall allowed her to see the hard-packed dirt floor, covered in places by straw. The walls were log and stone, and attached to one rough slab of rock were huge rings from which thick chains hung. A meat hook dangled from the ceiling.

This was a werewolf containment lair. She knew because she had one.

Her memory came back in a series of slaps against her brain. She'd been running from The Aegis. Looking for Luc. She'd been caught. Shot. And then Luc was there. They'd actually held a conversation, though the details were a little hazy.

She sniffed the air, got a lungful of burning hardwood mingled with the musky scent of warg, and the very male scent of Luc.

Something thumped above her, followed by the creak of a door opening. Groaning, she rolled onto her back, clenching her teeth at the wash of pain through her right side. Luc, wearing jeans and a blue flannel shirt, clomped down the stairs with a steaming bowl of what smelled like rich, meaty soup in his hands.

"You're awake." His words came out as a grunt.

"Yeah," she said hoarsely.

"You're pregnant?"

"Yes."

Oh, God, she'd told him. Her memories churned, and so did her stomach. He'd asked if she was going to kill the baby if it was born human, and his voice had been as cold as the draft blowing across her face. Thing was, the baby probably would be born human—not because the father was turned, but because *she* was. He believed she was *varcolac* because he'd seen the mark she'd had tattooed on by a warlock who specialized in mystical markings. Thankfully, during their sex-fest in Egypt, Luc hadn't questioned how a warg could infiltrate The Aegis, but then, he hadn't asked anything about her. Not even her name.

Luc shoved his shaggy black hair back from his face and kneeled next to her. "I brought you some stew."

The savory aroma of rabbit filled her nostrils, and though her mouth watered, she didn't feel like eating. She wanted to go back to sleep, even though pain wracked her and her skin was so sensitive it hurt to lay on the lumpy pallet where she could feel every individual piece of straw. "I'm not very hungry."

He doubled up the pillow behind her to elevate her head and he put a spoon of stew to her lips. "You need to eat so I can give you some medicine. Don't worry," he said, when she opened her mouth to protest, "it won't hurt the baby." He took advantage of her open mouth to shove the food inside.

Even though she wasn't hungry, she moaned at the taste. "That's good."

"Isn't hard to put some meat, water, and potatoes in a pot." He dipped the spoon in the bowl and caught a large chunk of rabbit. "You'll eat this entire thing."

His command rankled, and though she scarcely had the energy, she squirmed into a sit. "I appreciate your saving my life, but you didn't have to kill the Guardian, and—"

"I haven't saved it yet."

A chill washed through her, countering the fever and making her sweat ice. "What are you not telling me?"

"You could still die. Probably will."

"Don't sugarcoat it or anything."

His expression was devoid of emotion, reminding her of how coldly efficient he'd been while blackmailing her into sex with him. But that icy demeanor had turned into something hot and passionate once the demon war ended and lust had taken him. "I never do."

She took the bite he offered, more to give herself a chance to think than anything. "What are my options?" Though she tried to keep her voice level, there was a humiliating tremor hanging on to the end of her question.

"We need to get you to Underworld General."

The demon hospital? The very idea frightened her more than death did. "I don't know..."

"There's no choice. I've already rigged a sled to the

back of my snowmobile. We'll leave after midnight when it's fully dark, and hope there are no Guardians waiting to ambush us." The spoon clanked in the bowl as he fished for another bite. "If we were closer to the full moon, you could shift. Heal your wounds."

A curious warmth settled on her skin, and she knew that if she could actually shift during a full moon, they'd either tear each other apart or they'd tear up the night with passion. She'd bet on the latter.

The warmth turned into a tingle, and she gasped. Oh, God, how could she have forgotten? "Luc? What day is it?"

He frowned. "Why?"

"Because—" She broke off with another gasp. The pain, the tenderness she'd felt . . . it wasn't from the wound. Her skin stretched, and her muscles cramped up hard. "Oh, damn."

Luc's eyes shot wide. "Kar . . ." His voice was a low, deadly growl, tainted with just a touch of anxiety. "Tell me you're not doing what I think you're doing."

"I wish I could," she whispered.

Snarling, he leaped to his feet and reeled backward. "No." He shook his head, teeth bared. "You're not—"

"I am." Joints began to pop, and muscles ripped off the bone, and she clenched her teeth against the searing agony. "I'm a . . . Feast warg."

A Feast warg.

Cursing violently, Luc grabbed one of the wall chains and hooked the manacle around Kar's ankle as she bucked and writhed. The sounds of her bones snapping, her skin splitting, and her fur erupting filled the small space, and he cursed even louder so she could hear every fucking syllable.

A Feast fucking warg!

Jesus. He took the stairs three at a time and jogged to his bedroom, where he jerked open his bureau drawer and palmed his Beretta. At the back of the sock drawer was a small, hand-carved wooden box, and inside were six silver bullets.

He'd need only one.

Nasty snarls echoed up from below, as well as the sound of claws on the stone. The chains were made to hold him, but she was a different creature. She was stronger, meaner, rabid. Worst of all, a Feast warg's bite was venomous to other wargs. Just a scrape of their teeth would kill a normal werewolf in seconds.

Feast wargs were the monsters in garden-variety werewolves' closets.

Because of that, both *varcolac* and *pricolici* trained special teams of operators to search out Feast wargs during the nights of the new moon, after they'd turned, because they were impossible to detect while in human form. As a result of the merciless execution teams, they'd been hunted nearly to extinction, their bodies just as vulnerable to a silver bullet as any other werewolf. They were so rare, in fact, that Luc had never come across one—that he knew of.

Until now.

Oh, he'd sensed the werewolf in her, but she'd hidden her "special" secret well.

Dammit! Luc's steps were heavy as he exited his bedroom. Outside, snow roared out of the darkness to slap the window, and the wind howled as though trying to get his attention. Beneath the floorboards, Kar's howls got what the wind didn't, and he tightened his grip on the pistol.

She's pregnant.

Fuck. Didn't matter. She was a killer.

So are you.

Ignoring his internal voice—what some might call a conscience, but his had taken leave a long time ago—he lifted the hatch. Kar's snarls grew louder and more violent. He moved carefully down the stairs, weapon at his thigh, finger poised over the trigger guard.

She was in the corner, her red fur gleaming in the light from the fire. She was huge, the largest female he'd ever seen, and as she went up on two sturdy legs, she towered over him. Rarely did he get to see a fully transitioned warg through human eyes, and even when he did, he had little time to admire it since he was always caught up in his own transition.

But now...now he could appreciate Kar's powerful form, her muscular build and sleek fur. Her massive head hung low, her sharp, intelligent gaze tracking him as he eased to the side, seeking the best angle to get a clean shot. He might be a brutal asshole, but he didn't want her to suffer.

Without warning, she lunged.

In a single, smooth motion, he swung the pistol up and targeted her broad chest. She drew short in a clank of chains and went down on all fours with a snort. He swore confusion swirled in her blue eyes, turning them murky. Why? She should be furious, trying to rip him limb from limb.

A low, keening whimper came from deep in her chest.

As a paramedic, he was used to pained noises from his patients. For the most part, he'd hardened himself, had erected a force field that bounced suffering right off it and kept him suitably neutral. Or maybe he just didn't care. Hard to tell anymore.

But the sadness in Kar's mewling cry somehow penetrated his numbness, and as she backed up, he frowned. Then let out a curse on a long exhale.

She's pregnant. Shit. He had no idea if pregnancy made females more docile, and somehow he doubted it, but one thing was clear: she wasn't trying to antagonize him. What was her game? Had she come to Canada to kill him but missed her chance when he chained her before she could?

Not wanting to put her down until he got the truth, he lowered the weapon. "You," he muttered, "are really fucking lucky that I'm in a good mood."

Twelve

By the time Con and Sin made it to the safe house, it was fully dark, and nothing was chasing them too closely, though they'd seen a pair of raptor horrors flying overhead, their twelve-foot, leathery wings skimming the treetops as they searched for Sin. Con hated the fucked-up creatures that had given rise to the Mothman legend; they were hard to kill and always reeked of rotting flesh. Probably because they liked to wear the skins of their victims.

Sin was still engaged in iceman assassin mode, but every once in a while, her gaze would grow haunted, and her "don't fuck with me" mask would slip. The slaughter of a dozen innocent wargs had shaken her, and Con wondered how often that happened.

He tried not to think about it as he studied the two-story log cabin that nestled into the banks of a mountain lake. "Doesn't look like Rivesta is home." Then again, the half-breed Nightlash sorceress rarely was. She had a dozen homes, spread out all over the world and Sheoul, and she preferred the warmer climates. For June, it was strangely cold.

"How do you know her?"

"Family friend," he replied.

Sin raised a black eyebrow. "*Intimate* family friend?"

"Once." Rivesta wasn't your average Nightlash. She'd inherited their streak of cruelty, but her human side tempered it and made her fragile enough to know who she should and shouldn't fuck with.

Which meant that sleeping with her wasn't nearly as dangerous as bedding a purebred Nightlash.

He found one of Rivesta's charms hanging from the bough of a fir tree. He gestured to Sin. "Give me your hand."

Sin did so, without argument, which told him more about her mental state than anything, and his gut knotted. Not long ago, he'd have been glad for her silence and her cooperation. Now he wanted the feisty little demon back.

Cursing to himself, he gripped her wrist. His pulse raced as he lifted her hand to his mouth and took her finger between his lips. Her dark eyes flared as he pierced the pad with his fang. Her blood hit his tongue, and he nearly groaned. Quickly, before he lost himself to lust, he opened up his own finger and touched them both to the muslin bag above their heads. Their blood seeped into the charm, and there was a pop, a flash, and they had five seconds to cross the invisible threshold.

They darted onto the front porch, and a pop behind them let him know that the barrier was once again closed.

Cautiously, he pushed open the door. Rivesta's spell worked against supernatural creatures, but not humans, which meant hunters or burglars or squatters could have broken in. "I'll clear the upstairs if you do the down," he said, and Sin slipped away like a phantom.

Damn, she was amazing, and he found himself staring after her, his heart racing more than it should.

Calling himself all kinds of stupid, and a couple extra types of moron, he willed his pulse to throttle down and mounted the spiral staircase. He cleared the bedroom and bathroom and met Sin downstairs, where she was standing in the center of the great room, gazing into the cold fireplace and hugging herself as though chilled.

On the floor were the smashed remains of her cell phone. "Battery's dead. Case was cracked."

"So you punished it," he said wryly, but the dead battery was not good news. They now had no way to get help.

"Hey." He reached for her, and, as usual, she stepped away, and he let his arm drop. "We'll be fine. Nothing is getting past Rivesta's barrier." At least, not until the assassins after her realized they could send in humans. "Why don't you get some rest, and I'll come up with a plan to get us out of here."

"Sleep is for the weak, and you can stop treating me like I'm a child." She wheeled away and produced a dagger from out of nowhere, as far as he could tell. "I'm going outside to patrol the area."

"Sin," he said wearily. "Stop. You said you're drained. You need to rest."

She stopped, but she was facing the door. At some point, she'd tied her hair up in a messy knot so the ends were dangling over a spiky, tribal tattoo on the back of her neck, and he suddenly wanted to free those wild tresses and bury his face in them. In her. "I need to do *something.*"

"Going outside and getting yourself killed isn't that something."

She rounded on him, all spitfire and hell on legs, and yeah, be careful what you wish for. "Did you see those people, Con?" She gestured to the window and the wilderness outside. "Are you forgetting that butchered child? Who cares about me? Who gives a crap if I live or die? It's those people who matter!"

"Dammit, Sin. Yes, they matter. But so do you. People care." She snorted, and he grabbed her, used every ounce of restraint he had not to shake her. "Your brothers care—"

"They want to care, but they don't. How can they?" She batted his hands away and stepped back. "All I've done is cause them trouble. Okay, there's Lore. He might give a shit, but he's mated now and he doesn't need me."

"Trust me," Con said. "They do care, and they *do* need you."

Doubt burned in her eyes, but abruptly, the light flickered out, and he knew she was thinking about the warg child again. "Doesn't matter." She dug the map out of her pocket. "Let's go to Germany. There was an outbreak near Berlin."

"We can't just waltz out the front door. We need a plan. Rivesta has hidden exits. We'll find them and come up with a way to get us out of here. Just take a breather first. It's best if we can wait for first light." Too many demons could see better at night than in the day, and the time when they were most blinded was as the sun was just breaking over the horizon.

She glared at him, one finger caressing the hilt of her blade, and he wondered if she was considering stabbing him with it. Then, as if a switch had been thrown, she made the blade and map disappear, and the anger drained from her expression. She was the most mercurial female he'd ever known.

"I need a minute," she said crisply. "Alone."

He let out a frustrated sigh. "I'll raid the kitchen and see what we've got. Stay in the house." When she stiffened at his command, he added, "I mean it, Sin. If you try to leave, I *will* give you that spanking I talked about at the hospital."

The light of battle sparked in her eyes, triggering a primitive response inside him, one that demanded her capitulation...beneath him. He should never have threatened a spanking, because now his hand tingled with anticipation and his cock hardened and his entire body primed for sex.

"I'd like to see you try." Sin's husky voice shot straight to his groin, and so had all his blood, because his brain was flipping through a lot of spanking scenarios now.

"I don't try, Sin. I *do*. Remember that."

"Whatever," she muttered, as she did a crisp about-face and strode out of the kitchen. He watched her swaying retreat, which did nothing to cool the heat in his veins.

Though it was the last thing he wanted to do, he turned away and started pawing through the cupboards, which were crammed with canned and boxed goods. The freezer was nearly as packed, but mostly with unidentifiable raw meat. Grimacing, he closed the door. He'd eaten some questionable things in his life, but you never knew what demons considered to be food.

The fridge contained mostly bottles of water, soda, and beer. Con grabbed two Cokes and went back into the living room, where Sin was sitting on the couch.

The scent of blood was thick in the air.

Her *dermoire* was writhing, and a thin laceration in the perfect shape of a Z split a circular symbol at her shoulder in half. Blood beaded along the seam, but it was the six-inch gash just below in her biceps that had his attention.

He dropped the sodas on the massive dining room table and crossed to her. "What did you do?"

"Leave me alone."

Ignoring her, he grabbed her arm and applied pressure. "You've got to stop this, Sin. Where's the knife?" When she didn't say anything, he barked, "Where's the fucking knife?"

"There isn't one!" she shouted, jerking away from him. The laceration grew another inch and widened more, as though it were being cut from the *inside*. Holy shit.

Before she could stop him, he swiped his tongue along the wound, and instantly, it sealed.

"You asshole!" Sin shoved to her feet, looked at her arm, and just beneath where the cut had been, another started, growing quickly from a tiny quarter-inch line to a good two inches in length in a matter of seconds.

"What are you doing?" Con grabbed for her, but she sidestepped like a dancer.

"I said, leave me alone."

Idle down. Just back off. The taste of her was still on his tongue, heightening every one of his senses and emotions, which included anger, and she didn't need him lashing out. Her stubborn ass would clam up tighter than, well, a clam. "Not until you tell me what's going on."

She looked up at the thick log rafters for a long time before saying softly, "It's my guilt."

"Your what?"

"It's how most of my guilt comes out." She dropped her gaze back to him. "I've trained myself not to feel it. Guilt, sorrow, regret. But they need to be released, so they present as pain."

Con drew a sharp breath. He'd heard of that before—manifestation of certain emotions as physical symptoms instead of as true emotion. And if that was what was going on, she was feeling a *lot* of guilt. Blood streamed down her arm and dripped to the floor, yet she didn't seem to notice. When he reached for her, she skirted away from him.

Fed up and frustrated, he dove for her, took her down to the couch cushions, yanked her arm up, and once again licked the wound closed.

"Stop it!" She wriggled, jerking her leg up to cause some damage in his fun parts, but he was ready, and he pinned her legs down with his weight.

"Dammit, Sin, you need to feel."

"No, I don't." She rocked her head up, trying to bite his arm, but he shifted, and her teeth snapped on empty air. "Do you think I could do my job if I broke down in tears every time I killed someone?"

Fury ripped through him. He couldn't—wouldn't—judge her for the job she did. He hadn't been an angel himself. But she was cheating herself, and cheating all the victims of the epidemic she'd started.

"So everyone who's died because of the disease you caused gets nothing?"

"Nothing?" she asked, incredulous. "I *bleed* for them."

"Really?" He looked at her arm, which had cut open

again. "Do you think there's enough blood to cover the deaths of all the wargs who have come through the hospital? How about the child we just saw slaughtered?"

"Shut up," she rasped.

He swiped his tongue over the blood again, and she bucked, but he didn't budge. "You're going to feel it, Sin. I promise you that."

"Fuck you."

"Feel it," he said, his voice low and harsher than he intended. "Remember everyone who has died."

"No."

Her arm split. He licked. "I won't let you bleed. *Feel it.*"

"You're one to talk," she snapped. "How bad do you feel when you kick your human friends to the curb with lies?"

"We aren't talking about me, Sin."

"You want me to be miserable?" she yelled. "Do you hate me that much?"

"No!" he shouted back. "I care that much." He froze, unable to believe he'd just said that.

Sin blinked, her lush eyelashes framing the surprise in her eyes. Then she slapped him with her free hand hard enough to jar his teeth. "You bastard. You lying bastard. I get that you owe Eidolon some big debt, but I'm not stupid enough to fall for crap like that."

"Jesus. I didn't say I was in love with you or anything." Oh, hell no. Never. "But I don't hate you anymore." And *when* that had happened, he wasn't sure.

"Why not?"

"You might have started the epidemic, but you didn't mean to."

Beneath him, her body relaxed, just a little. "Then why do you want me to feel all that guilt?"

"Because it's not just guilt you're locking up inside you. It's everything. You need to let it out and learn to trust your feelings."

Her skin split. "No." Some of the resolution had seeped out of her voice, but clearly not enough.

Lowering more of his weight onto her to keep her held down, he dragged his tongue up her arm. "Give it up, Sin. Feel."

"I . . . If I think about that kid, the things I've done . . ." Her entire body started to tremble, and her eyes grew liquid.

The sight of her, so conflicted, clawed at him, and he eased away—and she dumped him on his ass on the floor. With near-vamp speed she was up and tearing toward the stairs.

He leaped to his feet, grabbed her, and spun her to face him. "No more bullshit, Sin. Feel what you've done." He took her hand and pressed it to her chest, where her heart was pounding painfully fast. So was his. "Let yourself feel something for someone else."

"I hate you." Her voice was so shaky he could hardly understand her.

"Then that's something," he said softly.

Abruptly, her eyes filled with tears. "Con . . ." She swallowed, over and over.

"Let it happen."

"I'm . . . afraid."

On impulse, he folded her into his arms. "Let it go."

For an unbearably long time, she shook. And then she cried out an agonizing, terrified, animal-like wail that made his heart clench.

"It hurts," she moaned. *"Oh, God."*

Her sobs came hard and fast, and he supposed he should

be taking some measure of pleasure from her pain, but all he wanted to do was make it stop. Maybe he'd made a huge mistake. He almost released her, almost apologized, but when she started to push away, he tightened his arms around her. She was strong, and as her struggles grew more frantic, he had to crush her to him.

"Let go!" She tried to throw herself backward, tried to kick him, claw at him, bite him. He took it all, let her do as much damage as she wanted to. "Let...go..." The order came out as a moan and a plea, and as her struggles weakened, she began to sob again.

"Sin," he whispered into her hair. "Shh..." Relaxing his grip just a little, he hooked a finger under her trembling chin and lifted her face to his. Black eyes swam in tears that left a trail down her cheeks.

Without thinking, he kissed her wet face, first one side, then the other.

"No," she groaned, but her body sagged against his. And when he pressed his lips to hers, she clung to him as if he were a life raft and she was drowning.

He licked at her lips, easing his way in, not wanting to rush this. In his arms she felt tiny, fragile, in a way she never had and in a way he hadn't believed possible, and some crazy instinct surfaced, making him want to take care of her, pamper her, and make her strong again.

Though she wasn't actively participating in the kiss, she wasn't fighting, either, and he took his time, nibbling at her mouth, stroking her lips, her teeth, and, finally, her tongue. He began an easy rhythm in and out of her mouth, and slowly, so slowly, heat built and she began to respond.

Sin's hands eased up his back, tentatively at first, but as

the kiss deepened, intensified, her touch became firmer, until she was rubbing not only her palms against him, but her breasts against his chest.

"That's it," he whispered against her lips. "Touch me."

Sin dropped her hand to his fly, but he gripped her wrist to stop her.

"Not there. Not yet."

"But—"

He shut her up with another kiss, this one more urgent, as he carried her to the floor. With one hand, he cupped her buttocks and tucked her beneath him, and with the other, he cradled her head, holding her for his kiss.

Her thighs cradled him in a tight fit, her soft sex rubbing, driving his hips forward even though he wanted to keep this whole thing at a leisurely pace. But his loins were already full, his animal blood ran thick and hot in his veins, and the mountains, the wilderness around them, called to his primitive nature.

It demanded that he take her with surety, a rough joining that would make them both howl. And as she came, he'd take her blood, too...

The idea made him run both cold and hot. He wanted nothing more than to fill up on her as he filled her up. But, as always, in the back of his mind was the fear of addiction, something he knew he was precariously close to.

He couldn't be responsible for another death caused by his careless hunger for a female's blood.

Sin's slick tongue flicked over one of his fangs and then ran up and down it, stroking, and he moaned, forgetting everything but her. Right now, he needed to concentrate on making her feel good. On making her forget the horrors of the day and the horrors yet to come.

The hardest thing he'd ever done was keep from tearing off her clothes and plunging inside her, especially when she began to rock against him, her lean form undulating in sinuous waves. A softly uttered "No" accompanied every roll of her hips. Her body was willing, but her mind still hadn't accepted this. If he did what his body was demanding, a hard, fast fuck, she'd be on board. But the tenderness was scaring her.

"Easy," he murmured, as he kissed a trail down her jaw, to her throat, where her pulse beat madly beneath his lips. "If you truly don't want this, I'll stop. But it's time for you, isn't it?"

He knew it wasn't. Oh, she was giving off the usual succubus fuck-me vibes, but not in desperate, take-me-now quantities. But she was nervous, afraid, and she needed an excuse to go with this because she wanted to, not because she required it.

"Yes," she rasped, the lie seeming to catch in her throat.

"Then I'll take care of you," he murmured. The problem, he realized, as his hunger surfaced, would be taking care of himself.

Sin was scared to death.

It took a lot to terrify her. But somehow this sexy dhampire who was kissing her senseless was making her squirm with anxiety and need that went deeper than the physical. He'd forced her to confront emotions she'd never wanted to experience, and she was still reeling from that, trying to stuff those feelings back in the box they'd been locked in for so long.

Cold, hard-core sex would help make that happen.

Con reared back, just a little, so he could peel off her top and bra, her ultrathin leather dagger harness, and then her boots, pants, and thigh and ankle sheaths. He made a messy pile of her weapons, something that made her twitchy, but then he was touching her again, and her weapons were forgotten. Her heart pinged around in her rib cage as he slid his long, talented fingers up and over her breasts. She inhaled, taking in the musky scents of aroused male and battle that still clung to Con's bronzed skin. Lust tackled her, turned her muscles to Jell-O, and made her core run wet.

Writhing, she dropped her head onto the hardwood floor with a frustrated curse. "Stop teasing." She went for his pants again, but he stopped her, his grip on her wrist ruthless almost to the point of pain.

"I'm going to make love to you, Sin. We're not going to fuck. We're taking it slow, with lots of that foreplay I talked about."

Her chest constricted with alarm. "Why?"

He made a sound that was something between a chuckle and a purr. "Only you would question extended erotic play." His fingers delved between her legs, feathering over the fleshy lips of her sex. "And I intend to turn you into my personal playground."

Oh, Jesus. "I . . . can't." She didn't know how. But more than that, making love would leave her open, vulnerable. Fucking was easy, two bodies slapping together to reach a brief moment of pleasure. Making love involved emotions tangling and minds meeting until the orgasm was more than physical . . . and she wasn't good at that at all.

"You can, and you will." He peeled off his jeans, leaving his lean, toned body completely naked, his silver eyes glittering in the moonlight streaming through the windows, his fangs glinting wetly. Deep-cut muscles flexed from his neck, to his arms, to his abs, where a thin line of blond hair beckoned her gaze lower. His cock was so rigid that it curved into his stomach, the veins throbbing with the intensity of his arousal. He looked like a god, a devil, a wild animal intent on taking what it wanted.

And yet, there was an underlying tenderness in his expression and in his touch as he prowled up the length of her body. Something lurched in her chest. Her heart, something she'd believed to be completely insulated, was reacting to this man in a way it never had before.

Panic wrapped around her, and with a cry, she shoved him away and scrambled to her hands and knees. Terror made her awkward, and she slipped while trying to get to her feet. A low, dangerous growl sounded behind her, and she screamed just before Con's heavy body covered her so she was belly down on the floor. One hand yanked her arms above her head, pinning her, while the other delved between her legs.

"Please, Con," she begged, but she wasn't sure what she was pleading for. She tried to break his grip on her wrists, but her hips rose to meet his fingers as they penetrated her core.

His breath was hot and desperate against her ear, and she realized he'd bitten her lobe, was using his mouth as yet another way to hold her. She made a sound of equal desperation, a high-pitched plea for more. For less. She didn't know which.

The fact that she'd made that much noise at all was a sign that she was in trouble.

She'd always been silent in her passions, but Con had

a way of coaxing things out of her, whether she liked it or not... and *oh, yes*, she liked that...

He controlled her with the weight of his body, his strong legs that caged hers together, and those fingers that began an erotic glide in and out of her sex. She wouldn't come from what he was doing, but he could get her so close that she could explode the moment he entered her if even a drop of pre-cum eased from the tip of his cock.

Moaning, she shifted her butt toward his shaft, which lay heavily in the crease of her thighs.

"Not yet," he murmured. "Almost." His tongue made a slow, wet stroke around the rim of her ear. "Do you promise to be good?" He squeezed his hand around her wrists as emphasis.

"Yes," she groaned. "Just fuck me."

His deep laughter vibrated her organs deliciously. "There will be none of that."

"I so want to kill you right now."

This time, his laughter was silent, but she felt it in the rise and fall of his shoulders on her back. Carefully, he released her and slid down her body. His lips kissed her spine, his tongue licked her skin, and his fangs scraped her hip. What the— She tried to push up, but he palmed the small of her back and pressed her down while slipping his other hand beneath her belly to lift just her hips.

When he nibbled her butt cheek, she yelped. "What are you doing?"

"Kissing your beautiful ass." And then his tongue was between her legs and she cried out at the wonderful sensation. The tip flicked over her clit, and then slid back to delve in her slick heat.

"Oh, God." She shuddered at the lash of his tongue as

he repeated the sequence. Each flick, each stroke, each penetrating thrust wrung a different sound from her, and holy hell, why had she ever thought that foreplay was a ridiculous waste of time?

"Do you like this?" he said against her intimate flesh, the vibration roaring through her and bringing her as close to orgasm as she could get without semen filling her.

Frustration put an edge on her reply, which was more of a shout. "Yes!"

Suddenly, he flipped her so she was on her back, her legs flung wide, and his mouth was between them. An animal purr rose up from him as he licked and sucked, and she screamed when he pushed two fingers inside her.

"Con, I need...need...you."

He lifted his head, the silver in his eyes swirling with molten heat. "Foreplay first."

"But I can't come that way."

His smile was pure evil. "Yes," he insisted, "you can." He rose up between her legs, blocking the white moonlight streaming in through the front window blinds. His cock was a thick, dusky column against his bronzed skin, and her throat tightened and her mouth went dry as he fisted it and began to pump.

Holding her gaze with his, he took her hand and replaced his with hers. "Stroke."

She didn't even consider disobeying his guttural command. She squeezed his hard flesh from base to tip as he thrust into her fist. His breaths became ragged, his surging motion less coordinated, and he threw back his head and let loose a roar that shook the house. His come spurted onto her belly, a hot, pumping cream that tingled. He shuddered, jerked, until finally he gripped her wrist and made her stop.

He was still hard, his shaft bucking in her grip. "I can control how much semen I release," he breathed. "A benefit of being a dhampire."

One of many bennies, she was discovering. "That is so cool." She arched her hips and wrapped her legs around his thighs. "You can still come inside me, right?"

"I *will* come inside you," he said. "But not yet."

"Damn you!" She swiped at him, only a little playfully, but he caught her hand, kissed her knuckles, and dove back between her legs. His tongue was a merciless whip on her tender, swollen flesh, and just as she was about to start sobbing with frustration, he smoothed his hand up her belly and swiped his finger in the warm pool of wetness he'd left there.

His lips latched onto her clit, and he sucked hard, his tongue circling and flicking...and then he inserted his finger deep into her core. It was as if lightning had struck her. Every cell in her body exploded with ecstasy, her blood boiled, and pleasure shot up her spine and came out her mouth as a scream. His finger swirled inside her as his mouth continued to work on her flesh, and she came again, over and over, her body bucking uncontrollably, until finally, mercifully, he stopped, and she lay limp on the floor.

He crawled up her body, his muscles tense, bunching as he moved. "I'm not done with you, sweetheart," he growled. "Not. Even. Close."

A tremor shook her body at the undercurrent of possession in his voice. He wasn't done because he hadn't gotten what he wanted out of her yet. And as she looked into his heated gaze, she knew what he wanted.

Her soul.

Thirteen

Sin's broken, whispered words, "I can't," when he'd said they were going to make love instead of get down and dirty and violent had sucker punched Con. He'd known at that moment that no one had ever taken time with her, had ever shown her any kind of compassion or attention during sex, and she didn't know how to handle it, accept it, or feel deserving of it. For the longest time, he'd assumed her tough exterior was a defense against the things she did and saw on the job, but now he'd glimpsed something inside her—an extremely low measure of self-worth.

And Con was at least partly to blame.

His own words, spoken just before they'd first had sex, came back in a sickening rush. She'd asked him about his motives, and he'd been crystal clear. *I don't want to get to know you. I want to fuck you.*

How many times had she heard that in her life? How many times had a male dismissed her as a person and valued her only as an object to rut on? The answer, he knew, was *too many*, and while he couldn't erase all of them, he could make up for his own shameful callousness.

"I see you, Sin," he whispered. "I see *you*."

He didn't know if she heard, but before she could recover from the half-dozen climaxes he'd given her, Con stood, scooped her into his arms, and sank his fangs into her throat. She gasped, a sweet feminine sound that nearly took him to his knees again. He mounted the stairs two at a time, stalked to the bedroom, and eased them both onto the bed. At some point, she'd grabbed one of her daggers, and he wondered if she thought she needed protection from him . . . or if being armed was a habit that had risen out of living a dangerous life.

Gently, he extracted the blade from her hand, which still left her with her primary weapon—her gift. She didn't protest, though she did note exactly where he had set the dagger on the nightstand.

Using his thigh to separate her legs, he sank between them. His shaft slipped between her swollen folds, and instantly, she locked her legs around his waist, urging him, tempting him. He didn't tease. Her spicy blood mingled with the taste of her orgasms, feeding his desire.

His stomach and buttocks tightened as he concentrated on maintaining control, on sliding into her slowly instead of slamming home and fucking her into the mattress like instinct demanded of him. He'd taken things slow to this point, and he wasn't going to stop now.

Not yet.

Her hot core clamped around him, sucking him deep and shredding his control. His body hummed with lust and new energy as her blood filled him. Deep inside, the connection with her intensified. He felt drugged, wanting...needing...more. It was as if every swallow made him hungrier instead of sated. Oh, this was bad, very bad...

Sin's *dermoire* lit up, and her warmth joined the hum in his veins. "Almost, Con," she breathed. "It's almost gone."

He had to stop. He was about two swallows from no return. She must have sensed his reluctance, because she fisted his hair and held him.

"This time, we finish it."

Last time, he'd had the willpower to pull away, but then, he hadn't been buried deep inside her. Now, he was helpless, a slave to the pull of her blood. He swallowed, again and again, knowing he'd crossed a line.

"It's done," she gasped. "The virus...it's...gone."

He barely heard her. Ecstasy had taken over, had engulfed him in a vortex he couldn't escape. More...he needed more.

Sin cried out as pleasure swamped her. That was the danger of this addiction...The victim would feel nothing but euphoria and orgasms as they were drained to death.

Gods, no!

Con roared as he ripped his fangs from her throat. His entire body convulsed, and instant craving began again. He swiped his tongue over the punctures, savoring the last taste he could ever have of Sin.

Anger, frustration, and lust combined into a massively caustic mood, but somehow he managed to take it easy instead of pumping into her with punishing thrusts. But maybe in a way the gentle rhythm *was* the punishment. Forcing her to accept kindness might actually be cruel. It definitely wasn't what she wanted.

"Harder," she moaned, and he intentionally pulled back, holding her on the very edge.

"Am I your first?" he whispered, some deep, selfish part of him wanting to know for sure, wanted to hear her say that he was the only male who had ever made the act about more than tab A into slot B.

She threw her head back, exposing her long, graceful neck and making her hair spill like black silk across the red satin duvet. "Con—"

"Tell me." He ground against her, took her breast into his mouth, and suckled until she whimpered. "Am. I. Your. First?"

"Yes." That one barely audible word was loaded with a lifetime of emotion: regret, anger, sorrow. For a moment, he thought she was going to break down, but then her fingers raked down his back and ass, and he shuddered at the pleasure. "Now, please..."

He should have felt victorious, but instead, he felt like a bastard. Furious at himself, at her, at the entire world, he broke loose, hammered into her, and the result was electric. A shout tore from his throat, and he blew apart into a million pieces. Sin joined him, the effect of his seed splashing inside her instantaneous and magnificent. She shattered, her body clenching, her core milking him so hard he came again.

When it was over, when his senses came back online, he realized that beneath him, she'd stiffened. He inhaled, needing to know where her emotions were, and yeah, mingled with the heady scent of sex was an acrid note of anger.

Well, you wanted her to feel. Said you'd make it happen. Promised it would happen.

For the first time in his life, he wished he'd broken a promise.

"You son of a bitch," Sin rasped.

"Yes, I'm a son of a bitch for making you come."

"That's not what I'm talking about, and you know it." She felt naked—well, more than physically, anyway. He'd somehow stripped away some of her emotional shielding, leaving an exposed gash.

Con lifted his head, and she saw something sad in his gaze before he rested his forehead against hers, eyes closed. "Tell me."

He didn't have to say anything else. She knew what he wanted. She trembled, and he simply held her, breaking her down with the force of his will and the strength of his embrace. "They . . . leave me."

His eyes popped open. "Who leaves you?"

"Everyone," she whispered. "If I care about them, or if I want them to care about me, they can't. They leave me." God, she couldn't believe she was spilling her guts like that. The emotional laceration he'd made was bleeding out, a steady trickle of words she couldn't stop.

Smoothly, he rolled them to their sides and his hand stroked her back, coaxing more out of her. "You have Lore."

"He left me, too."

"Lore? What happened?" He tucked her face into his chest, the best thing he could have done, because she couldn't talk while looking at him. When she said nothing, because she couldn't find the words, he prompted her with a light caress over the base of her throat. "Start with something easy. Like when you were a child."

She nearly laughed, because that hadn't been easy at all.

"Come on." His voice was gruff, commanding, but somehow encouraging. "Tell me about your parents."

"Oh, that's a good one." Sin focused on his sharply defined pecs as she spoke. "My mom was human. And batshit crazy. She fucked a demon she thought she'd summoned, and when she learned she was pregnant, she tried to abort. She couldn't, and she ended up giving birth to me and Lore."

"She knew you were demons?"

"Yeah. She seriously believed she'd screwed Satan. Everyone thought she was insane. So after she tried to kill us by abandoning us in the snow as newborns, my grandparents adopted us, named us Sinead and Loren, and locked her up in an asylum."

"Did you grow up thinking you were human?"

"Yeah." Sometimes, when the doctors thought her mother's treatments were working and she was getting better, they'd let Lore and Sin visit. But the visits always turned ugly. "The only time we questioned ourselves was when we got to see our mother, and when no one was around, she'd tell us she wished we were dead. That we were the spawn of the devil."

Con's hand froze on her back, and he swore. "That must have hurt."

She shrugged, but yeah, it had hurt. Lore had handled it pretty well, but Sin would cry for days after the visits. "My grandparents helped us through it."

"Your grandparents sound like they were good people."

"They were." When she tried hard enough, Sin could

still smell her grandma's homemade cookies. Could remember the hugs, the bedtime stories. The secret laughs her grandparents would sometimes share. They'd loved each other so much. They'd never had a lot of money, but the hard times only brought them closer.

"And then my mom escaped from the hospital. Lore and I were eighteen, two days from our nineteenth birthdays and still living with our grandparents when she broke in and killed them. The only reason she didn't kill us, too, was that I rolled over just as she was trying to stab me in the heart. The knife went into my shoulder. I screamed, and Lore came from his bedroom to tackle her."

Con pressed a kiss into her hair, and it was so tender, so intimate, that she sucked in a harsh breath. Con seemed to realize what he'd done, his big body going taut, as if he couldn't believe his own action. "I'm sorry," he said roughly, but whether he was sorry about kissing her like that or about her past, she didn't know.

Either way, it made her uncomfortable. And maybe a little...warm.

"'S'okay. No big." But her bravado was false, and she wondered if he knew that. The truth was that, at the time, she'd been devastated beyond consolation. She'd gone into some sort of shock that lasted for weeks. If not for Lore forcing her to eat, to live, she might have died. "Lore took care of me. We stayed in the house for a little over a year, and then we found out that everything our mom had said about us was true."

She'd never forget that night. It was a full moon. Foggy. Creepy. Her right arm had started to burn, and she'd watched in horror as red welts boiled up in her skin. Lore had come home from his job at a factory, and he'd stumbled into the house, his face wrenched in pain, his arm burning like hers.

"Some of the memories are fuzzy." She traced Con's ribs with her fingers, needing to put her hands to work because she couldn't reach her dagger, which she liked to flip out of nervous habit. "But some are crystal clear. We developed our *dermoires*, and a desperate...need. Lore had it the worst. He fought what was happening to him, and he went into this wild rage." She shuddered, remembering how his skin had turned red, shot through with black, bulging veins. His eyes, glowing crimson fire, had targeted her for death. "I guess purebred Sems go kind of crazy during their first maturation cycle, and they need lots of sex to get through it. Lore...it was different for him." At least, it was different while he was inside the house. After he left, she could only guess at what he'd done. "He tore the house apart. I think I only survived because I played dead. I left the house after he did, but I got home before him. It was a couple of days, I think. When he came back...." She took a deep, ragged breath.

"Where have you been?"

"I don't know. Everywhere. Nowhere." He looked around the kitchen. "I did this?"

She nodded.

"Sinead, I'm sorry." He put his face in his hands. "I... killed and...I did terrible things."

"So did I," she whispered. Two days spent in Boston's Irish Slums had left her shaken.

His head came up, and he reached for her. She flinched away from him, not wanting him to touch her filth, but he misunderstood, and his face fell. "I'm so sorry..."

"I—I need to—" She couldn't finish. She just wanted

to climb into bed and pray that when she woke up, this would all have been a nightmare.

She'd gone to bed, and when she got up the next morning, Lore was gone. The note on the table said, "I can't risk hurting you. I love you."

"He packed a bag and left. I didn't see him again for more than three-quarters of a century."

"Seventy-five *years*? Jesus. What happened to you?" When she didn't answer, because her throat had clogged up, Con lifted her face to his and brushed his lips over hers, devastating her and making the lump in her throat even bigger. "You can tell me. Please, Sin."

She had to swallow several times before her voice would work. Finally, she tucked her face against him and said, "I...told you I left the house for a couple of days right after our weird change, right after Lore hurt me."

Con stiffened. "He didn't—"

"No...God, no. He was enraged, insane, but there was nothing sexual." As Con relaxed, she continued. "Afterward, I needed something, but I didn't know what." She clung to Con as if she were drowning. "I was a virgin. I hadn't felt arousal before. Not like that, anyway. And sex wasn't something my grandparents ever discussed. All I knew was that, inside, I was on fire. I was cramping and aching, and right away, I was drawn to every man I saw."

She closed her eyes, hating to go back to the worst time of her life. "I was terrified. I ended up in one of Boston's Irish slums..." She'd been feverish, in pain. She'd grabbed the hands of several men, begging them for something she didn't even know how to put into words. She'd been spared the physical transformation Lore had suffered, but no doubt she'd seemed like a crazy person, and one man had struck her hard enough to make her nose bleed. Another had been seduced by the pheromones she'd been putting out, but when he'd tried to take her into an alley, a woman, presumably his wife, had caught them, and Sin had been forced to flee.

She'd finally made it into the seediest part of the slums, which smelled of slaughterhouses and factory smoke, and two young thugs had whisked her behind a corner store and given her what she'd needed.

She'd cried for hours, huddled behind some boxes, confused, afraid, and physically sated but mentally tormented.

"Gods," Con whispered, and she realized she'd spoken aloud. "That was your introduction to sex?"

"Oh, it wasn't all bad," she said, unable to keep the sarcasm out of her voice. "Imagine my shock when they climaxed... and I did, too." A hot tear squeezed from her eye. She was disgusting. A horrible creature who got off no matter who—or what—fucked her or how much they hurt her.

"You can't fight your nature, Sin. You are what you are."

"So there's nothing about yourself that you hate?"

"Yeah," he ground out. "Yeah, there is. What happened after that? Did you search for your own kind? Or try to?"

"I didn't know what my kind was, and I never got the chance to find out." She wiggled her toes against his, such a curiously intimate, random thing to do. Mainly because she'd never, not once, remained in bed with a man like this. Was rubbing toes something normal lovers did? "After Lore left for good that morning, I felt dirty and disgusting, not worthy of staying in my grandparents' house any longer. I wandered around the city, living like a stray dog. You know, sleeping under bridges and doing tricks for scraps of food."

She hesitated, measuring his reaction, but all he did was rub her back in soothing circles. Relaxing a little, she continued.

"One day, a man approached me. He was well dressed, spoke with a European accent, and he said he could take care of me. I was starving and desperate, and I went with him. Turned out he was a demon. A slaver. I never even knew what species he was—he was *ter'taceo*, so he never looked anything but human." She resumed skimming her fingers over Con's ribs, counting them idly. "He was nice at first, got me to trust him. And then he started using me. Once we learned the extent of my gift, and of my need for sex, I became his prize assassin."

Again, she waited for a reaction, but none came.

"He dealt with a lot of demons, and I saved up enough money to pay one of them to do this." She rubbed her hand over the tattoo on the back of her neck. "It's enchanted. The demon imbued it with magic to ease my need for sex."

Con trailed a finger over the pattern, and pleasant tingles followed its path. "I'm sorry it didn't work."

She frowned. "It did work. You should have seen me before."

A mild curse came out on a long exhale, and Con's touch grew more tender. "What happened next?"

"I was with him for thirty years, and then he sold me to someone else after I tried to escape one too many times. My new master was such a douche. He totally got off on locking me up and denying me sex."

This time, Con's curse was loud and nasty. "Why?"

Her stomach churned at the memories, at the helplessness and humiliation. "Punishment. Fun. I don't know. He'd wait until I was writhing on the floor, begging for relief." She laughed bitterly. "Thing was, I didn't care if relief came in the form of sex or a bullet."

But what that experience had taught her was that she would never again be at anyone's mercy when it came to sex. Now that she was free, she would never be owned, especially not by someone who would be the sole provider of the very thing she needed to survive. No one would ever have that much control over her again.

"Where is he?" Frost could have formed on Con's words. "I'll tear out his spinal cord and strangle him with it."

"Aw, that's sweet." She snuggled up to him, something she'd never done with anyone, but now wasn't the time to think too hard on that. "But having him offed was the first thing I did when I took over the assassin den." She'd paid Lycus well for that job.

Slowly, the tension drained out of Con's muscles, and he let out a long, shuddering breath. "How did you end up there?"

"The asshole sold me to Detharu—the assassin master I took over for after Idess killed him."

"If Idess made the kill, why isn't she in charge of the assassin den?"

Sin squirmed a little before she caught it and forced herself to stillness. "Idess wasn't cut out for the job, so I volunteered."

"But did you want it?"

She wiggled her fingers, feeling the weight of the ring.

Felt heavier than usual. "It's a great gig for someone like me."

She really hadn't answered the question, but Con didn't call her on it. "So how did you meet up with Lore again?"

"He joined up with Deth twenty years later. And it was my fault." She'd gotten herself into some serious trouble with Deth and had been desperate enough to seek Lore out. Bitterness had built up over the years, and in a lot of ways, she'd hoped he'd turn her down, just to give her another reason to hate him for leaving her.

But he'd been willing to do anything to make his abandonment up to her, and he'd agreed to help find a way out of her contract with Deth. Unfortunately, there hadn't been a way, and he'd signed on as an assassin in order to save her life.

"I'd lost my temper and killed one of Deth's buddies. He was going to sell me to a blood gallery—"

"*A what*?" Con snarled, and she swore she heard the slide of his fangs shooting out of his gums.

"You sound like you're familiar with the galleries."

"You could say that," he muttered. "I've done a lot of stupid shit in my life."

And frequenting a place where drugs were available to anyone who was willing to give up their blood—and bodies—to feeders like vamps, would be pretty stupid, in Sin's opinion. She'd been to a few while hunting targets, and while most had standards and strict rules, like how you couldn't kill the junkies, they were still little more than underground cesspools. And in the really bad ones, where the druggies weren't exactly volunteers, the victims rarely survived more than a couple of days at the hands—and claws—of the vampires and demons who used them.

"Well, obviously, I didn't get sold. Lore signed up with Deth to save me."

"He must love you a lot to have done that."

"He felt guilty for leaving me the way he had. And you know what's so shitty about the whole thing?" She said that as if *all* of it hadn't been one big, stinky pile of ghast-bat guano. "At first, I was just happy that since he was tied to Deth, he couldn't leave me again." Shame welled up like acid in her throat, and she curled in on herself—as much as Con would let her, anyway. "They always leave, Con. Always."

Fourteen

The damned Harrowgate wouldn't open. Which meant a human was nearby and Lore would have to wait until the human—or humans—left the area. Great. He was going to be late for breakfast with Idess at her favorite Italian restaurant.

He tapped his boot on the stone floor. Stared at the walls, which were pulsing with crude neon outlines of the street map of Rome. There were three Harrowgates in the area, but this was not only the closest to the cafe, but it was also the only one that was aboveground. He might be forced to get out in one of the sewer Harrowgates and hoof it back in this direction.

Shit.

He was just about to tap one of the other Harrowgate symbols when the gate shimmered and opened into an alley. He stepped out quickly—the stupid things had been known to solidify and chop people's limbs off. Or worse, slice people in half.

It was late morning in Italy's capital, and as Lore emerged from between the buildings and onto the shop-lined sidewalk in the Trastevere district, the scent of coffee and baked goods tickled his nostrils and made his stomach growl. Every time he ate here with Idess, he felt like a damned king. Before they'd met, he'd been content with bologna sandwiches and cheap fast food. His angel had introduced him to the finer things in life, and he was rapidly becoming spoiled.

He strode up the walk, weaving among crowds of people... and then he stopped. His scalp tingled and his adrenaline kicked in, and something definitely wasn't right. He'd spent thirty years as an assassin, and he had one hell of a sixth sense and self-preservation instinct, and his oh-fuck meter was spiking off the charts.

Casually, he eased into a recessed doorway, putting his back to the building. His hackles raised as he scanned the street, and his heart stopped when he saw Idess moving toward him, her normally sexy, rolling gait stiff and forced. A *ter'taceo*, a demon in a human suit named Marcel, walked beside her, one hand gripping her upper arm, the other in his pocket. Lore knew exactly what the assassin—one of Sin's own—was concealing because Lore had worked with Marcel before: a pen that shot out a retractable six-inch bolt meant to go through the eye, through the back of the skull, or into the heart. It was a quick, relatively bloodless way to kill if used right, and Marcel never fucked up.

Slipping into stealth mode, which meant controlling his breathing, his thoughts, and even his heartbeat, Lore blended in with the crowd. He strolled past Idess, whose gaze never wavered from looking straight ahead, even though she was aware of Lore's presence. He kept an eye out for anyone who might be working with Marcel, Lycus in particular. The warg and the Sensor demon had been doing a lot of tag-team killing over the years... some of it just for fun.

Tugging the glove off his right hand, Lore did a slow turn in the crowd and eased up behind Marcel, whose unremarkable height, looks, and mousy brown hair allowed him to become practically invisible in a group of people. But Idess was tall, striking, and she definitely stood out. Males eyed her with lust, women with envy, and Lore was going to have to use every bit of his stealth skills to get her out of there and get Marcel dead.

Good thing just a brush of the fingers would end the guy—Lore didn't even have to fire up his killing gift, which was cool, because Marcel didn't deserve the energy it would require to do so. No one who touched Lore's female did.

Lore allowed himself a grim smile as he "accidentally" bumped into Marcel and allowed his hand to graze the demon's arm. Instantly, the guy dropped, and in the resulting rush of people who stopped to help, Lore grabbed Idess and quickly slipped into the alley and into the Harrowgate. He wasn't worried about the body—as a *ter'taceo*, Marcel wouldn't disintegrate; he'd most likely be taken to a human hospital and then to a human morgue, and no one would be the wiser.

Once inside the Harrowgate, Lore didn't allow Idess a single word as he wrapped himself around her and kissed her desperately until they both needed a breath.

"What happened?" he finally said, as he caught her long brown ponytail, which was held by gold bands spaced every six inches, and drew it over her shoulder. "What did he want? Did he hurt you?" If so, Lore was going to regret not causing the bastard a whole lotta pain before he died.

"I'm fine." She reached past him to tap the symbol on the wall that would take them to Underworld General. "He said I was going to be bait. For Sin."

"Son of a bitch." Lore slipped his glove back on to prevent any accidents in the hospital. Idess and his siblings were immune to his touch, but everyone else was at risk.

Idess curved her hand around his waist, her honey-colored, almond eyes full of concern as she looked up at him. "Have you heard from her?"

He shook his head. "It's not unusual to not hear from her for days, but with assassins after her..."

"She'll be fine. She's tough. I should know," she said wryly, and Lore smiled despite his worry. Sin and Idess had fought it out, and the results hadn't been pretty.

Sin was tough, street smart, and hard to kill. But obviously, the people trying to kill her had stepped up their game, and it wouldn't be long before the roll of the dice went in the bad guys' favor.

The Harrowgate opened up into the emergency department, but Lore didn't step out. "Stay here, babe," he said to Idess. "It'll be the safest place for you until this whole thing is over."

She crossed her arms over her chest, and his gaze went automatically to her breasts, which were now nicely plumped by her biceps. Yeah, he was a sex demon. Shoot him. "What are you going to do? And eyes up, mister."

Busted. "I'm going hunting." He gave her a quick peck on the lips and then a gentle nudge out of the gate. "I'm going to see how many assassins I can take out before they get to Sin."

"Be careful."

"Always, angel cake. Always." He smiled as the gate shimmered shut.

Kar's entire body was on fire. Not with fever, but with need. Man, she hated waking up the morning after a Feast moon shift, but usually she woke alone in her own house. This time, she was in a male's lair, naked, and surrounded by his scent.

She was also alive.

Luc hadn't killed her.

She sat up with a start, found herself looking into his furious golden eyes. He was crouched over her, as naked as she was. Werewolves always came out of their transitions horny, and clearly, Luc was reacting to her, ready to answer her call.

His hand shot out, and suddenly she was on her belly, his heavy body pinning her to the pallet. He held her down, controlling her with a grip on her throat and chin as he popped her hips up.

She stifled both a groan and the urge to grind her butt against his erection. Another more vicious urge welled up in her, and she wrenched her arm behind her to claw him in the thigh. He pinched her earlobe between his teeth in response, a punishing nip that only made her want him to bite harder.

"Why didn't you tell me?" he rasped against her ear. "Who sent you?" His hips rocked back and then rammed forward. He entered her, burying himself all the way to his balls, and she cried out at the erotic invasion.

"No one sent me," she moaned. "I swear."

He pulled back again, until only the thick head of him was inside her, and she quivered, shoving her hips back to take more of him. He denied her that, holding himself out of reach. "I don't believe you."

She snarled in frustration. "It's true, you jerk."

He slammed home with a ruthless thrust, and she nearly climaxed. His lips brushed her cheek. "I could kill you right now. Just a twist of my hands is all it would take."

"Will you let me come first?" She couldn't believe she'd said that, but her body was screaming for release, was teetering on the very edge, and he was just being cruel.

"We'll both come." His teeth sank into the back of her neck, holding her in the most primitive way possible as he pumped into her...slowly. Way too slowly for her to get what she needed, damn him. After several excruciating minutes, he released his bite hold. "How did it happen?"

"How did what happen?" she asked between panting breaths.

Luc kept one hand on her chin, but slipped the other down her belly and between her legs. "Your turning."

Right. That. He flicked his finger over her tight knot of nerves, and she whimpered. "My Aegis partner and I were battling a wizard." *Oh, yes, right there...* "After we killed him, I found a woman chained in his basement. She begged me to kill her. Said she would turn into a were-wolf in a few minutes. I thought she was crazy. It was still weeks until the full moon." Pausing to catch her breath, she squirmed, chasing Luc's elusive touch. "She turned and bit me." Thankfully, Kar's partner, Emilia, had been searching the mansion's attic, so she hadn't witnessed the attack.

"And you didn't tell The Aegis?"

Son of a bitch. How could he sound so calm and unaffected while Kar could barely get her lungs to work? "Luc, please…"

Rearing up, he gripped her hips with both hands and hammered into her. Finally, oh, finally! The wet sound of his cock sliding through her core blended with the snap of the fire and the slap of their flesh coming together, and she'd never heard anything so erotic in her life. Her sex contracted with the beginnings of her orgasm, and Luc fisted her hair, drew her head back, and tilted her face around to kiss her.

It was rough, a kiss meant to punish and dominate, and it worked. She was more than ready to submit to him as long as he relieved her of this delicious agony.

He clipped her lower lip with his sharp teeth, propelling her to the very brink of climax. "I'm going to ask you one more time. Did you come here to kill me?"

The rough, guttural words sent her over. "No!" Her cry of denial and of pleasure filled the tiny basement, and then he joined her, roaring into her mouth and filling her core with his hot seed.

Her orgasm went on and on—one of the benefits of becoming a warg was longer, stronger orgasms. She thought maybe he came again, too, but she was too focused on her own pleasure, and when it was over, he collapsed on top of her.

When she could breathe again, she shoved him and rolled away, taking the blanket with her. A twinge of nausea made her swoon as she sat up, and she winced as she tucked her legs beneath her and brought the blanket up to cover her breasts.

Luc reached out and tugged the blanket down to her waist. "Don't hide from me."

She jerked it back up. "Don't tell me what to do."

He stretched his long, muscular body out and propped himself on one elbow. Between his legs, his thick sex lay, still semi-erect, on his thigh, though she tried not to stare. "You sought me, not the other way around. And you've lied to me."

More than you know. Guilt and anger at being called out made her cheeks hot, and with a snarl, she yanked the blanket down so it pooled in her lap. Despite their love-making, his gaze heated as he took in her breasts, the soft swell of her belly.

"Good girl," he purred. "Now, tell me what happened after you were bitten."

"Why?"

"I'm curious. I've never encountered a Feast warg before. Did you know what you were bitten by?"

Even though she wasn't cold, she shivered. "Not really. She looked like a werewolf, but I knew she couldn't be. I mean, it wasn't a full moon, right? And when nothing happened to me during the full moon, I figured I was safe." And relieved. Being bitten by any underworld creature, especially demons, usually wielded nasty results.

"Did you tell anyone?"

"My dad." She fisted her hands in the blanket to keep from fidgeting. "He's a Guardian. He's why I was in Egypt in the first place. You know, when we met. We were there for training." She'd been raised in Texas, born to an American mother and an Italian father, but after her parents divorced when she was a teen, her father had taken her to Italy with him. It was there that he told her the truth of what he did for a living, and she'd joined up with the demon-slaying organization as soon as she was out of school.

"And?"

"And he didn't know what I'd been bitten by. He did research, but in the meantime, I shifted on the night of the new moon. I was freaked. Woke up in Spain, with no idea how I got there. There was this woman with me... She was a Feast warg, too. She explained what was going on...Right after that, I got this weird feeling inside. I could sense dozens of others like me. She took me to someone who put the born-warg mark on me so that anyone who sensed werewolf in me would never suspect what I'd been turned into. She said we had to stay hidden and secret because we couldn't let The Aegis know about us, and regular werewolves would hunt us."

Luc's voice deepened, and his eyes flashed. "That's because Feast wargs were bred to kill us."

"The first ones were," she agreed, a little testily.

"So you're saying that none of you are out to kill us?"

"Oh, we want to kill you. It's instinct." She sighed. "That's what makes us so different from regular were-wolves. You shift and want to hunt...hunt pretty much anything that moves. We want to hunt only other werewolves. Which means we don't usually attack humans, which has allowed us to stay so secret. And rare. Our numbers are shrinking rapidly."

A wicked smile turned up one corner of Luc's mouth. "Then maybe you should bite people to make more of you."

She grimaced. "I would never put anyone through this." When he looked away, just a flicker of his eyes toward the floor, suspicion bloomed. "Have you ever turned anyone?"

"Wasn't intentional," he muttered.

It usually wasn't. "Did you claim First Rights?"

First Rights, according to warg law, stated that a warg who turned another had the legal right for one year to either claim the newly turned warg as a mate, or kill them without consequence. Of course, the term "mate" was more accurately described as "sex slave," when claimed under First Rights. She'd heard of many females taken under First Rights clauses being held in shackles until they went into season and got pregnant, which was how a true, permanent bond was formed.

"Nah. She hunted me down to kill me, but she was already mated to my boss, Shade."

"Your boss? That must have been awkward."

He shrugged and trailed a knuckle over her exposed calf, and her flesh prickled under his touch. "Was your mate a Feast warg?"

Her heart gave a great thump. Her mouth went as dry as the ashes in the fireplace, and this time, when she tugged the blanket up, it was because she needed a shield, some sort of barrier, flimsy as it was, between her and the male in front of her.

"Kar?"

She'd rehearsed this, had a story prepared about her mate and how they'd gotten together and how he'd died, but now her mind was a blank and her heart was pounding and the only thing she could do was blurt, "I didn't have one."

Luc went very still. Even the air around him seemed to go dead. "So . . . no breeding heat?"

She could practically see the wheels turning in his head. If she got pregnant outside a breeding heat, she could have gotten pregnant at any time. Which meant—

Luc lunged across the pallet and gripped her shoulders in a bruising hold, his eyes flashing. "Who is the father, Kar?" Her throat had closed up, making speech impossible, and he gave her a little shake. *"Who?"*

"You are," she finally whispered. "This baby is yours."

This baby is yours.

Jesus. Luc fell back, nearly tumbling off the edge of the pallet. Son of a bitch! He'd been so careful in his life, had always chosen bedmates that weren't even close to their season. And if his partner was of a species that didn't have "seasons," he could still sense fertility, could tell when any female was ripe for breeding. But for some reason he hadn't known Kar had been fertile when they'd fucked like animals for that half hour.

"How?" he asked, his voice shot all to hell. "I would have sensed your fertility."

"My periods stopped when I was turned. I thought I was infertile. It wasn't until after I became pregnant that my Feast buddies told me fertility and pregnancy are random."

"Random." He laughed humorlessly. "That's just great."

"Fuck you." Kar scrambled to her feet, taking the blanket to wrap around herself. "It's not like I did this on purpose."

No, she probably hadn't. And he knew he was being an ass, but she'd blindsided him with this news, and really, he'd never been anything *but* an ass. He stood, and she shrank away from him, as though she was afraid he was going to strike her, and he realized how insanely furious he must appear. He carefully schooled his expression and concentrated on keeping his voice level.

"The baby is why you're really here, isn't it? It has nothing to do with the epidemic."

"No, I'm here because of SF. I'm afraid for my child, and you do work at Underworld General." She took a ragged breath, and he realized she looked paler than she should. "And after The Aegis found out about me, I needed help, and you were my best hope."

He narrowed his eyes at her. "Is that why you didn't attack me when you shifted?" He'd thought her behavior was odd, but now it was making sense.

"I think so. Pregnant females don't usually try to rip apart their cubs' father."

Father. Turning away, he jammed his hands through his hair, over and over. "Fuck," he breathed. "Just . . . fuck."

"That's what got me into this mess in the first place." She tightened the blanket around her even more, as if the flimsy thing could protect her. "Look, I didn't mean to cause you trouble. If you'll let me stay for the next two nights of the new moon, I'll leave after that. I just can't be out roaming around or I'll kill wargs."

Leave? Man, he might not have wanted this to be happening, but it was, and no way was she taking off with his kid.

Yeah, because he was great father material.

He grabbed his jeans off the floor where he'd left them when he'd stripped down. He'd known she'd wake up with postshift lust, and truth be told, her desire had affected him, too. In the basement's cramped space, he'd been overpowered by the scent of a female in need. And wasn't he quite the gentleman for offering his services.

"You're not going anywhere," he said, stepping into his pants.

"Excuse me?"

"Just what I said." He threw on his flannel shirt. "Were you planning on telling me? If The Aegis hadn't discovered your secret, would you have hunted me down to tell me I knocked you up?"

The stubborn light in her eyes was answer enough.

"You weren't going to tell me," he growled.

"Oh, please," she scoffed. "Don't play the injured party here. You blackmailed me into fucking you, and afterward, you walked away without looking back. You didn't even ask me my name."

That was because he'd heard another Guardian say her name, so he knew it . . . but yeah, he had been a little on the silent side. "What, did you want my phone number? You wanted to go out on a date? Because you didn't ask me for anything, either."

"You didn't give me a chance! You were dressed and gone before I even found my underwear. You certainly didn't bother to turn around and say something like, 'Hey, if you end up pregnant, I'd like to know.'"

"Well, now I know."

"And? You going to marry me?" Venomous sarcasm laced every word. "Move me into your cabin and build a nursery?"

Marriage? A nursery? What he was going to do was break out in hives. He hadn't let himself want anything like that until Ula, and when she was killed, so was his desire for a family. He'd turned vicious that day, had never clawed his way up from the downward spiral of anger.

"Yeah," she said bitterly. "That's what I thought. I told you because I need help. But I don't expect anything else from you."

"It's my kid," he gritted out. "You're not taking it anywhere."

"See," she spat. "This is exactly what I didn't want to happen. A child is not property. Just because it's yours doesn't make you a parent. My father treated me like a possession, nothing but a successor for him in The Aegis, and I will never allow my child to be raised like that. It's better to have no father than a bad one."

She'd spoken of her father earlier, but not with the same resentfulness, and suspicion bloomed. "He's the reason The Aegis found out about you."

"Yes." She blinked, and Luc thought maybe she was trying to keep tears at bay. "I really do think he was trying to get help for me. He'd heard that the R-XR was experimenting with cures."

"But The Aegis turned on you."

She nodded. "My cell felt betrayed. Like I'd been some sort of spy."

Yeah, Luc could imagine that when an organization that had been hunting supernatural baddies for thousands of years learned a werewolf had been knowingly working for them, they wouldn't take it well. "I'll keep you safe, but that means staying with me. No running off on your own."

A flush washed over her, and she swayed, but when he reached for her, she stepped out of his reach. "It's just morning sickness," she said, and then cleared her throat. "If I'm going to stay, we'll need to talk about this."

Luc started for the stairs. "We will." When he could wrap his mind around it.

"Sooner is better than later. Besides the nine-month timer, there's a plague and Aegis Guardians are after me."

"I know."

"But?"

Christ, couldn't a guy get a moment of peace? "But I'm not a talker."

Suddenly, she was in front of him, eyes glinting with anger. "Well, too bad. There are some things you can't run away from."

Run away? He hadn't run away from anything since he had turned. Before that, though... "I'm no coward," he growled.

"Really? Because I didn't know that running away from every female in your life was a sign of bravery. Or am I wrong? Has there ever been *anyone* with whom you didn't fuck and run to avoid emotional commitment?"

Fury lit him up, set his jaw so hard he thought he heard his molars crack. "You don't know anything about me," he gritted out.

"I know your kind. The Aegis is full of them. So tell me, how close am I?"

Too close. Way too close. He'd spent a lifetime avoiding emotional connections. Even as a paramedic, he didn't have to get involved with his patients. They were his for a few moments, but he got to drop them off and never think of them again.

And even Ula, the female he'd wanted to mate with, had been more of an escape from loneliness than a love match. He'd liked her, found her challenging, but love? Not even close.

"Drop it, Kar."

She laughed. "No wonder you live out here in frozen desolation. The land is just like your heart, isn't it?"

Ignoring her barb, Luc mounted the steps, needing to get away but knowing that what she'd said was spot on.

There were some things you couldn't run away from.

Fifteen

They always leave, Con. Always.

Sin's last words before she drifted off to sleep stayed with Con, had him nearly shaking her awake to tell her he wouldn't leave. But it would be a lie, because he never stuck with anything. So why in hell did he feel like saying that to her?

Because Sin had lived a waking nightmare, that's why. As he fell asleep, he'd thought about everything she'd told him, had nightmares about it, and now, as he prowled the house in the early-morning gray light, seeking out all of the secret exits, he couldn't stop thinking. Sin was still sleeping, but he knew she'd awakened several times during the night.

Once, she'd sat up from a dream, panting and holding her hands over her ears as though trying to block something out. Another time, she'd taken her Gargantua-bone dagger off the nightstand and held it against her chest, cradling it like a teddy bear, before falling back to sleep.

Those images haunted him as much as the things she'd told him.

She wasn't an assassin because she wanted to be. She'd been sold into it. She wasn't master of her den because she wanted to be. She'd done it to spare her brother's mate. And because she was who she was—tough, intense, determined—she'd made the best of the situations. Self-preservation instincts hadn't allowed her to feel sorry for herself or to feel anything or, probably, to even think much on what she'd done or had to do.

And he'd gone and torn down the one defense she had to protect herself.

Fucking idiot.

"Hey." He whirled around, unable to believe she'd caught him by surprise. She stood at the base of the stairs, clothed, wet hair up in the messy knot she favored, a splash of shy color on her cheeks. She didn't look like a hard-as-brimstone, cold-blooded assassin. Probably because she wasn't a cold-blooded assassin like he'd once thought. No, she looked like a woman who had been well loved for the first time and wasn't sure how to deal with it.

Yeah, well, neither did he. He'd been with a lot of females. Too many couplings had been nothing but one-nighters where they didn't even exchange names. But he'd also made love to sensual, experienced females he'd liked. He'd spent hours in bed with them, hours talking, playing, doing real "date" stuff. But with the one exception so many centuries ago that had ended in disaster, he'd always kept relationships casual.

Suddenly, this thing with Sin did not feel casual.

The things she'd shared had leveled him. She had mad skills when it came to killing and surviving, but she had little practice with emotion or relationships, and she was lost. Yet she'd opened up, trusting him with a piece of her past, and he knew how monumental that had been for her.

It was a mistake for him to have coaxed any of it out. She needed her thick walls, and who the hell was he to try to breach them?

An arrogant bastard, that's who.

She'd been a challenge. A puzzle he'd wanted to solve, a code he'd wanted to break.

Well done, asshole.

He'd had a human friend once, back during the Civil War. John had nursed an injured coyote back to health, taught it to trust humans despite Con's warning to scare it off, throw rocks at it . . . whatever it took to keep it safe. And one day, it approached the wrong human and was killed.

Con hoped he hadn't created a coyote out of Sin.

"Hello . . . Con?" Sin waved a hand in front of his face.

"Ah, hey. Sorry." He gestured to the stove. "I made breakfast." If powdered eggs and dehydrated hash browns could be considered food.

Wordlessly, she slipped past him, and he caught the fresh scent of lavender soap from her shower, and underneath the floral notes was the earthy tang of their love-making. His blood stirred and heated, but he kept his baser instincts leashed as Sin scooped up the eggs and potatoes onto a plate and scarfed every bite. When he shoveled more onto her plate, she didn't argue.

"Have you thought about who's after you?"

She looked up at him, one dark eyebrow cocked. "Um . . . assassins?" Her fingers slid absently over her breastbone, and he tracked the motion with greedy eyes. "Speaking of which, I lost another one this morning."

"Should I offer my condolences?"

She snorted. "Hardly."

He propped one hip on the counter and folded his arms over his chest. "Well, here's the thing. I get that they want your ring, but that doesn't explain the horse guy who tried to kill you and then save you. It also doesn't explain my house."

"I know," she muttered. "Someone who wants my job wouldn't blow up a house with me in it. It would make finding the ring nearly impossible."

So someone wanted her dead, and not for the ring. But why? Unless...

"Valko," he snarled.

"The *pricolici* leader?"

He nodded. "With you dead, he might hope that no cure would come for the turneds." Rage filled him, made all the more potent by the fact that he had no proof of his suspicion, and by the fact that he could do nothing about it at the moment.

Sin was a hell of a lot more level than he was, shrugging as she finished eating, giving him time to cool off. He watched as she washed her dishes, taking an extraordinarily long time.

She was stalling.

Finally, after she'd put away her plate and fork, cleaned the sink, and wiped the counter, she swung around. "Thank you."

He shoved his hands into his jeans pockets. "It was just breakfast."

"That's not what I'm talking about." She looked down at her boots. They were scuffed, beat to hell. Con had never worn a pair of shoes long enough for them to look like that. "I've been an ass to you, but somehow you've put up with it. You've helped me when you'd have been well within your rights to kill me for what I've done to the wargs. So...um...thank you."

Coyote.

Her admission cracked his heart right open. He should throw rocks at her, should be thinking only of ways to make her raise her defenses again, but instead, he was thinking about wrapping her in his arms and never letting her go.

You'll let her go. When her coffin is lowered into the ground. Fuck.

Rocks. He had to throw rocks. Maybe pebbles.

"Sin—"

She held up a hand. "Whatever. I'm done talking about it. We should go." She brushed past him, and the moment they touched, it was like an electric jolt went through him. His brain short-circuited, and without thinking, he tugged her against him and tried to ignore the sound that his vampire senses picked up: the *thud whoosh* of her heartbeat. They definitely needed to go. They had to contact Eidolon, too, who would probably be going crazy about now. But Con's body was tweaking out, his fangs were thrusting downward, and if he could get a taste of her first...He leaned in, slowly—

"Yo." Sin slapped her hands on his chest. "Ah...do you need to feed?"

The vein in her throat pounded, and her pulse became a roar in his ears.

"Con?"

A wash of red colored his vision, the color of merlot. Or blood.

"Con!" She slapped him hard enough to rock his head back and clear it enough to think. "What's going on? I can sense your hunger, but it's weird."

"Damn." Stepping away from her, he scrubbed his hand over his face and wondered how the hell he was going to explain this.

"Hey. Straight up, what's going on with you?"

She deserved to know the truth. He'd asked too much of her, and it was time to give back, even if he had to spill another of the many dhampire secrets that kept his race shrouded in mystery and, to outsiders, very grounded and stable. Nothing could be further from the truth.

"You know how I said that dhampires don't mate with each other?" His voice was gravelly, as though every word was being dragged from between his lips. "It's because males become addicted to blood. If we feed from one host more than a few times, it takes root."

"So . . . why would that be a bad thing if the couple was mated?"

"Because the male can go out of control and kill the female while feeding." Shit, this was hard to talk about, and not because he was violating some ancient dhampire rule. He was way too intimate with the consequences of addiction. "That's why there are very few mated dhampire pairs."

"How could there be *any*?" Her eyes widened with curiosity, and for the first time, he could see a little of Eidolon in her as she dug into the mystery. "Do the mated males feed from other males and females to keep from getting addicted to their mates?"

He nearly laughed. "That only works temporarily. Eventually addiction happens because feeding and sex are intertwined. At that point, males inject a venom that bonds the female to him and he to her, and that ends the addiction."

"Then what's the problem?"

"There's a catch." Strange how nothing good came without strings. "We don't produce the bond fluid until we become addicted. By then, your control is shot and what you crave is the high you'll get when they die. So instead of injecting the bond fluid, you run the risk of draining the female and killing her instead."

She hooked her thumbs in her front pockets and propped a hip against the kitchen's log entryway as though settling in for a long convo. Which wasn't going to happen. "You sound like you know something about that."

"It's how my mother died. My father killed her."

A thousand years ago, before the two dhampire clans had merged, his parents had belonged to separate clans, both from royal blood. It was hoped that by mating his parents, the clans would join peacefully. It went well...Con and his younger brothers, Dubdghall and Eoin, had been conceived without his father succumbing to addiction, mainly because he took his pleasures—sex and blood—from other females except during his mother's breeding heats. And then, during his mother's fourth heat, his father lost control, and instead of bonding with her, he drained her.

"Oh, wow," she said, her dark eyes shifting from the rapidly lightening dawn back to him. "What happened to your father?"

"The death of the female ends the addiction, but he couldn't live with what he'd done. He destroyed himself." That was the understatement of the century. Con's father had burned himself alive.

Sin rolled her bottom lip between her teeth, suddenly looking a little pensive and, for the second time in the last few hours, vulnerable. "Have you ever..."

For a long time, he considered his answer. For an even longer time, he considered lying. And then he hurled the answer like the rock he needed to throw. "Yes."

"Did you bond with her?"

"No." He hadn't gotten the chance...Hell, he hadn't wanted to. He'd wanted blood and sex from her, but not a lifetime commitment. And even then...the desire for sex hadn't even been a fraction as intense as what he wanted from Sin.

"Did she die?"

"Yes."

"Your fault?"

"Yes."

He expected her to react with disgust, but she just cocked her head, stared at him, and then gave a definitive nod.

"I've killed a few dudes after I slept with them. Mostly it was because they tried to kill me." She shrugged. "It happens. You shouldn't punish yourself."

It was his turn to stare. Every time he thought he had her figured out, she did a one-eighty and reacted in the exact opposite way he'd anticipated. He loved that. No one had ever kept him on his toes the way she did. Even if she was utterly annoying about it.

"I knew better, Sin. I knew what would happen if I fed from her too many times, and I did it anyway. I wanted to take feeding to the very edge, to see how far I could go without crossing the line. I played with her life, and she's the one who lost."

"And that was how long ago? Have you done it since?"

"It was eight centuries ago, and no." He pinned her down with his eyes, making damn sure she understood what he was saying. "Until you."

Oh, yeah, she got it, inhaled a ragged breath and swallowed hard. "Are you..."

"Close." Too fucking close. Even now he was inching toward her, his mouth watering.

"And what, exactly, does that mean?"

"It means I have an overwhelming desire for your blood. *Only* your blood. Eventually, feeding from anyone else will make me sick. Probably already will. The addiction grows with each feeding. It's like a drug. I'll need more and more, until I can't stop."

"Is the only way out to kill the female or to bond?"

"It's possible to detox. But it takes a long, miserable time. Some dhampires have died before the addiction broke." Kicking the habit wasn't easy, and even once it happened, dhampires couldn't so much as be in the same room as the female whose blood addicted him, or it started up again, even more fiercely.

"Well, I guess it's a good thing the virus is out of your blood."

"Thank the gods." He gestured toward the back door before he lost himself to temptation again. "We'd better go." He paused. "How long before you need sex again?"

"Several hours, probably. You seem to have some powerful juice."

It was such a male thing to puff up with pride over that, and sure as shit, he did. "I'm not surprised."

She rolled her eyes. "Of course you aren't."

"Ah, hey..." He eyed her curiously, realizing that what

he was about to ask her probably wouldn't rub her the wrong way, but he wasn't sure he truly wanted to know the answer. "What about vampires? Pure vamps. Does their...juice...work for you?"

"It does," she said, and he had to bite back a growl at the unwelcome images burning into his brain. "The effect just doesn't last very long."

Not surprising. Vampires didn't produce sperm, but since they ingested blood and any other liquid they wanted to drink, their bodies produced fluids like anyone else's. They could cry, piss, spit, and ejaculate, all in smaller quantities.

"Why do you ask?"

"Curious."

She started toward the concealed door at the rear of the house with a shake of her head. "You medical people are way too curious about stuff like that."

Funny, but even though he'd been working as a paramedic for years, he hadn't ever considered himself a "medical person." The job had been...a job. A hobby with a bonus of a massive danger element involved, which was cool. But now that he thought about it, the life had seeped into his bloodstream, and the fact that half of his favorite TV shows were on the Discovery Health channel should have been a clue.

The other half of his favorite shows were on the Playboy channel. He mentally measured Sin for a naughty nurse outfit, and when she gave him a sultry glance from over her shoulder but kept walking, her rear swaying temptingly, he knew he'd been caught.

"I'm a succubus," she called out in a teasing, singsong voice. "I know what you're thinking."

"Of course you do," he muttered as she opened the

door, which was concealed on the outside by a vine-covered trellis. As they stepped out, he halted, sniffed the wind, but nothing unusual was on the crisp, morning air.

"Do you sense anything?"

"No," she said, "but—" She cut off with an *oof*, and he whirled to her, a cry of his own somehow making it past his heart, which had jammed up in his throat.

Sin staggered backward, her face pale and twisted by pain, her chest caved in by what looked like a pool table's eight-ball—with spikes. It was a demon weapon, designed to punch through armor and skulls. Once the victim was impaled, the spikes would grind, slowly, so the victim died in excruciating pain.

Sin sank to her knees, her mouth working soundlessly. Fear strangled him as he hooked her beneath her arms and dragged her inside the house.

"Sin? *Sin!* Hold on. Just...hold on." *Shit!* He lay her on the braided carpet in the living room as gently as he could. Blood streamed from her mouth, and each breath wheezed loudly through her closing airway.

Oh, gods, she couldn't die now. She'd been through too much, had led a miserable life, and she deserved better than this. Fighting the urge to panic, he called on all his medical training and reached deep for the clinical detachment he always had when treating patients.

It didn't work. Inside, he was terrified. Outside, he was sweating bullets. But at least his voice was level, and he hoped Sin was fooled.

"I can't remove the thing," he said calmly. "You'll bleed out. I'm going to get help."

Her trembling fingers closed around his wrist. "No," she rasped. "Too...dangerous."

"If I don't, you'll die." This time, his voice wasn't so calm.

"Don't...leave...me."

They always leave me. A lump formed in his throat. "Listen to me, Sin. I swear, I'll come back. I won't leave you."

A single tear dripped down her cheek as he squeezed her hand and leaned over to brush his lips across hers. A deep, primal rage rose up in him. He would get her brothers, and he would tear apart the bastard who had done this to her.

The pounding on Eidolon's apartment door came as he was getting ready to leave for the hospital. At this hour of the morning, pounding was not good. He was getting a late start, but he'd been up until three A.M. with a full emergency department. Diseased and injured wargs had been crammed into every nook and cranny, and as he was leaving, injured demons had come in as well—demons caught up in the escalating warg civil war.

The only good thing that had happened in the last few hours was that his father had gotten Eidolon, Wraith, and Con a reprieve from torture, and he'd pulled some strings and gotten the Carceris to lay off until Justice Dealers could determine whether or not the Warg Council had a case against Sin. It wasn't much, but at least she didn't have to run from the demon jailers for now.

He just wished he'd hear something from her.

Tayla answered before he did, but her shout kicked him into high gear, and he jogged down the hall, nearly tripping over Mange as the dog darted between rooms, chasing Mickey, Tayla's ferret. Eidolon cursed when he saw Con standing in the foyer, bloody and holding his arm at an awkward angle.

"What happened? Where's Sin?" Eidolon caught Con by the wrist and powered his gift into him. Con hissed as the pain started.

"Call your brothers. Come with me. She's dying."

"I'm on it," Tay said as she flipped open her cell phone. "I'll have them meet us at the 84th Street Harrowgate."

The desire to rush to Sin's rescue was nearly overwhelming, but after years of yanking Wraith out of deadly situations, he'd learned to be prepared. "Tell me what happened," he said with a calm he didn't feel, but Con jerked away.

"We have to go. Now!"

The guy's eyes were wild, his panic rattling Eidolon as much as anything. Con was always level. Gently but firmly, Eidolon shoved him against the wall and started the healing process again. "Listen to me. You're no good to her if you're dead. This will just take a minute."

"She might not have a minute," Con rasped, but he didn't fight. "She's been hit by an *exomangler*. It's ripping her apart."

Eidolon's blood pressure bottomed out. He'd seen the damage those things caused, and it wasn't pretty. "What happened to you?"

"Had to go through a forest full of assassins, all lined up to kill Sin."

Tay came down the hall, her blood-wine hair up in a ponytail. She was dressed for battle, including red leather pants, jacket, and weapons tucked everywhere. "All your brothers are on the way."

Eidolon breathed a sigh of relief. He'd expected Lore

and Wraith, but Shade was iffy. He wouldn't want to leave Runa and the kids.

"Wraith is leaving Serena and Stewie with Runa, and Kynan will stay in the cave, too."

Good. Nothing was getting past Ky. Eidolon checked his watch. Gem was on shift at the hospital, so no worries there, and Idess was all but living at UG because of the overload of souls needing guidance out of the hospital and into the light. It was also the safest place for her now that she was basically human, and the assassins after Sin had taken a new tack to get her by using family.

Con's last wounds sealed up, and they were out of there. They met Eidolon's brothers at the Harrowgate just as E's cell rang. Gem.

He flipped open the phone. "Quickly."

"The disease is affecting born wargs now," Gem said.

Eidolon's chest constricted, and he could barely speak. "What happened?"

"It's Bastien." There was a rare hitch in her voice. "It seems to be moving even faster than the original strain. E... he's not going to make it."

Holy hell. "I'll be there as soon as I can."

The call-waiting beep sounded as he entered the Harrowgate, and he switched over.

"It's Arik. We have trouble."

"Thank you, master of the obvious. My hospital is overrun by victims of the warg conflict. I have to go—"

"It's not that. SF... it's affecting born wargs now."

Eidolon slapped his hand on a glowing patch in the black stone that amounted to a Hold button for the Harrowgate door, which, if closed, would cut off the phone's signal. "Fuck me, I know."

"Not in this lifetime." Arik took a deep breath. "Our specialists are freaking out. Born wargs share a lot of genetic code with wolf-shifters. Wolf-shifters share a lot of genetic material with leopard and other shifters. And as you know, all shifters are related in some way to anything that can shift."

Iced adrenaline trickled into Eidolon's system. "You think SF is going to jump species."

"Yes. And once that happens, there's nothing to stop it from jumping to humans."

Or to any other creature on the planet.

Including Sems.

Someone had run over Kar with a truck while she was asleep. That had to be what had happened, because she'd woken up on Luc's couch feeling like, well, she'd been run over by a truck.

She'd followed him upstairs and ignored his stomping around while she showered and dressed in a pair of his sweats and a green flannel shirt, both of which swallowed her whole. He'd thrust a bowl of stew at her, stared until she ate it—and then watched, wide-eyed, as she promptly threw it all up.

The morning-sickness thing was weird—she'd had a couple of bouts of nausea around the time she found out she was pregnant, but she'd been fine since. She would have chalked it all up to nerves, except that now she was so miserable that death was starting to look good.

"Kar?" Luc's deep voice was a strangely soothing murmur in her ear. "You were moaning in your sleep... *Holy fuck*, you're hot."

"Not hot," she mumbled. "Cold. Need a blanket."

She heard him shuffling around, felt a blanket come down over her, and then he was nudging her head up. "Hey. I have some Tylenol. You need to take it."

Her stomach rolled. And then she coughed...so hard her ribs screamed. "Luc...do I have an infection? From the gunshot?"

"You shouldn't. It healed with your shift." He frowned as he thumbed up her eyelids. "Your pupils are dilated." He sank down next to the couch and peeled the blanket away from her chest. "I'm going to take a look at you."

She felt her shirt being unbuttoned, and despite her misery, she smiled. "Any excuse to get your hands on me."

"I don't need an excuse. You're easy."

"You—" Her eyes flew open, but when she saw the rare smile turning up his lips, she knew he'd been teasing her. Which was weird, because she would not have taken him as the playful kind. "You should smile more often."

"Can't." He grunted as he opened her shirt to expose her chest. "My face might freeze like that."

She laughed, but immediately cried out at the pain that wrenched through her abdomen.

"Shit." Luc jerked his hands away from her. "Did I hurt you?"

"No," she croaked. "Hurt to laugh."

His gaze swept her with the intensity of an X-ray machine, and she suddenly felt like he was seeing all the way through her. "I'm sorry. About everything."

About the baby, was what he meant. "Don't be." She swallowed, and grimaced at the sudden soreness. "The sex was great. You were only my second, but it was so...

good." Another swallow, another grimace. "And the baby is the best, most normal thing that's happened to me in years."

Luc averted his gaze, so it was impossible to tell what he was thinking as he finished unbuttoning her shirt. He peeled the flaps open to reveal an odd bruise around her navel... and the color drained from his face.

"What?" she whispered. "What is it?"

"SF. Jesus Christ, I think you have the virus."

Sixteen

Massive bleeder. Pulmonary contusion. Pneumothorax.

Voices and strange words pierced Sin's fog of pain. She thought she heard Con, and maybe Shade. Or Eidolon? A sudden, hot agony electrified her body, and she screamed. And screamed.

Until blackness took her.

Waking up took a long time. Between the buzz in her ears and the raw ache in her throat, it seemed as though she was stuck in a state of nothingness for an eternity. Gradually, she became aware that she was sore, thirsty, and on a bed. She blinked, opened her eyes. She was in Rivesta's master bedroom. Standing around her were her brothers. All of them. And Tayla. And Con.

"What...happened?" Her voice sounded rusty. Beat up. And it became even more so when Con sank onto the bed next to her and took her hand. His fingers slid over her wrist as if checking her pulse, but unlike the times he'd done it in the past, there was more tenderness than professionalism in his touch. "Why are you all here?"

"One of Bantazar's assassins hit you with an *exomangler*," Lore said. "He's dead."

"A lot dead." Wraith snorted and high-fived Lore. "Massive deadness."

Sin could only imagine. And boy, was her imagination entertaining. Bantazar really was a grade-A prick, and his assassins weren't any better. He was probably still pissed that she hadn't taken him up on his offer to screw him for the names of assassin masters who were bidding on the big werewolf contract.

She rubbed her chest, where she remembered being hit by something that had felt like a cannonball. Aside from a little tenderness, she'd never have known she'd nearly had a tunnel drilled through her.

But…wait…the tenderness…there was something deeper there, and abruptly, she drew a harsh breath. It was the sensation of losing a lot of assassins. Unfortunately, she wouldn't know who until she got back to the den or talked to someone who knew.

Right now, it wasn't important, anyway. Fewer people trying to kill her was a good thing.

She put the dead assassins out of her mind and cast her gaze between her brothers. "So you all came?"

"It's what we do," Eidolon said simply.

Uh-huh. There was a catch. There had to be. "Okay, so you healed me. Thank you. What now?"

Wraith looked up from studying her Gargantua-bone dagger. "How did you escape the infernal fire?"

"Infernal fire?" She frowned, and then that horrible screech she'd heard at Con's house pierced her memory as if the sound were right there in her ear. "Holy shit, that's what destroyed Con's house?"

Con cursed. "I should have known. I've seen what that shit does."

"So have I," Wraith said. "But I've never seen anyone escape it."

"Con's escape tunnel," Sin muttered. "The heat couldn't get to us, and by the time we were out of it—"

"We were too far away from the house for the spirits to grab."

"Someone wants you really dead," Wraith said.

"Okay, so now that you've saved my life and pointed out the glaringly obvious, why are you still here?"

They all exchanged glances, which couldn't be good. Finally, Shade cleared his throat. "Con said you healed a warg."

"Did he also tell you what happened to her?"

"Yeah," Eidolon said. "But I'm not sure how much difference her survival would have made. The virus has mutated. It's affecting born wargs now."

The information drilled a hole in her more efficiently than the *exomangler* had. She exhaled shakily and tried to keep her voice above a whisper. "So what now?"

"We're going to have to take some drastic measures. We can't afford to waste more time looking for infected wargs, and it's getting too dangerous for you. I got the Carceris off your back temporarily, so we'll bring you into the hospital and find some volunteers to infect and then cure, so I can work with the killed virus."

"Getting volunteers to be willingly infected with a fatal disease won't be easy." Con shifted on the mattress, causing her to roll toward him a little more. The contact comforted her, made her wish he'd stretch out beside her.

"Want me to grab a volunteer?" Wraith asked, and Sin had a feeling his "volunteer" wasn't going to be a willing one.

Con's mouth tightened. "I can point you toward a couple of Warg Council members I'd like to 'volunteer.'"

"We're not forcing anyone." Sin sat up and grimaced. Someone had put her into clothes that weren't hers. Which made sense, given that everything she owned was at the assassin den. But whose brilliant idea had it been to put her in a hideous, pink, floral T-shirt? With *glitter*. At least the jeans fit. "I've fucked over enough people with this."

"How about Luc?" Wraith sprawled in the bedside chair, legs spread, arms splayed wide, as if he didn't have a care in the world. "He's running on borrowed time as it is."

Lore swung around to him. "Why's that?"

"He made me swear to kill him when he lost his humanity. Which pretty much happened when Aegi scum killed his would-be mate."

"Hey," Tayla huffed. "Aegi scum present, you know."

Wraith grinned, and Sin got the impression that those two took a lot of pleasure in needling each other. "So let's say we get our volunteer," she said, "cure the disease, and a truce is called in the civil war. Will the Warg Council still want my head?"

Con reached for a glass of water sitting on the bedside table, and handed it to her. "I'll talk to them."

"And the chances of them backing off?" Shade asked.

Con's expression was grim. "Not good." He stroked the back of her hand absently, but Sin noticed that her brothers' eyes zeroed in on the action. Impossible to tell what they were thinking. Well, Wraith was clearly amused, but the others...not so much. "As soon as you find a volunteer and we confirm a cure, I'll go to them. I have a little clout and some of the members owe me."

Sin's eyes stung. He was willing to use up some favors for her? All of these guys were willing to help her? Once again, emotion overwhelmed her, and she vaulted out of bed. "I need a glass of water."

Never mind that she had one in her hand. She needed to get out of there. She was on emotional overload and short-circuiting was a danger.

She took the stairs down two at a time and darted into the kitchen, where she backed into a corner and stood there, panting, wondering what in the hell was going on with her. She didn't know how long she'd been there when she heard someone coming down the steps. Too light for any of the guys.

Tayla.

"I'm surprised they sent you," Sin said when Tay entered the kitchen. "I was betting on Lore or Shade."

"I had to convince those two to stay." Tay rolled her eyes. "Which was easier than convincing Con not to chase you."

For some reason, that made Sin all warm and fuzzy.

"Eidolon, of course, wanted to come check your vitals. I think Wraith just wanted to make fun of you."

Sin snorted. "And you?"

Tayla's hand dropped to her thigh holster, where the hilt of a dagger protruded from its leather housing, and Sin instinctively tensed. But the slayer's fingers only played with the sleek wooden handle. Still, her gaze was steady, fearless, focused like green laser beams, and the way she was studying Sin was almost adversarial.

"Wraith and I don't agree on much," she said slowly, "but we do have a meeting of the minds—feeble as his is—when it comes to protecting the family."

Okay, Sin knew where this was going. "And you're afraid I'm going to hurt my brothers. Yeah, yeah, Wraith already gave me the hurt-them-and-you'll-be-sorry speech, so save your breath."

Tayla's fingers continued to caress the weapon. "Look, I know you don't want to talk—"

"You don't know anything," Sin snapped.

One eyebrow arched up. "I think you'd be surprised."

"Really? Why don't you share."

Tayla hopped up on the table and folded her hands in her lap as though settling in for a nice, long lecture. Great. "Okay, here's the deal. My mom was a junkie. I was born on the floor of an abandoned warehouse, addicted to heroin. I grew up in foster homes and on the streets. I was abused. I did drugs. I stole. I was always in a lot of trouble. When I was a teenager, I watched my mom be torn apart by a demon. A Soulshredder. After that, I was even angrier. I joined The Aegis and killed every demon, vampire, and shapeshifter I could get my hands on. Eventually, I met Eidolon, discovered I had a twin sister, and learned the demon who tortured my mom was also my father. How's that for a start?"

Christ. No wonder Tayla's emerald eyes were those of a warrior. She might not be as old as Sin, but she'd fought just as hard to survive. Grudging respect for her sister-in-law softened Sin's demeanor. "You have my attention."

"Good. Because I was royally pissed off for a long

time. At the world, at humans, at demons. I hated everyone and everything."

"Yeah, well, that's the difference between you and me," Sin said, crossing her arms over her chest. "I don't hate the world."

"No, you just hate yourself." Before Sin could even attempt to deny that, Tay asked, "What do you think of Lore?"

Sin blinked at the rapid change of subject. "What?"

"Lore. Do you respect his feelings? Do you think he's a bad judge of character?"

"I've always trusted his judgment. Why?"

"Because he loves you. So if he's a good judge of character..."

Sin rolled her eyes. "Please. Spare me the psychobabble and pep talk. I'm not going to off myself or anything. I'm free now, and life is good."

"Is Con part of it? Your good life?"

Butterflies flitted in Sin's stomach. The sensation was weird, almost panic-inducing, but at the same time, it was strangely...pleasant.

"I don't know what you're talking about."

Tayla leveled a flat stare at Sin. "I'm neither blind nor stupid. I saw the way you freaked when he offered to do something nice for you."

"Doesn't matter. He doesn't want me. Not like that."

"How many bullshit flags do I have to throw down? You didn't see him when he got to our apartment. He was terrified for you. I thought he was going to explode out of his skin while the boys were working on you. And just a minute ago, I saw how he looked at you. He might not want to admit it, even to himself, but there's something there. Let him in, Sin. I know it's hard. Giving myself to Eidolon was the toughest thing I've ever done. But I haven't regretted it. Not once. Con's a good guy, and you can also trust your brothers."

God, this was getting so old. "I don't need—"

"I know. You don't need them." Sarcasm laced Tayla's words. "You don't need anyone. But you know what? They need you."

"Why does everyone keep saying that?" Sin slammed her glass of water on the counter, sloshing liquid everywhere. "They've done fine without me."

There was a long silence, and then Tayla smiled, but it was a sad upturn of her lips. "No, they haven't. Their sick, twisted brother, *your* brother, Roag, nearly destroyed their lives. And he tortured and killed Shade's sister. But in a way, he brought Lore and you to them. If they can turn Roag's deeds into something positive...Let's just say they need that." She closed her eyes and took a ragged breath. "My father was a monster. I can still taste my mom's blood on my tongue because it was so thick in the air. But because of him, I have a sister. The fact that some tiny bit of good came out of the horrors he inflicted on me and my mother has kept me sane and kept me from wasting my life on bitterness."

Sin turned away, unable to think too hard about what Tayla had said. Because for as much as Tayla and Sin had in common, they couldn't be more opposite. Sin *had* wasted her life on bitterness.

Maybe Tayla was right. Maybe it was time to accept the good things that had come into her life instead of shoving them away. Her brothers were tight, and though things had been rough for a while, the way they'd ultimately accepted Lore into the fold was absolute, like he'd never been missing. Maybe they'd accept her like that.

A strange frisson of longing shot through her. She hadn't had a family, a real family, in more than a hundred years. Then again, the very idea made her break out into a cold sweat.

And then there was Con. She'd told him things she'd never told anyone. She'd done things with him she'd never done, and her body heated at the memories. He'd protected her when he could have killed her. He forced her to confront things she didn't want to . . . and even though it totally wasn't cool, no one else had ever bothered to go that far with her. Not even Lore, who wanted to be close but was too afraid of pushing her away.

Con pushed, and instead of running, she'd pushed right back.

"Sin?" Tayla's hand came down on Sin's shoulder. "Are you okay?"

Instead of replying, Sin asked a question of her own. "How did you let Eidolon in?"

A blast of affection flowed over Sin like a blanket, and that weird, warm longing came back. "I realized I was a better person when I was with him. So I told him my darkest secrets. I let him see the worst sides of me. And he wanted me more than ever."

Sin had already told Con her secrets. He'd seen her at her worst.

And he'd said he wouldn't leave her.

She turned around, looked at Tayla. Looked at the stairs that led to the room where her brothers and Con were gathered. Where they'd taken care of her. Saved her life.

She was in a house full of people who were there for

her. The knowledge leveled her. Laid her out like she'd been kicked in the head.

She really did have a family, and the emotional tether between her and them was getting stronger. Tightening. But would it become an embrace, or a noose?

⌒

Con paced in the bedroom, weaving between the Sem brothers as he waited for either Tayla or Sin to return. Relief that she'd survived the assassin attack was tempered by the fact that she seemed to have reverted to her distant self, the Sin that no one could get through to.

Maybe Tayla was having some luck. He didn't know the Guardian well, but he did know she was tough, and she hadn't had an easy life. It was possible that she could relate to Sin on a female level no one else could.

The brothers were all watching him speculatively, but he ignored them. "Those bastards we killed outside the house, they were all assassins?"

Lore nodded. "I checked their bonds. The ones who hadn't disintegrated before I got to them, anyway. Three worked for two different masters, but the other four belonged to Sin."

"Son of a bitch." He paused. "Did you see a dude on a stallion?"

The brothers all shook their heads. "Why?" Lore asked.

"I saw what looked like a knight on a horse when my house was firebombed. He barely missed Sin with an arrow, and then when we were under attack at the warg settlement, he saved us. I'm confused as hell. Do you know of any assassins who work from horseback?"

Lore folded his arms over his chest, which was criss-crossed by a loaded weapons harness. Not even Wraith was that well armed. Of course, Wraith didn't need to be. "No, and that would be a stupid way to do business for an assassin. Not very subtle."

"We need to get Sin out of here," Con said. "It's only a matter of time until assassins get past Rivesta's barrier."

Eidolon nodded. "We'll get her to the hospital. She'll be safe there." He turned to Wraith. "See if you can find Luc. If he's cool with it, we can run the infection experiment on him."

"He's not going to be cool with it," Wraith said. "But I'll see what I can do."

No, Con did not see Luc volunteering. The guy was truly an *all-for-one-and-one-for-me type*, and risking his life for complete strangers wasn't in him. And though Con might not say it to Luc's face, he really didn't want the warg to volunteer. Luc had grown on him. Like a fungus, maybe, but still...he'd grown.

"How's the virus?" Eidolon asked Con. "In you. Is it under control?"

Jesus, how could he have forgotten to mention that earlier? "It's gone. Since last night."

"Then you won't feed on Sin anymore, right?" Shade's dark eyes fixed on Con, and somehow...Shade knew. He was well aware of the addiction issues. But how?

Con glanced between the other brothers, but as far as he could tell, they didn't know, nor had they picked up on Shade's underlying concern. "I don't need her blood anymore," he assured the demon. "Now, we'd better go."

Shade blocked the door. "Hold on, dhampire." The shadows in the male's eyes writhed madly, and Con knew what was up before Shade said it. "So you're done with the feedings. But what else is going on with you and her?"

A knowing smile curved Wraith's mouth. "Duh. He's boning her."

"How serious is it?" Lore asked, and no, this wasn't embarrassing at all.

"There's nothing going on." He hoped he sounded more convincing to them than he sounded to himself, because there *was* something going on between them, no matter how much he tried to keep it from happening.

"Good," Shade said. "You know I like you, man. But you have...issues. If you hurt her..."

Shade didn't need to finish his sentence, because the warning in the brothers' eyes said it all. Con would die. Painfully.

Lore moved forward, and Con stiffened. "You've been taking care of her. Thank you. But you should know that if you're looking for anything other than sex from her, you're not going to get it."

For some bizarre reason, that struck a nerve. Sin was more than a hole to drill, and though Con got what Lore was trying to say, it still shifted his temper into overdrive as his own shame over how he'd once treated her heated his cheeks.

"Yeah?" he spat. "And why is that? Maybe it's because you abandoned her when she needed you the most, and now she thinks everyone will do the same?"

The temperature in the room dropped to subarctic levels, and a range of emotions, from guilt to fury, crossed Lore's face. "You don't know what the fuck happened."

Con got right up in Lore's grille, his anger mounting as everything Sin had told him roared back. Instinct made him want to defend her, avenge her, and prove that Lore was wrong about getting nothing but sex from her.

Even though Lore had to be right.

"I know that people owned her, tortured her. I know she cradles her dagger like a stuffed animal when she sleeps because she doesn't feel safe. I know you left her like a coward and then sat on your ass feeling sorry for yourself while she was fighting just to survive—"

Lore's gloved fist slammed into Con's jaw. Con lurched backward, caught himself, and returned fire with a jab to the gut and an uppercut to the chin. He ducked another of Lore's punches, but took a boot in the chest hard enough to make him suck air.

"Stop it!" Sin rammed Lore into the wall and turned on Con, shoving him against the opposite wall. "What's this about?"

"Just a little alpha posturing." Lore shot Con a glare, and Con nearly went at him again.

Sin narrowed her eyes at both of them, then settled on Con. "Just keep in mind that Lore is not a warg. Winning a fight does not give you special privileges."

Con blinked and then grinned as the impish twitch of Sin's mouth brought dawning realization—she remembered the battles followed by sex in the warg village.

Lore dabbed blood from his mouth with the back of his bare hand. "What the hell are you smiling about?"

"Trust me, you don't want to know." Then, in front of everyone, he grabbed Sin and kissed her, not caring—actually, taking a perverse pleasure in the fact—that her brothers were tense as nocked arrows. "You," he said against her lips, "are wicked."

And he was so screwed.

Seventeen

"Go to hell, Valeriu. And take the Sigil with you." Kynan slammed the satellite phone down so hard that a piece of plastic snapped off it and pinged off the stone wall of Shade's Central American cave. Cursing, he checked to make sure the phone still worked. It did, but damn, he was pissed. Beyond pissed. And he hoped to hell Serena hadn't heard him telling her father to bend over for Satan's big stiffie.

But fuck if he was going to take orders from the R-XR again.

Picking up the phone, he sank down on the leather couch that ran the length of the cave's living room wall. He started to dial Tay's cell phone number... and froze at the hair-raising rumble of a growl.

The women had heard the intruder before Kynan did. It wasn't that he wasn't alert; it was just that Serena was a vampire with uber-sharp senses, and Runa was a werewolf with ultra-sensitive hearing even when she was in human form.

Which she wasn't right now.

Runa, thanks to military experimentation immediately after she was bitten by a warg—Luc—had been altered. She still shifted into a raging beast on the three nights of the full moon, but she could also shift at will. The way she just had.

Her snarls echoed off the smooth rock walls of the cave. Kynan, drawing his Sig, darted to the kitchen, where Runa was standing on two strong, toffee-furred legs, teeth bared. Behind her, Serena, fangs bared, blocked the door-way to the bedroom, where Runa and Shade's triplets, and Serena and Wraith's son, were sleeping.

The narrow entryway filled as someone stepped inside. Kynan held his breath, letting his finger ease from the trigger guard to the trigger.

He damn near sighed with relief when Runa's brother and Kynan's old Army buddy Arik stepped out of the shadows. Arik wore a standard-issue beige T-shirt with his cammie BDU pants, an M-9 Beretta at his hip, but his hands were empty, and when he held them up, Ky lowered the weapon.

"Take it easy." Arik's voice was the calm, soothing drawl of a police negotiator talking someone off a ledge. But Ky knew Arik well enough to recognize a rare note of stress. "I'm not here to take you in, Runa."

Kynan angled his body so he could cover the cave entrance. "Are you alone?"

"Of course I am," Arik snapped. His muscled arms bunched up hard, as though he was prepared to end any further doubt with his fists. Because of the charm, Kynan couldn't be injured—unless he *wanted* to be injured. He hadn't had a decent challenge in months, and he almost hoped Arik would throw a punch just so Ky could work off some aggression.

For a long moment tension circulated in the cool air, and then Runa shifted back into her petite human form. Ky and Arik averted their gazes as Serena handed her a robe to replace the clothes that had been shredded by her shift. One of the babies started crying, and Serena disappeared back into the bedroom.

"I'm sorry, Arik," Runa said, the rustle of cloth on skin mingling with her voice as she shrugged into the robe. "You startled us. And the R-XR does want me as a lab rat."

He had the grace to blush. "It's not an issue now."

"So, what, have I been given a pass? And you can look at me now."

Arik's mouth tightened into a grim line. "You haven't been given a pass."

Runa froze as she tugged her caramel-colored hair out of the back of the robe, and Ky's pulse picked up. He didn't want to believe that the man who used to be his friend had come to grab his own sister, but a lot of things he hadn't wanted to believe had proved to be true over the last couple of years.

"Why are you here?" Kynan tapped the pistol against his thigh, drawing Arik's gaze. "You've got five seconds to fill us in."

Arik's pause lasted four. "I refused to give up Runa's location, and they threatened to lock me up until all of this is over. So I walked."

"You're AWOL?"

Arik nodded, and Ky let out a low whistle. Absent without leave was a serious offense in the regular military. But from the R-XR? The paranormal unit played for keeps and without oversight. It could do anything it wanted to Arik, and no one would argue or even know.

The only thing that might save him was that the people who worked for the R-XR were specialists and worth their weight in gold. And Arik, an ex–Delta Force operative who could learn any demon language after hearing only a few words, was priceless.

Runa ran to Arik and folded him into her embrace. "You can stay here, Arik. For as long as you need to."

Arik cocked a dark eyebrow at Kynan. "And what does your bodyguard have to say about that?"

"Brother," Kynan drawled, "it ain't me you need to worry about."

"Shade will be fine," Runa said, as she drew away, and Ky hoped she was right. Arik and Shade weren't the best of friends; Arik still hadn't forgiven Shade for his role in turning Runa into a werewolf, and Shade had a total distrust of the R-XR.

"Do I get to see my nephews?"

"They're in the bedroom with Stewie." Runa's champagne-colored eyes lit on a rattle on the floor and then flicked back to her brother. "You haven't met Wraith's son, have you?"

"Nope."

"Okay, hold on a minute." Runa went into the bedroom, leaving Kynan and Arik alone.

Ky gestured for Arik to follow him into the living room. Once there, Ky pivoted, putting himself in line to keep an eye on the doorway. "Tell me everything."

Arik rubbed his hand over his dark, military-short high-and-tight. "Have you spoken with the other Elders recently?"

"You could say that," Kynan said.

"Did they tell you The Aegis is taking orders from the R-XR now?"

"Val mentioned something about that. But I don't know why The Aegis is going to be the R-XR's bitch. We didn't get that far into the conversation."

Arik glanced through the doorway at the bedroom Runa had disappeared into. "You know born wargs are now being affected by SF, right?"

"Yeah. And there's a danger it'll jump species."

"There's no time left to find a cure."

Kynan exhaled slowly, as if that would put off what he knew was going to be very bad news. "What are you saying?"

"I'm saying," Arik said gravely, "that the powers that be are done waiting. They're mobilizing forces and joining up with The Aegis to go out on a search-and-destroy mission. If a cure for this disease isn't found *now*, they intend to eradicate every werewolf on the planet."

⌒

They had just gotten to the mountainside Harrowgate when Tay's phone rang. She peeled away from the group to answer, and through the static and in-and-out reception, she could barely hear Kynan's voice.

"Tay? Where are you?"

"Montana. Are Runa and the kids okay?"

"They're fine. But The Aegis has been trying to contact you—" As if on cue, her phone beeped, and the caller ID identified her supervisor, the head of the New York State cells.

"Yeah, Richard is on the other line—"

"Don't answer!"

Jesus. Okay...Ky never got excited like that. "Ky, you're making me nervous." He was making everyone nervous—they'd gathered around, and Shade was about to grab the phone from her.

"Look, I got a call from Val earlier. He said the R-XR and every military supernatural unit in the world is heading up an operation, and that The Aegis was going to be taking orders from them."

Tayla snorted. "Bullshit."

"That's what I said. Val told me to fall in line, and I told him to go to hell. Right after that, Arik showed up."

She lowered her voice and turned away so Shade wouldn't flip out. "At the cave?"

"Yeah. He's here because he refused to hand over Runa. Apparently, the R-XR and The Aegis are sending out extermination squads to kill all wargs, born and turned."

"Oh, shit." Tayla paused, the implications of what Kynan had just told her flashing like a movie in her head. A horror movie. The worldwide slaughter would be off the scale. "We've got to stop them."

"I tried," Kynan said. "I just got off a conference call with the Sigil."

"They're not listening to you?"

A sound of frustration came over the airwaves. "Tay, I used all my clout. I swore to leave the fucking organization, but they aren't budging. They're serious about destroying the wargs."

"Is that why Richard is calling? To get me to organize my cell for a warg hunt? Because I won't do it." Ky paused, and a chill skittered up Tay's spine. "Ky...what are you not saying?"

"They know you won't cooperate. Richard wants you to head back to your cell's HQ."

"And then what?"

"They plan to hold you until the massacre is over. They don't want you interfering. Tay, hold on." She stood there, stewing, while Ky spoke in low tones to someone else. When he came back on the line, he sounded like he was speaking between clenched teeth. "Arik's got some interesting intel. The R-XR indicated that there's a massive gathering of wargs in Canada. Do you know anything about it?"

"Canada?" She frowned, and then scowled when Con grabbed the phone from her.

"Kynan? What about Canada? Isn't that where you told the Warg Council there was a Feast warg?" Con listened for a moment. "She's a Guardian? And wait...what? Holy shit." Con closed the phone.

"What's going on?" Eidolon asked.

"Luc." His gaze drifted to Sin, and Tay recognized that look. The dhampire was falling, and falling fast. "We need to get to his place."

"Why?" Tayla was confused as all hell.

"Man, I can't believe I didn't put this all together sooner," Con said. "Luc...in Egypt. He banged this Guardian who was a werewolf—"

"We don't have any werewolf Guardians," Tay interrupted.

"Not that you knew of. Apparently, she was hiding it."

"You can't hide it. We make sure every Guardian works at least one night of the full moon."

Con nodded impatiently. "She's a special breed. They turn on the new moon. Kynan went to the Warg Council to ask about her. She was heading to the Northwest Territories. So the borns and turneds both sent out extermination squads to kill her. But the thing is, I think she was heading there because that's where Luc is. She's the werewolf he had sex with."

"So she's leading packs of werewolves right to him," Wraith said.

Con's voice went low. "And worse, both warg sides know the other one is there. They're amassing an army."

"That's where they're going to fight their civil war," Sin said, and uttered a dark curse. "Werewolf Armageddon."

Eighteen

"Well?"

Luc tossed a log onto the fire and cast a glance over his shoulder at Kar, who was curled up under a blanket on the couch. The fire was roaring hot, and Luc had moved the couch closer to the hearth, but she was still cold. It was all he could do not to stretch out with her and add his body heat to hers. He wanted to—if she had SF, he'd already been exposed. But she wouldn't let him come near.

The odd thing was, she wasn't nearly as sick as she should be if she'd contracted the disease. Maybe it wasn't SF. Or maybe it affected Feast wargs differently. Either way, he needed to get hold of Eidolon. He'd called the hospital and E's apartment, but nothing. And no one seemed to know where he was. Hell, he couldn't get hold of any of the brothers. Or Con. If he couldn't get hold of Eidolon soon, he was going to have to make a run for the Harrowgate in the daylight, slayers or no.

"Luc, we need to talk."

"You're sick. You need to rest."

She struggled to sit up, and he leaped to his feet to help her. "Don't touch me," she said, but it was too late. He eased her into a sitting position and stepped back.

"Kar, you really need to rest. If this is SF—"

"If it's SF," she said quietly, "then what I need to do is talk."

Well, that sobered him right up. She wanted to keep her mind off it, and he was a big bastard if he didn't let her. "Okay, yeah. What do you want to talk about?"

She looked at him like he was an idiot. How females could manage that even when they had exhaustion circles under their eyes and fever rashes on their cheeks, he had no idea. "Are you still singing that same tune? I can name fewer things we *don't* need to talk about than what we do."

"Is this about the kid? Because I don't see the big deal. You stay here, have it, and we raise it."

Kar buried her face in her hands and shook her head. "How long has it been since you were human?"

He blinked at that. "I was twenty-four when I was bitten. That was in 1918."

It was her turn to blink. "Wow. You're *old*."

"Thank you," he muttered.

"How have you managed to not knock up anyone else in all that time?" She narrowed her eyes at him. "Or do you have a bunch of puppies running around?"

He tossed another log onto the fire, even though it didn't need it. "No, I don't have any offspring."

"Do you remember what it was like to be a kid? To have parents?"

The fire crackled and hissed as though taunting him to answer Kar's idiotic questions. He grabbed up a poker and jabbed at the logs. "It was a long time ago."

"That's not what I asked," she said quietly.

"The turn of the century wasn't a good time to be the eighth son in a poor family." Not at all. He'd been raised on a farm in the Midwest, had been introduced to backbreaking work before he was three. His parents were as good as they could have been, but when every daylight hour was taken up with work, either on the farm or in the kitchen, there wasn't much time for play or hugs. At sixteen, he'd left home, joined the military, and never looked back.

Except…he had. The soldiers he'd fought with in France had become the tight-knit family he'd never had. At least, until they started dying in battle. A massacre had left him alone and injured, wandering through the woods in an attempt to escape the enemy. He'd been found, but not by a human foe.

A werewolf had attacked him. He'd managed to fight it off, but then he'd lain there, so mangled that when the human enemy did find him, they'd left him for dead.

He'd shifted into a werewolf that night, healing his wounds, and he'd awakened the next morning lying among the shredded remains of a dozen American soldiers.

Soldiers he'd killed.

Sickened, frightened, and confused, he'd gone AWOL. He barely remembered how he'd survived after that, running only on instinct and the desire to kill the monster who'd infected him. Three years later, his sire was dead, and Luc had returned to America.

"What happened?" Kar asked.

"I went to war, was bitten by a warg, and when I came

home, I learned that four of my brothers and sisters, and my mother, had died of influenza. My oldest brother was killed in a farming accident. And my father was nursing what was left of his mind."

Luc had tried to help, had chained himself in the barn on nights of the full moon, but in his third month, he'd broken free, killed livestock, and bit his youngest brother, Jeremiah. What happened next had pushed Luc over the edge and right into a solitary existence.

Jer had turned into a werewolf that next night, had killed their father and sister. When he woke up and realized what he'd done, he'd taken his own life.

Luc sank to the floor and leaned back against the couch cushions. "And because of me, because I bit my brother, I lost the rest of my family."

"Hey," Kar said gently, as she lay her hand on his shoulder. The intimate, comforting gesture startled Luc, made his throat close up a little. She had every reason to hate him, to use him for protection and nothing else, but she was still trying to make the best out of a shitty situation.

"What?" He pulled away, twisted around so he was facing her.

"I know you don't want this. A baby wasn't exactly on my to-do list, either." She rubbed her belly, and a tiny smile crimped her mouth. "But I love the little tadpole now. I want it, and I'll do anything to protect it. That means I'll protect it from you, too."

"You think I would harm my own kid?"

"Not intentionally. You'd be protective and fierce and possessive. But Luc, if you can't love it, if you can't connect with it, you *will* harm it."

Luc stared into the fire. The flames licked the logs,

eating at the wood and putting out so much heat that surely it could melt the wall of ice inside him. Kar was right. The kid would probably be human—it needed parents who could love it.

Which was why he'd been so okay with having cubs with Ula—she'd been *pricolici*, so the offspring would have been raised in the harsher world of the warg, where the males existed to protect, not nurture. Luc could definitely protect.

Nurture? He closed his eyes, but they flew open when Kar took his hand and placed it on her belly.

"You can't feel it yet. It's not even a bump. But it's there. Your baby."

Something inside him cracked a little. But that tiny fissure felt like an earthquake in his soul. *Your baby.* What if he didn't like it? What if he couldn't love it? He jerked his hand away like the thing inside was a viper.

"I...ah..." He leaped to his feet, at a complete loss. Then he spun toward the door. "Do you hear that?"

Kar looked up, her expression filled with skepticism. No doubt she thought he was trying to weasel out of the conversation. "Hear what?"

"I don't know. Could be a branch dropping from a tree." The storm had died down, leaving only silence in its wake. He eased cautiously to the window, but he kept his back to the wall as he peered out.

Kar pushed to her feet. "Do you see anything?"

A glint of metal against the field of white brought his hackles up. "Stay down."

Kar sank smoothly to her haunches, her Aegis training and warg instincts kicking in. "What is it?"

"I think the slayers have found you."

"Damn them," she breathed. "Where are your weapons?"

"You mean, besides the rifle and shotgun propped next to the door, the six other shotguns and pistols on the wall, and the crossbow in the corner stand?"

She gave him a dry look. "Yes, besides those."

"I have a chest full of various blades in my bedroom, and in the metal chest downstairs, I have dynamite."

"Seriously?" she asked, and when he grinned, she returned his smile. "Awesome."

He nearly laughed, something he hadn't done in a long time. But damn, how many females actually lit up like lanterns when you mentioned you had explosives in the house? "I need you to go downstairs and keep quiet. I'll see if I can get them out of here."

"I don't think so."

"Do it," he barked. "The basement is concealed—they might suspect you're here, but even if they come in, which they won't, they wouldn't be able to find you."

"Luc, I don't think that's a good idea." She eyed the weapons near the door. "I might be pregnant, but I'm not helpless."

"This isn't because you're pregnant." Humans treated pregnant women like they were made of glass, but even before he'd been turned, he'd known they were tougher than that—he'd seen his mother go through three pregnancies, working just as hard on the farm as his father had, right up until she went into labor. And warg mothers were even tougher than that, fighting and hunting until the day they gave birth.

"Then what?" Suddenly she stiffened, and a low, lethal growl rumbled in her chest.

"Kar? What is it?"

"Werewolves." Her eyes flashed, and her lips peeled back from her teeth. "It's not The Aegis. It's wargs. I feel them. A lot of them."

A block of ice dropped into the pit of Luc's stomach. "Exterminators. The teams they send to destroy Feast wargs." And then he felt it . . . a wave of violence crashing into him like a tsunami rising up out of hell. His blood thundered in his veins, his skin grew tight, and his joints stretched to the point of pain.

"Luc," Kar gasped, and he spun to her. She doubled over, clutching her stomach. "I feel . . . a shift. It's like I need to . . . kill."

When too many wargs got together to fight, everyone shifted, no matter the time of month, the time of day. Kar definitely didn't need to be out there killing with her venomous bite. "Get below!" His voice was distorted, mostly snarl, but she understood and crawled down to the basement. With long, claw-tipped hands, he slammed the hatch shut and rolled the rug over it.

Lurching, he threw open the door even as his body clenched, on the verge of contorting into his beast form.

The forest all around had come alive, was teeming with movement. On one side, *varcolac*, distinguishable from the born wargs by their varied sizes and colors of fur, and on the other side, *pricolici*, mostly dark, all massive, and ready to charge the others.

"What the hell!" Luc swung his head in the direction of the shout. Six humans—Guardians, if their wealth of weapons was any indication—stood near the river, in the middle of what was about to be tooth-and-claw hell.

Luc stepped outside just as the two warg sides met. The

Guardians sprang into action, sending crossbow bolts into the fray. But one wheeled toward Luc, pistol trained.

Luc's only thought as the bullet tore through his chest was that for years he didn't care if he lived or died. Now he cared, but it might be too late.

The Harrowgate opened up to snow on the ground, blinding sunlight in the sky, and the clean, crisp crack of gunshots on the wind.

Con plowed through the shin-deep snow at a near run, with Wraith on his heels. Sin, E, Lore, and Shade were close behind. Tayla had gone to UG to round up medics.

Don't be too late. Don't be too late...

As they got closer, the unmistakable sounds of battle vibrated the air. Screams, bloodcurdling snarls, and the scent of blood guided them. Luc's cabin was maybe fifty yards ahead when Con's muscles vapor-locked, and he gasped and tripped over his own feet as he stumbled into a tree. Sin caught him, her strong body bracing against him.

"What's wrong? Con?"

He couldn't answer. His throat had closed up so that the only sound he could make was a growl. He was shifting and there was nothing he could do to stop it. He could only lessen the damage, and as quickly as he could, he stripped out of his shirt and pants.

"What's going on?" Sin's voice seemed distant, and then Eidolon yanked her away.

"The warg battle. He's shifting. He'll be fine. We have to go—" The sound of gunfire cut him off, and then wood sprayed in shards next to Sin's head. "Shit! Slayers."

Slayers who had tried to kill Sin.

They tried to kill my female.

Didn't matter that the thought was insane. That it wasn't true. That it could never *be* true. Something dark reached up and grabbed Con, squeezed rational thought out of his brain, and before he'd even fully shifted, he launched himself at the group of humans engaged in battle with dozens of wargs. The scene was chaos—wargs fighting each other and slayers in snow that had turned to pink, bloody slush.

He leaped, mouth watering as he prepared to bite right through a slayer. In midair, a gray mass of fur broadsided him. The warg's teeth clamped onto his shoulder and his claws dug into Con's ribs, and crazily enough, it was the damned slayer who brought down a blade and separated the warg's head from his neck, probably saving Con's life.

Faintly, he heard Eidolon order his brothers to gather the Guardians without killing them, something about Tay and Ky wanting them alive, and then another *pricolici* slammed into Con, and nothing mattered but the battle. The crunch of bone between his teeth, the taste of blood on his tongue.

He didn't know how long the battle had raged when he felt a sting in his flank. Spinning, he rounded on the source... Sin?

She stood a few yards away, a crossbow trained on him. Searing agony stole his breath as his body turned inside out, twisting and morphing until he was back in his human form. She'd hit him with an Aegis morph dart, and damn, it hurt to shift with unnatural speed like that. He went to his knees, the icy snow scraping his bare skin. A god-awful snarl sounded behind him, and Sin, moving with catlike grace, launched a morning star at the charging warg while shooting another with the crossbow. The injuries wouldn't be fatal, but the wargs fell to the ground, incapacitated by her well-placed strikes.

"You're...damned good," he rasped.

The cold-induced blush in her cheeks gave her a fresh, playful expression as she tossed him his clothes. "I'm made of awesome." She offered him a hand. "Sorry about the dart, but Eidolon doesn't know which of these werewolves is Luc, and he needs your help." He could be macho and not take her help, but right now, his leg didn't feel stable, he was sore from a dozen claw and bite wounds, and, really, he'd take the excuse to touch her. "I thought shifting healed you."

The world tilted and spun a little, and shit, stop the ride, he was ready to get off.

"We all heal at different levels depending on our species and type of wounds. Trust me, I healed a lot in that shift." Not as much as he'd have liked, but at least he wasn't bleeding. He grunted and came to his feet. All around, the battle raged, and Sin took down another warg with a targeted shoulder shot as he plucked the dart out of his thigh and tossed it to the ground. "Has anyone checked the cabin for Luc?"

"Not that I know of." She frowned. "Looks like the *varcolac* are retreating."

Yeah, they were. The ground was littered with bodies and injured wargs, some of whom were starting to shift as the battle waned. He tugged on his jeans and whipped the shirt over his head. "Come on. Let's search the cabin."

Sin shook her head. "I'm going to help out the guys. You go." Before he could argue, she was off and running.

"Sin!" he called after her. "Be careful. You still have assassins after you."

She flashed him a wave with one hand and took down a warg with another.

Christ. The female was going to give him a heart attack.

Nineteen

Con sprinted to the cabin, his heart pounding at the sight of blood splashed on the snow, the door, and the entryway of the cabin. Luc lay stiffly on the floor, bleeding from an apparent gunshot wound to the chest.

"Hold still, buddy." Con sank down on his heels and slapped his hand over the bubbling wound. "Eidolon! Shade!" The brothers were still engaged in battle, now mostly defending the *varcolac* that were trying to flee.

Keeping an eye on the situation outside, because it would suck to get attacked while he was rendering aid, he ripped open Luc's shirt to expose the bullet hole. Luc moaned as Con performed a rapid exam, gently rolling the heavy-ass warg to check for an exit wound. Sure enough, the bullet had blasted a mangled hole through his shoulder blade.

Finally, the two demons jogged over, leaving Wraith, Sin, and Tayla to clean up. Looked like staff from UG had arrived, too. "What do we have?" E asked.

"GSW to the right upper chest. Through and through. He's got blood in his airway, and his breaths are rapid and shallow." Not that any of that mattered, since Shade and Eidolon would be able to get inside Luc and use their gifts to heal him quickly and efficiently.

They both palmed Luc's arms, the symbols on their right hands glowing intensely. Luc groaned, but his eyes were bright as they locked on Con's. He mumbled something about a car. "Under... the rug."

"Hey, man, it's okay—"

He shook his head. "Let her... out. Name's... Kar." *The Feast female.*

"We got Luc," Shade said. "Go ahead and handle whomever he's got stashed under the rug." Shade frowned down at the warg. "Hell's fires. You think you know someone..."

Eidolon muttered something about Shade's BDSM cave, but Con ignored them to roll back the thick, knotted rug. There was nothing there but wood planks.

Sin and Wraith stalked through the door, and behind them was Lore, hauling a medic duffel over his shoulder.

"UG staff is patching up wargs, and all surviving Guardians are tied up," Wraith said. "But they could probably use some medical attention. Especially the one dipshit with the idiotic Mohawk. He lost a lot of blood."

"Because you ate him," Sin said wryly.

Wraith blinked with exaggerated innocence. "Fighting makes me hungry."

Con's own mouth watered at the sight of Sin, all fresh from battle, her eyes bright and hair wild. She pointed at the floor. "Oh, secret door!"

"You can see it?"

"You can't?" Her expression of innocence matched Wraith's, and yes, those two were definitely related.

Lore punched her in the shoulder. "Stop being an imp." He moved toward Con and set the bag down on the floor. "Assassins are trained to recognize the spells cast around hidden entryways. Luc's secret door glows like a neon sign to us, but few others would see it. She's messing with you."

"You ruin all my fun." Sin scowled at her brother as she bent to trace her fingers along what Con assumed was the edge of the hidden door. Then she thumped her fist on a board. Thumped on another. And another. The third time was the charm, and suddenly, the door popped up, a three-by-three square. "And yes, I knew where all the secret doors at Rivesta's were. I just liked watching you look for them."

Sin really was an imp. Con peered down the hole, the darkness no match for his vamp vision. He didn't see anything, but he heard a heartbeat, soft breaths, and he smelled the bitter spice of anxiety.

And sickness.

"Kar?" he shouted down. "My name is Conall. I'm a friend of Luc's"—he ignored Luc's snort—"and it's safe to come up." There was no answer. He glanced at Sin. "I'm going down."

"Be careful."

"You two are just so cute," Wraith drawled.

Con ignored the demon and dropped into the hole, not bothering with the stairs. He landed in a crouch, fully prepared for the throwing knife that whooshed over the top of his head. He whirled to face the thrower, whose arm was cocked back and prepared to launch another blade. Before she could, he had her in a headlock and pinned, face-first, against the wall.

"Be nice," he growled into her ear. "I'm not going to hurt you."

She snorted. "What makes you think you could hurt me?"

Her arrogant, wiseass comment reminded him of Sin. "I'd ask who you are, but something tells me you wouldn't answer and I think I know anyway. I'm going to release you and head back upstairs, where Luc is being treated for a gunshot wound. If you want to see how he's doing, you'll come up, and you won't try to fillet me again."

She drew a harsh breath. "Is he okay? Who are you?"

He paused at the sound of Luc's ferocious curses from above. Luc was a terrible patient. "He'll be fine, I'm sure. He's got a doctor and medic from Underworld General working on him. I'm his ambulance partner. Now, are you going to play nice?"

She nodded, and he released her, stepping back quickly in case she decided to strike out. If she was anything like Sin, she'd nail him in the balls. Fortunately, she didn't attack. In fact, she remained against the wall, forehead against the stone, her body trembling.

"Hey. Are you okay?"

"Yeah." Squaring her shoulders, she swung around, and though she was pale and unsteady, she moved toward the ladder.

"You're sick."

"Just woozy from the shift."

Con got that, was still suffering the effects himself. But he sensed more was at play here, and the sharp tang of illness was in the air. He gestured for her to go first, and he followed.

When he emerged, Luc was sitting with his back braced against the wall, an IV attached to his arm, and

Lore, Shade, and Wraith had gone. Con must have had a questioning look on his face, because Sin said, "They're dumping the slayers in the nearest town. Wraith is going to scramble their memories so they don't remember what happened."

Eidolon looked up from mopping blood off Luc's chest. "You'll need to contact the Warg Council to have them collect the dead. We can't leave them here for humans to find. Not in these numbers."

Wargs were one of the few paranormal species that didn't disintegrate when they died in the human realm, which usually wasn't a problem because autopsies revealed nothing strange. But an investigation into a battle of this size wouldn't be good no matter how much damage control The Aegis applied.

Luc shifted his worried gaze to the female, whose sunken eyes and flushed skin were even more noticeable in the daylight. For as long as Con had known Luc, the warg had been a loner, and with the exception of one *pricolici* female, he'd never latched onto his bedmates. They were lays, and that was it.

But the way he was watching Kar, with hunger, a trace of affection, and a glint of shame, definitely made her more than a bedmate.

She moved to Luc, and though it was obvious that she wanted to touch him, she didn't. "Are you okay?" She swiveled around to Eidolon. "Is he?"

"He'll be fine," Eidolon said. "Sore, and we should get him to UG sooner than later, but yeah."

Luc dropped his head back against the wall as though exhausted, but Con sensed coiled tension in him. "Doc. You have to do something for Kar. She's sick."

"Sick?" Eidolon shoved to his feet. "With what?"

"I think it's the virus."

All heads swiveled toward Kar, and Con's gut twisted. "Must be early stages."

"Which means there's hope." Eidolon's voice gentled, but never lost the no-nonsense doctor edge. "Kar, do you mind if I take a look at you?"

She studied him warily. "You're a demon."

"I'll try to keep my forked tongue and cloven hooves out of sight," Eidolon said.

"Kar." Luc's voice was as soft and gentle as Con had ever heard it. "He's a doctor. The best person in the universe to handle anything you've got."

Doubt and suspicion warred in her expression, and then she gave a slow nod at Eidolon. "You should know that I'm pregnant."

Gods, it just kept getting worse. Sin closed her eyes, her shoulders sagging, and Con had the oddest urge to draw her into his arms. Though maybe it wasn't so odd anymore. He was much, much more deeply involved with her than he should be.

Eidolon guided Kar to the couch, retrieved a stethoscope and thermometer from the medical bag Lore brought, and began an exam. When he lifted her shirt and saw the faintest shadow of a bruise around her navel, he frowned. "This must be very early. When would you have been in contact with an infected warg?"

"Two weeks ago. My partner and I chased a demon into a sewer and were attacked by a sick warg. He clawed me, but when I didn't have any symptoms later, I figured he didn't have the disease."

Eidolon shook his head. "The timing isn't right. This

acts fast. You'd be dead by now if he was the one who infected you."

Kar shrugged. "I don't know what to tell you. I didn't go on any Aegis hunts after that, and then I've been locked up with Luc, so unless he has it, there's no way I got it from anyone else."

"Maybe the fact that you're a Feast warg is making the difference." He gestured to Sin. "Can you get inside and take a look?"

She nodded, sank to her knees beside Kar. "This shouldn't hurt." Gently, she gripped Kar's wrist, and her *dermoire* lit up. She closed her eyes, and for a good two minutes, she did nothing but scowl and shake her head. Then, suddenly, her eyes flew open and she sucked in a startled breath. "Oh, oh, man. E, *Kar* doesn't have the virus. The *baby* does."

"What?" Luc tried to absorb was Sin was saying, but he'd been in the medical field long enough to know that an unborn baby contracting a virus while the mother didn't was nearly impossible. "How?"

Eidolon repositioned himself to insert the tympanic thermometer into Kar's ear. "Sin, you're sure the virus is present only in the fetus?"

"I'll check again." Sin concentrated, her *dermoire* glowing fiercely. Her glyphs might be faded replicas of her purebred brothers', but they lit up just as brightly. "Yeah. Those little strands are running through the baby and floating around in the baby water."

"Amniotic fluid," Eidolon said. "How is the virus not moving through the placenta and umbilical cord?"

She shook her head, bit her lip, and the glyphs on her arm began to writhe. "What's the placenta? A pancake-shaped thing?" At Eidolon's nod, she frowned. "They're... getting attacked. By... I'm not sure what the things are. They're all in Kar's bloodstream but not the baby's."

"Antibodies," Eidolon breathed. "Holy shit, Kar is producing antibodies!"

Kar scowled. "I don't understand. What's happening?"

Eidolon's voice went deep, but with an undercurrent of excitement that gave Luc hope. "Up until now, no one who has contracted the virus has produced antibodies to it. But you... you're the exact opposite of a regular warg. It might be different if *you* had the virus, but since your baby does, your body is fighting it off. Is the father a warg?"

"It's mine," Luc said. Con's surprise was tangible, a burst of static in the air, but wisely, the dhampire kept any smart-ass comments to himself.

"Since you both turn at different times of the month, I'm going to guess that conception didn't take place during a breeding heat?" Eidolon asked. Kar blushed, turning her already fevered skin even redder, and she nodded. "Okay, then, this is starting to make sense. I know nothing about Feast wargs, but obviously, they can give birth to babies who are born wargs, even if the father is turned, and even out of heat. The virus must have entered your blood and passed to the baby, but in the meantime, your body produced antibodies, which killed the virus in you—"

"But not the baby," she finished. "Can you cure it? Can you save the baby?"

Luc didn't like the dismal expression on Eidolon's face. "Doc?"

"I don't know. Sin, how advanced does the disease seem?"

She shook her head. "Not very. It's weird. The virus is reproducing, but it's being killed, too." She swallowed. "But it's reproducing faster than it's dying. Eventually, the baby is going to, ah . . . be in trouble."

It was going to die.

Luc might as well have been stabbed in the gut. He'd only just learned about the baby, but although doubt sang through him about his abilities to be a good father, he had no doubts that he didn't want it to die.

"Please," Kar whispered. "Can you do something?"

Sin and Eidolon exchanged glances, and Luc's stomach clenched. "What? What's going on?"

"Sin has successfully cured one warg whose disease wasn't advanced."

"There's a 'but' at the end of that sentence," Luc growled, his worry adding a rough edge to his voice.

"But," Sin said, "I've killed others I tried to cure. I could kill the baby, and maybe even Kar."

Luc shook his head. "Then no. You're not doing it."

Kar shoved to her feet and moved away from Sin and Eidolon as though needing distance from the bad news. But when she spoke, her voice was steady as she faced off with Eidolon. "What other options are there?"

"We can wait for a cure." Eidolon tucked the stethoscope and thermometer back inside the bag. "But it could come too late. We aren't even close. We have a better shot at a vaccine, but that won't help the baby. Sin really is your only hope."

Luc tugged the IV catheter out of his hand and stood. "And if we don't agree to this?"

"The baby *will* die. But Kar will probably be safe."

Luc cursed. He looked over at Kar, whose expression was remote, not giving anything away, but she was rubbing her belly, probably not consciously, and he knew exactly what she was thinking. She wanted to go for it.

"Can we get a minute?" he asked, and everyone but Kar drifted to the other side of the room. He drew her toward the fireplace. "How are you doing?"

"I'm scared." She looked down at her stockinged feet. She was wearing his wool socks, which were twice as big as her feet, and they looked adorable on her. *Adorable?* Shit, he hadn't even known that word was in his vocabulary.

He took her hand, and though it felt awkward, it also felt... good. "You don't have to do it, Kar."

"Yes, I do." She inhaled deeply, blew the breath out for a long time, as though gathering the courage to speak. "I hadn't planned to tell you about the baby. At least, that's what I told myself. But I didn't have a choice. Not really." She paused, let a few heartbeats pass, enough that Luc got antsy before she swallowed audibly and continued. "I was faced with a pregnancy I didn't know how to deal with, because of what I am. I'm out of a job, The Aegis is hunting me, and if my father knew... he might see the baby as a monster. I could have gone to my mother, but she doesn't know what I am, and I don't know what she'd do if she found out. And how could I take care of the baby on the nights I shift? I know regular werewolf mothers don't shift for a few years after giving birth, but I'm a different breed. God, I'm babbling. I know I am." She tried to back away from him, but he gripped her hand tighter, forcing her to stay.

"Finish," he said quietly.

She sighed. "It's just...I knew I couldn't do it alone. My only choice was to find you...or let The Aegis find me. Better for them to kill me before I give birth than to kill me and do God knows what with the baby."

The very idea chilled him to the bone. That she'd been so desperate as to even think of allowing those demon-slaying scumbags to kill her...Jesus. "I won't let them touch you," he swore. "I will keep you safe no matter what."

"I know. Maybe it's hormones, maybe it's some sort of warg connection...but whatever it is, I know that about you. And I don't want to lose our baby."

He traced a finger over the lush curves of her lips. "I'm glad you told me." Holy hell, he couldn't believe he'd just said that. "I can't promise you a white picket fence and flowers and poetry," he said gruffly. "All I have to offer you is..." He made an encompassing gesture around the cabin. "This. Some weapons and rabbit furs and me. But nothing will get past me to you or our kid." Nothing. For the first time since becoming a werewolf, he'd lay down his life for someone else.

Gently, he tugged Kar into his arms, suddenly liking how she felt there. "And if anything ever happens to me, you still won't be alone. Those people standing over there listening to every word we're saying? They will make sure you're safe and cared for. I promise." Damn, he was shocked to discover that he meant what he'd just said. At some point, even as he watched his humanity fade away, he'd learned to trust the people who ran Underworld General.

"Thank you."

"God, Kar, I should be thanking you. It's been a long time since I had something to live for. So you'd better make it through this."

"I will."

Before he broke down and looked like an idiot Con would make fun of for the rest of his life, Luc stepped away and gestured to the group of eavesdroppers. "Let's do it."

Twenty

Luc and Kar's conversation sat in Sin's gut like a hot coal. She knew little about Luc, except that he'd always been gruff and unfriendly. But the way he'd spoken to the female—yeah, Sin had eavesdropped, BFD—had been a shock. Not just the words themselves, but the affection threaded through the gruffness. He wasn't used to caring about someone, and Sin could totally relate to that. It was foreign territory, and it made sense to tread carefully in situations where land mines made every step hazardous.

One wrong move could result in suffering and utter destruction.

Con didn't seem to be unmoved either. He kept looking between Luc and Kar, his face expressionless, but raw pain and understanding flickered in the silver of his eyes.

"We're doing it," Kar repeated. "Cure my baby."

Sin guided Kar back to the couch and sat beside her. Luc took her other side, and Sin got a lump in her throat when he took Kar's dainty hand in his big one. Eidolon came around front and kneeled before her.

"I'm going to get a blood sample before Sin starts, okay?"

Kar nodded, but the fear in her face was obvious. Eidolon took a deep breath, and when he spoke, he still sounded like a doctor, but a nice doctor. One who wasn't being all superior, like he usually was.

"Kar, I know this is hard. You're a Guardian. We're demons. Natural enemies. But you're also a werewolf. You've obviously accepted that, so you're going to need to accept your place in our world."

"But—"

He gripped her shoulder, gently but firmly. "I know. We're demons. I get that. You probably saw my mate, Tayla, when you were in Egypt. And I'm sure you've heard she's half demon as well as a Guardian. But she didn't know she was a demon when we met." A wry smile turned up one corner of his mouth. "Trust me, we didn't exactly have an easy path. But eventually, she accepted it. We're not the monsters you think we are."

That wasn't entirely true. Sin had met a lot of monsters in her life, and most of the time she felt like one herself. But no, for the most part, Eidolon and his brothers, his staff, were no worse than a lot of humans, and in many cases, a lot, lot better.

Kar turned away like she wasn't sure how to respond, her gaze lighting on Luc. And then she turned back to Eidolon, resolve burning in her eyes. "I'll have to take you at your word for now, but what it comes down to is that I would make a deal with the devil to save my child, so do what you have to do, Doctor."

Good for her. Sin waited until Eidolon finished taking blood before engaging her gift. Man, it was weird threading her power through Kar to the tiny fetus. The virus floated around inside the womb and inside the baby, and for a moment, Sin didn't do anything. Yes, she'd cured the warg in Montana, but she'd killed two others. This was a baby, one the parents were desperate to save, and if Sin made one little mistake, used too much power, not enough...

"Sin," Con whispered into her ear. "You can do this."

God, how had he known what she was thinking, what she needed? Grateful for his encouragement, she sent a controlled burst of power into a mass of virus strands. They ruptured, coming apart in pieces as others rushed in, almost as if they were trying to help. Fucking demon virus was *freaky*.

She was about to hit another cluster when Kar stiffened, her back arching so violently Sin heard the crack of spine.

"She's seizing," Luc barked, and suddenly, Kar was falling backward, her body flopping. Her skin turned red, hot, and her eyes rolled up into her head.

Con gripped Kar's wrists and pinned them to the couch while Eidolon gripped her legs. "Hurry up, Sin!" Eidolon grunted as Kar thrashed. "We need to finish—"

He broke off as Kar roared, exploding out of her seizure. Eidolon flew into the air, coming down awkwardly against the stone fireplace, and Con rocked backward into the wall. Kar, a mass of teeth and rage, lunged at Sin, her hands wrapping around her throat.

"My baby!" she snarled. "You're hurting it!"

"Kar, no!" Luc wrapped his arms around her, but he couldn't break Kar's stranglehold on Sin.

Eidolon spoke sharply. "Fever delirium. Luc, pin her!"

Sin's lungs burned. Panic frayed the edges of her consciousness, which was starting to fade. Her gift flared, her instinct to kill Kar, but instead, with the last bits of concentration she had, she struck out at the virus strands in the baby, exploding them like little bombs.

Somehow, Eidolon managed to pry Kar's fingers away from her throat, and Sin took several grateful gulps of fresh air. Luc bore Kar to the couch cushions and even as Sin sucked deep breaths, she gripped Kar's ankle and started work again.

It seemed to take forever, and by the time the last virus strand was a crumpled, shrunken little string, she was shaking and her power was nearly drained.

"It's...done," she breathed. The world spun, and as she keeled over, Con was there, tucking her against him, stroking her hair, and wow...to have someone catch her like that...it made her world spin again.

Kar groaned as Eidolon dug through his medical duffel. "The baby," she rasped. "How is the baby?"

"It's fine." Sin cleared her throat, which was still tender. "I think it'll be fine."

Then Con, smiling broadly enough to flash those sexy fangs, shook his head. "Who would have seen this coming? Luc the family man."

Luc snorted. "Trust me. I would not have bet on those cards." He inclined his head at Sin. "Thanks." The word was barely more than a grunt, and a stranger on the outside might have doubted his sincerity. But his hands trembled with the emotion that wasn't in his voice, and his throat worked on audible swallows that spoke volumes as he twined his fingers with Kar's.

Just a few days ago, Sin would have been rolling her eyes at the intimate, tender gesture. Now, she just remembered how she'd awakened after being hit by the *exomangler*, and Con had been at her side, holding her hand the same way.

"Just lie still," Eidolon was saying to Kar. "I'm going to take some blood from you. And then we need to get you to the hospital for more tests. The fact that you were producing antibodies to this virus is major."

"Won't it take some time to make a vaccine?" Sin asked.

"If it can be done, yes, but I've got demon magic and bone devil eggs at my disposal. I should be able to test the first batch of vaccine within a day or two if all goes well."

"Bone devil eggs?" Kar asked, and Eidolon nodded.

"They're what we use instead of chicken eggs to develop vaccines. They cut incubation time by two-thirds."

"You said *if*," Sin said. "Why?"

"Because I can't guarantee it. I think it's likely, but I'm not going to make any promises."

Sin's stomach turned over. And as the others went back to taking care of Luc and Kar, Sin backed up until she bumped into the door. While no one was looking, she slipped out, needing space, but once she was out in the cold, where the coppery zest of spilled blood still hung in the air, there was too much space. Too much blood, too much death.

All of which she'd caused.

She stood there, taking it all in, watching as the UG staff tended to the injured and dragged the dead into the forest, where they could be hidden from human eyes.

On her arm, her *dermoire* tingled, a precursor to the pain that would erupt.

Feel, Con had said.

And yeah, she owed these people that.

Grief welled up in her, a massive wave of agony that burst out as a sob. She ran, stumbling, into the forest, and by the time she was deep in the bush, she was bawling so hard she could barely breathe, and tears were trailing down her cheeks.

"Con, I hate you for this," she whispered. She'd worked so hard to protect herself from pain, and now it seemed like that was all she could feel.

She sucked in a shuddering breath, desperate to get herself under control, and then...the air went still. And colder. Her breath formed an icy fog, and right behind her, a horse screamed, a godawful, evil screech that Sin felt deep in her marrow. The distinct whistle of a missile made her heart skip a beat a split second before an arrow punched into the snow between her feet. Secured to the end of the arrow was a twisted piece of sinew from which something shiny dangled.

Knowing she was a dead woman, Sin turned.

The horseman came out of the trees like a wraith, with brimstone smoke as an escort. He drew his mount to a halt, and the giant white beast reared up, flashing hooves larger than an old Chevy's hubcaps. When the horse settled, the rider removed his great helm. Long white hair spilled out over the male's broad shoulders, which were covered in armor, and just like in the mountains of Montana, it was dull, sooty, and an oily, bloodlike substance oozed from the joints and cracks.

His eyes glowed with an unholy sanguine light, the same as the stallion's. His face should have been handsome, but his smile was pure malice as he inclined his head, gave Sin a two-finger salute, and then wheeled his mount around and disappeared as if the forest had swallowed him whole.

Unbelievably, Sin was still alive.

"What. The. Hell." Eidolon's voice startled her, and she spun to find him and Con standing behind her. "Was that the horse guy who's been stalking you?"

"Yeah. And I'm getting tired of his games." Covertly, Sin dashed away her leftover tears as she bent to tug the arrow out of the snow and snap the gold object off the twine. "It's some sort of coin. Well, half a coin." She rubbed her finger over the broken, zigzagged edge. "There's writing on the back. *She who... blood... carries... spread plague... battle breaks... seal'd.*" Eidolon frowned, and Sin returned the look. "What? Why do you look like you licked a Mondevilin piss pod?"

"It sounds vaguely familiar."

"We'll have to figure it out later," Con said. "We need to get Sin somewhere safe. We've been here long enough to make me nervous."

Eidolon's expression took on a sympathetic cast. "Yeah, I'm worried about the damned assassins, too. We'll get Sin to UG—"

"That won't be necessary," Sin interrupted. "I'm not going to be in danger from my assassins anymore."

"Why not?" Eidolon asked.

"Because," she said quietly, "I'm going back to the den."

"Like hell you are," Con and Eidolon said simultaneously.

Sin jammed her hands onto her hips and glared at

them both in turn. Maybe if her eyes weren't swollen and her face damp from tears, she might have looked a little fiercer. And Con wouldn't feel like such a piece of shit, because he knew damned good and well that every single tear was on his shoulders.

"This is my choice," she said. "Everyone will be safer if I go back to the den. I've made up my mind."

Eidolon gave her a look that was pure big brother. "You don't need to go back there, Sin. We'll find a way to make it safe for you."

Con sure as hell agreed with that. "They can't touch you at the hospital. Go with your brothers."

"I *am* going back there. It's my job."

"Bullshit." Gold flecks kicked up in the black of Eidolon's eyes, and Con braced himself. This could get ugly if the guy started ordering Sin around. "You will not—"

"E," Con interrupted. "Could you give us a second?"

Though Eidolon's expression was as frosty as the breeze that stirred up the snow around them, he nodded. "I'll take Luc and Kar to UG. You two can meet us there."

Once he was out of sight, Sin huffed. "Good cop, bad cop doesn't work on me. You're not going to change my mind."

"First of all," Con growled, "I'm not the good cop. Second, I know I'm not going to change your mind. But at least tell me the truth." He wanted the truth because he *did* plan on changing her mind.

"I just did."

"Tell me the rest of it."

She curled her hands into fists and got that stubborn set to her mouth, the one that made him want to kiss her just to make it go away. "I don't know what you're talking about."

"Don't do this," he gritted out. "You've made a lot of progress. You know, with your brothers."

Pink splotched her cheeks, and she averted her gaze. Kicked at the snow. "You don't understand."

"Then make me understand. Because even if you go back to the den, we still don't know what's up with the horse guy or why someone besides your assassins wants you dead. So you should be at the hospital with people who care about you right now. Not in your assassin den, all alone and hiding from your brothers."

The color in her cheeks deepened, and she lifted her angry gaze to him. *"Hiding?"*

He stepped closer. "Hiding."

"Maybe I just don't want to be treated like a child by them—"

"Then stop acting like one!" he shouted. Her head snapped back as if he'd slapped her, and he pressed his advantage, stepping into her. "You don't want to be owned, possessed, chained, but what the hell do you think you're doing to yourself? You're going back to your den to be free? How are you free if you can't go anywhere without worrying about being killed by your own assassins? You're still a slave, Sin. But this time, it's of your own making."

Her dark stare flared with fury. "I told you why I took the job—"

"Yeah, yeah. You took it to spare Idess." He knew he was being a dick, was once again doing a repeat of what he'd done at Rivesta's, but dammit, she had a shot at having a family. And if she went back to the den and shut herself off, she'd close down again, maybe tighter than ever this time. "But you know what? I think you'd have taken it anyway. You couldn't even deal with your feelings, so how would you have dealt with the real world if you were out in it instead of living in a cave where you had a great excuse to not hang out with your family?"

Her eyes went steely. "God, you're such an asshole sometimes."

She'd called him that before. Had called him worse. But this time, it actually hurt. Because she was right. "Don't do it, Sin. Just . . . don't."

"I think," she said, in a soft voice he hadn't expected, "you're forgetting that I couldn't get out of my job if I wanted to." She dragged her hands through her hair, which glinted with bluish highlights in the sunlight that squeezed between the treetops. "This is pointless. I either go to the hospital and be a prisoner there, with my brothers as jailers, or I go to my den, where at least I'm my own warden."

"No." He couldn't let her go. He couldn't—

The hairs on the back of his neck stood up, and an animal growl rose up in his throat before he could stop it. He spun around, instinctively tucking Sin behind him. The sight of Bran standing in the shadows with two male dhampires came with a gut-wrenching blast of dread.

"It's time, Conall."

"Con?" Sin tugged on one of his belt loops. "Who are these douche bags?"

Was it wrong for him to want to smile at that? *Nah.* "The ugly one would be my clan leader," he said quietly.

"Stay here." He moved to Bran with swift, sure steps. *Show no weakness.* "I'm not ready."

"Your state of readiness is irrelevant," Bran growled. "Our first female has gone into heat. The rest will be ready to breed by the end of the week. We need you."

The idea of having sex with anyone but Sin made him cold inside. Hell, the very thought of even *feeding* from anyone else made him ill. Which wasn't a good sign, and somehow, Bran was aware of the reason for Con's reluctance. His dark gaze zeroed in on Sin, then cut sharply to Con when he stepped in front of the dhampire leader to block the view.

"The Warg Council is on our backs as well." One of the other males, Enric, if Con remembered right, gestured in the direction of the cabin. "The *pricolici* and *varcolac* both want our allegiance in their war. We need the Dhampire Council to assemble."

Con shook his head. "So we refuse to take sides."

"We've already been drawn into it. We have dhampire females mated to *pricolici*," Bran said, and Con thought about Sable, hoped she was okay. "Some are fleeing with their families to our lands, and others are dragging dhampires into the conflict."

Con drew in a ragged breath. He might be able to put off yet another breeding heat, but there was no stalling when it came to a matter of politics and possible war. His people needed him. He'd felt disconnected from them for so long that he could barely consider them his people anymore, but ultimately, he *was* a dhampire, and it was time to take the long overdue reins.

The sound of Sin's heartbeat, so loud and tempting even at this distance, reminded him that it was a very good time to get away from her and fulfill his destiny. But the words wouldn't come. *Yes, I'll go with you. Yes, I'm ready. Yes, let me bend over and take it up the ass for the dhampire race.*

Not a single word formed on his lips.

Bran's hard gaze zeroed in on Sin. "That is the demon female you're working with?" His nostrils flared, and he cut quick looks between Sin and Con, and *shit*... Bran knew Con was teetering on the brink of addiction. Hell, he was probably already over the edge.

"Yes," Con ground out.

"Is the virus out of your blood?"

Con opened his mouth to say yes, but suddenly, Sin was there. "No," she said. "One more feeding should do it, though. So whatever you need him for, it can wait."

"Sin—"

She covertly pinched his ass, shutting him up and nearly making him jump. Bran glared, and when he said nothing, Sin made a shooing motion with her hand. "Run along. Leave us to it."

Bran practically shook with rage, which, to Con, was a combination of funny and oh-fuck. Finally, Bran snarled, "You have until tomorrow to put your affairs in order, Conall. If we have to seek you out, you'll be kept in the *lunecrate* for a year."

Bran and the males left, and Con let out a soft curse. The *lunecrate* box was the fun punishment place for dhampires. Shoved inside the iron cage during the full moon, a dhampire was left for three days of madness, unable to hunt, howl, or even move. By the time the dhampire recovered from the trauma, the full moon had come again.

Sin's hand came up to his shoulder, a tentative, surprisingly gentle touch. He turned into her. "Sin . . . *fuck*."

"Yes."

Confused, he frowned at her. "What?"

She pressed her curvy body against him, and his body sparked to instant, fierce life. "Make love to me."

"Right here?" He hoped she didn't notice how strangled he sounded.

"Well, not this close to the cabin." She placed her hand over his heart, and the wolf in him howled. "Please. It sounds like you have some sort of crisis to handle, and I have to go, so it might be the last time for a while."

Or forever. The unspoken truth hung in the air between them, literally visible in the fog of their breath. He still didn't want to let her go, but Bran's untimely visit had clarified things. A lot. If Sin went to the hospital, she'd be accessible to him, and he didn't think he had the willpower to stay away. Going to the den would be best for both of them.

"Yeah," he rasped. "Fuck, yeah."

She dragged her finger down his chest, made a playful flick at his waistband, and then took off in a dead run. A few yards away, she cast him a sultry glance over her shoulder . . . and his prey drive activated. He caught her as she wove between the fir trees and he took her down to the fluffy snow. Once down, she didn't fight him. Instead, she flipped him so he was on his back, and though it was freezing, he wasn't cold at all as she tore open his pants and released his raging erection.

Then she stood, peeled off her pants. The sight of her straddling him, her sex spread and glistening, nearly made him come. "You need to feed, don't you?"

"I can't." His voice cracked humiliatingly. "Not from you."

"You don't have to drink. I just want to feel your fangs in me one more time."

"Sin," he groaned, but he couldn't deny her, and besides, this would be the last time. After this, he'd go to Scotland and never see her again, so her life wouldn't be in danger—from him, at least, and eventually, his cravings for her blood would die.

Though he knew his desire for *her* never would.

"I can't wait to feel you inside me," she whispered.

He groaned again, and as she walked up his body, his breath grew hot. Strangled. And as she lowered herself, he stopped breathing altogether.

His hands actually shook as he cupped her gorgeous ass to hold her steady. She put her sex against his mouth and he kissed her, pure heaven. Then he penetrated her with his tongue, wielding it as he would his cock for a few strokes before swiping the flat of his tongue up her valley.

"God, that's good," she rasped, even as she shifted her weight to put her femoral artery over his mouth. He could still taste her, and as his fangs unsheathed, he allowed himself one more quick taste, a flick of his tongue over her clit.

Then he sank his teeth into her thigh, relishing the spill of her lifeblood into his mouth. Her spicy taste mingled with that of her arousal, and his hips began to pump of their own accord, seeking the place his tongue had just been.

Sin's blood hit his bloodstream like a shot of heroin, both satisfying his hunger for her and intensifying it, strengthening his addiction to her. At the same time, her incubus pheromones hit him, and his erotic hunger warred with his blood hunger. She moaned, tipping the scales. Thank the gods he'd fed this way, because he'd have to stop feeding to fuck her. Had he taken her by the throat or wrist, stopping might be impossible.

Reluctantly, he disengaged his fangs, licked the punctures slowly, and continued the journey to her sex. Gently, he spread her, speared her with his tongue, and let her ride him until her desire forced her to take more aggressive action.

She tore away from him and backed down his body, dragging her mouth over his chest, abs, until his shaft slid between her lips. Holy *damn*, that was good. Her tongue flicked over the head of him, and then she took him deep. The sucking sensation was exquisite, and he had to pant through the pleasure to keep from coming. Finally she lifted her mouth away, but before she seated herself, she scooped some snow.

He arched an eyebrow, and she gave him the wickedest smile he'd ever seen as she formed a small, loose ball. He nearly swallowed his tongue when she spread herself with her fingers and inserted the snowball into her core. Jesus. He'd done a lot in his thousand years, but this? This was a first.

Taking his shaft in her hand, she guided his cock inside her. She was slick, hot, and when the head of him kissed the ice, the erotic contrast made him hiss in pleasure. Slowly, she rocked back and forth, and though her feet and legs had to be freezing, she didn't complain. Didn't seem to notice. Each downward stroke gave him that *a-fucking-mazing* mix of hot and cold, and each time he struck the snowball, she whimpered.

"Where...ah, yeah, right there...did you learn that?"

Leaning forward, she brushed her cold lips across his. "I slept with this pack of ice trolls once, and—" At his insanely jealous curse, she laughed, a pure, tinkling sound. "I'm kidding. It was just a sudden flash of brilliance." She sat up on him again, closed her eyes, and threw her head back. The slender arch of her body was a graceful line against the wild backdrop of the trees and distant mountains, and once again, the wolf in him howled. "I never get to play like that."

With a tortured groan, he gripped her hips and guided her faster. "Play all you want." And then it struck him; she wouldn't play like this again. She'd be back to screwing males because her body demanded it, back to hating who and what she was.

And the idea that she would be screwing any male other than him put acid in his stomach and a serrated growl in his throat.

"I love it when you growl like that," she breathed. "Mmm...Con..."

Despite his possessive fury, hearing his name on her lips sent him over the edge, and his climax blasted through him. He bucked hard, his hips coming out of the snow. Sin cried out, but he slipped his palm into her mouth, and she bit down, muffling the shout that might have attracted attention from the medical team still combing the area for the dead and injured.

The erotic pinch of pain set Con off again, igniting a chain reaction in her and a series of orgasms that kept milking him, dragging out his orgasm for so long he thought he might have blacked out.

Gradually, she sank down on him so they were chest to

chest, her face buried in his neck, and even though they were half-dressed, lying in the freezing snow, this somehow felt like the most intimate position—and situation—they'd been in. He could hold her like this forever.

Or, at least, until they either froze to death or Eidolon found them and killed Con.

"I've always been quiet during sex," she murmured.

"Sweetheart, you just defined the term 'screaming orgasm.'" He felt her smile against his skin, but he couldn't find anything amusing about it. This was just one more example of how he'd broken through her shell, and probably not for the better. And wasn't he a massive ball of indecision? Because he couldn't decide if it was best for her to feel again or not. She needed to be happy, to have a family. But she also needed to protect herself.

He sighed, and Sin joined him. "I know," she murmured. "We need to get back to the cabin."

"I'd give anything to be able to make love to you without worrying about what's next," he said, kissing her neck lightly. "To just lounge around and do nothing but touch you. Feed you. Watch movies."

She chuckled. "Sounds so normal. I wouldn't know what to do." She lifted her head, stared into his eyes, and her smile faltered. "What if... What if I could get out of my commitment to the Assassin's Guild?"

Grief hollowed out his chest, turning it into a bottomless pit as he brought his hand up to cup her cheek. Even if she could get out of it, he couldn't get out of his own obligations. And he definitely couldn't risk hurting or even killing Sin. "Don't. Let's not go there."

She nipped the pad of his finger. "Come visit me. You can come to the den—"

"Sin..."

"Please." The strain in her voice matched the pain in her eyes. "I'm not...I'm not ready to give you up."

God, his heart broke wide open, and he heard himself reply with a serious disconnect between his mouth and his brain. "Yeah, I'll go to you," he said.

But it was a lie.

Twenty-one

The emergency department was in chaos when Con stepped out of the Harrowgate, leaving Sin inside, her lips swollen from his good-bye kiss.

Don't think about it.

Not thinking about it actually turned out to be easy, given the crazy medical situation. The injured wargs from the battle in Canada had been triaged, were lying around the emergency department on stretchers and on the floor, lined up all the way down the two hallways leading from the area.

Con immediately jumped in to help, and it was nearly four hours before the situation was under control. He spent the next hour with Bastien, doing what he could to comfort the warg until Con called time of death. Afterward, Sin's brothers, Tayla, and Luc joined him in the waiting area.

"Where's Sin?" Shade asked as he stripped off his bloody surgical gloves.

Con's own gloves got tossed in the trash, and man, he couldn't wait to get in the shower. "On her way to the den."

Eidolon swore. "I thought you were going to talk her out of that. She didn't need to go back there. She'd be safe here."

Unbelievably, Lore came to Con's defense. "She's better off there. She needs to get back to normal."

Normal. What a fucking joke that was. Her normal was pain and isolation. And meaningless sex. Probably with that Lycus guy. Jealousy expanded in Con's chest as an inappropriate blast of heat curled through his veins. There had been nothing meaningless about what he and Sin had done at the mountain safe house. Or in the snow. Every cell in his body vibrated with hunger for her, both for her body and her blood, and just thinking about it was revving him up again.

"What about you, Con?" Shade asked, and Con took two deep, calming breaths before he answered.

"What about me?"

"You aren't a danger to her, right?"

"No," Con said levelly. "I'm not." But even he didn't believe his own words.

Wraith flipped a blade in the air, a very Sin-like move. "Okay, what the fuck is all the subtext here?" He blinked when everyone stared at him. "What? Like I don't know what subtext is? I watch movies."

"That's because you can't read," Tayla said brightly, and the demon shot her the finger. One on each hand.

E and Lore returned their focus to Con with varying expressions of confusion, and Shade looked like he might want to rip Con's throat out. Yeah, Con's secret was about to be revealed.

"Male dhampires are prone to blood addiction if they feed off the same female host more than a few times," Shade said. "Isn't that right, Con?"

Eidolon swore under his breath. "How did I not know that?"

"Ever had to chain up a female dhampire and, ah, coax out her deepest, darkest secrets?" Shade asked, every word laced with dark sarcasm. "Well, that's why."

Con's entire body jerked with surprise. "You tortured a dhampire?"

"Trust me, she didn't get anything she didn't want." Shadows writhed in Shade's eyes as he locked them on Con, as if daring him to challenge him.

"There were things Shade had to do before he met Runa," Eidolon said quietly. "So let's drop it."

Damn. Con had seen Shade's little BDSM cave hideaway once, but it hadn't occurred to him that Shade had used it for anything other than pleasure. And what did E mean by "had to"? Con wondered what other information Shade had gotten from the dhampire female.

"So?" Shade asked. "Are you a danger to our sister?"

Con struggled to keep his voice level, to convince these guys that he was no threat to her. To convince himself. But the image of her being with other males was making his blood boil and his temper flare.

And he was . . . hungry.

"I am not a danger," he swore. "I'm never going to see her again."

Lore's gloved hand worked into a fist at his side, something Con had noticed he did when he was agitated. "Why not?"

"I'm quitting Underworld General as of now, and after

I take care of a few things, I'm going back to my clan's lands in Scotland."

"Ah...does Sin know?"

"No."

"Fuuuck." Lore scrubbed that gloved hand over his face, looking suddenly worn out.

"You son of a bitch," Tayla snapped, her green eyes blazing. "She cares about you. And you're going to slink away without telling her?"

"Yeah, it's a dick move," he said. "But I can't see her again, Tayla. I'm already too close—"

"Fuck that. You could have told her. You could have warned her." When Eidolon slung an arm around her shoulder, she softened against him, but it was obvious she still wanted a piece of Con.

Shit. He didn't know why he'd lied to Sin, except that he didn't want to hurt her after they'd just had mind-blowing sex that had actually meant something.

He was such an asshole.

"Are you coming back?" Luc asked.

"No. Come tomorrow night, a ritual will bind me, as a Council member, to the land and the clan. I won't be able to leave except for short periods."

"That sucks." Luc's voice was gruff. "Bad."

"It's what I've wanted all my life," Con said, but his voice was hollow, wooden. Because no, he didn't want this anymore. And truthfully, he wasn't sure he ever had. His rebellion against the clan had started early, peaking with his edgy, idiotic flirt-game with addiction that had ended so badly for Eleanor and had gotten him kicked out of the clan. He'd lived off the chain ever since, leaving smoke behind him as he burned a path of death wish.

"If you change your mind," Shade said, "we'd like you back."

Con swallowed. For how long had he told himself the job was temporary, that eventually, he'd move on, because that's what he always did? But now, hell, these people felt like family, and the hospital like home.

"I'll remember that," he rasped.

Lore looked down at the floor, and when he glanced back up, his expression was almost...friendly. "Are you sure there's nothing you can do? About Sin, I mean. The addiction—"

"Nothing." Con backed up toward the Harrowgate. Good-byes had always been easy for him. A simple see-ya-around, and then he was out of there. But this was different. And he didn't want to do it. "I gotta go. I, ah... yeah. See ya."

The brothers looked skeptical, and Con couldn't blame them.

Sin didn't go back to the den. She needed to, she knew that. But she wasn't ready yet. For some reason, the hospital called to her, and while she could come back anytime she wanted to, she knew that once she'd gone back to the den, she'd harden, would avoid the hospital, her brothers, and the place would once again be nothing but a cold building.

She wanted just a little more time to indulge in silly sentimental wanderings before she had to banish fuzzy warm feelings from her life forever.

She'd taken the Harrowgate with Con, had kissed him good-bye when the gate opened up into UG's emergency department, and had watched him step out. Once the gate closed, she waited a minute, opened the door, and while chaos reigned, she slipped out and down a hallway.

She wandered around, until, oddly, she found herself in the nursery. It reeked of baby powder and disinfectant, but it was empty and was the last place anyone would look for her, so she sank into a rocking chair and, utterly exhausted, she closed her eyes and rocked.

"Sin?"

Startled, she sat up, blinking as she got her bearings. Where was Con? Her body burned, ached with succubus needs that he'd been so good at fulfilling...Oh, right. He was gone. Her heart sank as she remembered saying good-bye to him, knowing the whole time that it wasn't the see-you-later kind. It had been nice of him to lie, though.

Disappointment tempered her lust a little and, still dis-oriented, she looked around. She was in UG's nursery. Shade and Lore were standing in front of her, and Lore held out a Styrofoam cup of coffee. Freaky. She glanced at her watch. Twelve hours. She'd been asleep for twelve hours.

"Hey." She gratefully took the coffee.

"A janitor found you," Shade said. "How are you doing?"

I'm sleeping in a freaking nursery and I miss Con. "Peachy." She scrubbed her eyes with the heel of her palm. "Any news? On the vaccine?"

Lore nodded. "E was up all night working on it, and the R-XR even allowed Wraith to bring specialists from USAMRIID into the hospital to help."

"They'll be mind-wiped, of course," Shade said.

Sin sipped the coffee, hissed when it burned her

tongue. "What's going on with the warg war and the military action against them?"

Lore whistled, loud and long. "The last few hours have been fucked-up. The war is dragging a lot of different demon species into it. Some that are loyal to the borns, some who are loyal to the turneds, and some who just like to fight. Both sides have hired mercs, too."

Shade nodded. "It's already getting messy and spilling over into the human world. The Aegis is working overtime on damage control, but people are seeing shit they shouldn't be seeing. Religious fanatics are screaming about the end of the world, governments are trying to deflect, but it won't be long before someone catches something on video and it ends up on the Internet or some crap."

"What's going on with the R-XR?"

Shade growled. "Arik, that bastard, is holed up in my cave and won't leave." He clenched his fists as though imagining his brother-in-law's neck in them. "And Runa won't let me kill him."

"That's too bad," Sin said, but Shade totally missed the sarcasm and nodded.

Lore rolled his eyes. "Shade's cave is filling up, between Arik, Luc, Kar…"

"Good thing I have the cave set up for a warg shift," Shade muttered. "Kar's Feast shifts are insane."

"Luc mentioned that Feast wargs are bigger and stronger."

Shade snorted. "No shit. She nearly tore the hooks out of the stone. It would have been better to put her in Runa's cage at our house, but it's not safe yet."

"So the R-XR and The Aegis are still trying to exterminate the wargs?"

"Until E starts the vaccinations, yeah," Shade said. "He's hoping to start testing today."

"Are Con, Wraith, and Eidolon still in trouble with the Carceris?"

"Eidolon and Wraith will be fine." Shade patted his BDU chest pocket and pulled out a pack of gum. "They'd have risked a lot more to make sure you were safe."

So yes, they were still in trouble, and she felt guiltier than ever. *Thanks, Con. I appreciate having these horrible feelings.*

She shouldn't ask. She really shouldn't. The fact that her brothers hadn't mentioned Con's name should be a warning sign. But then, she'd never been one to obey signs or take hints.

"What about Con?" she blurted, her heart pounding wildly, because at this point, she needed to let him go. She'd go back to her den and back to her life, and he'd go back to being a paramedic and dealing with his dhampire clan stuff.

But she really, really couldn't bear the thought of sleeping with someone else. Or of being alone.

Shade's expression shuttered, and her lungs struggled to take in a breath. "What about him?"

"Is he...is he here right now? Working?"

"No." Shade revealed nothing in his voice or his eyes, but Lore had a tell when he was nervous, and the way his left pinky flexed totally gave him away.

"What's going on?" she growled. "And don't BS me."

The boys glanced at each other, and after a little shuffling of their feet, Lore said, "He left for Scotland."

"He's not coming back," Shade said. "He quit."

"Oh my God." Her heart jerked painfully against her ribs. "He wouldn't quit. He loves it here."

"Dunno what to tell you. His clan will perform some sort of ritual tonight that'll bind him to them."

"No." Her dazed mind refused to believe he'd leave the hospital. Sure, she'd planned to stay away from here, but some small part of her had taken comfort in knowing that if she did come back, he'd be here. Even if they couldn't be together, *he'd be here.* "I'll go to him. Talk him out of it." And jump his bones while she was at it.

"Sin," Lore sighed, "it's too dangerous."

"I don't care about my safety!"

Shade stiffened. "*We* do. If you haven't figured that out by now—"

"I know." Her voice was soft, but firm, a copy of Con's soothing medic voice she'd somehow learned. "But I really can take care of myself."

"But Idess can't," Lore said, and then he winced, closed his eyes as if he just realized what he'd said.

"What? What do you mean, Idess can't? Dammit, bro, what the hell is going on?"

Lore and Shade exchanged glances, and she wanted to scream. Stomp her feet. Throw a little-girl temper tantrum because they were certainly treating her like she was a delicate tot. "I swear, I'm going to knock your heads together so hard you'll be hearing tweeting finches for a year. Now *tell me!*"

Shade's mouth twitched in a half-smile, and she figured he was picturing her trying to slap down two demons who were twice her size, but Lore didn't appear so amused. Probably because he knew she could do it.

She shoved to her feet. "Well?"

Lore sighed. "Your assassins went after Idess."

She felt all the blood drain from her face. "What happened?"

"Marcel tried to take her off the streets of Rome a couple of days ago. It was nothing I couldn't handle, but Idess is human now, and she's vulnerable."

Sin sagged back down into the rocker. "Fuck. I'm so sorry Lore." He took her hand, squeezed her fingers, and in that one gentle gesture, there was more love than she'd ever felt from him. Not because it hadn't been there, but because she could finally see it.

She'd been so blind. So stupid! Sin clutched Lore's hand like a lifeline. "I'll fix this. I swear I'll fix it."

Lore narrowed his eyes at her. "What have you got planned?"

Sweat dampened her temples. "Don't worry about it."

"Why do I feel like there's something you're not telling me?"

"Because you're paranoid." She paused, her brain working overtime to process everything she'd just been told. "Marcel worked with Lycus a lot. Do you think he was involved in Idess's attack?"

"I didn't see him. But if he was involved..."

"Yeah, I know. I'm out of here."

He wanted to argue; Sin knew it. But he was still working off the guilt he felt for leaving her so long ago, something she'd been content to let slide for all these years. Shame burned her cheeks, and she swore that after this, she would do whatever it took to finally release him from the obligation he felt for her. She'd been so wrong to let him continue to try to make it up to her, when he'd made up a thousand times over.

Now it was her turn to make it up to him.

Sin was greeted at the den by scowls, growls, and curses. Not the vulgar kind; the actual, may-your-bile-sacs-explode-and-poison-you-to-death kind.

"I love you guys, too," she'd called out as she stalked down the dark hallways to the throne room. Once inside, she collapsed against the door, her breathing fast and heavy, her hands shaking like a rookie on her first kill mission.

What the hell? She'd been rock solid for a hundred years, and she'd expected to get back to the den and immediately shift back into the assassin mode that had kept her sane—and alive—for so long.

Not so much.

Angry at her own weakness, she called for Sunil and waited, pacing next to the hearth, taking care to avoid the trapdoor in front of the hideous throne Deth had commissioned to be made out of the skeletons of humans and several species of demons.

She couldn't stop thinking about Con, wondering what she was going to say to him when she saw him. She probably wouldn't say anything at first. Her primary goal at this point was to get him inside her. Her brain was rapidly turning to a hormone mush, and any arguments she tried to form for getting him to go back to UG were interrupted by images of him naked.

Sunil finally appeared, and he approached warily, moving like a cat caught out in the open. If he had a tail, it would be twitching madly.

"Hey, boss." As always, his voice was a deep rumble, his words precise.

She cut to the chase, not wanting to be here for one second longer than necessary. "My assassins wanted me dead."

"Yes," he said sadly. "People are angry. We need work, and we need it badly."

"I know," she said, sinking into the chair. "I've been a terrible master."

His ears twitched the way they did when he was uncomfortable. "Not terrible. Just too nice."

She gave a startled laugh. "That's something no one has ever said about me."

"Glad I could be the first." He cocked his head and studied her. "So why am I here?"

"First, I need to know who has been trying to kill me."

"Everyone," Sunil said simply.

Sin shifted, winced at the poke of some creature's finger bone in her butt. "Including you?"

"Yes." His brown cheeks darkened with a blush of crimson, and his nervousness was now fully explained. She had the right to torture or put down every assassin who had tried to kill her. "You know I like you, Sin, but I have a family to feed."

"I know. I wouldn't have respected you if you hadn't tried." Oh, the assassin code was interesting, wasn't it?

"So," Sunil prompted. "Am I here to be tortured? The Peelers have been anticipating your return."

She shuddered. Those unholy, eyeless demons lived for torture. They were also bound to the den, so Sin hadn't found a way to get rid of them. "I want you to take over as assassin master."

His golden eyes flared, the pupils elongating and then rounding out again. "You can't be serious."

"Very."

"But . . . why?"

"My reasons are my own."

"There are only two ways to escape the life," Sunil pointed out.

"I'm aware of that, and I don't plan on dying."

Sunil started to reach inside the tattered wool trench coat he'd worn since World War II, but dropped his hands at his side. "I can't use a weapon against you."

"I know." Idess had been the exception to the *slave-can't-harm-master-in-the-den* rule. She'd been human when Deth bonded her, and humans weren't meant to carry the assassin-bond. "But you can shift, and as long as I allow it, it should be fine."

He hesitated, which was one of the very reasons she'd chosen him for this. Accepting the job meant he'd be stuck, the same way she had been. He'd have to move his family to the den in order to be with them, and he'd have to assign them bodyguards any time they left. But it was better than belonging to someone cruel, who would use your family against you, like Deth had.

"If you don't want it, I'll send for Tavin. He's the only other person I'd approve of." The blond Sem was new to the den, but his contract was huge—he was an all-purpose, anything-goes slave until he went through *s'genesis* and was freed from the contract. But he was very young, so he had a good seventy years to go until he went through the final maturation process.

"Agreed. He'd be a good master." Sunil grinned. "But I think I'd be a better one."

"Then let's do it."

Sunil bowed his head. "It has been an honor to serve you."

"The mushy stuff is embarrassing. Let's get it over with."

Closing his eyes, Sunil stepped back. A sudden stillness came over the dank air in the chamber, and then a massive vibration shook the big male. A moment later, he was gone, and there was a six-hundred-pound tiger in front of her. He bumped his head up against her hand, bucking her palm until she scratched behind his ears.

"You shithead," she murmured.

She could have sworn he smiled as he rubbed his cheek against her and then took her hand in his mouth as tenderly as he might carry a fragile egg. He used his sharp teeth to tug the ring as far up her finger as it would go, to the very tip.

Then he bit down.

The crunch of bone echoed through the chamber, or maybe it just echoed in Sin's skull. She clenched her teeth to keep from screaming. Fiery agony shot up her arm, and when Sunil let go, she fell back, clutching her bloody hand... which was now minus the first joint of her left ring finger.

"Put pressure on it," Sunil said, his voice raspy from his shift back to his human form.

"I am," she gasped. Fuck, it hurt.

He held up her severed digit. "Do you want it back?"

Sin sagged against the stone wall to keep from falling over. "Keep it... for snack time or something," she gritted out.

Sunil grinned. "Couldn't your brother reattach it?"

"Probably, but I don't have time for that. It's just a finger. No biggie."

"Thank you," he purred. "And, Sin, if you or Lore ever need any of my services, for you... half price."

Despite her pain, she laughed. "You are a true mercenary. Take care, Sunil." She paused at the door. "Also, fair warning: If I find out that someone from this den was in on the attack on Lore's mate, I'll kill them, so be prepared to look for a replacement."

Sin hurried down the den's halls, her thoughts racing. She had to get to Con, but first, she had a warg to grill. The walls were a blur, the people she passed not worth saying good-bye to. She'd liked some of her colleagues while she'd worked *with* them, but the dynamic had changed when she'd taken over, and for the most part, they'd treated her as the enemy.

When she passed by one of the two sleeping quarters, she slowed, sensing that the one person she wanted to see was inside. She shoved her aching hand in her pocket and stepped into the room.

"Lycus."

He spun away from his open chest of weapons, his movement so smooth she wouldn't have known she'd startled him if she didn't know him so well. "You're back. I didn't know."

"Clearly."

His toothy smile nearly made her shudder. "I'm glad you're safe."

She cocked her head and studied him, his handsome, hard face, his dark, soulless eyes. "Why don't I believe you?"

"I don't know." He rolled one powerful shoulder in a nonchalant shrug. "I've made it clear that I want you. If you're dead, I can't have you."

"You can't have control of the den, you mean." He shrugged again, but she didn't expect him to deny it. They both knew the deal. "I'm curious, Lycus…where's Marcel?"

Something flashed in Lycus's eyes, but it was gone before she could read it, and in an instant, his expression was neutral again. "Don't you know?"

"I know he was responsible for an attack on Lore's mate."

"Then I assume Marcel is dead?" He narrowed his eyes. "You suspect me of knowing about the attack."

"You're a rocket scientist, aren't you?" She started moving, a slow circle around him that he tracked with his gaze. "What would you say if I've decided to hand over control of the den?"

This time, his grin was genuine. He moved to her, slid his hand around the back of her neck, and for a moment, she thought he was going to kiss her. "I'd say you won't regret it, baby."

She pulled her hand out of her pocket and flashed her ringless finger at him. "I won't."

Lycus's eyes shot wide open, his expression filling with rage, his hand tightening on her neck. "You *bitch*!"

Twisting, she wrenched away from him, settled in a defensive stance, his chest of weapons behind her. "Don't do it, Lycus. You know the penalty for injuring another assassin in the den." Not that she was an assassin any longer, but she was entitled to safe passage until she was inside a Harrowgate.

"I'll kill you, Sin. I will have your head within the week."

Smiling, she eased backward, next to the chest.

Keeping an eye on him, she reached inside, removed a clay bottle. "Infernal fire, huh? For some reason, I'm not surprised to see this."

"So?" he snarled.

"You know it's forbidden to use this in the human realm."

"Which is why I don't use it there."

"Oh, I think you did. The question is, why. Why would you want me dead in a way that would mean you couldn't get my ring?"

He took the bottle from her, and she could practically feel the hatred rolling off him, scorching her skin. "You little succubus whore. You should have taken me up on my offer to become my mate. Now you're dead. And I think, just for fun, that I'll have your body stuffed and preserved, and the things I'll do to you..." His voice lowered to a creepy, shiver-inducing whisper. "You'll be my blow-up doll, baby. Forever."

She hit him. Decked him. And then she got the hell out of there. She wouldn't belong to anyone in life...or death.

Twenty-two

Con's boots felt like they were full of lead as he trudged across the rocky grounds of the dhampire sanctuary in northern Scotland. The evening breeze brought with it the scent of the ocean, the bite of salt air, and the stench of angry wargs.

Thatch-roofed cottages dotted the mossy countryside, but it was the larger, wooden motte and bailey structure that Con was heading toward. At the base of the grassy hill, where fog had settled like soup in a bowl, heavy trestle tables and chairs were visible in the mist like mountain peaks poking out of a cloud deck. No matter what the weather, dhampires preferred to be outside, whether they were conducting business meetings or celebrating a holiday.

Now, the members of the Dhampire Council were gathered in the area, as were several Warg Council members, including Valko and Raynor. As Con drew closer, the familiar sensation of his skin tightening grew stronger.

"*Conall.*" Valko's deep voice cracked like a whip, and everyone turned to Con. "Where the fuck have you been? Did you know there's a war going on? The damned *varcolac* attacked us."

Raynor swung to Valko. "Because *someone* leaked the fact that only we are affected by the virus! You knew what would happen, and now you're using the attacks as an excuse to exterminate us."

Valko scoffed. "It wasn't the *pricolici* who leaked the information. But we *will* finish this war. Your curs are already on the run after the battle in Canada—"

"No," Con interrupted. "The Aegis and human military will finish it. The virus has mutated, and it's affecting the *pricolici* now."

Every drop of color drained from Valko's face. "What? Are you sure?"

"Very."

Valko's legs seemed to give out, and he sank onto a bench. "Have you found a cure? A vaccine? Where is Sin?"

Hearing Sin's name come from the warg scum cranked up Con's temper. "Why do you care? You wanted her dead."

Valko's eyes nearly popped out of his skull "She's dead?"

Con didn't answer. "Tell me who you hired, Valko." He moved toward the warg, prepared to beat a confession out of him, but Raynor blocked him.

"Has a vaccine been developed?"

"It's close," Con said tightly. "And the irony is that if the vaccine works, it's all because of the Feast warg you both tried to kill."

That shut everyone up—everyone except Bran, who barked out a laugh until someone called his name.

A gangly blond female was loping toward them, her coltishly long legs eating up the ground. "My lord," she panted as she halted in front of them. "There's trouble... a female demon on the property."

A lick of unease went through Con, but he tamped it down because no way would Sin have come here—

"She's demanding to see Conall," the girl finished, and Con swore.

"Damn you!" Sin's outraged curses carried on the wind, and despite Con's increasing anxiety, he felt a flicker of a smile touch his lips. At least, until he saw her, struggling against the grip of two big males, a trickle of blood at the corner of her mouth.

Rage rolled in like a thunderstorm, roiling up from his gut and crashing into his skull. His feet were moving before his fury-soaked brain knew what was happening. He tore off across the wiry grass, each step parting the wispy tendrils of fog that skimmed the ground.

"Release her," he roared.

Enric stepped back, but the other, Baine, gripped her tighter. Sin took instant advantage of having a free arm and decked him with a right hook and a knee to the groin. Baine fell to the ground, one hand clutching his face, the other cupping his balls. Enric struck out at Sin, but Con, his blood still running hot, tackled him, knocked him clean out with a flurry of blows. He was going to kill Enric for touching Sin. He was going to rip his—

"Con!" Sin grabbed his arm, halting his attack as the Council members from all three societies came running.

Body still wired for battle and clamoring to turn his

fellow dhampires into mulch, Con lurched to his feet, hoping someone made a move on him or Sin. She stood in front him, her raven tresses spilling over her shoulders and onto the black leather sleeveless top she wore. A savage light glinted in her equally black eyes, as well as something just as primal, something that called to the male animal in him: desire. And, when he caught the scent of her blood, hunger.

He should have stepped away from her. Instead, he closed the distance between them. "You shouldn't be here."

"I had to find you." She licked her lips, the pink tip of her tongue catching the blood in the corner of her mouth. His gaze zeroed in on the action, and his loins filled with heat and his fangs pulsed, and he felt himself fuzzing out, leaning toward her, mouth watering, cock hardening.

He barely managed a grunted "Why?"

"I couldn't let you do the oath thingie." She spoke on a whispered breath, her face tilted upward, and he wanted to kiss her, claim her, right there against the rugged backdrop where his people had been mating for centuries. "I can't stand the thought of you losing your freedom."

Bran clapped his hands, the harsh crack drawing Con's attention. "Get her out of here."

Raynor reached for Sin, and oh, *hell no*. Con put himself between them, fangs bared. He didn't say a damned word. Didn't need to. Raynor backed off, but hatred blazed in his eyes. Icy, ancient hatred that Con had no explanation for, but right now he didn't give a shit.

Wheeling around, he gripped Sin's arm and marched her away from the group. Gods, her skin was hot in his palm, and it radiated right to his groin. "You need to leave." His voice was guttural, barely controlled. "Now."

"No." She dug in her heels and jerked them both to a halt.

He blinked. *"No?"*

"I..." Her gaze dropped to the ground and she shifted her weight, and suddenly he was struck by a blast of need that came off her in an atomic shock wave. "It's time. I... I need you."

Fierce male pride made him puff up like a rooster. "You don't *need* me." He clenched his fists to keep from grabbing, kissing, doing that public thing he said he'd never do. "You could have anyone if that were the case. You *want* me."

She snorted, an automatic response no doubt, but then her chin trembled, softening her appearance, and once again, he felt like a bastard. "Yes, okay? I want you. I know you have that"—she lowered her voice—"issue, but we can find a way around it. You don't have to bite me..."

His mind whacked out at the mere thought, and suddenly he could hear the pump of her heart, the swish of her blood running like raging rapids through her vessels, and, around him, he sensed Bran and several other dhampires closing in.

"Back away from her, Con," Bran barked. There was a dagger in his hand, and he was focused on Sin. The icy fingers of déjà vu wrapped around Con, strangling him. Following Con's mother's death at the fangs of his father, the Dhampire Council had taken a hard stand on addiction.

No more attempts at rehabilitation.

They killed the source, which killed the cravings. Con hadn't lied when he'd told Sin he was responsible for Eleanor's death. He just hadn't killed the leopard-shifter female himself.

Bran had done it with a blade through the brain stem. They hadn't even given Con a chance at bonding with her.

Con pushed Sin behind him and backed them both up toward the Harrowgate. "I'll handle this, Bran."

"You know the law," the big male said.

"I *will* handle this."

"See that you do," Bran said, as he ran his finger along the edge of the blade. "Or I will."

Sin had no clue what that craziness had been all about, but she kept her mouth shut as she and Con entered the Harrowgate, kept her mouth shut as he tapped out the map until the gate opened up into London's east end, kept her mouth shut as he stiffly led her to a flat half a block away.

As he closed the door behind him, she studied his tense demeanor, the way his chiseled features sharpened even more when he was angry. But she couldn't tell if his anger was directed at her or not.

The question was answered when he stalked to her, all sensual energy and rolling muscle encased in faded jeans and a tight black tee. His lips came down on hers, and she opened for him, met his tongue as she plastered her body against him. Desire roared through her, flaming hot, hotter than it had ever been with anyone, even at the height of her need. This was different. As pure as the snow they'd made love in.

Con held her tight, and while his hands stroked her back, they didn't stray. He dragged his mouth along her jaw, down to her neck, and then he kissed her there, right over her jugular. "That was stupid, Sin," he murmured against her skin. "You shouldn't have gone to Scotland."

"We're here, aren't we? Where we should be."

His entire body tensed, and he pulled back. "Yeah. But—" His gaze dropped to her left hand, and he snatched it up. "What the fuck?" He was staring at her fingers—or more accurately, her missing finger. His voice degenerated to a guttural rasp. "What happened? Who did that to you?"

"I did it to myself," she said gently. "I gave up my assassin master ring."

"Oh, Jesus. We need to get you to UG—"

"There's nothing that can be done, and you know it. It's healed." She waggled her fingers. "And I have nine spares."

Con closed his eyes, and when he opened them, they were the somber gray of an overburdened rain cloud. "I'm sorry."

"Don't be. You were right. Just because no one owned me didn't mean I wasn't a prisoner." She eyed the full-sized bed that was pretty much the only furniture in the studio apartment, and tugged him toward it. "Now," she teased, "I'm ready for you to do more of that foreplay thing you've been bragging about."

He stopped her, halting suddenly a few feet from the bed. She turned to face him and sucked in an appreciative breath at the sight of him, his gaze dark and predatory, his fangs extended. He looked half-wild, wholly primitive, and, God, he was so hot. His nostrils flared and his lips parted, and she wondered what he was thinking.

A glance at his groin gave her a pretty *big* clue as to the state of his mind.

And that fast, she forgot about the foreplay, because she needed him inside her. *Right now.* She reached for him and he hissed.

"Have you fed recently?" she asked, the idea that he'd taken nourishment from someone else punching her in the gut. Of course he'd have to. The addiction issue would forever keep him from being able to dine on her. Well, he'd just have to settle for bagged blood, because he was *not* sticking those fangs in anyone else. "Con?"

"No," he rasped. "I'm hungry, Sin. Not just for blood... for you."

For her. He wanted her. He didn't just need her; he *wanted* her, the way he'd made her admit to wanting him. A startling jolt of joy kicked her pulse into high gear, but it was cut short by a blast of heat and desire that came off him. Lust tore through her in a twisting, writhing tangle, and she moaned. Her vision alternately sharpened and blurred, and the scent of the aroused male in front of her flowed through her like an aphrodisiac syrup.

She took a step toward him, but her legs went rubbery and her feet felt glued to the floor. Weakness meant she was so far gone that, at this point, she didn't have the strength to even make it to a Harrowgate to find a male. Good thing Con was here, good thing he was who she wanted, and good thing he liked it rough.

Twenty-three

Con stood with his back to the door, so close to it he could reach behind him, open it, and run. Which, if he was smart, he'd do. But Sin's pheromones had hijacked him, his lust was boiling over, and that, on top of the blood addiction, kept him frozen to the spot.

She moaned again, and the sound made his groin throb. "Con, *now*. It's been too long."

"I know." He took a step closer. He could have her. He just wouldn't feed. And then he'd find a way to explain to her that she needed to stay away from him, or her life would be in danger.

The logical thoughts slid like a drop of oil over a gallon of water, fragmenting, becoming slick and thin and lost as the more primitive instincts drove his body and brain.

She tossed her head, flinging her hair away from her neck, and his line of sight narrowed, focused, filled with only her. The whoosh of blood through her veins became a beacon for his growing hunger. The pump of her heart thudded so loud it seemed to affect his own pulse rate.

"Now."

Another step. His brutal erection punched painfully hard against his zipper. Another step. She might as well be a she-wolf in heat, and the male warg in him couldn't resist. He was starving, needed her so badly.

If I touch her, I'll kill her.

Violently, he shook his head, shattering his runaway fears against the inside of his skull.

"Please." Her pheromones were clouding his head, making his heart pound and his skin shrink.

His gaze locked on her throat. His lips peeled away from his fangs. *Bite. Drink. Kill.*

No! Reeling backward, he crashed into the wall. "I can't." She reached for him, and he hissed. "Don't. Don't touch me, goddammit!"

Sin recoiled, hurt flashing behind the haze of need in her eyes. "You want me to go find another male?"

Another male? Oh, hell no. "I'll kill him." His voice was smoky, gravelly, as if it had been plucked from the pits of hell.

"Then what?" Sweat beaded on Sin's brow, and she winced as she wrapped her arm around her belly. She was hurting. "Con, you've got to—"

"I can't!" he roared. "Don't you get it? I'm not strong enough."

"So . . . let me get this straight." She threw her hand out to catch herself against the wall and she spoke between panting breaths. "You won't fuck me, but you don't want anyone else to either."

That about summed it up. "Damn you," he growled

angrily. "You shouldn't have gone to Scotland. You shouldn't have forced this choice on me." He wasn't being fair, and he knew that. But he was pissed at himself, at her, at the alignment of the planets and the fate that had brought this all about.

Her head came up, and defiance flashed across her face. "I'm so sorry I need something you can't give me so you're feeling inadequate and grumpy." She started toward the door. "Go to hell. No, wait, that's where I'm going, because I'm sure I'll be able to find some hot demon who can give me what I need."

He snapped, his control shredded beyond repair, and he pounced, taking her down to the floor and tearing at her clothes. Beneath him, she writhed greedily, wrapping her legs around him and thrusting her breasts up into his palms. He tore open the fly of his jeans and entered her hard, and they both cried out. She was hot. Wet. Perfect. His pulse roared in his ears and his vision sharpened—hell, all of his senses heightened to the point of sensory overload as he pounded into her with raw, punishing violence usually reserved for moon fevers.

His fangs shot out as he peaked, and he dove for her neck. Somehow, he dipped into his last reserves of control, and he bit into his arm instead, coming even as pain streaked through him.

Sin joined him with a scream, and as he pumped, taking himself to another, she came again. But when he should have felt sated, he only felt a burning need coiling inside him. Possessive fury tightened his muscles. Heated his blood until he was fevered.

He tore his mouth away from his arm. "Mine. You're *mine*, Sin. No one else will ever touch you, do you

understand? You belong *to me*. You'll bond with *me*."
Everything but the ecstasy was a blur as he bit into her
shoulder, barely able to keep from taking a vein. Behind
his teeth, the bond glands tingled. His next climax was
hard and powerful, but as Sin's sex clenched around him,
he noted—barely—a change. She whimpered through her
orgasm, and then she was struggling to get out from under
him.

"No," she moaned. "Please, no."

The despair in her voice pierced his Neanderthal brain.
What was he doing? Blinking, he tried to bring himself
around. Was he...yes, he was biting her. He released her
with a hiss of panic, but the glands were pumping, and
horror filled him as he felt the hot sting of a drop of bond
fluid drip into the bite he'd left. Oh, *shit*! Maybe it wasn't
enough. She hadn't gotten a full dose—

"Get off me!"

He scrambled off her, his mind spinning, his body
cramping and whacking out with the need for her blood.
He'd tasted it, but he needed more. At the same time,
shame ripped him apart. It was not okay to bond with
someone without their permission. He'd be as bad as all
the scumbags who had owned Sin over the years.

She rolled away, grabbed at her clothes, and eyed him
like he was a monster. "What did you do to me?"

Gods, he couldn't even look at her. "Sin..."

"What did you do?" she screamed, shoving to her feet.

"I tried to bond you to me...I stopped before it went
too far, I think—"

"You bastard," she whispered. "You fucking bastard."
She jammed her legs into her pants. "You want to own
me, just like everyone else. I'd be just another possession,

wouldn't I? And what will you do when you get tired of me?"

He didn't think that was possible, but right now, she wouldn't believe his denial, and he couldn't blame her at all. "I'm sorry, Sin." He stood, zipped up, hated himself for how his hand shook.

"Sorry?" She snorted. "You're such a hypocrite, Con . . . You accused me of having a wall around my heart, but do you even realize that you do the same thing? You take risks with your body because you won't with your heart. You can't get attached to anything, so you're always changing up cars, jobs, friends." She snorted again. "Friends. What a joke, huh? That's why they're human, isn't it? You don't have to keep them for long if you're always having to dump them before they get suspicious."

Shock rippled through him. She was right. Holy shit, she was right on the money. He lurched backward, slapped by the stark truth she'd hit him with. He wasn't easily bored . . . he was just too damned afraid to get attached to anything. Gods, what a selfish piece of shit he was. He'd forced Sin to confront her fears, her feelings, and all the while he'd had the same issues. The same wall.

For far worse reasons. He'd gotten himself addicted to a female's blood, and then, after she'd been killed and he'd been banished from the clan, he'd spent his life blaming everyone but himself for all of it. He'd thought he was carefree, happy, experiencing life just to prove that he didn't need anyone or anything.

You are a spoiled wretch who should have been brought to heel centuries ago. Bran had been right. Just like Sin.

But now, more than ever, he couldn't weaken. Not when it came to her. He wanted her so badly it hurt, as if his heart had been wrapped in razor wire. She didn't deserve a spoiled, selfish wretch like him, and he couldn't bond with her even if she wanted him to. He couldn't tie her down like that.

And he couldn't be with her without being bonded to her.

"You're right, Sin." Gods, his chest ached. He rubbed it, and it felt caved in. Hollow. "So there's nothing left to say. You should go."

He was pretty sure she'd take him up on that, but sure as Sheoul smelled like brimstone, she was Sin, so she did the exact opposite. She finished dressing and planted her feet.

"I don't think so. You accused me of running from things, and now you're doing the same thing? You need to *feel*, Con," she said, hurling his words back in his face. "You don't get to throw me away because I refuse to be a possession. Owning a person is a way to have them without admitting you feel something. So no. You don't get to do that. You can have me, but only because you want me and I want you. I get the addiction thing, but you know what? Somehow we'll handle it. Maybe Eidolon can help. Or a sorcerer. I know a few good ones."

Jesus. She was serious. Even after what he'd just done, she still wanted to be with him. It was tempting, so fucking tempting, and he'd always been a gambler. But he would not gamble with Sin's life.

"The clan will kill you, Sin. They don't allow addiction. And even if I manage to get cured, I can't be near you or it'll start up again."

"I'm not afraid of your damned clan."

No, she wouldn't be, would she. His stomach turned

over at the realization that there was only one thing he
could do now. He had to throw rocks. And this time,
he had to aim well. Better to see her hurt than dead. He
opened his mouth, but nothing came out. *Man up, asshole*. Yeah, because it was so manly to kick a female while
she was down.

"You don't get it, little demon." He deliberately made
his voice toneless, but it took effort, and he prayed his voice
wouldn't break. "You were right. You'd be a possession to
me. I do care for you. Now. But in a few months, maybe
a couple of years, you won't appeal to me anymore. I'll
want something shiny and new. Probably taller. Blonder."
Yeah, that rock had sharp edges.

A flush spread from her forehead to the swells of her
breasts, and she stepped back with uncharacteristic awkwardness. "What are you saying?"

"I'm saying I shouldn't have let Luc talk me into that
bet. I never should have fucked you even though that's
all any succubus is good for." A soft gasp escaped her,
and shame made the ground shift beneath him. Instinct
made him want to fold her into his arms and fix her hurt,
but instead, he steeled himself to finish it. "What? Why
do you look so surprised? You *are* a sex demon. Did you
think we could ride off into the sunset, set up a house
and fuck up a bunch of kids? The only thing I've ever
wanted from you is sex and blood. Fucking and feeding
go together for me, and since I can't feed from you anymore . . ." He gestured to the door. "Get out, and don't ever
come near me again."

Before his eyes, Sin changed. Left the building. The
female who had finally found a bit of softness, kindness,
and acceptance disappeared behind a cold, remote mask.

Only the very slight tremor in her fingers as she jammed them into her pocket gave away any sign of emotion. He thought she was going for a weapon—he certainly deserved it.

Instead, she drew out a neatly folded square of bills. She peeled off two fives and dropped them on the floor. "The ten bucks I owe you."

She walked out of the flat and out of his life. When the door closed, so softly he barely heard it, he retched. Barely made it to the toilet.

He'd done it. He'd finally thrown the rock that hurt her. That drove her away for good.

Sin didn't cry. She couldn't afford to. Not yet. She had to talk to her brothers.

Her *brothers*.

It struck her that not only did she feel the need to go to them, but for the first time, she truly acknowledged what they were. Yes, she'd known they were siblings, but at some point, they'd actually become family to her. And crazily enough, her first instinct was to go to them.

And didn't it just figure that the first one she ran into at UG would be Wraith.

"Smurfette!" He grinned as she stepped out of the Harrowgate. "Where's Con? Some warg was just here and he said Con left the sanctuary with you." When she didn't reply because her throat had closed up, Wraith's smile faltered, and his voice gentled. "Lore's here. I think he's in E's office."

She started down the hall, and Wraith fell into step beside her, his silence both surprising and oddly comforting. When she got to E's office, though, Shade was there instead of Lore.

Shade pushed himself off the wall he'd been leaning against. "Where's Con?"

Why was everyone so freaking curious about him? She wanted to scream at them to shut up, but the moment she let loose, the waterworks would start and all those emotions Con had wanted her to *feel* would lay her flat. "Not important," she said crisply. "What's up with the vaccine?"

"Initial immunizations have begun," Eidolon said from behind his desk. "A lot sooner than I expected. So far, the two males I vaccinated and then exposed to the virus are fine."

"You actually got volunteers for that?"

"Heh. Volunteers. Funny." Wraith's grin was pure evil. "They were both on Carceris death row. By volunteering for the testing, they got their sentences reduced to life in prison."

Personally, Sin would rather have death, but whatever. The fact that death row in a Carceris jail lasted only a week probably scared the poor bastards enough to make them volunteer. Well, that and the fact that the Carceris's main means of execution was to toss the victim into a pit as bait for the hellhounds.

If you were lucky, they only tore you apart. If you weren't lucky, and they were horny...

She shuddered. Little frightened her as much as the unholy canines. But she did find it amusing that the souls of evil humans who had tortured animals and were sent to Sheoul-gra got to spend a lot of time in the pits with the beasts. She'd always loved the whole an-eye-for-an-eye thing.

Shade shoved a stick of gum in his mouth. "Now, what happened with Con? Raynor said—"

The only thing I've ever wanted from you is sex and blood. Dammit. She didn't want to talk about it. And yet, her mouth opened up and words came out. "He's at his apartment." The tears she'd been holding back finally erupted, but she dashed them away before Eidolon could hand her a tissue. "He tried this...bond thing—"

"What do you mean, he tried? Against your will?" Shade's voice degenerated into a dark rumble. "And what *the fuck* happened to your finger?"

"I had to get the assassin ring off so I could go to..." Con. She'd done it, in part, so she could be with him. What a freaking idiot she was! Anger and misery tightened around her chest, making it hard to breathe.

A snarl from behind her startled her. "I'll kill him," Wraith said.

Shade tossed his gum wrapper into the trash. "I'll help."

"We'll make it a family fun night," Eidolon drawled, his voice calm, cool, and serious as shit.

Gold flecks peppered the blue of Wraith's eyes, and he flicked his tongue over the point of one fang. "I told you I won't let anyone fuck with my family, Sin."

At the time, he'd said those same words to her. Meaning that he didn't want *her* fucking with his family. And now...*she* was the family. "Don't. Please." Somehow she kept her voice from cracking. "I just want to forget."

They stared at each other in silence for a while, and then Eidolon cleared his throat. "I discovered how you came into existence."

It was an abrupt shift of subject, but a welcome one. Eidolon was good at that. "Do I want to know?"

Shrugging, Eidolon leaned back in his chair and stee-pled his fingers over his chest. In the short time she'd known him, she'd learned that when he settled in like that, he was gearing up for a medical lecture.

"You told me your mother used a demon herb to attempt an abortion," he said. "The most common plant used for that purpose is skullwort, but it's meant for demon physiology, not human. When ingested by most demon species, the mother's body becomes hostile to the fetuses. But in a human it does the opposite. It strengthened the demon halves of you and Lore instead of destroying them. And because it's a demon chemical compound, it reacted... badly... with your human half. I suspect your mother ingested the herb immediately after conception, and likely a couple of times after that. The herb is loaded with hormones, and it apparently retarded the normal progress of gene development that should have turned you into a male."

Retarded. Nice. "So if Lore and I shared the same womb, why would it affect me and not him?"

"You're fraternal, not identical. You have different genes that are susceptible—or not—to different things. Same thing happens in alcoholic human mothers. She might give birth to one twin with fetal alcohol syndrome, while the other has no symptoms at all." Eidolon shifted, sitting forward in his chair again. "There's something else. Unlike Lore, you're not sterile."

She blinked. "Then why haven't I gotten knocked up, like, a million times by now?"

"Because you don't ovulate, but you do have viable eggs. You can have a family, Sin. You'll just have to go through an in vitro procedure."

"That's not going to happen." Not only did she not want kids, but who would she have them with? No one but Con had ever wanted to be with her. She'd never wanted to be with anyone but him. And in the end, he'd rejected her. Left her, the way he'd said he wouldn't do.

God, how could she hate someone and ache for them at the same time?

A hot, angry flush settled over her skin, and she knew she was going to burst into tears again.

"I have to go." She leaped to her feet, making a slashing motion with her hand when her brothers tried to stop her. She needed to be alone. Like she'd always been.

Sin hightailed it through UG's halls as fast as she could without looking like a complete idiot. It was only as she entered the emergency department, where the Harrowgate was, that she realized she had nowhere to go.

She'd lived for so long at the assassin den that she had no other residences. In her haste to get out of the den, she'd left her clothes, her few trinkets, and all her weapons—except what was on her body and a few spares she kept at Lore's place—behind. Now she was homeless on top of everything else.

"Sin."

She wheeled around. She wasn't overly surprised to see Raynor, the dude she'd seen in Scotland, standing there, but still a ball of "oh, shit," dropped into her gut. He'd been waiting for her. The hunter's gleam in his eye was a dead giveaway.

"Are you here about the vaccine?" It was a lame question, but she was on the verge of tears over Con, was unnaturally nervous, and her guilt over the fact that she'd started a plague that had killed hundreds, maybe thousands, of his people still ate at her.

"Yes, thank you for asking." He moved toward her, and she felt like a rabbit in a wolf's sights. "You destroyed a lot of lives, including those of many of my friends and family."

"I know," she said. "I'm sorry—"

"That's not good enough, you little bitch," he snapped, the sudden change in him putting Sin on edge.

Somehow, she kept her expression and voice neutral. "Is that why you're here? Because you want your pound of flesh from me?"

"That's exactly why I'm here. I have a proposition for you."

"Whatever it is," Sin said wearily, "you can shove it up your ass."

He laughed. The dude's moods flip-flopped like a dying snake. "Trust me, you want to hear this. If you don't, more people will die." He headed toward the parking lot, obviously expecting to be followed. Sin nearly didn't. But she had a feeling he wasn't bluffing, and she couldn't be responsible for more deaths.

Once they were in the parking lot, he stopped near an ambulance. The stall next to it, where the rig she and Con had taken should have been, screamed with emptiness, reminding her of Con, of being in the back of the rig, of his hands on her.

Stop it. Grow a fucking pair of balls and get over your tender feelings. Good plan. She'd let Raynor take the brunt of her misery.

"Okay, dickhead," she said finally. "What do you want?"

"I want the born wargs to be destroyed. It's time the balance of power shifted and turneds took over."

"That's all? Well, good luck with that. I want world peace and for people to stop making bad Batman movies, but guess what, buddy, I'm screwed, too."

"Sarcastic little wench. I *will* get what I want, and you're going to give it to me."

"I don't think so." She jammed her hands into her pants pockets. Her left hand felt weird and she wondered idly when she'd get used to the missing digit. "I mean, the 'me giving it to you' part. I *am* a wench."

Raynor snorted. "Only a demon could be proud of that."

God, this guy was slime. How had Con not killed him before now? Con. *Stop it!* "What do you want? I'm bored. You've got ten seconds to tell me why I'm here."

"You're here because I want you to create a virus that affects only the *pricolici*."

Not just slime, but delusional. The parking lot vehicle entrance flashed, and an ambulance zipped through, pulling to a stop in the unloading space near the doors to the ER. Sin's pulse went a little crazy as she peered into the cab to identify the medics. Con wasn't one of them. Not that she'd expected him to be, but she couldn't help but look.

Stop. It.

"You do realize," she said, turning back to the warg, "that the last time I created a virus, it jumped species."

"It won't if the *pricolici* are contained."

Sick bastard. "Okay, for shits and giggles, what in the hell makes you think I would ever do that?"

Raynor smiled. "Because you're going to become my personal assassin."

"You should see Eidolon for a brain scan or some-thing." She watched the medics unload some sort of hid-eous, skeletal demon out of the ambulance. "Because you're fucked in the head."

The warg's voice became an eerily calm drawl. "Did you know that when a born warg hides the fact that her off-spring were born human, she is committing a crime punish-able by death? She and her offspring are chained to stakes on the eve of a full moon, and once the pack shifts, they are torn apart. And eaten. It's a painful, gruesome death."

Sin didn't allow her expression to change, but inside, she was sweating bullets. "So?"

"So I know Conall's little family secret. I have a spy inside the *pricolici* pack you and he visited. And I know all about his granddaughter, Sable."

Oh, holy shit. "And what do you think you know?"

"I know that at least one of her twin cubs was born human." He leaned forward. "Because my brother was the father."

Sin's throat closed up, but she managed a raspy "What?"

Raynor cast a glance at another vehicle coming in through the parking lot gate. "I was there. I watched The Aegis kill my brother, and I kept an eye on her for months—"

"Why?" Sin interrupted. "What would you have to gain? Or are you just some obsessed, creepy stalker?"

The warg's gaze drifted, softening his expression. "Do you know what it's like to be invisible, demon? I was on the Warg Council when it was even more of a joke than it is now. We were allowed to sit in on meetings, but we had no input, no vote, no voice when even the dhampires, who aren't even full wargs, had more power than we did. I needed every advantage, every bit of ammunition I could get, no matter how insignificant it might have seemed at the time." His eyes refocused, bitterness burning in them once again. "So I watched Sable, and when she disappeared with Conall for a few days and returned to the village with the infants, I suspected that she'd had one or both of the cubs turned and tattooed. But it wasn't until Con's appearance a few days ago, followed by her rapid departure from the village with her family, that I knew for sure. And I *will* spill the little secret."

"Bastard." Sin drew her right hand out of her pocket, preparing to fire up her gift and fry the fucker. "You wouldn't—"

"Oh, I would. I'll tell her pack what she's done, about Conall's part in it, and I'll take you there to watch. He might even be put to death with them."

"Unless I work for you."

"Exactly. And don't even think about harming me. My second-in-command is only one of several people I've told, and if anything happens to me, she'll make sure Sable's secret is made public." He drew a delicate choke chain from his jacket pocket. A fucking dog collar. "Once you put it on, it would be in your best interests to not allow me to be hurt or killed, because what happens to me, happens to you."

Enraged, Sin instinctively engaged her power. Heat spread from her shoulder to her fingers, following the track of her glyphs. If she looked, she knew they'd be glowing and writhing as though alive. "You son of a bitch."

"That," he said icily, "would only be accurate if I were *pricolici*."

She stared at the collar dangling from his fingertips, her heart rate spiking. How could this be happening? After a hundred years of slavery, of belonging to so many different masters, she'd finally found freedom, and now she was faced with slavery once again. Worse, she'd freaked on Con over a bonding issue, something that might have been constricting, but that would have been far preferable to what Raynor was trying to force upon her.

"Well?" he asked. "Will you serve me, or will you let Sable and her son, and perhaps even Con, die?"

Her mind screamed and her body trembled. She had no choice. Not really. Maybe if she agreed, it would buy some time for Con to get his family to safety.

"Yes," she ground out. "I'll do it." He tossed the collar to her, and her fingers shook as she fastened it around her throat. A cloying, strangling sensation washed over her, a feeling of being caged and smothered, and she doubled over and lost the contents of her stomach.

"There, there," Ray said, as he stroked her back. "You just saved lives. That's nothing to feel sick over."

"I'm going to kill you," she swore. "Someday, I'm going to rip your throat out with my bare hands."

Ray shrugged. "Until that day, you're mine. And I plan to use you until you drop."

Use her. Oh, God, if he touched her like that...she shrank away from him, unable to bear his hands on her for one more second. She didn't know how she'd manage to have *anyone's* hands on her now. Not after Con.

His glare was full of righteous indignation. "Don't worry, I wouldn't touch you with my dick if it were on fire and you were wet for me. I don't screw demons. But don't push me, Sin, because I have friends who do."

Twenty-four

Sharla LastNameDidn'tMatter rubbed her naked body against Con's, exposing her slender neck. "Take me, Conall."

He needed to. Badly. His body wasn't responding to her sexual invitation, but he could force himself to at least take blood from her. The lack of feeding was making him weak, but so far, his stomach had rebelled against everything he'd put in it, from food to the few swallows of blood he'd taken from a human male vagrant last night after he'd kicked Sin out.

The fact that he'd expelled her to save her life didn't make him feel any better about it.

Sharla's hands slid up his bare chest and then down, over his tense abs to the waistband of his jeans. She was practiced...as a swan, a human who willingly submitted to the blood and sexual needs of vampires in exchange for the high they got, she knew what was expected of her. But Con didn't want anything she was so boldly offering.

He still wasn't sure how he'd managed to get himself inside Revenant, an underground Goth club, not with the dark circles under his eyes and the sunken hollows in his cheeks, classic signs of vampire starvation that usually meant no admittance. Clubs couldn't afford to have their customers ripped apart by out-of-control feeders. But he supposed the fact that he was a regular had given him a free pass, and it hadn't taken long for the swans to find him. He'd seen other vampires feed from Sharla, knew she could handle rough.

His fangs extended, and he wondered if she could also handle dangerous.

Tilting her head, Sharla stood on her toes so her throat was only inches from his lips. Her blood thudded through her veins, filling his ears with the sweet music. He only wished Sin was the one playing it.

"I'm ready." Her voice was husky, needy, and full of futile desperation, and he wondered if he'd taste drugs in her blood.

Con swallowed dryly, which seemed so odd with the way his mouth was watering. He needed this, but it felt so wrong, as if he were being unfaithful to Sin.

In a way, he supposed, he was.

Sharla's fingers tightened on his hips, urging him on.

The door flew open. Crashed into the wall behind it hard enough for plaster to fall to the carpet. Con whirled, instinctively tucking the human behind him. His heart pounded, his breath rasped in his throat, and when he looked into the hard, frosty eyes of the male in front of him, he knew he was dead.

Shade's gaze shifted to Sharla. "Get out."

"Go fuck yourself, asshole," she spat, stepping out from behind Con, but staying close. She was mouthy, but not stupid.

Con gripped her shoulder and nodded. "Go."

Glaring at Shade, she gathered up her clothes and shoved by him, not bothering to dress. Shade shut the door, and Con braced himself for a fight. In his weakened state, Con couldn't put up much of a battle, and Shade would kick his ass. Thing was, he couldn't dredge up much give-a-shit.

"I'm surprised you're alone," Con said. "Figured all of you would want a piece of killing me."

"For what? Trying to bond with Sin against her will, or for hurting her?"

"Both."

"As tempting as it is, I'm not here to kill you. She begged us not to, and we owe you for saving her life." Shade dug in his jacket pocket and pulled out a bag of blood, which he tossed on the bed.

Con drew a harsh breath. "Is that..."

"Sin's."

Surprise rocked Con back a step. His entire body trembled, and it took everything he had to not pounce on it. But he definitely couldn't yank his gaze away from it. "I can't. I'm trying to detox."

"You're a mess. Drink it. Come back to the hospital with me, and we can detox you there. You'll have a better chance at success, and it'll be faster and a hell of a lot less painful. We've gotten a lot of experience with Wraith."

"I'll deal. Can't go to the hospital." Not with Sin around. It would be like waving a red flag in front of a bull. "And I'm not touching that."

"Don't be an idiot. Drink the fucking blood."

"No."

Shade came at him, and Con met him, head-on. They were nose to nose, chest to chest, and Con could feel the aggression rolling off Shade. The demon wanted to shed blood as bad as Con wanted to drink it.

"Are you completely suicidal?" he growled. "You're suffering, and you don't need to. Sin wouldn't want to see you like this."

Sin would probably *love* to see him like this.

"Step off, Shade." Con's adrenaline rose in an angry tide, his hunger cresting, his fury at himself peaking with it, creating a caustic temper that had him ready to knock the demon's teeth in.

Shade shoved at Con's chest. "You stupid son of a bitch. You know detoxing by yourself is risky as shit, and the only fucking way we're letting you live is if we know you aren't a danger to Sin, so drink!"

Con swung, and it was on. Fists flew, and furniture broke as they threw each other around the room. Con's waning strength became a factor, and it wasn't long before Shade was straddling him, forearm over his throat as he jammed the bag into Con's mouth. Con shook his head, his teeth firmly clamped shut, but Sin's heady scent was all over the unit, and his fangs remained elongated no matter how hard he willed them to retract.

Shade was ruthless in his determination, and he kept pressure on the bag, scraping it back and forth across Con's mouth. Finally, the plastic snagged on the tip of one canine, and a drop of blood dripped onto his tongue. Con's entire body jerked as if an electric current had shot through him.

Game over. Delirious with need, he gripped Shade's wrist and held his hand steady as he bit deeply into the bag. Sin's essence flowed down his throat, lighting him up from the inside. He moaned at the taste, at the relief from the painful hunger that had ridden him hard. He wished Sin were here. Wished he could sink into her body as he ravaged her throat. He'd take her hard and fast, listening to her screams of pleasure...her screams...her blood.

Con...stop. The voice barely penetrated his feeding frenzy. Sin was beneath him, her struggles ineffective against his new strength and need.

Yo, get off me. No, not happening. He'd have to bite again, because the vein he was at had run out...Maybe he'd drained her. Terror welled up through the bloodlust, piercing the addiction.

"Con! Fuck!" Male voice. Deep.

Con blinked, coming out of his haze to see Shade beneath him. Con's erection was pushed hard against Shade's thigh, and yeah...not cool.

Panting and shaking like a leaf, Con scrambled off him. "Ah...I don't...that was, ah...not for you."

"I fucking hope not," Shade muttered. He rolled easily to his feet, seemingly unperturbed, but then, he was a sex demon, and Con doubted much fazed him when it came to that. And seeing how Con was a thousand years old and had done pretty much everything, it shouldn't faze him, either. Except that Shade was the brother of the female he craved, and...yuck.

Con remained on the floor, sitting on his haunches. He scrubbed his hands over his face, suddenly exhausted. "Gods, I hate this."

"Come to the hospital." The black leather of Shade's

jacket creaked as he folded his arms across his chest, and
Con knew this argument was a losing one. But his stubborn self couldn't cave in that easily.

"I can't."

"You let Sin warm up to you, and then you smashed her
under your boot." Shade's already deep voice dropped an
octave. "The least you can do is get yourself clean. And,
buddy, I told you, kick the habit so you aren't a danger to
Sin, or we'll put you in the ground."

Fair enough, and no less than what Con deserved.
"The detox...it'll be ugly. You'll have to keep me caged
or bound."

"I'm pretty much an expert at that." There was a glint
of wry amusement in Shade's eyes as he gestured to the
door. "Let's go."

Sin needed sex.

The need wasn't so bad yet that it hurt, but it wouldn't
be long before the cramps, sweats, and nausea hit her.
She'd put it off because the idea of being with anyone
other than Con made her sick.

It made her cry, too, but she wasn't about to admit that
to anyone. Not even Lore.

She'd spent the night at his place, the North Carolina
shack he rarely used anymore now that he lived in Italy
with Idess. Thankfully, he'd stayed away, even though he
probably knew she'd been there. Still, he and the other
three brothers had tried to call her about every fifteen
minutes, and she finally had to shut off her phone just to
keep her sanity. This morning when she'd checked her
messages, she'd found forty.

She'd deleted them all without listening. But the text message she'd just gotten from Shade as she sat at the bar in a demon club made her heart stall. Apparently, Con was at UG, and it would be best if she stayed away.

No problem. Being felt up by the handsome, crimson-skinned Sora demon behind her was what she wanted to be doing anyway.

Her heart knocked on her rib cage, calling her a liar.

The Sora's strong hands gripped her hips, his broad chest blanketed her back, and the bulge in his jeans was an insistent prod on her ass. Not long ago, she'd have responded, would have had him in the bathroom or on the dance floor, making use of his multitalented tail by now. Instead, all she could think about was Con.

"Bastard," she snarled into her beer mug.

"That's not a nice thing to say to the male who is going to make you scream his name," he said, as he nuzzled her neck. His teeth clinked against the chain around her throat, and she swore she felt it tighten.

She drained her beer as his hand slipped under her leather skirt, his fingertips brushing the silky material of her underwear.

Pain streaked through her, radiating from the male's hand all the way to her organs, which suddenly felt like they were shifting, rearranging, tying themselves into knots. Gasping, she leaped off the bar stool and dashed outside, where the unique, moldy smell of Bangkok made her stomach rebel on the cobblestone walk. What the hell was going on with her?

Taking great gulps of polluted air, she sagged against the side of the building, which housed an underground prostitution and drug parlor in the front, and the demon dance club in the back. The sounds of the raunchy night-life drowned out the throbbing pulse in Sin's ears; it was four a.m., and this section of the city was still alive. Every vice, every fetish, no matter how illegal and disgusting, could be satisfied in Bangkok, and the universal truth remained in effect here: wickedness preferred the cover of darkness.

As the nausea waned, Sin's needs came back front and center, an aching, shivery presence. She'd never hated what she was more than right now. Before Con, her body had been a tool, something as impersonal as a hammer. Now it felt like hers, like she finally owned it, controlled it, and the idea of sharing it with anyone but Con...

Fuck. *Get over yourself.* She brushed by the bouncer at the door and strode directly into the crowd of people writhing on the dance floor. Seizure-inducing lights flashed to the techno-pop beat of the music as Sin eased against a large male Bedim. They were a sensual, dark-skinned race whose young males were forced out of their community for ten years to experience life outside. Upon returning, they would be given a harem of females, but until then, they had to find pleasure elsewhere.

He turned into her, his masculine smile something that should have started her engines. Her body was full of need, but as he smoothed his palms down her bare arms, only cold shivers followed.

"Touch me," she growled, and he grinned, moved his hands to her breasts.

Instantly, her stomach rebelled again, and she tore away from him, panting, praying she wouldn't lose the rest of her liquid dinner all over the dance floor. Quickly, she grabbed another male and swung him around. She palmed his groin... and lost it. Totally blew chunks on his spandex zebra tights. Which, really, needed to be put out of their misery, because hello, the '80s were long gone.

Humiliation rocked her, and she stumbled out of the bar. Her lust hadn't eased, and neither had the want for Con. Had he bonded with her after all?

A horrible thought spun up. When male Sems bonded to a female, they couldn't so much as get it up for any female other than their mate. What if female Sems went through something similar? Something that would make her unable to ever sleep with another male?

Head swimming with the horrific possibilities, she hopped a Harrowgate to UG.

When she stepped out, she saw Tayla speaking with Serena, who was holding a squirming Stewie in her arms. Knowing at least one of her brothers would be nearby, Sin looked around and, sure enough, Eidolon, dressed in his usual green scrubs, emerged from one of the exam rooms.

Sin marched up to him. "Where is Con?"

Eidolon handed a chart to a nurse. "He's detoxing. You can't see him."

"I don't care if he's dancing ballet in the cafeteria. I need him."

"Sin, you can't. You'll only set him back—"

"I don't care!" She was practically shouting now, and her sisters-in-law were moving toward them. Dammit. She didn't need more witnesses to her weakness and embarrassment. She'd find Con on her own. She shoved past her brother but he grabbed her arm and swung her back around.

"I won't let you near him."

"Then you can watch me die." She broke away from him, unable to bear his touch, not because it made her ill, but because she couldn't deal with affection right now.

His eyes narrowed. "What are you talking about?"

"Remember when I said Con tried to bond with me? Well, it looks like he didn't just *try*. He *did*."

For a moment, Eidolon stood there, frowning, and then his eyes shot wide. "So you can't..."

"No, I can't."

"Fuck."

"Exactly. Now where is he?"

Twenty-five

Con hadn't expected to be housed in a room decked out like a Hilton hotel suite or anything, but he had figured the Sem boys would at least provide him with heat.

Not so much.

Apparently, ice-cold temperatures helped hasten blood addiction detox. How, Con didn't know, but he half-suspected the boys were torturing him, and it was working. He was freezing his ass off. Well, he froze when he wasn't sweating out a fever.

Shivering in the scrubs E had thrown at him, he paced back and forth in the room, where all the furniture except a bed had been removed. He was chained to the floor with a manacle around his ankle that allowed him to move around—but only during the short periods of lucidity, like the one he was experiencing now. Usually, he was a violent, pissed-off animal, and when he felt the starvation begin to ride him again, he'd hit a call button, and one of the brothers, along with several orderlies, would chain him to the bed, sedate him, and jam a feeding tube down his throat.

The human blood they forced into his stomach was keeping him alive, even though most of it came back up.

Fuck, he was miserable. He'd looked in the bathroom mirror, had barely recognized the gaunt face or the hollow eyes staring back at him. He was so weakened that after only a couple of minutes of pacing he'd have to rest, but then, his periods of noncrazy lasted only about five minutes, anyway.

He glanced at his watch. In about ninety seconds, he'd slide back into insanity, where nothing but hunger, violence, and Sin existed.

Sin.

He ached for her. His entire body felt bruised, and the center of his chest stung, telling him his yearning was more than physical. He missed her, couldn't stop thinking about the stupid little things, like how she smiled. How she ate. How her voice went low and smoky when he touched her. Holy hell, he would give anything to be with her like a normal person.

But that would never happen, and he was the world's biggest dumbass to even fantasize about it. The best he could hope for was to get clean and spend the rest of his life ruling the dhampire clan. Participating in the mating rituals with females he probably wouldn't even like.

The door swung open, and Eidolon strode in. "Get on the bed."

It was a little early, but Con didn't have the energy to argue. He lay stiffly as Eidolon strapped him down... extra tight.

Con glared. "What, is circulation in my extremities an option now?"

Eidolon tugged hard on the leather strap that crossed over his chest. "Sin's here to see you."

"What?" Con's voice was strangled, and it had nothing to do with the final strap Eidolon was tightening over his neck. "No! You can't let her—"

"Too late." Sin swept into the room the way she always did, like a storm cloud that stirred up everything and everyone around it. She was wrapped like a gift in black leather, from her zip-front, sleeveless corset and matching miniskirt to the sleek boots that came up to her knees, revealing a toned expanse of thigh he remembered touching. Kissing. Remembered those legs wrapping around his waist and resting on either side of his head.

Fever swamped him, his fangs sliced out of his gums, his vision trained on her like a laser sight, and his entire body strained against the bonds. "Get out."

Eidolon complied, even though he wasn't the intended recipient of Con's order. He did, however, shoot Con a deadly look of warning before he closed the door behind him.

"Wow," Sin said, her high-heeled boots clacking on the floor as she approached. "I didn't expect a party or anything, but I figured you might be able to handle a hi."

"I'm serious," he gritted. "Get out."

"Well, you know what?" She tied her hair up in a knot. "I would, except that you fucking bonded me to you or something, and I need to borrow your dick for a minute."

His cock jumped excitedly at her news, but Con frowned. "I couldn't have bonded with you. The addiction would be gone."

"Yeah? Then explain to me why touching other guys makes me hurl?"

Touch? Other guys? He knew she'd have to, but to hear her say it, to know she'd tried... A terrible pressure condensed in his chest cavity and his skull, and then he heard some sort of monster in the room—

"Hey." He blinked at the sharp sting in his cheek, saw Sin standing beside him, palm open and ready to strike again. "That enraged snarling and trying to break out of your bindings is not attractive." She reached for the waistband of the scrub bottoms. He was already hard, painfully so, and okay, now he realized why Eidolon had left the hip strap unfastened.

"I'm sorry," he said, instinctively trying to raise his hips to help her tug his pants down, but Eidolon had left the leg and waist bindings too tight for any movement. *"I want to sink my teeth into your throat and drink until you scream for me to stop..."*

Had he just said that? Fan-fucking-tastic. Looked like he was in for brief periods of clarity followed by fun moments of murderous insanity.

Sin cocked a dark eyebrow at him. "You really know how to charm a girl." Rolling her bottom lip between her teeth, she turned back to his hips, where his cock was now free, the waistband of his scrubs sitting uncomfortably snug just beneath his balls. For some reason she seemed hesitant to touch him.

"What..." He swallowed, teeth clenched, because he was in a moment of nonhomicidal existence, and he wanted to stay there. "What's wrong?"

"Nothing." She shook her head briskly and then gripped his shaft. The feel of her warm, soft palm on him made him moan, and her relieved smile made him do it again.

"Now, Sin," he whispered. "Before I lose control again."

Sin didn't argue. She stepped out of her panties, careful to not let them catch on her two thigh holsters, hiked up her skirt, and climbed onto the bed. Straddling his hips, she guided him inside her.

Oh, yeah...she was warm and wet, and her body was so made for this. Made for him.

"Sin..."

"Shh." She threw her head back and rode him. "I can't...listen to your voice. Not now." With every glide of her sex along his shaft, her boots rasped against his hips. He wanted to touch her, to take fistfuls of her blue-black locks and hold her for his kiss, his bite.

He howled in frustration, his fingers curled into his palms so hard it hurt. But the pleasure built, the waves of it growing larger and crashing into him faster as she rocked on top of him. She slapped her hands on his chest, digging in with her nails, clinging to him as little mewls erupted from her parted lips.

This was good, so freaking good. He strained, trying to pump his hips, match her rhythm. His fingers stretched, but all he could reach was the hilt of one of her daggers. If he could get it, he could cut himself free. Then he could have her the way he wanted to—

"Please," she gasped. "Come."

His body obeyed, a slave to her desire. His climax was so fiery hot that his pleasure was almost pain. Sin cried out, her body arched, a long, graceful work of art. As the orgasm—actually, he thought she had three or four—waned, she shuddered and collapsed onto his chest. Inside, his heart went wild, as though it could get to her. But deeper, something more sinister awakened, the need to sink his teeth into her and drain every last drop of blood. If she inched up, just a little more, she'd be in range of his mouth—

"Con?"

"Hmm?" Just a little more—

"What are we going to do?"

Do? He was going to taste her... That's what he was going to do. Sin swallowed hard enough for him to hear. He'd swallow, too, big, satin gulps... *Stop it!*

"Con? Is there any way out of this bond?"

Bond. *Bond.* Shit! Shocked out of his evil thoughts, he sucked in a sharp breath. Regret and pain and about a million other emotions twisted through him. They were truly fucked. His cock twitched inside her heat, as though adding on a silent, *literally.* She needed sex and could get it only from him, but he was blood addicted and would kill her if he wasn't chained. They were in for a lifetime of, well... this.

And that was assuming his clan didn't hunt her down and kill her.

"No," he croaked.

She raised her head, her black eyes liquid. "So for the rest of my life, I'm basically as chained to you as I am to—" She broke off, but at the same moment, he noticed the collar around her neck. It was a warg collar, developed by the same demons who originally bred Feast wargs.

"What. The. Fuck?" His voice was so dark, so warped that he could barely understand it himself, and Sin sat up quickly. "Who enslaved you?"

Her fingers flew up to touch the collar, and then she jerked them back and scrambled off him. "It's just a dog collar. Current fashion."

"Don't fucking lie to me!" he roared. He was going to kill the fucker. Whoever it was, he was dead. Except, Con couldn't kill him. Couldn't even feed the bastard his own teeth, because whatever he did to the master, the pain would be felt by Sin.

Sin slipped on her underwear. "Con, it's okay."

"Bull-fucking-shit, it's okay!" God, he wanted to spill some blood, and it was actually a relief that it wasn't Sin's he wanted to spill. *"Tell me."*

Sin avoided eye contact as she tugged his scrub bottoms up. "Raynor."

"How?" Con asked between clenched teeth. "How did he get you?" With her hatred and fear of slavery, there was no way she'd sign up for a life of ownership for anything less than the threat of death.

But she didn't fear her own death . . . so she was protecting someone.

"Who did he threaten to kill, Sin? One of your brothers? Tell me. Now." Misery clouded her eyes as she finally turned to him, and his gut wrenched. "Me? Is it me?"

"Sable," she whispered. "Sable and her child. Maybe you as a bonus. Raynor knows. You should also know that the person who blew up your house and tried to kill me is a born warg named Lycus. I just don't know *why* he wanted me dead like that."

"Valko." He let out a long, vile string of curses in several languages. "I'd bet my life that Valko put him up to it. He wanted you dead so you couldn't help find a cure for the disease."

Soul-destroying anger turned his blood to acid and corroded most of what was left of his lucidity. He'd been betrayed by the Warg Council, his family was in danger, and Sin, who had finally, after a hundred years, escaped the bonds of one monster, was now bound to two. The rage mounted, and along with it, the need to feed, and his gaze zeroed in on Sin's throat.

This had to end, and while he wasn't sure how to get Sin out of the bond with Ray, he knew exactly how to get her out of the one that tethered her to him. Because he'd lied. There *was* a way out. His fingers stroked the dagger he'd worked out of her sheath and slipped beneath his leg. Before he fell completely into the black hole of bloodlust, he growled, "Get Eidolon. And Luc."

She nodded, making the ends of her ponytail swish against the neck tattoo he always wanted to lick. He panted, breathed through the madness that was suffocating him. He couldn't let her leave without letting her know...

"Sin, I...shit..." He breathed hard, sucked in three massive lungfuls of air, and then stopped breathing when her fingers closed around his.

"What is it?"

"Those things I said...at the apartment. Didn't mean them. I had to chase you off...so my clan wouldn't kill you."

Tears swam in the black depths of her eyes. "Oh, Con," she whispered. "We can never be together if I'm not bonded to you, can we?"

"No," he gasped.

Her throat, her creamy, delectable throat, worked on a hard swallow. "Then...bond with me. Do it. Finish it so it goes both ways."

Jesus. What she was asking, just...Jesus. His own eyes stung at the magnitude of what she'd just said. After all her fighting, she was willing to give herself up to him, to give up the one thing she'd prayed for her entire life: her freedom.

Con would *never* take that from her.

"Yes," he lied, and wasn't he getting good at that? "Not now...hungry. Later. You need...to trust me." He squeezed her hand, hyperaware of her pulse under the pads of his fingers. "Mine..."

She said something, but he didn't know what. A mist of red washed out his vision, and his brain went too fully animal to think. All he knew after that was hunger and hatred.

Con was a disaster. No matter what Eidolon did, the dhampire was growing more violent and weaker. Very little blood would stay down, and Eidolon was so desperate that he'd even tried feeding the guy Lore's blood, hoping the similarity to Sin's would have some sort of positive effect.

Nothing.

Then, in a strange, trancelike moment of clarity, Con had told him about Sin's new bond with Raynor and then asked him to take and store samples of everything, from blood to saliva to semen. Now Eidolon stood outside the door to Con's room with Shade, Wraith, Gem, and Kynan, waiting for whatever Luc was doing inside to be done. Con had been tight-lipped about his reasons for the samples and seeing Luc, and Eidolon had to wonder if Con's mind was starting to go.

Eidolon hoped not. Con swore he'd break the bond-gone-wrong with Sin, and that had better be true. As for the other bond, the one with the werewolf... Eidolon forced his anger to remain on a slow simmer until Wraith and Lore got some useful intel on the guy and the collar he'd used on Sin.

"Hey." Speak of the demon, Lore rounded a corner, a stack of papers in his gloved hand. "Got some info on this Raynor cocksucker."

Wraith cocked an eyebrow. "Did you use your assassin contacts?"

"And the Internet." Lore grinned. "Seriously, I'm pretty sure the invention of cyberspace was the work of the devil."

Eidolon wouldn't doubt that. "Where's Sin?"

"She's in the day care, helping Serena and Runa with the kids."

The day care had been a new addition to the hospital—Serena's idea. She and Runa spent so much time at UG that it made sense to create a safe place for the babies to play. Plus, it made life easier for the employees with kids. Serena helped out when she and Wraith weren't off treasure hunting—or just hunting. Runa now ran it, and Idess helped out since she worked at the hospital anyway.

Eidolon still shook his head in amazement every time he walked into the day care to find Wraith or Shade cuddling and feeding the babies. Shade had always loved kids, but Wraith... E never thought he'd see the day that Wraith would be comfortable and happy with a fragile infant in his arms.

For Eidolon's part, he couldn't wait to get Tayla pregnant. His Seminus urges to reproduce with his mate were growing more intense, and Tay was finally starting to come around now that her twin sister, Gem, was sporting a baby bump. Just thinking about his mate growing heavy with his son made Eidolon restless, and Tayla was probably lucky she wasn't here right now, or he'd have her against the wall, doing his best to make it happen.

Gem stopped playing with one of her black-and-blue braids to settle her hand on her belly. "Lore, what did you learn?"

"That this guy is good at keeping his hands clean." Lore handed the papers to Shade to pass around. "His photo is there, suspected residence, favorite hangouts. He owns an auto salvage yard in Pittsburgh that's making a tidy profit. He's got a lot of enemies, but they drop like flies. Nothing can be pinned on him, but his trail reeks of assassins."

"And you would know," Kynan muttered, but it was a good-natured ribbing, and Lore's lips quirked up as he flipped off the human. They used to be bitter enemies, and though they weren't exactly friends, they got along and actually sparred in UG's gym from time to time.

Eidolon turned to Wraith, who was messing with his iPhone. "Have you learned anything more about the collar around Sin's neck?"

"No," he said, not looking up from the device. "The demons who made it are, like, legendary. I can't find any proof that they even existed."

"Well," Gem said, "until a couple of days ago, we didn't have proof that Feast wargs existed, either."

Yeah, that had been a total shocker. Luc and Kar were now staying at Shade and Runa's New York house until Tayla and Kynan could get The Aegis death order against Kar called off. So far, doing so was a low priority—The Aegis and the military were still trying to decide if wiping out wargs was a desirable course of action, even though

Eidolon's vaccine had tested well and was being manufactured with the help of USAMRIID. Complicating matters was the fact that both paranormal agencies were scrambled by troubling developments, apparently unrelated to the warg virus, in the human world.

The Nile was running red, and though scientists had determined that the cause was red toxic algal bloom, they couldn't explain how it happened overnight. Worse, the toxins were being spread by wind, and the normally mild effects on humans and animals—respiratory irritation—had become deadly. Naturally, thanks to the emergence of Sin Fever, The Aegis and R-XR were quick to blame demons on the new troubles, as well.

Shade crossed his arms over his chest. "So what you're saying is that you don't know how to remove the collar or release Sin from the warg's bond."

"That's what I'm saying," Wraith grumbled. He hated not finding what he was looking for. Granted, he'd had only a couple of hours, but he wasn't the most patient demon in the world, and with Sin's freedom and, possibly, her life on the line, Wraith was wound especially tight. "Tonight, Serena and I can snoop around the Horun region of Sheoul. Most of the legends regarding the Feast wargs and their creators originate there."

The door to Con's room opened, and Luc stepped out. "It's done." His voice was strangely raw.

"Ah, what's done?"

Luc stared at Eidolon, and he could have sworn that the warg's eyes were a little bloodshot. His color was definitely mottled, a rare sign of emotion in the usually unflappable warg. "He didn't tell you?" When E shook his head, Luc swore. "That fuck. He made me do it, E."

Alarm clanged through Eidolon. *"Do what?"* He didn't wait for Luc to answer, threw open the door, took three steps, and froze.

"Hell's fucking rings." Shade rushed to Con's bed, his arm glowing, and Eidolon fired up his gift as well. "What the fuck did you do, Luc?"

"You can't help him," Luc said. "I broke his neck after I shoved the blade through his rib cage. I thought you knew."

Eidolon shook with demonic fury as he rounded on the paramedic, and he knew his eyes had gone red. "Why did he do this, and damn you, why'd you help him?"

"He said something about breaking a bond with Sin and keeping her safe. I owed him—I owe all of you—for saving my life. For saving Kar and the baby. So he asked me to do this, and I did." Luc's voice caught, just a slight tremor most wouldn't notice. "He made me swear to take his body to his clan within the hour."

"Oh my God." Every head snapped around to Sin, who stood in the doorway, hand over her mouth and horror in her eyes. "He's not... He can't be..."

Lore caught her in his arms as she broke into a high, keening wail of grief that sliced into Eidolon's heart like a scalpel blade. His connection with his purebred brothers had always been strong, but he'd never had the same physical link with Lore or Sin. But for the first time, he felt Sin. Felt her pain.

And when he glanced at his brothers, he saw that they felt it, too.

"Con!" Sin screamed his name over and over. Her throat hurt and her eyes felt like they were going to pop out of her head from the pressure of her shrieks, but all that mattered was getting to him. She jerked out of Lore's arms and ran to Con's side, her foot slipping in blood that had pooled on the floor. "No, Con, no!"

Dazed, terrified, and desperate, she grabbed Lore's hand. "Bring him back!" She mashed Lore's hand onto Con's thigh. It was still warm. There was a chance. There was! *"Do it."*

"I can't, Sin." Lore gently peeled her fingers off his. "The blade . . . It's your Gargantua-bone dagger."

Impossible. Her hand went automatically to the empty sheath at her thigh. Oh, God. That son of a bitch had lifted it off her somehow.

Luc cleared his throat. "He made me use it. Said that way Lore couldn't bring him back. Something about the dagger having magical properties that would thwart Lore's gift."

Sin barely heard Luc's explanation, barely heard anything but the silent screams in her ears. "You bastard!"

She launched herself at Luc, but Shade caught her before she reached him. Still, the intent to harm Luc was there, and the Haven spell kicked in, making the writing on the walls pulse as pain ripped into her skull like claws shredding her brain. Agony blacked out her vision, and she hit the floor with a crack of kneecaps and a cry. Shade's arms tightened around her. And then, through the pounding in her head, she sensed the others, Eidolon, Wraith, and Lore, ease onto the floor around her. Someone took her hand. Someone else palmed her shoulder. And then someone else . . . Wraith, she realized, tucked her head against his chest as her world shattered into a million pieces.

Twenty-six

For a thousand years, Con dreaded the three nights of the full moon that turned him into a creature feared by humans and demons alike. It wasn't that he'd hated being the creature, or even that he hated the agony that accompanied the transformation—it was that he'd despised the thirty seconds of vulnerability that came with each change.

Now, as he opened his eyes to stare at the dark sky and rising moon, he offered a silent hello, because night was now his new best friend, and daytime was his enemy unless the ritual was completed. Instinctively, he took a breath, even though he didn't need to. He put his hand over his heart, even though he knew it wouldn't beat.

A boot nudged his hip, and he shifted his head on the ceremonial pallet to look up at his childhood buddy, a wiry male whose hair was covered by a blue do-rag. "Hey." Well, at least his voice still worked.

Aed grinned. "How's it feel to be on your second life?"

Wincing at the stiffness in his muscles, Con sat up. "Feels like I wasted the first one."

"Better make up for it with this one, *ayech*?" Aed's accent was a blend of Scottish, Danish, and something else that made half of what he said sound like gibberish to Con, who, unlike his old friend, had spent enough time with humans in the modern world to cultivate an accent that didn't sound like it came straight out of *Beowulf*.

"Yeah." Con tested his new limbs, stretching as he sat on the wood and deer hide pallet, but he felt much the same as he had before he'd *gone to the night*. "Luc. The warg who brought me..."

"He was given safe passage. He's away."

Good. Man, that damned warg had *not* wanted to do as Con asked. Con had been forced to remind him that Luc owed him after the avalanche save, not to mention that Con had been there to help at the cabin, saving not only Luc but Kar and the baby, as well. Still, Luc hadn't gone easily into it. His last words had been *I hate you for this, you motherfucker*.

Con winced at a sharp hunger pang in his stomach. "And you were given the honor of seeing to my birth." A vampire birth. And one that was required to take place on dhampire ground. If Con hadn't been brought back here before nightfall, his life would have ended for good. No second chances. Which was what had happened to his daughter centuries ago.

With a grunt of assent, Aed crouched, drew a blade across his wrist, and the effect on Con was instantaneous. His fangs punched down, his mouth watered, and a low, famished growl rose up in his chest.

The blood of a dhampire was required for this part of the ritual, was crucial in imparting an extra layer of protection, something that would separate him from regular vampires—an immunity to holy water and the ability to walk in the sun, which apparently hearkened back to the oldest vampire legends. Con would still be susceptible to the other usual vampire threats—fire, decapitation, wooden stakes, but...yeah, who wasn't?

Con gripped his friend's arm and brought his wrist to his mouth. It was good, but nothing tasted better than Sin.

Damn.

What was she thinking right now? He wished he'd been able to tell her about the dhampire's second chance, but all he could do was try to tell Sin, in those last seconds of lucidity, that he would be back. That she was his, but this time, there would be no bonds of blood or magic or chain-link collars.

Now, no longer dhampire, Con would be banished forever from dhampire lands, sent into the night like his brothers before him, like his cousin Aisling, who he was supposed to have replaced on the Dhampire Council.

He no longer had to serve the dhampires, and he felt as if some huge weight had been lifted from his shoulders. He palmed his chest, where his heart no longer beat, and smiled. Son of a bitch, this was what he'd wanted all along. Why he'd been so reckless with his life. Oh, he'd wanted to have fun, do everything he could do, but fear had never been in play.

Because deep down, he knew that death was only temporary. If he died, he could come back, and then he'd be free of dhampire life forever.

Excellent.

He would now be governed by the Vampire Council, his story that he was turned by a vampire, sire unknown. Even the vampires didn't know about the dhampire's second chance.

"That's enough, there, boy." Aed gripped Con's hair and tugged him off his wrist. He licked his own wound to seal it, and then helped Con up. "What now?"

"Now," Con said grimly, "I go to kill a werewolf and claim my woman."

Sin felt like hell and didn't look a whole lot better.

She hadn't wanted to leave the hospital, and God, how crazy was it that not long ago she'd done everything she could to avoid the place, and now all she wanted to do was stay?

Her family was there. And it was all she had left of Con. Funny how losing him had made her realize that, bond or no, she was linked to him. He'd owned her heart, and now that he was gone, it sat like a useless lump in her empty chest cavity, a stray organ with no reason to beat.

Well, that wasn't entirely true. There was always revenge.

She didn't know how long it would take, but she would make Raynor pay for her pain. The thought made her bare her teeth in some twisted, grim resemblance of a smile as she hoofed it along the inky streets on the outskirts of Pittsburgh. His summons had come in the form of radiating pain from the collar while she'd been in Eidolon's office, where she'd spent the night. She'd never been alone; her brothers had made sure that one of them had always been with her.

It was Eidolon who had been there when the summons came, and he'd been furious, but as he'd walked her to the Harrowgate, his hands behind his back and his face pinched in concentration, she'd seen a spark of wickedness in his eyes that would have chilled her to the bone if she'd thought his mind was working against her.

"Let us know your location," he'd said. "Take your time getting there, and get Raynor to lay out his genocidal plans."

"I don't understand..."

"Just do it." He'd shoved her into the Harrowgate, leaving her cursing and nearly in tears—again. Not because of Eidolon, but because everything seemed to remind her of Con. The Harrowgate, because she'd been in it with him. The hospital, because he'd worked there. Scrubs, because those were what he'd died in.

Oh, God.

Desperate to not lose him, she'd asked him to complete the bond with her. Instead, he'd killed himself, and she didn't need to be a brain surgeon to know why. He hadn't wanted to take her freedom away. She'd been so damned insistent that no one would ever own her again, would never be the sole provider of the one thing she needed to survive, and he'd taken it to heart. He'd made the ultimate sacrifice in order to honor what she'd said.

And she'd never gotten the chance to tell him that the reason she'd wanted the bond wasn't because there was no other choice. It was because she loved him.

She. Loved. Him.

It was something she'd never thought could happen, and she'd realized it too late. If she could go back in time, to his apartment, she'd change everything. She'd be his, he'd be hers, and he wouldn't be dead. It was possible, even, that a stronger bond with Con would have prevented Raynor from having any hold on her.

She was such a fool!

Fueled by hatred and regret, she stopped in front of the chain-link gate of the junkyard her collar had led her to. Raynor was inside, no doubt about it. After looking around to make sure no one was watching, she dug the new cell phone Shade had given her out of her backpack and dialed Eidolon. "I'm here. Some sort of auto yard outside Pittsburgh, near the Gerunti Harrowgate." Sin had no idea why some of the gates were named after demons, but then, she didn't care. Would be nice to find a Seminus gate, though.

"Good. Be careful." Eidolon hung up before she could say anything else.

She pushed open the creaky gate and moved between the junked autos. Movement surrounded her, people watching from shadowed recesses and concealed perches. No doubt they were *varcolac*, patrolling for enemies like junkyard dogs.

She found Raynor near the trunk of a trashed Corvette. Smoke from a cigarette wafted up from his hand, and he smiled as he took a drag. Hatred rolled over her with such intensity that it stung her skin.

"I'm here, asshole," she snapped.

He blew out a stream of smoke. "Took you long enough."

"What do you want? And why are we in a damned junkyard?"

"Because I own it."

She glanced around, took in the rusted piece-of-shit

cars, skittering rats, and rotting tires. "You should be so proud." He slapped her so hard her teeth rattled and her eyes stung, but she refused to react except to say saucily, "You must have heard how I like foreplay." Except she didn't. Until Con. *Oh, God*. Her knees nearly buckled, and she had to lock them in order to stay upright.

"I hope you like it a lot, because with your mouth, you'll be getting it nonstop."

"Goody," she said dryly. "Because I so love a man who needs to prove his masculinity by beating on women. Do you hit children and kick cats, too?"

He laughed. "You're no woman. You're a half-breed abomination who's lucky enough to have not been caught by a Purifier yet."

Purifiers were demons—of any species—who hunted half-breeds for fun or money or just a twisted sense of responsibility. In the demon world, anything mixed with human blood deserved to die. And she *had* encountered Purifiers before. She'd just killed them before they killed her.

"So, is that why I'm here? So you can use this half-breed freak as a punching bag?"

"I'm going to take you to the warg village you visited with Conall. You're going to infect a few *pricolici* with something that will spread to others."

Her cheek throbbed from his blow, and she tested a tooth with her tongue. "Are you completely stupid? We went over this before. The last time I did that, the virus mutated. What makes you think this will be any different? You could end up killing your own people."

Raynor took a drag on his cig, and Sin suddenly wondered if turned wargs got lung cancer. She kind of hoped so. "And I told you: not if the *pricolici* are contained. The warg version of Dragaica has just started." At what must have been a what-the-hell-is-that look on her face, he rolled his eyes. "Romanian midsummer festival," he said, as if she should know all about Romanian holidays. "Very important to born wargs. In the town you visited with Con, the largest *pricolici* gathering of the year will take place, and now that immunizations against SF have begun, there is even more reason to celebrate. Nearly every *pricolici* in the world will be there." Raynor paused to take another drag, and Sin felt bile rise up in her throat, scouring it raw with disgust and hatred. "We'll bar the gate, they'll get sick, and they will die within the confines of their own walls. The beauty of this is that even though all *pricolici* won't be destroyed, the race will be weakened, scattered to the winds, and the *varcolac* will finally become the dominant warg species."

"You," she said hoarsely, "are a sick fuck."

Raynor shrugged. "Eye of the beholder." He frowned, and at the same time, Sin picked up the sound of . . . a scuffle? Muted . . . and from several directions, but definitely fighting going on. Cursing, Raynor threw his butt to the ground, grabbed Sin's arm, and dragged her toward the rear of the junkyard.

Out of nowhere, Wraith appeared, blocking Raynor's retreat. "Hey. Where ya goin'?"

Ray's hand tightened on Sin's biceps. "One of your brothers, I'm guessing?"

"Yep. The mean one. Oh, wait, they're all mean." She grinned. "You are so fucked."

Ray snarled at Wraith. "You do realize that if you hurt me, she suffers."

"Yeah," Wraith drawled. "Sucks, because I would love to beat you to a pulp."

All around, the shadows stirred, and from them the rest of her brothers, plus Kynan, Luc, Tayla, and a guy she thought might be a Guardian, surrounded them. "Thought" being the key word, because the tall, blond male looked an awful lot like a vampire, and she didn't think The Aegis employed the bloodsuckers. Though she supposed that if they could keep a half-demon in charge of an entire cell, a vamp might not be a big deal.

Sin slid her gaze to Eidolon. Next to him were two female Judicia, their green skin eerily luminescent in the moonlight. Then she heard the click of weapons being brought to bear, and damn if she didn't nearly have a heart attack.

Men in black SWAT-like gear swept through the compound like ants. That would be the R-XR. Here? Working with demons?

"What's going on?" Raynor practically screamed. "You're killing my men!"

"Only the ones who fight back," Kynan said. "The rest are being rounded up. If they're productive, harmless members of society, they'll be freed."

Shade snorted. "Something tells me a lot of them are going to rot in some military testing facility."

"Release them, and I'll free Sin." For emphasis, Raynor jerked her roughly against him.

"Sorry, buddy," Eidolon said coldly, "but the time for negotiation passed when you put that collar on her."

"If you touch me—"

"Yeah, yeah, she dies, yadda, yadda." Con's voice came from behind her, and Sin whirled—or did as best as she could while still being held by Ray.

"Con?" she gasped.

He moved like a ghost through the maze of vehicles, hand around the neck of a badly beaten male, the one from the warg village and the dhampire grounds. "What, you thought you could get rid of me so easily?"

She smiled so big it hurt, and tears sprang to her eyes, and geez, she was a faucet lately. "How? Oh my God, how are you here?"

Something was different about him. He was still as sexy as ever, but maybe a little paler. And the way he moved... Before, he was like a panther in motion. Now, he was a phantom panther... silent, more sleek and deadly. As if his most potent, most powerful elements had been distilled, leaving nothing but raw grace and an overpowering presence. God, it was so hot. Her sex drive, which had been as dead as she thought he was for the last twenty hours, roared back to life.

"Long story. When I called Eidolon a few minutes ago, he said you'd be here, so here I am." He shoved the male forward. "Brought you something. This is Valko, if you don't remember. He's going to call off Lycus." Con's hand slammed into the warg's throat. "Aren't you?"

Valko grunted. "No, I'm not. And if you kill me without a formal challenge, you'll face a death sentence, dhampire."

"Vampire. And I'm not going to kill you." Con smiled, flashing fangs that seemed a little larger than before. "I need you alive so you can take any punishment handed down to me, Wraith, and Eidolon for keeping Sin out of Carceris hands." He glanced at Eidolon. "Volunteers are allowed to do that, right?"

Eidolon grinned. "Hell, yes."

"I will never volunteer," Valko snapped, and Eidolon shrugged.

"You will if you want your SF vaccination."

"I already got it."

"You got a B-12 shot. Con's idea." He slid Con an approving glance. "Good thinking, man."

"Thank you." Con's voice was pleasant, as if he wasn't gripping an enraged warg in the middle of a situation so tense the air seemed heavy. He shoved Valko to the ground and gestured to Raynor. "Release Sin. This is your last warning."

"I will not. And if you slipped me a damned vitamin shot, your sister dies with me."

"You, unfortunately, got the real thing." Eidolon stepped forward with the green demons. "And I'd like you to meet my other sisters, Omira and Ravan."

Right...Sin remembered something about Eidolon growing up with Omira, but Ravan had been born long after he left the fold.

Raynor snorted. "Do I look like Captain Kirk? Because I already told Sin I don't do demons. Especially not ugly-ass green ones."

Omira laughed, a curiously beautiful sound, given that, really, she wasn't all that attractive. "My brother was right. I'm going to enjoy this." She dug inside her leather satchel and drew out a thin, gold rope in the shape of a figure eight. "A charge has been brought against you by... well, all those present. The charge is conspiracy to commit genocide. I do find you guilty."

"What?" Raynor's voice was strangled. "You can't do that! Who are you?"

Eidolon patted Omira on the shoulder. "She's a Justice Dealer. She can definitely do it."

Ray's eyes nearly popped out of his head. "No. The Carceris must jail me first, and then—"

"The Carceris is called in only to capture those who have charges pending, who are wanted for questioning, or who must be held during an investigation or trial." She moved toward him. "Because I heard your plot, I have the authority to be judge, jury...and executioner."

Someone must have given a silent signal, because her brothers and Kynan rushed Ray, and Con tore Sin from the warg's grip. He held her so tightly she could hardly breathe, but she didn't care. Didn't matter. All that mattered was that he was alive.

"I've got you," he murmured into her hair. "I'll always get you."

She'd have melted at his words, but Raynor was getting manhandled, and in response, her arms ached, the joints feeling stretched, her upper arms and legs bruised as the boys took Raynor to the ground. It was obvious that they were holding back, trying to be gentle, but Ray was fighting them.

"If you kill me, she dies," he screamed, and yeah, that was a concern.

"Just watch," Con said. "Every member of the Judicia uses restraints similar to what the Carceris has. They nullify all magic and all supernatural and natural abilities. As long as he's wearing the rope—"

"The bond with him will be severed," she finished on an excited breath. Somehow, Ray broke away and struggled to his feet, and okay, she was sick of this. "Guys? Hurt him! I can take it."

Lore wrenched Ray's arm behind him, and yep, that freaking hurt. Ray's snarl was cut off, and for a split second, she thought one of her brothers had slammed a fist into his throat. But when, out of the corner of her eye, she saw Lycus retreating behind a crane and spurts of blood shooting out from Raynor's ripped-out throat, her breath became a knot of fire in her own throat, and she realized what had happened.

She and Raynor had just been killed.

Twenty-seven

Con wasn't sure what happened. All he knew was that Sin was dying, even as Eidolon and Shade tried to save Ray, their *dermoires* glowing so brightly Con had to squint. Wraith, Lore, Tayla, and Kynan tore off, presumably after the assassin.

"Use the cuffs," he yelled at Omira, who hastily looped one of Ray's wrists with the gold twine. But it was too late. Sin convulsed, gave one last gurgled cry, and then went limp. Con's vampire senses noted the sudden silence at the cessation of her heartbeat, the lack of vibration as her blood pooled in her veins, and terror obliterated everything but the need to save her life.

Gently, he lay her on the ground, and though he knew her fate was tied to Ray's, he began CPR. Frantic curses and barked orders came from Shade and Eidolon as they worked on Ray, but even from where Con kneeled on the dirt, he could see that the warg was not coming back.

Not with the way his head had been shorn nearly off his shoulders by something that looked like a razor-sharp boomerang.

The collar around Sin's neck popped off, indicating a total disconnect from Ray, but the damage had been done.

Won't give up. Will never give up.

"Con, we got it." Eidolon's glowing hand came down on Sin's shoulder as Shade's splayed on her belly.

Con felt Shade's power going deep, grabbing at the organs and forcing them to work. "Fuck," he muttered. "I can make them function, but if I stop..."

"They stop," Con whispered. Sin's heart was beating, her lungs were breathing, her liver was filtering. But not on their own. "Maybe I can turn her into a vampire. Maybe I can force her to drink." Even as he said it, he knew he was grasping at straws. Demons couldn't be turned, and even if her human half allowed for it, the chance of it working on someone who had died was practically zero.

At Sin's feet, Lore hit his knees, a sob breaking from deep in his chest. "Sin, damn you." He tore off his glove and gripped her ankle. "This works only if the death is natural, but since the warg's death was, and with you guys helping..."

"Maybe," Shade grunted.

Yeah, Ray's death wasn't exactly natural, but Con got what Lore was saying. The warg had been killed by a normal weapon. He hadn't died of a curse or spell or mystical disease. Sin's death had come via a mystical connection... to a natural death.

Son of a bitch. There were way too many *if*s and variables here.

"Save her." He gripped her hand so hard that if she could feel it, it would hurt. "Please."

The "please" wasn't necessary and he knew it. These guys would give their own lives if it meant saving hers. But Con would beg for anything right now.

Beneath his hand, the signs of life were there—she had a pulse, a heartbeat, and her chest rose and fell, but it was all artificial, forced by her brothers. Lore was panting, sweat running from his temples, teeth gnashed together.

"Come on, come on," Eidolon muttered.

Lore groaned. "So…close…"

Impulsively, Con leaned over and kissed her. It was cliché and corny and Sleeping Beauty on crack, but he needed her to fight. *To feel.*

Tenderly, he closed his mouth over hers. Nothing happened, but he wasn't about to give up. He nudged her lips with his tongue, stroked them gently at first, and then more urgently. Something burned in his eyes…tears? Yes, bloody hell, he was crying like a baby, and soon, the taste of Sin mingled with the salt of his tears.

Refusing to break contact, he pulled her into his arms and rocked her, even as he kissed her. Even as her brothers lit up the old junkyard with the power of their gifts.

And then…he felt it. A stir deep inside. She twitched. Once. Twice. And then she gasped into his mouth, and her black eyes flew wide open.

Ear-shattering whoops came from all around, but Con was silent as he tugged her tighter to his chest. He would never let her go again. Never.

Her arms came around him, and though she didn't say it, he knew she felt the same way.

Sin felt like she'd gone a couple of rounds with a Gargantua demon. Everything ached, but mostly her ribs and throat.

Throat. Hadn't Raynor's ripped wide open?

Groaning, she finally pulled back from Con. Well, she tried to, but he held her so tightly she had to smile. "Con? You're smothering me."

"If you were being smothered, you couldn't speak." But he loosened his grip enough for her to look up at the wall of people standing around them as Con held her on the ground.

"What happened?"

"You sort of bit it," Wraith said. The announcement was delivered with a certain nonchalance, but the tension in his expression said he wasn't as detached as he'd sounded. Aw, big bad Wraith had been worried about her.

Which meant things had been really dire. A sinking sensation made her gut plummet to her feet. "Lore? Did you..."

"Yeah. But if not for E and Shade, I couldn't have done it."

Oh, shit. Lore's resurrection gift came with one hell of a side effect. He'd spend days in bleeding, writhing misery, which was why he rarely used it.

"Lore, I—"

"Don't." He crouched beside Con and her, and gave her a smile that held no regret. "We've had so much guilt between us, have felt like we owed each other so much. Time to let that go. I did what I did because I love you. You'd do the same for me. Let's put the past behind us for good."

A huge sob escaped her, and Con released her so she could throw herself into Lore's arms. She held him like she hadn't since before their transformation, since before they learned they were demons. "I love you," she whispered. "I don't think I've told you that before."

"You didn't need to." He held her for a moment longer, and then passed her back to Con.

"I feel like a football," she muttered, as she dabbed at her eyes. But she wouldn't change a thing. Except the subject, away from so much sap. "So, what happened to Lycus? Where is he?"

Wraith snorted. "Between a Chevette and a Mustang. And on the hood of a Thunderbird. And all over the grille of a—"

"Got it," she said, holding up her hand. Not much made her queasy, but being brought back from the dead seemed to be wreaking havoc with her stomach.

Wraith gestured to Valko, who now sat chained to an old Ford pickup. "I got him to talk. He admitted to getting Lycus to kill you. Guess the *pricolici* were going to forgive his crimes and put him on the Warg Council if he did. They were also going to try to buy him out of assassin service from the new master."

"Which is why getting my ring wasn't an issue," she mused. "He wanted it, but probably figured that either way he was getting a good deal. Asshole." She hoped the punishment Valko was going to "volunteer" for was really painful. "How did you guys manage to get the R-XR here?"

"Arik," Kynan explained. "Once we had your location, the R-XR tapped into government satellites to determine how many enemies we'd be up against, and since there were a few dozen, they called in a local team to back us up."

Tayla snapped her stang into its belt sheath and slung her arm around Eidolon's waist. "I'd have called in the local Aegis cell, too, but The Aegis is still fired up about what happened in Canada with the wargs. Wraith wiped the Guardians, but Command still knows something went down to cause injuries and the one dead Aegi. Didn't think it would be wise to give them a shot at revenge."

"Does this mean Arik is in the clear and can get the hell out of my cave?" Shade asked, and Kynan nodded.

"They couldn't afford his loss anyway."

Luc parted the crowd and strode up to Con. With a guttural curse, he hauled off and punched him in the shoulder. "That, you asshole, is because you made me kill you and didn't bother to mention you wouldn't stay dead."

Sin punched Con, too. Same place. Maybe vampires bruised easily. "Yeah. Would have been nice to know."

"Sorry," he said sheepishly, and then he kissed her, long and hard, and she forgave him. "I promise to make it up to you."

"Dude." Luc stepped back, hands up. "You don't need to make it up to me."

"So," Lore said, as he jammed his hands in his jacket pockets. "I hate to be a party pooper, but I'd better head home."

Oh, damn. Sin hated what he had to deal with now. "I'll take care of you. Idess doesn't need to see what you're going to go through." Besides, Sin had nursed Lore through recovery before.

"I agree." Lore looked up at the cloudless night and sighed. "But you know her. She'll want to be there."

Of course she would. Sin would go through the poison pits of eastern Sheoul to be able to take care of Con if he were suffering.

"I have a better idea," Eidolon said. "Come to the hospital. We'll all take care of you."

Wraith gave an enthusiastic nod. "E's liberal with the painkillers."

"Yup," Shade agreed.

"We won't take no for an answer." That from Eidolon, who was using his no-nonsense doctor voice, which somehow still rang with compassion.

Lore stood there, emotion playing across his face, probably just like hers. He'd allowed their brothers in before she had, but he'd been alone for so long that, clearly, he still hadn't gotten used to the way they rallied together as fiercely as they fought.

"Okay," he said roughly.

Kynan shouted at the R-XR guys to wrap it up, and gestured to Tayla and the Guardian vampire, who joined in the gathering of wargs.

"You guys go ahead," Sin said. "Con and I will be at the hospital later."

"You sure?" Shade asked, and Con nodded.

Sin could tell the guys wanted to argue, but they left with Eidolon's sisters, leaving her alone with Con. Relatively alone, anyway. Kynan, Tayla, and the military dudes still milled around the junkyard, but they didn't seem to be paying any attention to them.

Con opened his mouth to say something, but Sin spoke first. "I'm so sorry," she said. "I shouldn't have fought you when you wanted to bond with me at the apartment. I should have done it. I should have—"

Con put his finger to her lips. "Shh. You spent most of your life belonging to someone, and belonging to me was the last thing you needed."

She couldn't help but smile. "Still, it was stupid. I should have trusted you then. But, Con, you didn't need to kill yourself. And how *did* you become a vampire?"

"I can't say."

"Can't, or won't?"

His gaze glinted with diamond shards in the light of the moon, holding hers with its intensity. "Can't."

Sin's first instinct should have been to get angry, but he'd asked her to trust him, and she'd have to trust that if he could tell her, he would. In any case, the important thing was that he was here, not dead. Well, sort of not dead.

"So . . . no more blood addiction?"

"Nope."

"Do you still have to do the thing with your clan?"

"Nope."

"But do you still need to feed? Like a normal vampire?" *Say yes.*

"Yep."

Her heart gave a happy thump. "Do you need to feed soon?"

His fangs flashed. "Oh, yeah." The way he said it made her shivery. Melty. Total putty.

"Then maybe we should go?"

"Good idea." He caught her, hauled her against him. "I love you, Sin. I don't ever want to lose you again."

"You won't," she whispered. "Because I love you, too. And that's something I never thought would happen."

"Then let's go, and I'll show you exactly how much I love you."

Since Sin didn't have a home, and Con's had been destroyed—and because there was no way in hell he was going to take her back to the London flat—Con had checked them into a five-star Manhattan hotel. He booked the room for the night, but after six hours of indulgence—in bed, the shower, the sofa, the floor—they headed to the hospital to check on Lore.

As Sin had predicted, he was in misery. He looked like he'd been tortured for days, but thanks to meds, Shade's gift, and Idess's bedside vigil, Sin said Lore didn't look half as bad as usual.

Which was fucking scary, given that Con had seen roadkill in better shape.

Sin and Con didn't hang around; no doubt Lore didn't need gawkers. They slipped out of Lore's room and headed for the Harrowgate. He planned to take her to an early breakfast, and then they were going to stay at Shade and Runa's house. It was a temporary arrangement until he and Sin could find a place to live, but Shade and Runa were generous enough to let them shack up as long as they wanted. Besides, Luc and Kar were staying there, too, so the place was already in use.

Horror Hotel, as Wraith called Shade's house. "Vampires, demons, and werewolves check in...and then they make out, and—"

Serena had dragged him away, whispering something in his ear that had made him let out an erotic growl, and then they were gone.

As Con and Sin approached the Harrowgate, it flashed and a tank of a blood-bay stallion leaped out, scattering staff and patients. Atop the horse sat a massive male in hard leather armor. His hair was short, reddish brown, and his eyes were as black as Sin's.

"What the hell are you doing?" Eidolon shouted, but the big male swiveled his head and focused his gaze on Sin with such intensity that Con stiffened.

"Why is he looking at you like that?"

"I…ah…" She slid him a timid glance. "I sort of slept with him once."

Con took a deep breath and tried to rein in his desire to rip out the horse guy's throat. "Where'd you find him? EviLove.com?"

"Hey, that's not funny. I know people who use the demon dating service."

The entire hospital seemed to go still, watching and waiting, and what the hell was up with Sin and guys on horses anyway? "Well, who is he?"

"War."

Con stared at her. "War. Just…War. What kind of name is that?" *Nope, not jealous at all of muscle-bound handsome guy.*

"Yeah, you know, the original War. Second Horseman of the Apocalypse?"

Con nearly swallowed his fucking tongue. Everyone else in the ER scrambled backward. Even Eidolon backed up a step as the guy swung down from the horse. Christ, standing, the guy was damned near seven feet tall.

"Sin," he said in an impossibly deep voice. He approached her, bent to kiss her cheek, and Con bristled.

"Big horse," Con ground out. "Compensating much?"

The guy straightened, shot Con an amused smile—the

fucker had some seriously white teeth—and turned back to Sin. "I need the object my brother gave you."

"That tool with the dissolving arrows was your brother?" Sin dug the gold piece out of her pocket. "Is this it? This coin?"

"Yes." He took it, and Eidolon sucked in a strangled breath as he put two and two together.

"A Seal. Gods, that's a Seal."

Con felt the blood drain from his face. "A broken Seal." White horse. Bow. Holy shit. "Conquest. Your brother is Conquest."

"His real name is Reseph," War said, "but he's also known as Pestilence in some interpretations of the Four Horsemen of the Apocalypse."

Eidolon's voice was stunned, toneless. *"She of mixed blood who should not exist, carries with her the power to spread plague and pestilence. When battle breaks, conquest is seal'd. Isagreth 3:17, Daemonica."*

War shifted, and his leather armor squeaked loudly in the otherwise silent ER. "It's what was engraved on the back of this Seal."

Slowly, Sin pulled her right arm out of her jacket and raised her sleeve to reveal the circular glyph that had split open so badly at Rivesta's cabin. The scar that ran through it was an exact replica of the broken edge of the Seal. "I'm the reason it broke," Sin rasped.

"Yes. You are what we call an *agimortus*, a catalyst of sorts. Your actions put into motion an event that caused my brother's Seal to break."

"Wait," Con said. "So why was he trying to kill her? He was there when my house blew up...He tried to shoot her."

"We were all trying to kill her," War said. "No offense to you, Sin, but we wanted to prevent the Seal from breaking. Contrary to a lot of religious interpretations, we're neither good nor evil until the Seals break."

"And then?"

"And then it's time to bow before whatever God you believe in."

Sin's dainty eyebrows slammed down in a frown. "Why did Pest save me from assassins in Montana if he was trying to kill me?"

"By then, the Seal had already broken. At this point, your life or death isn't important, but he did want you to have the coin."

"Why?"

War rubbed his thumb over the writing on the Seal. "A message to me," he said quietly.

"So, are you still planning to kill me?" Sin asked, her arm tensing under Con's palm.

"There's no point." He rolled one big shoulder in a shrug, and his mouth turned up in a smile that probably made females fall all over him. "Besides, it would be a shame to kill you."

Another growl formed in Con's chest, but Sin squeezed his hand, reminding him that she was there with Con, and she wasn't going anywhere. Not even for muscle-bound legend guy. Asshole. "What was the final straw that broke it?" Con asked, much more nicely than he'd have liked. And that note of awe in his voice ... seriously? Humiliating.

War slipped the coin into his horse's saddlebag. "It triggered when the disease jumped species and the two warg factions began to battle each other." He glanced at Eidolon. "Yes, we've kept up on everything that's happened."

"What can we do?" Eidolon asked.

"Pray." War mounted the horse. "And prepare your staff for mass casualties. Things are going to get a lot worse before they get better. *If* they get better." With a jerk of the reins, he and the stallion disappeared into the Harrowgate.

Everyone stood there for a moment, frozen and silent. When the ambulance-bay doors slid open and Blaspheme and Vladlena rolled a patient in on a stretcher, everyone finally leaped into action. Everyone but Con, who stared at Sin.

"There's never a dull moment with you, is there?"

She frowned. "Are you regretting—"

"No!" He cleared his throat and lowered his voice. "No. Never. Now, let's go feed you, and then I'm going to make sure that War asshole"—*freaking Horseman*— "never enters your mind again."

Grinning, Sin linked arms with him. "War who?"

Yeah, *War who.* As Con led Sin toward the Harrowgate, he had a feeling they'd not seen the last of him.

Twenty-eight

"Are you crazy?" Sin asked Lore, as they stood in front of Eidolon's door. He'd just outlined his plan to her, and she was about to fall over. "I know they've been all brotherly and stuff, but they're never going to go for this. Never. And you're going to feel like an idiot."

Lore, wearing a form-fitting charcoal T-shirt, jeans, and combat boots, shrugged. "If they don't go for it, that's their choice, and I understand."

"Uh-huh." Sin jammed her fists on her leather-clad hips. "What does Idess have to say about this?"

"She doesn't know. I mean, she knows I plan to ask, but she doesn't know I'm asking right now. I don't want them to feel any pressure, and I don't want her to feel bad if they refuse. She'll be here in about fifteen minutes."

Sin just shook her head. Lore was in for one hell of a letdown. Their brothers had been a well of support, yes, but this . . . this was asking too much.

Con was already inside, looking fabulous in midnight jeans and a silver button-down that set off his eyes. Everyone was there in the living room—everyone but Idess. Even Kynan and Gem had come. And seriously, how could a pregnant chick look so good in Goth gear?

Taking Con's hand, Sin stood behind Lore, ready to be there for him when their brothers refused his request.

Runa and Shade were on the floor with their triplets, who were crawling around and playing with the dog and the ferret, who kept stealing their toys.

Eidolon was in the overstuffed leather chair with Tayla on his lap, while Wraith sprawled on the couch with a bowl of popcorn, his arm flung around Serena, who was holding a sleeping Stewie. "So, what's up? What's this favor you need?"

Everyone's eyes were on Lore, and Sin's heart pounded.

"Ah . . ." Lore shifted his weight.

"Spill, man," Shade said.

"Yeah, that," Lore muttered, and Sin groaned.

"What?" That from Eidolon.

"I need your sperm," Lore blurted. Shade, who had been drinking a soda, choked. Everyone else gaped. Sin groaned again. Tact had never been one of the items in her brother's chest of personality traits.

Finally, Runa said softly, "You want a baby."

"Yeah." Lore looked down at the floor, and Sin's heart broke for him. "You know I'm sterile. This half-breed shit. But Idess and I . . . we want a family. Since I can't give her that, I was hoping maybe . . . Well, the next best thing would be a brother." He took a deep, shuddering breath. "If you don't want to, I get it. It's cool."

The brothers all looked at each other. Then looked at

their mates. God, Sin could have cut the tension with a knife. She gripped Lore's hand in her empty one. "Hey, maybe we should go. Give them time—"

"No," Tayla said. "I don't think there's even a question." She smiled at Eidolon, who returned it with a crooked upturn of his lips. "If you need it, you got it." Her smile turned very, very naughty. "But you'll have to wait until we're done with it. We're going to be using it all for a while."

Eidolon lit up, and he pulled Tayla into a crushing hug, his palm going straight to her belly before glancing at Lore. "Yeah, bro, you got it. Maybe as early as tomorrow."

Wraith rolled his eyes at the happy couple, but after getting a nod from Serena, he turned back to Lore and drawled, "Hell, I'll give it up."

Shade shrugged. "Yup."

Sin sagged against Con, relieved, happy, and awed by this incredible family. How stupid she'd been to not want to get to know them.

"I have beer," Idess called out from the hall, and when she walked into the living room, Sin could only imagine what she felt at the grins that came from all corners. "Oh," she breathed, and cut her gaze to Lore. "You... asked...?"

Lore held out his arms, and she rushed to him, her eyes brimming with joyful tears. "Thank you," she said, to no one in particular. "Oh, thank you."

"Yeah, yeah, we're heroes," Wraith muttered, and then a bright, cocky smile lit up his face. "Oh, hey, I really am. Apocalypse, fallen angel, saved the world..."

Serena gave him a well-deserved jab in the side, and he "oofed."

Eidolon lovingly ran his hand up and down Tayla's arm, his fingers caressing the mate *dermoire* etched into her skin. "Can you believe how lucky we are? Seminus demons rarely take lifemates, but here we are, all of us mated."

"And alive," Shade added.

"*That's* a total shocker," Wraith threw in.

Gem laughed at Wraith. "Definitely a miracle. Especially in your case, dumb-ass."

"It's not a miracle."

All heads whipped around to a tall, stunning male who stood in the entrance to the living room. His thick blond curtain of hair fell perfectly around broad shoulders, and his black slacks and shirt had to be custom made to so perfectly fit his gorgeous body.

"Reaver," Shade ground out, and okay, this was the former fallen angel who had fought alongside Wraith in Israel. "I hate it when you do that."

Reaver grinned, a total panty-melter. "Why do you think I do it?"

Eidolon tucked Tayla tighter against him. "So why isn't our situation a miracle?"

"Because it's all fated, you silly demon. You all played roles in saving the world, and some of you have much more to do." He shrugged. "It's all good."

Wraith threw a handful of popcorn at the angel. "You know I hate the cryptic shit."

Suddenly, they were all pelting Reaver with food, and while they engaged in what was probably the strangest battle between angels and demons in history, Sin pulled Con into the hall, away from the laughter and curses.

"I haven't had a chance to thank you."

"Yes, you have."

"For saving my life, maybe. But not for giving me one."
She reached up and cupped his cheek. "Con, thank you. I
love you so much."

Warmth radiated from him, and Sin wondered why
she'd ever believed that vampires were cold. "We got a
good thing here."

"Yeah." Sin thought about her brothers, her sisters-in-
law, her new friends, and the fact that standing before her
was the most perfect mate on the planet. "I can't think of
anything better."

"It *could* be better...someday."

She narrowed her eyes at him. "What do you mean?"

"I mean, what Lore was just talking about—"

"Ah...I can't ask my brothers for sperm. 'Cuz with my
egg, that's just gross."

Con laughed, his fangs flashing sexily. "Not them. Me."

She patted his hand like she did with her baby nephews. "Sweetie, you're a vampire."

"Yeah, but I'm not a stupid vampire. I sort of planned
for this scenario."

"You've got some little popsicles?"

"Yup. I gave E samples of everything before Luc killed
me."

Her heart gave a great thump. She'd never wanted kids.
Had never even thought about wanting them. But as she
stood there with the male she loved, in a house full of the
family she never thought she'd have...she realized that,
yeah, she did want them. Maybe not today, but she and
Con had hundreds of years together, and in the meantime,
she had lots of nephews to play with. Well, to look at from
a distance, anyway.

"It's funny," she said, with a strange hitch in her voice, "but I never wanted to be tied to anyone. Never wanted to be owned or to belong to another person. But now I realize that belonging *with* someone is completely different. I belong with you, Con."

"And I with you."

He kissed her, sealing them together with a bond she didn't mind, and one that would never be broken.

The prophesies were there but no one listened. Until now.

They are the Lords of Deliverance and they have the power to usher in Doomsday...or prevent it.

Please turn this page for a preview of

Eternal Rider

Prologue

Her name was Lilith, and she was an evil succubus. His name was Yenrieth, and he was a good angel.

After hundreds of years of seducing humans, Lilith got bored. So she set her sights on Yenrieth, the ultimate challenge. He resisted. She pursued. He resisted some more. This went on for decades, until the inevitable happened. She was, after all, beautiful, and he liked his wine a little too much.

No one knows what happened to Yenrieth after their night of passion, but nine months later, Lilith gave birth to four children: three boys and a girl. She named them Reseph, Ares, Limos, and Thanatos. Lilith kept the girl, Limos, with her in Sheoul, and she placed the males in the human world, switching them out with the infants of wealthy, powerful families.

The boys grew into men, never suspecting the truth about their origins. At least, not until demons rose up, spreading terror and seeking to use Lilith's sons against the humans. Limos escaped from Sheoul, found her brothers, and told them the truth in that gossipy way females often do.

By this time, the brothers had seen their lands and families destroyed by demons and, blinded by hatred and the need for revenge, Lilith's children encouraged (manipulatively and forcibly, sometimes) humans to help them fight violent, never-ending battles against the underworld abominations.

This didn't go over well in the heavenly realm.

Zachariel, an Angel of the Apocalypse, led a legion of angels to Earth, where they met in battle with demon hordes. When the earth and waters ran red with blood, and humans could no longer survive on the poisoned land, Zachariel struck a deal with the devil.

Yes, that devil.

Lilith's children were to be punished for slinging mankind to the brink of doom in their selfish bid for revenge. Because they had nearly brought about the end of days, they were charged to be the keepers of Armageddon. Defenders or instigators, the choice would fall on their shoulders.

Each was given a Seal, and with each Seal came two prophecies. Should they protect their Seals from breaking until the prophecy laid out by the Bible came to pass, they would save their souls—and mankind.

But should they allow the Seals to be broken prematurely, as written in the Daemonica, the demon bible, they would turn evil and would forever be known by the names Pestilence, War, Famine, and Death.

And so were born The Four Horsemen of the Apocalypse.

"Mmm...I love that story. Doesn't it give you shivers when you hear it?"

Ares, seated at the bar of an underworld pub, tried to ignore the female behind him, but the rub of her breasts against his back and the slide of her dainty hands from his waist to his inner thighs wasn't easy to tune out. Her heat burned right through his hard leather armor.

"Yeah. Shivers." Some idiot read aloud the prophecy off the plaque that hung on the wall between two skulls every time Ares was in here... which was often. The tavern, kept in business mainly by Ares and his siblings, was his second home, was even known as The Four Horsemen, and for the most part, male demons melted into the background or scurried out the back door when Ares arrived. Wise. Ares despised demons, and that, combined with his love of a good fight, led to... *bad things*... for hell's minions.

But the opposite sex was a little braver—or maybe hornier. Female demons, shifters, weres, and vamps hung out twenty-four-seven in hopes of getting their hands, paws, or hooves on Ares and his brothers. Hell, Ares couldn't swing his dick without hitting someone out to get him. Usually he was a little more receptive to drinking, gambling, and general mischief, but something wasn't sitting right today. He was on edge. Twitchy.

He was never like that.

He was even in danger of losing the chess game he was playing with the pudgy pink Oni bartender, and Ares hadn't lost any game of strategy in... well, ever.

"Oh, War." The female Sora demon ran her tongue along the top of his ear. "You've got to know it makes us hot."

"My name," he gritted out, "is Ares. You don't want to be around on the day I become War." He moved his rook, tossed back half his ale, and was about to signal for another when the female's hand dropped between his legs.

"I still like War better." Her voice was a seductive trill, her fingers nimble as they sought the opening at his groin. "And Pestilence . . . such a sexy name."

Only a demon would think "Pestilence" was a turn-on. Ares peeled her red hand away. She was one of Reseph's regular bedmates, one of hundreds of Horsemen groupies who called themselves Megiddo Mount-me's. They even subclassed themselves according to who their favorite Horseman was; Ares's groupies liked to be called Mongers. War Mongers.

The bartender made a foolish move with his knight, and Ares hid a smile in his mug.

"Reseph should be here any minute," he told the Sora, and her lips curved against his skin on the back of his neck.

"Good. I'll play with *both* of you." The female, who looked like a cartoon devil, traced a long, black nail over the stallion tattoo on Ares's forearm. "I love this."

The horse was as much a part of him as his organs, whether Battle was on his skin or under his seat, and Ares stiffened at the sensation of both his arm and scalp being stroked. Any contact with the glyph sent a shock of sensation to the corresponding parts of Ares's body, which could be a real pain in the ass. Or it could be inappropriately pleasant . . .

Ares spun his mug down the length of the bar top and slid his queen into striking position. Triumph sang through him, filling that space in his soul that was always hungry for victory. "Checkmate."

The bartender cursed, the Sora laughed, and Ares got to his feet. At over six and a half feet tall, he dwarfed the demon, but that didn't faze her, and she plastered the entire length of her tank-topped, miniskirted body to his. Her tail swished on the cobblestone floor and her black horns swiveled like pointy satellite dishes, and if her gaze grew any hotter, his breeches were going to get real uncomfortable.

He despised his reaction to demons, had never truly warmed up to females who didn't at least appear to be human.

Some grudges lasted a lifetime.

"I'm outta here." Despite the chess coup, his unease was becoming an itch under his skin, the way it did when a global war escalated. Unable to remain still any longer, he flung a gold Sheoulin mark at the three-eyed bartender. "A round for the house. Give the females something to do while they're waiting for my brothers." Who were late, as usual.

Gently, but firmly, he dislodged the Velcro demon and strode out of the tavern and into perpetual twilight. Muggy, hot air that reeked of sulphur filled his lungs, and his boots sank into the spongy terrain that defined the Six River region of Sheoul, the demon realm in the Earth's core.

Battle writhed on his skin, impatient to run.

"Out," Ares commanded, and a heartbeat later, the tattoo on his arm turned to mist, expanding and solidifying into a giant blood-bay stallion. Battle nudged Ares with his nose in greeting—or, more likely, for sugar cubes.

"You forgot this."

Always ready to live up to his name, Battle bared his teeth at the Sora, who stood in the tavern doorway, her tail wrapped around the hilt of a dagger, which she dangled playfully. The blatant invitation in her sultry smile told Ares that she'd plucked the weapon from him herself, but he knew that. He didn't leave weapons behind. Ever.

Of course, he never got shit lifted, either. The female was good. Real good. And even though he wasn't normally into demons, he had to admire her talent. No wonder Reseph liked this one so much. Maybe Ares would make an exception to his no-demons-that-look-like-demons rule…

Grinning, he started toward her… and stopped dead.

The hairs on the back of his neck prickled in warning. With a furious scream, Battle reared up, and from out of the forest of shadowed trees, a buffalo-sized hellhound leaped through the air. Ares shoved the female out of the way, a stupidly protective instinct left over from his failed family days… and fuck, he needed to get his head out of his ass because he'd almost ended up between snapping jaws.

Ares and his sibs were immortal, but hellhound bites were poisonous to the Horsemen, causing paralysis, and then the suffering *really* began.

He dove to the ground as Battle struck out with a powerful hoof, hooking the other animal in the ribs and sending it tumbling into the tavern door. The fucking hound recovered so quickly that Battle's blow might as well have been a flea bite, and it targeted the Sora, who scrambled backward on her hands and knees. Her terror was palpable, like little whips on Ares's skin, and he had a feeling this was her first experience with a hellhound.

Hell of a way to pop *that* cherry.

"Hey!" *Distract.* Rolling to his feet, Ares drew his sword. *Provoke.* "I'm over here, you piece of shit mongrel." *Terminate.*

Anticipation gleamed in the hellhound's crimson eyes as it swung around, melting into an inky blur of evil. Ares met it head-on, with three hundred pounds of armored weight behind his blow. The satisfying crunch of steel meeting bone rent the air. An impact tremor shot up Ares's arms, and a massive jet of blood spewed from the hound's chest.

A bloodcurdling snarl ripped from its throat as it launched a surprisingly effective counterattack, slamming one huge paw into Ares's chest. Claws raked his breastplate, and he flew backward, plowing into a stone summoning column. Pain lanced his upper body, and then the hellhound was on him, its jaws snapping a millimeter away from Ares's jugular.

Foul breath burned Ares's eyes and frothy, stinging saliva dripped on his skin. The beast's claws tore at his armor, and it took every ounce of Ares's strength to keep the hound from ripping out his throat. Even with Battle striking at the canine's body, the creature did its damnedest to get a mouthful of flesh.

As hard as he could, Ares jammed his sword into the animal's belly and yanked the blade upward. As the beast screamed in pain, Ares rolled, twisted, and brought the sword around in an awkward arc.

Awkward or not, the strike cleaved the hound's head from its shoulders. The thing fell to the ground, twitching, steam hissing from its gaping neck. The spongy ground drank the blood before it could pool, and hundreds of blackened teeth sprouted from the dirt, clamped onto the hound's body, and began to chew.

Battle whinnied with amusement. The horse's sense of humor had always been perched on the gallows with the crows.

Before the earth could claim the beast, Ares wiped his blade clean on its fur, giving repeated thanks to whoever was listening that the hound hadn't bitten him. The horror of a bite was never-ending—the paralysis didn't stop the pain...or the ability to scream. Ares knew firsthand. A hundred years ago, he'd spent two weeks being fed upon, experiencing every excruciating bite that tore flesh, ripped apart organs, and snapped bones. With his ability to regenerate, he could have spent eternity feeding the entire pack. The torture had finally ended when his siblings destroyed the hellhounds and rescued him.

He frowned as a thought spun up. The vile canines were predators, killers, but they generally hunted in packs, so why had there been only one?

Ares glanced over at the tavern door. The Sora had disappeared, was probably pounding shots of demonfire in the bar, and hey, wasn't it great that no one had bothered to come out and help? Then again, no demon in his right mind willingly tangled with a hellhound no matter how much love they had for the slaughter—and most demons *loved* to slaughter.

Light flashed, and twenty yards away in a copse of black, twisted trees, a summoned Harrowgate shimmered into existence. Ares sheathed his sword as Thanatos emerged, throwing menacing shadows where there should be none. Both he and his pale dun mount, Styx, dripped with gore, and the stallion was breathing through bubbling blood.

It wasn't an unusual sight, but the timing was too coincidental for Ares's liking. "What happened?"

Thanatos's expression darkened as he took in the dead hellhound. "Same thing that happened to you, apparently."

Shit. "Have you heard from Reseph or Limos?"

Thanatos's light yellow eyes flashed. "I was hoping they were here."

Ares threw out his hand, casting a Harrowgate. "I'll go to Reseph. You check on Limos." He didn't wait for his brother's reply. He spurred Battle through the gate, and the warhorse leaped, his big hooves coming down on a rocky shelf that had been scoured smooth by centuries of harsh wind and ice storms.

This was Reseph's Himalayan hideaway, a giant maze of caverns carved deep into the mountains and drenched in ancient magic that made it invisible to human eyes. Ares dismounted in one smooth motion, his boots striking the stone with twin cracks that echoed endlessly in the thin air.

"To me."

Instantly, the warhorse dissolved into a cloud of smoke, which twisted and narrowed into a tendril that wrapped around Ares's hand and set into his forearm in the brown-gray shape of a horse tattoo.

Ares barged inside the cave entrance, and he hadn't gone a dozen steps when he froze, locked up hard as an electric current of ten-thousand-volt alarm shot up his spine.

Time to dance.

He was already in a dead run when he drew his sword, the metallic sound of a blade clearing its scabbard like a lover's whisper during foreplay. Didn't matter that he'd just engaged an enemy, he loved a good battle, craved the release of tension that hit him with the force of a full-body orgasm, and he'd long ago decided he'd rather fight than fuck.

Though he had to admit that after a good brawl, winding down with a lush, sultry female couldn't be beat. Maybe he'd head back to the tavern after this and find a War Monger after all.

Adrenaline pumping hotly through his veins, Ares took a sharp corner so fast he had to skid into a change of direction, and then he burst through the doorway to Reseph's main living area.

His brother, his hand wrapped around a bloodied ax, stood in the middle of the room, which was painted in a fresh, dripping coat of blood. He was panting, his shoulders slumped, head bent, white-blond hair concealing his face. Behind him, a hellhound lay dead, and in the corner, a very much alive one let out a gravelly snarl, its mouth a mass of sharp teeth.

Fuck. Reseph had fallen victim to a paralyzing bite.

The beast swung its shaggy head toward Ares. Red eyes glowed with bloodlust as it gathered its hind legs under it. Ares calculated the distance to the target in a millisecond, and in one quick motion launched a dagger that impaled the hellhound in the eye. Ares pressed his advantage, heaving his sword in a side swing that caught the creature in the mouth, slicing its bottom jaw clean off. The hound howled in agony and fury, but Reseph had already injured it and, weakened, it stumbled and fell, allowing Ares an opportunity to run his blade straight through its black heart.

"Reseph!" Leaving the sword impaled in the animal, Ares ran to his brother, whose blue eyes were wild, glazed with pain. "How did they get in?"

"Someone," Reseph groaned, "had to have...sent them."

That much was becoming clear. But very few beings could handle or control a hellhound. So if someone sent the beasts, that person was serious about putting Ares and his brothers—and maybe Limos, too—out of commission.

"You should feel special," Ares said, with a lightness he didn't feel. "You got two hellhounds, and I got only one. Who'd you piss off?" Gently, Ares wrapped his arms around Reseph's chest and lowered him to the ground.

Reseph sucked in a gurgling breath. "Seal. My... Seal."

Ares went cold to the core, and with trembling hands, he tore away Reseph's T-shirt to expose the chain around his neck. The Seal hanging from it was whole, but when he palmed the gold coin, a vibration, dense with malevolence, shot up his arm.

"This..." Reseph spoke between gritted teeth and rattling breaths. "This isn't...good."

No, it wasn't.

The countdown to Armageddon had begun.